Nella Bielski

After Arkadia

The
· Wickerwork ·
Tram

The
· Barber's ·
Hand

Translated by Jonathan Steffen
with the participation of
John Berger

VIKING

VIKING

Published by the Penguin Group
Penguin Books Ltd, 27 Wrights Lane, London w8 5tz, England
Viking Penguin, a division of Penguin Books USA Inc.
375 Hudson Street, New York, New York 10014, USA
Penguin Books Australia Ltd, Ringwood, Victoria, Australia
Penguin Books Canada Ltd, 2801 John Street, Markham, Ontario, Canada l3r 1b4
Penguin Books (NZ) Ltd, 182–190 Wairau Road, Auckland 10, New Zealand

Penguin Books Ltd, Registered Offices: Harmondsworth, Middlesex, England

First published separately in France by Editions Robert Laffont and Mercure de France under
the titles *Le Tramway d'osier* and *Si belles et fraîches étaient les roses* 1974, 1980
First published in Great Britain by Viking in one volume under the title *After Arkadia* 1991

Filmset in Monophoto Bembo
Printed in England by Clays Ltd, St Ives plc

A CIP catalogue for this book is available from the British Library
isbn 0-670-81615-9

The
· Wickerwork ·
Tram

· PART ONE ·

And she was no longer turning, the dwindling echoes of commands – One, two, three! – scarcely reached her mind, scarcely reached her muscles, until with a final spasm of the heart she surrendered herself completely to the feeling which had begun as a warm wave rising in her breast, almost a pleasant sensation, like a sudden welling of happiness, a mixture of sunshine and rain, myriads of gentle hands touching her, and she didn't have to think, she didn't have to react, she was sliding, she was free-falling, she was slowing down, and the voices were coming from miles away and everything was fading sparks and streaks of red.

'Jeanne!'

The thing that had fallen to the ground no longer answered to the name of Jeanne. It was nothing, answering nobody. The elderly dancing-instructor rushed across the hall towards her, and the lady at the piano stood up, knocking her music off the stand.

'Jeanne, my child, what's wrong? Where does it hurt? . . . Zenia Petrovna, call someone! Do something! . . . My God, she's as white as a sheet!'

He felt her chest. Her heart was still beating, if 'beating' was the word for such irregular contractions. She seemed to have broken nothing: her fall must have been extremely expert. But expert or otherwise, it was the end, and he knew it. When your heart packed up on you at the age of eighteen, you were finished in this profession. Jeanne wouldn't become a dancer, the great dancer he had predicted; and already he could see the moment when he'd have to tell her. With automatic movements he took her pulse, massaged her heart, prised open her teeth to put some drops into her mouth. What a mess. Such a marvellous body. The best bet he'd ever had. He lifted up her head again, calling for help once more, and from every side of the huge, empty hall with its glittering chandeliers the mirrored walls returned his gaze, his snowy head of hair, and Jeanne's body, dressed in pink and stretched out like a farewell. Then three doors opened simultaneously, and the doctor, Zenia Petrovna and the janitor came to take over. He straightened up again and left the hall without a word.

There was Jeanne's mother, too: he would have to break the news to her, talk to her. Right away. He had known her for a good number of years: she was still very young when he had met her, a pretty French governess in a Petersburg family – the family of the stage-manager of the Maryinski Theatre, where he was a well-known face. She was the daughter of a concierge from Limoges. The most marvellous legs she had, the kind of legs that he had only ever seen on French women; a mass of fair hair that tumbled down over her luminous face; and large grey eyes. She wasn't cut out for the gruelling life of a children's governess. He had noticed her courage and good humour right from the start. Then he had lost touch with her, not setting eyes on her again until that morning in Odessa years later when she came to see him at the Opera. She was just the same as ever – refined, elegant and optimistic; she told him she had a daughter, and that she wanted to arrange for her to have dancing lessons. He picked up a trace of an Odessan accent in her flawless Russian, which perhaps indicated that she had been living there for some time. How she earned her living, or who Jeanne's father was, she did not say. She had a three-roomed flat in Richelieu Street, just above the Naples Dairy Shop. He agreed to teach Jeanne, and, bachelor that he was, immune to all ideas of marriage, he took to visiting the mother and daughter for tea – and the daughter was growing up and displaying remarkable gifts. It wasn't a question of beauty: Jeanne's beauty was not of the obvious kind. Seen from close up, in fact, her face was rather unimpressive: the small features somehow didn't fit together, losing themselves in a maze of mobility. It was as if there were two Jeannes: one in the house in Richelieu Street and the other in the dancing-school at the Opera. Seen from a distance under the lights, her face redefined itself with brilliance and precision: it came alive, a face for the amphitheatre, for the arena − for the theatre, simply. Watching her dance, the old dancing-instructor would sometimes tell himself that Jeanne would become the first swallow of the spring of this new century − this century which had just been born and which promised, why not, a new kind of woman. When people pointed out to him that with her physique Jeanne would never make a professional dancer, he would reply by quoting Schumann: 'Whatever sounds beautiful fears no grammar, just as Beauty itself is not afraid of the Aesthetic.' Jeanne was a perfect pupil, a true student of classical dance, and yet there was something in the very least of her gestures that smacked of heresy, of an infringement of the laws of the dance; and even her teacher was unable to grasp the nature of this heresy, to give a name to the strange movements which she executed with such discipline, in lessons, just as at the annual concert at the Opera. With her, a simple *dégagé*, a turn, a bourrée step, a *fouetté* seemed to be a gift of nature, necessary, legislative, in a way: one might have thought them the projections, each time different and each time exact, of her soul. Jeanne compelled you to look at her, like those poems which open so bafflingly that you are hard put to read them at all, but which nevertheless demand to be read, again and again, drawing you on to the discovery of the key that will make everything clear.

And yet none of this turned her head. The confusion which she provoked in other people she put down simply to what she thought of as faults in her technique, or to her physical appearance, which she tended to perceive as rather awkward; and she redoubled her efforts, working herself to the point of exhaustion. And her everyday walk, her old-fashioned style of dress, the particular way she had of carrying her head – all these things spared her from being accosted in a city known for its loose morals. When she went into a shop, people would drop their voices, and the shopkeeper would speak to her with a marked solicitude, as though addressing someone suffering from a mysterious illness. Whenever she went out she wore a hat and a capeline with neither ribbons nor flowers, and the extraordinarily simple cut of the dresses which her mother designed for her so that she could get them on and off easily had everyone bewildered, as though a young girl from Dante's Florence had just strayed into the Odessa of the 1900s.

Jeanne had never gone to school. Of course she could read and write – although she made plenty of mistakes, and her French was better than her Russian. What really interested her were maths and astronomy, subjects she had taught herself from the textbooks which were her favourite reading-matter. Jeanne spent her free time on the roof, studying the sky night after night with the aid of a telescope which her mother had given her, and she wrote down what she saw in a small green notebook – her very first diary, which she hung on to for the rest of her life.

Her body was a curious mechanism, its supple, resilient spring wound up to the full. At the age of eighteen she didn't know the meaning of pain, and tiredness was for her nothing more than a sign that she should stop working her muscles for a moment. At which she would bury herself in the books and calculations which gave her a satisfaction close to joy. Her sensuality lay dormant: the sight of men had scarcely any effect upon her as yet. Her whole being was attuned to the single rhythm of the dance: it was calm, as beautifully balanced as a chessboard not one of whose pieces has yet been touched. And the presence of her mother, with her constant attentions, with her gentle hands, with her soft voice, created an ambient music in which Jeanne lived right up to the day of her fall.

Jeanne had no time to think about ambition, the all-consuming ambition which makes for the true artist. It was her mother who was ambitious for her. Regarding her daughter as a second self, Marie-Aynard saw in her a means to put her own life to rights – a way, perhaps, of redressing a wrong, of getting her own back at her mother, a corpulent, unhappy woman sitting in her concierge's lodge, always short of money, of getting her own back at her father, with his benevolent smile and his drinker's breath, of getting her own back with whatever means she had at her disposal, using whatever nature had given her in the way of brains and looks; and subsequently using her own daughter.

She had worked for so many women in the past, when she had been in domestic service: there were those who had no qualms about treating her as a servant, and then others, often the ugly and pretentious ones, who were more careful, envying her when they intercepted the long looks which men gave the young French governess – all those men who lost their heads so quickly when they were face to face with her and regained them so quickly when it came to getting involved. At a very early age Marie-Aynard learned to loathe the word Mademoiselle; and she learned how to harden her heart, lumping all men together as cowards, or, at the very best, weaklings. Sometimes it seemed to her that she just didn't know how to behave towards men, that she didn't understand the trick of keeping them, a trick which everyone else knew. At one point she went through a phase of being genuinely obsessed with marriage – ridiculous dreams of arriving at church in a beautiful long white dress, of fingers with gold wedding-rings on them as a sign that she belonged to someone and someone belonged to her, absolutely. Desperately needing someone to lean on – for she had no one at all, neither here nor in France – she wanted nothing more than to be 'taken under somebody's wing', as she put it; and she carried this madness to the point of actually refusing love. If a man fell in love with her and showed it, she would say, 'Another one, yet another one!' And inexorably, revelling in the act, she would throw the presents and flowers men gave her into the Neva. Jealous of her solitude, she would go down to the quayside, sit down at the water's edge, and send the bouquet of roses – so rare in that country – drifting down the river, one flower at a time. In winter she would strew them on the ice, walk all over them, and go back home without a second glance, feeling the relief of a duty accomplished.

One person and one alone knew how to touch her to the quick, knew how to remind her that there is more between a man and a woman than the symbolic ring of gold which unites them, knew how to make her laugh. He was invited one Saturday to a *dacha* at Pavlovsk which belonged to a certain stage-manager. Through a window he caught sight of a young woman in a light-coloured dress: she was running with the children under the trees, her long pony-tail bouncing on her back. This man was a 'littérateur', as the saying was in those days, best known for his articles in *Vedomosty*.

Shortly afterwards Marie-Aynard had an attack of appendicitis and had to go to hospital. He went to see her every day, talking to her about everything and nothing; and he didn't take her flowers, he didn't ask her questions. He didn't make a single promise – he was simply there. When she came out of hospital he was waiting for her in the entrance hall: he took her shoulder-bag and, without asking her opinion on the matter, led her to an apartment in Mokhovaya Street which was quiet and full of light. And surprisingly – or perhaps not surprisingly – there was a large bouquet of lilac and roses on the table.

Should she just go along with it, happy simply because he tore up the stairs two at a time whenever he came to see her? Or should she try to find a way of side-stepping his attentions? It took her some while to decide. Not a very long while, actually. Her madness took hold of her again, her cheerfulness changing into something bitter, very close to rancour: when he held her in his arms, she gathered herself to herself, closing up inside; and she answered his smile with a simple look, without even wanting to. She understood nothing of her own obsession, being unable to distinguish it from other, equally vague feelings; and on this point her natural intelligence was of no help to her.

And then the unforeseen occurred: she found that she was pregnant. Suddenly everything took on a different light, and what had existed between them returned once more, acquiring a new meaning – or perhaps one should say, acquiring a meaning for the first time. When she told him the news, he froze on the spot. His reaction was such that she was subsequently unable to recall the details of the scene. All that she remembered were the few words which decided the course of her life, once and for all: 'You can't keep it. It's for my sake that I'm asking you. For my sake, do you understand?'

As for her, she knew that from this point on she wanted nothing more than this: to have a child, safe in the knowledge that she would never be alone again in this country, in this world. A child. It would be hers, quite simply: it would be her possession, her purpose, her chance. At the age of twenty-five she became the mother of a little girl, and she clung on forever to the moment in which she saw the tiny blood-stained body which had just left her womb.

She settled in Odessa and got a job with a merchant marine company which plied the Marseilles line. She worked on a French-language bulletin published by the company. Her beauty did not diminish with age; she remained as calm as ever, at least to all appearances; and she was accepted into the 'better circles' of Odessan society – the world of academics, lawyers and doctors. Silent on the subject of her past and distant in her relations with men, she commanded a degree of respect which also protected her daughter, with her strange quirks, her astronomical tendencies, and her education, which had little to do with the time or the place in which she was living. Could one actually call it an education? Jeanne's mother knew instinctively that she had given birth to a soul whose development she would not be able to influence. She was content to stand back and watch her growing. Longing for freedom herself, she didn't want to pre-empt a single discovery of Jeanne's, preferring to wait until her daughter made it on her own – even if it was at the cost of a delay in her development which might take on the aspect of a certain immaturity. So Jeanne knew next to nothing about love, she didn't read novels, and she didn't feel drawn towards the various young girls who could have told her about it if she had become friends with them. Retarded by endless dancing exercises and the tiredness that ensued, her instincts lay dormant. Her diet was as healthy and simple as could be: fish, cream cheese and fruit. Jeanne was nothing but muscle and silky, delicate skin. Tall, with narrow hips and practically no chest, she looked like a teenager who was practising to be an old maid.

The day she fell on to the parquet of the classroom was the first day of spring: the briny air was incredibly pure, and a host of wild-cherry trees dangled their white blossom above the wooden palings. Jeanne, who had come round by now, looked out from the cab drawn by two Oriol trotters as it quickly covered the four *versts* from the centre of town to the *dacha* by the sea where she was to take the few weeks' rest which the doctor had just ordered. Her gaze still somewhat fuzzy, Jeanne watched the houses slipping by: they were a bit chilly in winter, but they came into their own in the spring – houses with something so Italian about them that one might have been looking at a stage set. But today the well-known spectacle of these streets was no longer the same for Jeanne. The contours smudged into one another, and the colours did not succeed one another naturally, as though the greens and blues of the Odessan spring had been adulterated with water, even at times with ink. The fall she had just had had been her first encounter with death, a sign that, from one instant to the next, everything can stop, just like that, for no good reason, just because of an invisible twitch of the threads that Someone holds in his hands. But she wasn't really thinking about these things in the cab: her mind was blank most of the time.

The cab gave a jolt which sent Jeanne sliding along the seat: she grabbed at her knee as if to keep hold of it, and the word *koleno* suddenly shot through her head. For a split-second it seemed strange to her, as did the part of the leg indicated by the Russian syllables. She clung to the word *koleno* as though it were a life-belt, repeating it several times and finding it irresistibly amusing; and then she hummed one of the waltz tunes which Zenia Petrovna played. Humming still, she closed her eyes. She saw a large room with neither floor nor ceiling, an indefinite space crowded with flickering candles, and flowers in disarray, and lace, and chance faces which slowly rotated – and suddenly she felt herself caught up in someone's arms, two arms without a head, and carried off. The cab was going down France Boulevard, a street which was tented with acacias and gigantic chestnut trees. On the corner of the street she saw a man, who raised his hat as she approached him. It wasn't the gesture that surprised Jeanne: it was the way the man was dressed – his suit, and his completely shaven head, to the lower half of which a ginger moustache appeared to have been glued. Jeanne would sometimes encounter boys like this in the corridors of the Opera as she came out of her dancing-class – actors, with something both studied and natural about them: you only noticed the disguise, you couldn't imagine them without it. The cab was going quite quickly: Jeanne turned her head to have another look at the man on the pavement, who was still standing with his hat in his hand. Now that it was too late, she felt suddenly intrigued by his salutation, and by the egg-like cranium which his raised hat had revealed; by the resplendently white spats, too, and the extraordinary number of gold chains which criss-crossed the waistcoat – itself striped

– in all directions. He wasn't from the theatre, that was certain, and he couldn't have been anyone her mother knew.

A moment later she forgot him, overcome with tiredness once more – not the joyous tiredness she loved, but a lassitude, an emptiness, a sort of hollow under the heart. There was only one thing she wanted: to get back to Beriozy as quickly as possible, take off her leotard, have a wash and go to sleep. Going more slowly now, the horses descended towards the sea along a narrow path, then followed a road which led between trees, parallel to the sea. Jeanne noticed women in white dresses carrying parasols, children in sailor-suits running along with hoops flying before them. A further ten minutes' drive took them to the front gate of the house.

The interior of the house, and the house itself, were modern: recently built, it was made of the porous stone which characterized the majority of buildings in Odessa and the surrounding area – a predominantly white stone, tinged with pink and nielloed with fossil-shells. It was very simple in design: just a row of five rooms whose windows and doors, framed by wooden columns, gave on to a terrace that was slightly raised. The house was given a fresh coat of whitewash at Easter every year.

The house was modern, but everything else – the front gate, the little summer-house in the garden, the close – bore witness to the past. Shortly after Jeanne's birth, when Marie-Aynard moved to Odessa and took possession of the property, there had been a fire. The original house, more substantial and far more attractive, had burnt to the ground. Only the things around it had survived. There was a peculiar charm about the contrast between the starkness of the new house and the ostentation of its setting – a charm which reflected perfectly the contrast between the mother and daughter who lived there.

Jeanne paid the cab-driver and turned her key in the little door. Marie-Aynard doesn't know what's happened yet, she said to herself: she won't be getting back till late this evening, after she's copied out the day's closing prices on the Stock Exchange in her office down at the harbour. Nastia wouldn't be waiting for Jeanne, either. The idea of walking into the courtyard at this unaccustomed hour of a Tuesday with her dancing-things in her hand filled Jeanne with a sharp sense of defeat, a realization of the irreparableness of what had just happened to her. She sat down cross-legged on the bare stone and began to cry. She cried for a long time, blowing her nose and swallowing the salty tears, more tears than she had ever shed in her life, until she suddenly noticed Nastia, who was standing there staring at her in bewilderment. Quickly she dried her eyes, forcing a smile to her lips, and assured Nastia that she was all right. She let Nastia undress her, telling her that Diaghilev wished to see her and that in preparation for this meeting she was in the process of working out an extremely complex routine. She mimed the sequence with her fingers on the kitchen table and then executed a few movements in the middle of the floor. Her movements lacked all verve: she barely sketched out the steps, doing it not for Nastia, and not for herself, but rather for an invisible third party who was hovering near – that Someone, perhaps. Look, she wanted to say, it's all over, you see: the spring is broken. And what happens now? It was enough for Nastia, however: her little Jeanne wasn't as ill as all that, thank God. Dancing, thought Nastia: what a waste of time, and what a wretched profession! She pitied Jeanne. Not simply at this precise moment: she had always pitied her, ever since the day Jeanne first took it into her head to become a dancer. Endless exercises, your hair all sticky with sweat, no hips, legs like a stork's, big feet – what misery for a woman! Now Jeanne's mother was a completely different kettle of fish – a fine-looking woman if ever there was one. Nastia's greatest pleasure in life was to brush out Marie-Aynard's long blonde hair, to put it up in airy chignons, to iron her clothes, to keep watch over her panoply of phials and pots of cream, to watch her leaving the house, dressed invariably as if she were going to a party. And Nastia would ask herself why it was that all the paths leading to the house weren't littered with wooers, rich, powerful, each more elegant than the last. Her faculty of imagination was expended entirely on Marie-Aynard. Sometimes, near the English Club in Deribassovskaya Street, she would pass a man with a particularly commanding presence or an especially handsome moustache; and whenever she did so, it was at Marie-Aynard's elbow that these men would take their place in her dreams, not at her own.

Nastia was thirty-nine. A country girl, she had been orphaned and taken in by her aunt, her sole remaining relation, who lived in St Petersburg. The aunt was a widow who ran a high-class grocer's shop on the Nevsky. She had a grown-up son called Constantine. Phenomenally lazy, he spent much of his time drinking and playing cards. But Nastia only saw his straw-blond locks and his sea-blue eyes. One day he made a grab at her in the corridor. With lowered eyelids, her heart beating wildly, joyously giving rein to all her fantasies, thanking heaven for having put her in his way, she had offered herself to him with all the naturalness of a plant turning to face the sun. He had consummated this act of near-incest with no little sprightliness – whilst his mother, fully aware of what was happening in the next room, wished she were deaf.

Living off this feast of sensuality, Nastia grew more beautiful with each passing day, asking nothing more of life than the sound of Constantine's voice and the feel of his hands, always rough and eager, which gave her such violent pleasure. She did everything about the house – the shopping, the housework, the cooking – and these duties were like a continuation of their intimacy, for every shirt she ironed, every patch of parquet she waxed, every log she lit existed only through him and for him. He would pull at her plaits, calling her 'My little sunbeam' as he tore open her bodice and buried his face between her cupped breasts; and she would laugh, whispering, 'Stop it, stop it,' whilst clinging to him with all the strength of her little hands.

And then came the blackness, the total numbness when one evening – an evening like any other – Constantine simply didn't return home. They informed the police: they looked for him everywhere. Nastia set out on foot to find him: she went through St Petersburg searching in every corner like a cat, making ever-smaller circles around the grocer's shop where she had been so happy. But he was nowhere. No one had seen him. Not among the living: not among the dead.

Not many weeks after her son's disappearance the aunt died of grief. It wasn't Nastia who inherited the grocery shop: she did nothing to make it come her way, having lost all interest in it. On the day she found herself with nothing to fall back on, alone and with a suitcase full of linen (Constantine's clothes) as her sole worldly possession, she put an advertisement in the paper; and she received a reply from Jeanne's mother, who was looking for a domestic. Jeanne had just been born. From that day forth Nastia's whole life revolved around ιMarie-Aynard and her daughter. The sun of her love set deep inside her: she never even spoke Constantine's name. Sometimes he would come back to her in dreams. These dreams simply caused her pain: she would wake up in the morning with a violent migraine, her mouth filled with an aftertaste of wormwood. Nastia was to know other men, but she never found anything that reminded her even remotely of what there had been between herself and Constantine.

On Sundays – not so often during the week – Nastia would go out. And when she did, she felt she had to rouge her cheeks and mascara her eyelashes, which were perfectly black as they were. She would go to the picture-house, spending hours there; and she would take all the imaginary lives and heart-rending loves very seriously. It's ever so sad, she would in-variably say to herself, but that's not it . . .

Whenever the family gave a dinner for their few friends – a French barrister who sat on the Commercial Tribunal and worked with Marie-Aynard in the export department; his wife; Jeanne's teacher, Victor Platonovitch; and a promising young man from the Faculty of Physics – Nastia remained at table with everyone else. It was Jeanne who, as the youngest, fetched things back and forth between the kitchen and the dining-room. Marie-Aynard chose Nastia's dresses at the same time as Jeanne's. And she taught the two girls the grammatical rudiments of both French and Russian.

The three women were always neat and tidy in their domestic arrangements, but never excessively so. The way each chose to live in the apartment could be seen as an expression, even an extension, of her personality. Thus the windows with starched canvas curtains, the monkishly narrow bed and a certain emptiness constituted Jeanne's domain. Marie-Aynard's was a great bed covered in lacework, the dressing-table crammed with little bottles, the flower arrangements, the conspicuously well-chosen dresses draped across a folding screen to air in front of a half-open window, a large number of engravings, Levitan's water-colour, *Thawing Snow with Black Bird*, the dressing-room in pale blue ceramics, and the bathroom fittings of elaborate copperwork. As for Nastia, what belonged to her was the very high rustic bed strewn with pillows, the big trunk in which the suitcase containing Constantine's things was kept locked, a photograph of herself at the age of seventeen – black eyes, mischievous expression, hair put up in a heavy bun, dimples, a smile at the corners of her mouth – and then the smell which pervaded the place, a smell of wild-strawberry soap.

There was something secret about their communal existence, something inaccessible to anyone else; something for which there was no word in the days in which they lived, at least no word that they were aware of, something which was almost bound to find its way into their lives, given their youth, their physical beauty, their solitude and their fear of men. One

stifling summer's day several years previously, Marie-Aynard
had fallen ill. She spent three nights in a raging fever which
was accompanied by loss of consciousness and delirium. Nastia
never went to sleep in all that time: she lavished a thousand
and one attentions on Marie-Aynard's enfeebled body, which
had grown more beautiful than ever. The moment that proved
to be the turning-point for Marie-Aynard was when, lying in
the darkness, she had the impression of being enveloped by a
smell of wild strawberries and dried herbs and by the soft feel
of a warm duvet; and the voices struggling to speak in her
conjured up a gamut of sensations of which she could, despite
her state, distinguish every note – notes which gently untied,
one by one, the knots and balls of pain which left her body on
that night of her recovery. The relief she had known so far was
this time of a completely different order – not localized,
coming quite naturally, as if of its own accord, and so total and
absolute in its power to assuage that Marie-Aynard fell straight
asleep. The next morning, she woke up with a clear head,
feeling right as rain. Nastia appeared in a shaft of sunlight
which was pouring through the half-open shutters, a steaming
cup of tea in one hand and the saucer with the jam in it in the
other. Smiling, she sat down on the edge of the bed; and
Marie-Aynard kissed her hair. Neither of them spoke; but the
ghosts of that night still hovered between them, giving an aura
of constraint to everything which had hitherto been so straightforward.

Jeanne was aware of this change, although she didn't really
understand it. For Marie-Aynard it constituted a watershed.
Her child was no longer enough for her. Neither was her job,
nor the life she led. Idly at first, then quite deliberately, she
began to scan the pages of the St Petersburg press in search of
Sergey Georgievitch Leontiev's signature. She wrote him
letters, never sending them. Across the years the smell of
Serge's tobacco came back to her, and the handkerchiefs he
used, black with a yellow border, and his face, serious and

thoughtful, and the times he caressed her, and his unmanageable hair, black with a few silver strands at the temples and the nape of the neck, and the hard gash of his mouth, so gentle to the touch, and his arms, which were stronger than the rest of his body.

She would look at Jeanne and ask herself: What is there of him in her? Not much, was the answer: not much of him, not much of Marie-Aynard herself. Perhaps there was just something, though: the way Jeanne had of smiling with one corner of her mouth, and her habit of screwing up her eyes when she laughed.

Marie-Aynard began to live on her own with nothing but this image for company, an image that was extraordinarily present, purified and indispensable. There were times when she would cry. She even began to draw away from Jeanne, although she didn't show it: inside herself she began to grow apart from her daughter, not so far as actually to make Jeanne suffer, but far enough to give her a secret inkling of having been abandoned. It was around this time that Marie-Aynard resumed her travels. She would feign illnesses, attacks of asthma, so as to be able to go off alone on a cure to Karlsbad or Yalta. At Yalta she at least had some sense of purpose. Serge had always loved the place, especially in September – 'the velvet season', as the Russians call it. She put up at a little boarding-house right close to the beach. She spent her time in a folding chair at the edge of the sea. Her desire to see Serge again was so great that the years separating her from her life in St Petersburg were simply elided, the intervening period concentrating itself into a single moment. There were times when she had to shake herself, rub her eyes and stop her ears so as not to hear Serge's laugh right next to her, the sound of his step on the stairs and then in the hallway of the apartment which she had so hated at first, as she had hated the clichéd role she had been obliged to play there – that of the foreign woman kept by a famous man. No, she had not known how to love Serge –

to love him to the point of loving what he wrote, what he said, to love him for what he was. Then what was the use of seeing Serge again? She might have considered whether she wasn't running the risk of finding herself face to face with a man who was growing old now, who was a father, yes, most certainly the father of other children, the husband of another woman. But she ignored all these questions. The important thing about this whole escapade was neither Serge nor Marie-Aynard, nor even the question of whether their love could be repaired. All she did was to snatch at the Serge who returned in gusts of wind throughout the day and night. There she was, far out, hurling a reply to the love that Serge had felt for her – a reply not composed of words, she could not think, she had no words – the reply of her senses, the reply of her body itself. She was rolling a ball of snow before her, a ball of snow which there would never be enough sun to melt. Seagulls skimmed the surface of the water, the water foamed among the broken rocks; and the seagulls were the grey envelopes of the letters which Marie-Aynard had received from Serge during her early days in Odessa and sent back unopened, the rocks were her own pride, shattered to smithereens ... Marie-Aynard spent hours sitting on the beach at Yalta that late September, nurturing the image of Serge's face above hers, his arms clasping her shoulders, his body streaming with sweat, and then his head upon the pillow, irradiated by a brilliant smile. That smile she remembered, and also the Marie-Aynard of those days – her spite, her conceit, her obsession with wedding-rings, her vengefulness. And Serge's letters seemed all the more wonderful to her because she couldn't conjecture what was in them, or the terms in which he might have described his love for her. *I don't want you*: could he actually have written those words? And what if it was a despairing attempt to get her to come back to him? What else could it have been?

Marie-Aynard was one of those women who are capable of

living a thousand lives. They don't age; they simply change, and of all the phases they go through it is perhaps the late thirties that are the most astonishing, time having just lightly sketched in the lines the wrinkles are to take, like the scarcely discernible creases in a newly folded sheet. Already an invisible painter has redrawn the features: there are days when this drawing appears, distinctly legible, but still so delicate that the slightest touch is sufficient to erase it. The shallow lighting of youth and the depth of field which comes with age intermingle, penetrating each other like two drawings on tracing-paper which, when placed on top of one another, produce a third: the woman's face. It vacillates at the whim of the hour or the day, reflecting tiredness or reflecting joy. Lost in her own thoughts, Marie-Aynard did not know that she was being watched and that the look trained on her with such insistence was that of the ideal spectator, capable of seeing everything that she was trying to run away from or cling on to – the concierge's lodge at Limoges, the damp and cluttered stairways of her childhood, the birth of her little Jeanne, the unopened envelopes of Serge's letters, addressed in his bolt upright hand, this whole dark forest of memories . . . A God was watching Marie-Aynard sitting on the beach at Yalta that late September in 1910. He had no idea of accosting her – nothing was further from his thoughts – nor of listening to her voice, or to what she might have to say. This God was mad, and thin, and hirsute. Well-built, with a healthy suntan and a gargantuan appetite. But he could eat nothing, nothing at all, in this dump of a town. The tiniest morsel he ate covered his palate with a greasy film, and he was damned if he was going to wash out his mouth with soap and turpentine as he did his paintbrushes. The sight of this grease, the smell of it, followed him every-where. Tons of oil must have been poured over the meats and pâtés and preserves which the local Tartars sold down at the quayside. You couldn't go out on to the street without seeing strings of sausages hanging everywhere, off-white or reddish-brown in colour, studded with fat melting in the sun. If it hadn't been for this woman who had popped up from nowhere with her folding chair and her parasol and her little basket, he would have been gone a long time ago. He had a bit of white left, and a few tubes of blue and green. He could then and there have primed a new canvas for the picture he was carrying within himself, without having to tramp through all those nauseating streets in search of an artists' shop. But he knew that it was not possible, not even thinkable, as long as that woman stayed there on the beach. If only she would go, he thought, if only she would clear the space, if only she would put a stop to the whirlwind of blues and whites which darted and receded and exploded into swarms of brush-strokes to veil the canvas stretched within him.

The woman got up, readjusting with a movement of her shoulder the silk scarf which had slipped down her back, folded up the chair, and picked up her basket. He watched her all the way as she left, not wanting to miss the least of her gestures, her long-legged stride clearly visible through the material of her dress, glued to her by the wind, the sand clinging in brown spots to the damp hem of her lace petticoats. He stood there watching her, and she walked out of his life forever. Only in novels do a man's and a woman's paths cross a second time. Never in real life.

Once she had gone, he left the terrace, feeling the sense of satisfaction which a good day's work brings; ate a tomato that was ripening on the window-sill, got changed in the twinkling of an eye, chucked everything that was lying about into the bottom of his trunk, settled his bill, and called a cab. Within half an hour he was down at the wharf, waiting for a boat. Ever since he had finished repainting the old church on the hill at Kiev, where he had been surrounded by lunatics as he worked (the church was situated within the precincts of a place 'for disorders of the brain'), he had felt his own soul somewhat eased of demons. It was as if he had managed to make them all, or very nearly all, take on a concrete form, plastering them in great black saucers on to the eyes of the apostles, venting his private fulminations in the golden streaks with which he painted the folds in their garments on to the ceiling above the choir. He must certainly be better now: how else would he have been able to respond to the blue-and-white charms of that woman sitting on the beach? As long as it just lasted, as long as he could take that shifting image, that moment's breathing-space, back with him to his studio at Kiev . . . He caught himself clenching his fist as though to keep hold of it, to safeguard that precious silence in the hollow of his hand. People arrived at the port, jostling one another, looking for somewhere to set down their luggage, masticating, talking in loud voices. The lunatics were so discreet, he reflected (not these ones, the ones up on the hill at Kiev): it was as if they knew quite well how not to make themselves understood. At dawn they would quietly appear, one by one, in the coolness of church, sitting down on the flagstones or the stone ledges that ran along the walls; and they would stay there without moving, their gaze fixed on the fresco, until the moment in the evening when, covered in paint, he would climb down from the scaffolding and share his meal of bread and cheese and pickled cucumbers with them. One of them, Andrey by name, who was both more ill and more effectual than the rest, would help him. He was the only one who really did. He erected and dismantled the scaffolding, fetched water, and even learned, in the course of time, to mix the paints. They needed so much of the stuff to cover all that space. And Andrey was the only one who asked the painter to take him with him when he left. He didn't, of course. You can take a homeless dog whose face haunts you; you can take a stray cat; you can take an injured bird – but a *man*? What are you supposed to do with a man? There's nothing on earth more cumbersome.

After the painter with the demons had left, it started to rain, even down on the beach. It rained the next day, and the day after that, and Marie-Aynard decided to leave Yalta. She couldn't rid her memory of Serge – she couldn't even put him back where he belonged – and so she went off to wait for him elsewhere, hoping to catch him passing by another day. And she wasn't all alone in this country: she had Jeanne, which meant a little bit of Serge. And Nastia, of course, her sister. From out of nowhere she had found a family here in this country which was not hers, but which was becoming hers more and more with every passing year. At the beginning she had felt the need to return to France. Little by little, the need had disappeared. Her father had died, and then her mother: she had nothing to go back for now, not even a distant niece or cousin.

She found herself thinking back to Corrèze, the village her mother came from, where she had spent her summers as a child. Her mother had supported them by doing the housework for the family of a lawyer who had a country seat there, with an estate, and woods, and a good number of horses which Marie-Aynard loved looking after. She treasured one image from this period, as precise as it was unforgettable. First thing in the morning. Sun not yet up. Stables still dark. Marie-Aynard gently pushes open the door. Right in front of her, her favourite colt and first playmate, Arthur. She can't see his head; just the line of his body trembling with joy at being let out at last to go and run in the fields.

Once, at the age of twelve, Marie-Aynard had had toothache. The only remedy her mother knew was to put warm compresses on her cheek and rub the affected teeth with cotton wool soaked in alcohol. Madame Seyn, the lawyer's wife, noticed that the little girl was suffering, and took her to her dentist at Limoges, paying for the entire treatment herself.

Madame Seyn had two grown-up sons, both married now and living in Paris: one was reading for the Bar, and the other was a doctor. She suggested to Marie-Aynard's parents that she should have the little girl to live with her. She sent her to a good school and had her taught the piano. As a child, Marie-Aynard was of a very tranquil disposition. Cheerful, extremely bright, tall, more than slim, she was completely lacking in awkwardness. On her, the simplest cotton dress looked stylish. At tea-times, when she would glide between the armchairs of the drawing-room with a plate of *petits fours* in her hand, everyone would compliment Madame Seyn on her discovery of this 'concierge's daughter'.

The years went by, and it was time to think about her future. Madame Seyn had the idea of giving her a situation as governess in the family of her barrister son, who already had three little girls. And so at the age of seventeen Marie-Aynard bade farewell to her parents, boarded the train on her own for the very first time, and got off at the Gare d'Orsay. The barrister's family lived in a large town-house in the Place Malesherbes. Marie-Aynard shared a separate apartment with the children, cut off from the rest of the house by an enormous corridor and thick oak doors. The children had their own dining-room, bathroom, and exit from the house, so that when Marie-Aynard took the little girls out walking in the Parc Monceau, she encountered no one, neither the servants nor the masters of the house. To Céline, Cécile and Laure, Marie-Aynard was like an elder sister, a friend who looked at the world with the same eyes as they.

Their mother, who came from an aristocratic family, was a woman obsessed with the premature collapse of her health: dried up, with a horsy face and big teeth in the Anglo-Saxon mould, she was an exceedingly difficult person. She spent the greater part of her time in the antique shops of the Faubourg Saint-Honoré, at the couturier's and in tea-rooms, in the company of ladies who bore a strange resemblance to her. Their looks apart, it was their heartlessness which created the resemblance.

Married to a wealthy man with considerable prospects, won

by him in the face of her prejudice against the bourgeoisie, Madame Yves Seyn – née Comtesse de la Chamallière – nevertheless remained a peculiarly dissatisfied soul. Obliged, albeit only once a year, to receive her in-laws in the salons of the house in the Place Malesherbes, a perfumed lace handkerchief pressed to her lips, she somehow managed to squeeze out a few words of politeness, trying all the time to avoid seeing Monsieur and Madame Seyn's features, which smacked rather too much of the Sinai Desert for her taste. Regrettably, the daughters to whom she had given birth in rapid succession scarcely resembled her at all. Ivory-skinned, raven-haired, and with the enormous eyes of Persian princesses, they owed nothing to the Faubourg Saint-Germain. In the bouts of enthusiasm which separated one migraine from another, however, Madame Seyn would go off buying expensive toys for them, or take them to the circus (which she found entirely acceptable apart from the smell), or of course stuff them with cakes that they didn't like. Marie-Aynard knew better: the little girls far preferred mustard. In the evening Marie-Aynard would make good the damage with the silent complicity of Céline, Cécile and Laure – giving them a purge, letting them get some fresh air in the garden, putting them to bed a little earlier than usual and telling them the stories they loved above all others, stories of her own invention in which the characters were not princesses but things like the kettle, for example, or the celebrated trio Fourchette, Allumette and Lunette.

Yves Seyn was forty years old. He had married Mademoiselle de la Chamallière for love. All that was left of that love was his three daughters. He didn't feel the slightest animosity towards his wife. Extremely taken up with his work (he practised international law), he had no great need of women. Yves Seyn had known Marie-Aynard as a girl: he would often see her when visiting his parents in Corrèze, and was quite familiar with the willowy little child she was then. Picking her up from the Gare d'Orsay, he failed to note any change in her.

He continued to treat her as kindly, even affectionately, as ever – very pleased for the sake of his daughters, who he could see were happy in Marie-Aynard's company. Whenever he happened to meet her with the girls, Marie-Aynard's extreme youth and natural grace, operating somewhere on the fringes of his immediate perception, would act upon him like a breath of calm, as when, walking through a forest, one experiences a sense of well-being without even needing to know the precise origin of the pungent odour that makes one look round, or the names of the trees.

At Easter every year Monsieur Seyn would accompany his daughters and Marie-Aynard to Honfleur, spend a day or two there, return to Paris to settle any outstanding business, and then, towards the end of the week following Easter Sunday, set off again to join his wife at Nice. He never admitted to himself that it was the former of these two trips that he preferred, and by a long chalk. He loved the noisy meals they took together in the little restaurant overlooking the cliffs, and the moment of arrival at the musty-smelling house, and the long walks through the woods where they would gather twigs to help kindle the logs which, being damp, were difficult to light.

After dinner, when Marie-Aynard had gone upstairs to put the girls to bed, he would sit for a long time in front of the fire. Marie-Aynard never came down again. An entirely straightforward observation, this, it led by simple antinomy to another, namely: she might have come down again and sat for a moment here. In fact, *here with me*, the 'with me' being tacked on later. Good God, there had only been two of these trips, two Easters of two days at Honfleur. Seyn couldn't believe it.

On the eve of his departure for Paris he left Marie-Aynard at the villa and took his daughters off to the High Street with a view to buying them something.

'Papa,' said Laure, the eldest, 'buy a present for Marie.'

'A present for Marie?' he said. 'That's tricky. What would you suggest?'

'Papa,' said Céline, who was the youngest, 'Marie's got no jewels, you know. Maman's got jewels and so've her friends and so's the cook and so's the chambermaid – everyone's got jewels except Marie.'

'She'd be so pretty with jewels,' said Cécile, who was the middle sister. 'She's the most beautiful lady in the world.'

'Marie's not a lady,' said Céline.

'What is she then?' asked Seyn.

'She's a fairy.'

Seyn bought a necklace of imitation pearls and brilliants which his daughters pointed out to him in a shop window, and then, taking the opportunity of an errand he had to perform for himself, went into a jeweller's. Comparing the false necklace with the ones he was shown, he chose the one most similar to it, genuine this time, in a black velvet case. He removed the jewel from its case and wrapped both necklaces in a bit of tissue-paper.

At dinner-time that evening he put the parcel on Marie-Aynard's plate. Father and daughters burst out laughing when Marie-Aynard unwrapped the paper to discover two similar pieces of jewellery. She forced a laugh out of herself too. She was touched, finding the two necklaces very beautiful, but she didn't understand their laughter, not knowing what the joke was all about.

Marie-Aynard got up and went around the table, kissing Céline, Cécile and Laure one after another. Seyn got up when she reached him; and as she offered her face to him, he kissed her on the corner of her mouth, his heart opening up so suddenly that he was astonished. Astonished, and annoyed.

Marie-Aynard had on a dress of red Scottish wool that evening. The red went well with the colour of her hair, the high neck set off her profile, but the two necklaces that the little ones begged her to put on as soon as she had finished her thank yous were too much. The fact was not lost on Seyn: he wanted to see the necklaces on Marie-Aynard's neck, but not like this. He wanted to see them on her bare neck. And more than this, he wanted with all the force of his being to stay with her, just the two of them alone together, without the girls, if only for one evening, here in the kitchen with its blue crockery, in front of the blazing fire. Once more he was amazed at the way these desires surfaced so clearly in his consciousness – so amazed that he couldn't even look at Marie-Aynard sitting opposite him, beautiful as she was that evening with the necklaces that were too much. Marie-Aynard concentrated on cutting up the meat on the girls' plates, pouring out water for them, passing round the bread. She too had to make an effort, if only to avoid looking at Seyn's hands, which were large, with long and delicate fingers, and the loose curls of his rather untidy hair, greying slightly with the years now. She had been familiar with this effort for a long time – ever since the year before, when, walking along the beach at Seyn's side, she had been stunned by his feet, by their phenomenal size, and by the unique manner he had of setting them down in front of one another, a manner that was rapid, nervous, and curiously careless. He was bantering away, something on the subject of seagulls, how big and voracious they were, an observation repeated in countless poems, and what on earth would poets do down at the seaside without gulls? Céline, Cécile and Laure ran on ahead, fooling about and laughing loudly. Marie-Aynard laughed too, at first. Then she stopped in her tracks, broke away from Seyn and went to join the girls. It's often the women who are quicker than the men.

The year that followed that first Easter at Honfleur was one long retreat for Marie-Aynard. She saw Seyn only very occasionally in Paris; and she clung more and more to the girls – kissing them, hugging them, stroking their curls. She couldn't bear to see them cry.

One time when Madame Seyn was entertaining, she asked Marie-Aynard to bring the little ones into the drawing-room so that she could show them to her guests. From outside in the corridor, just as she was about to enter the room, Marie-Aynard overheard talk of herself through the half-open door.

'What a marvellous governess you've got there, my dear. It's not every day you find one that good, you know.' The voice belonged to one of Madame Seyn's friends – very Saint-Germain. 'I must confess I envy you, seeing your little girls in such perfect health. Good appetites, you say, nicely behaved, and so cheerful! Let me know when you no longer have need of her services, could you? I'd be most grateful . . .'

With nothing in her head but these words – *when you no longer have need of her services* – Marie-Aynard ushered Cécile and Laure into the drawing-room, leading Céline by the hand. Wan-faced, unable even to conjure up the smile that politeness required, she made a brief curtsy and went off into a corner of the drawing-room to wait for the flood of compliments about the 'little treasures' to come to an end. A moment later she saw Seyn advancing towards her in company of a carefully dressed gentlemen who was as tall as he, but thinner. His eyes sparkled through a pince-nez with a little black chain – smiling, full of quite spontaneous curiosity, and touched with a hint of sadness which sometimes got the upper hand, as Marie-Aynard was to note by what followed.

Seyn asked her if she was well. Yes, perfectly well, was the answer. He introduced the new gentleman. The two planted, each in turn, a kiss upon Marie-Aynard's hand.

'Excuse me if I leave you,' said Seyn.

The gentleman gave himself out as Russian: he was a writer from Moscow, he said, although he was keen to point out that he was really a doctor by profession.

'You must travel a lot,' said Marie-Aynard, for the sake of something to say.

'Quite a bit. In Russia, mostly. It's so big that it's far shorter to go to England, for instance, than to Sakhalin. You've heard of Sakhalin?'

'Yes, I think so,' said Marie-Aynard. 'It's an island not far from America, isn't it?'

'Yes ... Yes ...' said the gentleman. 'What else do you know about it?'

'Nothing.'

'Don't bother to learn.'

He had an unusual way of saying his words, although his French was quite flawless. It was as if he was drawing them out to give himself time to ascertain what there might be in them to make him laugh. At any rate, Marie-Aynard felt at her ease with him, forgetting her mood of a moment ago. And, stand-offish as she was by nature, she talked to him about her childhood, about her mother and father; and she made him laugh with stories about Seyn's daughters. In passing she described to him the image she had of his country, Russia: a huge white plain being traversed diagonally by a bear.

'Diagonally?' he said. 'Why?'

He had taken off his pince-nez to wipe it. His eyes were completely wasted and very kind. Marie-Aynard had never seen such goodness in a single pair of eyes.

'I don't know,' she said.

She watched him all the time he was polishing his pince-nez with his handkerchief; and, seized by a boldness that was quite strange to her, she asked him, 'Are there many people in your country like you?'

'Like me? How do you mean, like me?'

'Good.'

'Mademoiselle, you don't know whether I'm good or bad.'

'Don't call me Mademoiselle. I don't like it.'

'What shall I call you?'

'Marie-Aynard. Or just Marie. Marie's better for you.'

'What do you want me to say, Marie? Come to my country and you'll see what the Russians are like, whether they're like me ...'

'What could I do if I went there?'

'The same thing as now, for a start.'

'Do you think so?'

'Why not? I could find someone among my friends that you'd be all right with.'

For Marie-Aynard, Russia became a place of refuge, a place of escape. She began to put money on one side so as to have the means to make the journey there. And it was only on that last evening Seyn spent with her and the children at Honfleur before departing for Nice that she decided she would have to ask him to tell her the gentleman's name and his Russian address.

'Do you remember that Russian gentleman? You introduced me to him shortly before Christmas. Who is he? Is he a friend of yours?' asked Marie-Aynard when she had finished cutting all the children's meat into little pieces.

'Not really a friend. An acquaintance, shall we say. I only know that he's a writer of very rare talent. An exceptional man. I've read some of his things. He came to me with a problem about copyright. That's how I got to know him.'

'Is his work available in French?'

'Yes.'

'Can you read Russian?'

'Yes.'

'Did you learn it just like that, all on your own? That must be difficult.'

'My grandparents came from Russia. They used to speak Russian amongst themselves. I understood it as a child. They were from Odessa.'

'And you've never wanted to go there?'

'I've been there. To Petersburg and Moscow. In winter it's marvellous . . . But you seem very interested?'

'Why did your grandparents leave the country? Didn't things go well for them there?'

'I don't think so. They never liked to talk about it. I always had the impression that they'd been very unhappy there.'

'And what did they do back there?'

'My grandfather was a tailor.'

Marie-Aynard was silent. Seyn too. She felt somewhat embarrassed at having carried her investigations so far. But she still hadn't asked him about the most important thing – the writer's address. What will he think? she wondered. That I'm wanting to see the gentleman again? So much the worse. Ought she to inform Seyn of her decision to leave France? Because for Marie-Aynard, the decision was already made. She didn't want to do so in front of the children – first reason. Second: she didn't want to hear Seyn telling her that she was right, and that he would help her. No, she'd manage on her own. All on her own. That evening she was fleeing from Seyn, as she would flee from Serge years later.

Marie-Aynard got up, said good-night, and let the little girls go on ahead of her. She was already climbing the stairs when Seyn's voice gave her a start.

'Marie-Aynard!'

She stopped and turned round to face Seyn, her blood running cold as she waited for what would happen next. He looked at her standing there at the top of the stairs, the candle in her hand illuminating nothing but her face and the two necklaces, the false and the genuine, shining with a single lustre.

'Good-night, Marie-Aynard,' said Seyn. 'Good-night, children, sweet dreams.'

'Good-night, papa!'

That night, after she had gone to bed and cried into the pillow, Marie-Aynard experienced what were perhaps the first symptoms of a condition which was later to take on the aspect of a neurosis. That night, however, her reaction seemed quite normal, a reaction of simple disappointment caused by the man she loved. To her nineteen-year-old eyes Yves Seyn was the last word in strength, the last word in desire, with his interminable feet. And the touch of insouciance that she had caught in his look had persuaded her into thinking that despite his position, despite his forty years, despite the manifest ease which characterized his every gesture, she and he – she, the daughter of a concierge, and he with his face of an unfrocked rabbi – were in some way alike. With the significant difference that it was in his power, and not in hers, to carry off the other, far away, to a country which did not exist but where she could already see herself, because all of those phrases – *when you no longer have need of her services, such a darling, your little governess* – would have no place there. She and he, the sea and the sand and nothing else – perhaps the rain, for she loved the rain and the sky – his hand holding hers tight, her face pressed against his sweater . . . In her imagination the scene ended there, almost nothing more than what she felt she had already had with him, just a detail altered here and there, and the distances made smaller. Instead of the rain, her tears soaking the pillow; in place of Seyn's hands, two necklaces cold against her breast. The room was damp. The hint of a gesture, the hope of a call: *Marie-Aynard!*

Despair is always full-blooded at that stage: it drowns itself in tears which are in part a happiness, whatever may follow. Twenty years later at Yalta, Marie-Aynard was past weeping; and yet the Marie-Aynard of those Easters at Honfleur and the Marie-Aynard on the beach at Yalta were one and the same person: with Serge, as with Seyn, she had never been prepared to struggle, preferring to nurse a broken heart from the outset. But what can one do for the heart? Does some miracle balm exist for it? Scarcely. Like dogs, we must treat our wounds ourselves, on our own, and leave them open to the air, exposed to microbes, leave them to get on with it! Jeanne was the daughter of Serge, and of Seyn, too. One's children are the children of all the men one loves, of all the men one has loved; the same thing happens with men: they love only one woman out of all those they have known, even if that one woman changes her form and name and person.

★

Since her fall on the parquet Jeanne had been pursuing her observations of the sky with redoubled energy. Jupiter was at its most visible at the time, and she spent hours focusing her telescope to catch, just for a few seconds, the luminous sphere; to see it slowly emerging into view, accompanied by its satellites – one, two, three – like so many silly geese all walking the same straight line. She would focus again and steal another look at the image: the ball rolling away, the geese following.

There was a considerable stir going on around Jeanne. Her mother, Victor Platonovitch and Nastia had all put their minds to making her forget about dancing in a gradual and painless way, and were trying to find other occupations for her. How could they guess that the decision had already been made, that it had already been accepted by Jeanne, during those hours she spent watching the stars? When she wasn't on the roof she would be helping Nastia in the kitchen, or watering the flowers; or she would go off into town – not to the centre, which she knew too well, but to the crowded and dusty suburbs of Sakhalintchik and Moldavanka, which were situated on a narrow, argilliferous strip of land at the edge of the sea. In the evening she would sit down on the sands and watch the fishermen going off for mackerel, the staple catch of Odessa. Before the fishing-smacks set sail she would see the fishermen seated in the bottom of their boats having a bite to eat, illumined by large paraffin lamps under shades of smoky glass. Then, when night had fallen completely, the boats would leave one by one, until at last Jeanne could no longer see the luminous globes in the blackness. By this time the smell of the sea in Jeanne's nostrils was like the smell of a conflagration. Jeanne was never hungry, but she sometimes got thirsty. And so, as it was a long way home from there, she would buy a copeck's-worth of fresh milk from a child street-vendor, drinking it down in a single gulp.

One evening, when the stars were already appearing in the

sky, Jeanne decided to return home on foot. She made her way down the Street of the Assumption, a narrow street whose houses with their ornate façades, separated by courtyards strung with washing which wouldn't dry, gaped like rotting teeth. At the end of the street she saw an open door with a sign above it in French: *Café*. Her mother often talked to her of Paris – its cafés with counters made of zinc, and chairs outside where people would go to meet each other when the weather was mild, or simply to be on their own. The sight of this sign, *Café*, sparked off in Jeanne an irresistible desire to go inside. She did so, pushing aside as she went the fine strings of bamboo which hung across the door, and found herself in front of a staircase, which she ascended without a moment's hesitation. A badly lit room opened up before her. At first she could make out only the white of the marble table-tops, the maroon of the long seats along the walls, a buffet counter of dark wood; and then two wall cupboards on either side of a French window which gave on to a courtyard where yellow dandelions were growing. The room was square and very large, with an upright piano on the left, and a chair piled high with sheet music.

There was no one in the place. Jeanne stood in the middle of the room for a moment, letting her eyes accustom themselves to the half-light. She went up to the piano and read on the lid of the open keyboard: BARCELONA. She read and re-read the word: there was the wind in it, and sails, and ships from former times, and unknown styles of dress, unknown continents, and a vast expanse of blue. Her head full of images, Jeanne sat down on a long bench in front of one of the tables, and waited. She took off her hat, putting it down beside her, ran her hands through her hair to tidy it, and checked that she had a little money on her in case she might have to spend something here. She picked up an ashtray and examined it. The ashtray, which was of copper, was in the form of a four-petalled flower: on two of the petals there was a Japanese woman holding an umbrella, and on the other two a bird displaying its long tail.

Five, perhaps ten minutes later she heard sounds coming from the stairway: footsteps and loud voices. A band of men burst one after another into the open space in the middle of the room – a confusion of hideous faces, beards, stale sweat, stinking feet, tobacco, and alcohol. They were dressed in bell-bottomed trousers that were staggeringly wide at the ankle – a quintessentially nautical look – with their top halves clad entirely as fancy dictated: jockeys' jackets, cowboy shirts, or just dockers' waistcoats of a dirty white thrown over their bare backs. They may well have been shouting and gesticulating, but Jeanne saw them as motionless, frozen to the spot: it was like a photograph, a nightmare vision, with Jeanne frightened to death and wanting simply to get out of the place as quickly as possible, and quite unable to move.

'Where's this mug of a Catalan, then? There are people here with a thirst on 'em, by –'

Jeanne could only catch the beginning of the sentence: the rest was as incomprehensible to her as some Martian idiom – a rapidly spoken formula with an incantatory rhythm.

'The tram's run over his balls,' said another voice, in a tone of bland reflection.

'He's still having it off with that fat bag of his!'

They sat down in a row on the bench – Jeanne might as well not have been there – squashing her from both directions. One of them, the man on her immediate left, landed slap bang on the rim of the hat she was carrying. They had a serious air about them, an air of preoccupation and complicity.

'Nice little chit!' said the ranter on her left. 'From a good family, I'll be bound!'

Jeanne had scarcely begun to unriddle the first words when her gaze was caught by a gesture, not exactly everyday itself, which her right-hand neighbour was starting to make: he was unbuttoning the opening at the top of his bell-bottoms. A conical object, rounded at the tip, obviously a piece of flesh, reddish in colour and veined with blue, but *alive*, made its appearance. Transfixed, unable to think, unable to react at all, Jeanne followed the sequence of movements made by the others, who, lined up along the bench, extracted from their trousers similar objects that were just as much alive. Jeanne came to herself at last and tore her gaze away; it came to rest on a figure standing at some distance from her on the top of the stairs.

'Get out, the lot of you!' Jeanne heard.

As if someone had waved a magic wand, or as if a sharp gust of wind had blown, scattering dead leaves from the pavement, Jeanne found herself sitting alone. She saw the men on their feet now, readjusting their clothes like so many submissive, shamefaced children.

'Scarper, lads – quick!'

The café was deserted once more. The stranger made towards the counter, opened the glass door of a cupboard near the French window, chose a glass, then another, bent down, got out a bottle, and filled the glasses with a golden-coloured liquid.

'Allow me,' he said, putting the glasses down in front of her. 'May I sit next to you? It's dark here.'

He went to adjust the wick of the oil-lamp on the table next to Jeanne's, and lit it.

'We can see better like that, can't we?'

Jeanne made no reply. She picked up her hat, mechanically attempted to put it to rights, blew into it a little, smoothed it with her hand again and again.

'Drink that, my dear,' said the man, pushing the glass nearer to her.

Jeanne took the glass, downed it in one, and coughed for a moment. She saw the man smile, she smiled herself – and suddenly she recognized him: it was the bald-headed man she had seen on the pavement on the day of her fall. He was

standing before her now, a glass in his hand. He asked her
once more if he could sit down next to her.

'Yes, yes, of course. So much ceremony after all that . . .'

'What are you doing here, I wonder?' said the man.

'I don't know.'

'You live in Richelieu Street, above the Naples. Your name's
Jeanne.'

'They've got good cheese – almost as good as in France, apparently.'

'I can't stand cheese.'

'That's a mistake. What should I call you?'

'Isaak.'

'Why is your head all bare? Have you lost all your hair?'

'No, I've got lots normally. But my head gets too hot.'

'Do you live here in this café?'

'No, but I come here a lot. The owner's a friend of mine.
He's a Catalan.'

'Where is he?'

'I don't know. Out doing something. He's just absent sometimes. Even when he is here, he's absent.'

'What does Catalan mean?'

'It's like saying Russian, or Georgian. A people who live in
the north of Spain.'

'So he's Spanish?'

'No, he's Catalan. Forget it.'

'Forget what?' said Jeanne.

'The lot! . . . All of it . . . Anyway . . .'

He seemed irritated.

'You mustn't go into places . . . places you don't know!
You shouldn't do it!'

'I saw the sign saying café and just went in. I thought cafés
were for everyone?'

'Young girls oughtn't to go into cafés.'

'In Paris, girls go into cafés whenever they want to.'

'In Paris maybe. Not here.'

'Are you annoyed?'

Isaak rummaged in his pocket a moment, took out a small, entirely black revolver, and put it down in front of Jeanne.

'Take that. With your brainstorms, you'll be needing it. Keep it on you at all times.'

Jeanne took the revolver, examined it carefully, turning it over in her fingers, and then set it down beside her hat.

'Is it real?'

'Of course.'

'Can it kill someone? Really? Pity I didn't have it a moment ago, I'd have –'

'Those men are my friends.'

'They are . . .? Who are you, Mr Isaak?'

'I'm in business.'

'Industry? Banking?'

'A bit of both.'

'I can't tell whether you're young or old,' said Jeanne.

'Thirty-three.'

'Pretty old,' said Jeanne.

'Terrifically.'

'I like you a lot.'

'I'm delighted. But you're a bit naïve all the same, or else just too young. I bet you don't even know how babies are made.'

'Babies? What babies?'

'You, for instance. Or me. We were both somebody's baby once.'

'Oh, I know that. My mother's name is Marie-Aynard, and I was her baby.'

'Your mother couldn't have had a baby all on her own. She needed a man for that.'

'Of course! In French, it's called making love. Get it? *Making love*. It's simple. In French, you make hats, you make revolvers and you make love. There's no word for that in Russian.'

'There are words, actually.'

'Are there? Well, you don't hear them very often . . . And what about you – do you have children?'

'No,' said Isaak.

'You see: you're exactly like me. You don't quite know how it's done. The whole thing – during, afterwards, before. Like me . . .'

Isaak smiled.

'Crazy . . . Are you just out of a convent?'

'I used to dance,' replied Jeanne.

'How do you mean, *used to*? Don't you enjoy dancing any more?'

'My heart isn't strong enough for it. Well, the doctor says it's not strong enough. He doesn't say it in so many words, he just hints . . . Everybody hints, but I know . . .'

'Would you like to dance for me?'

'What, here? Now?'

'Yes. Go on,' said Isaak.

Jeanne immediately set about undoing her laces, took off her ankle-boots, and, her legs encased in white stockings, stepped into the centre of the floor.

'Not very easy without music,' she said. 'You wouldn't know a tune, would you?'

'What kind of tune?'

'Anything. Just to give me the time. A waltz . . . Only to get going: afterwards I'll keep it here, and here.'

She gestured to her head and legs in turn.

'Can you play at all?'

'Yes, a little.'

'Let's do it this way: you play for a while. Say, two or three minutes. Then you stop playing and watch me. All right?'

Isaak lit the candles on the piano, placed his hands upon the keyboard, and considered for a moment.

He started playing a waltz as short and simple as a nursery rhyme, a tune that turned upon itself, unable to develop, arrested by some obstacle that rose up here and there in the cramped tempo. The Barcelona piano was very small and somewhat out of tune, but the interpretation itself seemed interesting to Jeanne. She just stood there listening to it, quite motionless, her entire attention focused on the obstacle, fascinated by it.

'Well, Jeanne, are you going to dance, then? Are you ready?'

'That tune, is it by you?'

'Scriabin.'

'Not bad. They didn't play us that one at the dancing-school. I'm frightened, Isaak.'

'Frightened, Jeanne? Well, that's no good.'

'I'm frightened. I don't know what of . . . Not of you, anyway!' she said, going up to Isaak. 'What did those men want of me? Tell me. Why were they acting so strangely?'

'Don't think about them. They're just poor devils. Unhappy men, Jeanne. Forget about them, please. Forget them.'

'I'll never forget them.'

Isaak started playing again, at first with one hand, barely brushing the keys; then with both hands, a completely different tune this time, which progressed of its own accord, without problems.

'Well, then? Shall we get on with it, Jeanne?'

'With what? I want to go.'

'But this is getting dramatic, my poor Jeanne.'

He had stopped playing.

'Not at all. I feel fine. I'd just like to go. Is there any way I could get home? It's late.'

'I'm busy this evening, but I could give you a lift. It's on my way.'

Isaak got up.

'What are you waiting for? Let's go . . . No, let me say something first: don't come here again. It's no place for you. You have your good areas: stick to them . . . Pick up your things, and admit that you've only got yourself to blame.'

Jeanne put on her hat, tightened her belt, slipped her revolver into the back of it, and, going right up to Isaak, said, 'You've been very good for me. If I had a friend like you, I'd show him the sky.'

'What sky?'

'I've got a telescope. A real one, a Zeiss. It's true, a real authentic one. One day in autumn I saw the aurora borealis.'

'The aurora borealis? In Odessa?'

'The aurora borealis in Odessa. Will you come to my house one day?'

'It's getting late, and I'm in a terrible hurry now. We must go, Jeanne.'

He took her by the hand and dragged her down the stairs.

'Your boots! You've forgotten to put on your boots! Go and get them, quick, and I'll wait here.'

He waited for quite some time.

'What on earth are you doing there?' he called from the stairway. 'Do you want me to help you?'

'No, no. Thanks. I'm done.'

Outside, night had fallen completely. The Street of the Assumption was lit by a single street-lamp. Near to the street-lamp was a resplendent carriage. Seeing Isaak, the coachman got down from the driving-seat and opened the door with an air of unconcern, whilst muttering under his breath, 'I've been waiting a long time, sir.'

'Get in, Jeanne,' said Isaak; and, to the driver, 'The London Hotel. First to the London Hotel. Then drop this young girl off near the Naples. You know the shop? It's in Richelieu Street –'

The horses set off.

'Is it loaded?' asked Jeanne, taking the revolver from her belt.

'No. There's no point.'

'Why did you give it to me?'

'Just as a present. A present for you. The bullets aren't on the open market, you won't be able to buy them. It's a completely new model. It's from America. If anyone ever threatens you, don't hesitate, just take it out and point it like this . . . You see?'

'It makes you feel stronger,' said Jeanne.

'What with your Zeiss, you've got the start of a collection there,' said Isaak.

He took Jeanne's hand and kissed it.

'I must leave you. Keep well. Goodbye.'

'Goodbye, Isaak.'

The first thing Jeanne did on waking the following morning was to look underneath her pillow. The revolver was there. She took it and ran through to the kitchen, where Marie-Aynard, in a pink dressing-gown, her hair carefully brushed, was drinking tea.

'Mother,' said Jeanne, putting down the revolver on the table in front of Marie-Aynard, 'I've met a man. He made me a present of this. He's –'

'What?' exclaimed Marie-Aynard. 'Are you quite well? What present? What man? What on earth are you talking about, Jeanne?'

'Don't worry. He's terribly well-bred. He's got a round head like this, completely shaven, and a moustache. You can't imagine how handsome he is! His name's Isaak.'

'My God!' said Marie-Aynard.

'I was bound to meet a man someday. You said so yourself.'

'A man! . . . That's all we need! . . . Jeanne, you're only a child.'

'That's not what he said to me.'

'What did he say?'

'That I was a woman, a real woman. Oh, and about children: you need –'

'You go off! You disappear for a whole day! I don't know which way to turn!'

'It's my way of relaxing. Didn't the doctor say I needed a rest?'

'But you're not resting! You're thinner than ever. And look at those rings under your eyes! Rings under your eyes at eighteen! You're a fright, you really are.'

'It's normal. I've met a man.'

'Where did you meet him?'

'In a café.'

'What café?'

'In Moldavanka. It wasn't like other cafés at all.'

'I can imagine!'

'Lucky, wasn't it? I'd like to have him here.'

'He said he'd come here?'

'No.'

'Where, then? I expect he's made a rendezvous with you?'

'No, he hasn't . . . He seemed very shy,' said Jeanne, retrieving her revolver, 'and – what shall I say? – disinterested. He's ever so nice, Mother, believe me, incredibly nice!'

'Just listen to her! You sound really smitten . . . His name's Isaak, did you say?'

'Isaak.'

'Isaak . . . Moldavanka . . . Not Isaak Storm, I hope?'

'Who's Isaak Storm?'

'The King of Moldavanka.'

'You see! I'm starting with kings!'

Jeanne sat down opposite Marie-Aynard.

'And kings give me an appetite! Is there anything to eat?'

'Bread, cheese, butter – look in the cupboard.'

Jeanne found some ham and smoked fish there too. She put everything on the table.

Marie-Aynard looked on in stupefaction as Jeanne devoured one gherkin after another, sliced herself some ham, poured herself out tea, cream – actually more cream than tea.

'Mother, I'd like to ask you a question.'

'I'm listening.'

'What's he like?'

'Isaak Storm? I don't know. I can't remember. He came into my office once to inquire about something. Something to do with ships coming in from Spain, I think.'

'I'm not talking about Isaak, I'm talking about my father. What's he like?'

'Your father?'

'Yes, my father.'

'Your father's very good-looking, Jeanne.'

'Handsome?'

'Clever . . . and handsome.'

'Did he leave you?'

'No.'

'So it was you who left him?'

'No.'

'What happened, then?'

'Sometimes it just happens that people separate, that life separates us.'

'Death separates. But life . . .? Tell me, Mother . . . Do you still love him?'

'Yes.'

'You must be unhappy.'

'Do I seem like an unhappy person?'

'No . . . Well . . . Not that one sees . . . Will you show me a photograph of him?'

'I haven't got one.'

'Have you no memento of him?'

'You.'

'Am I like him?'

'No. Well, that obstinate look you're wearing just now reminds me of him a little. Otherwise you're not like him.'

'And me? What am I like, Mother? Do you think I could be a pretty woman one day?'

'One day? You are already.'

Marie-Aynard got up.

'You're not annoyed, are you?' said Jeanne.

'Why should I be annoyed?'

'Well . . . All these idiotic questions.'

'They're not idiotic at all. I wonder why you're only asking them today.'

'Thanks.'

'What for . . ? I must be off. Don't forget to call by on Victor Platonovitch this afternoon. He came round yesterday evening wanting to hear your news.'

'I've got no news. I won't dance again, that's all. You're not too unhappy about it, are you?'

'What about you?'

'Me? I'm not. I've got used to the idea. Now I'll have to get used to another.'

'Another?'

'Yes, I'm going to be someone different . . . It'll have to be a real vocation . . . I'm going to do the same as you, Mother. I'm not going to rely on men.'

· PART TWO ·

The month of July 1914 drew nearer, with warm, scented nights under heavily overcast skies. The harvest promised well. Jeanne forsook the sky and from then on spent her time reading novels. Lying on her stomach in bed, she would devour book upon book, mixing French with Russian authors. Her new craving for printed matter was such that she even started flicking through the newspapers – the society pages, news reports, the movements of the Tsar's family, advertisements. Thanks to the advertisements, Jeanne discovered that mankind was extremely preoccupied with its physical strength, its digestion, its hair, the appearance of its skin, and its weight. The names of the majority of the products that the advertisements cried up – angiospermin, endospermin, monospermin, periospermin, aspermin, epi-spermin, gymnospermin or simply spermin, and which were designed to re-endow men with their original potency (IMPO-TENT? said *The Voice of Odessa*: AT LAST A CURE!) – had the same root. Jeanne consulted various dictionaries and discovered that the root in question meant both a physiological fluid formed of spermatozoa and the product of the male genital organs. If the stars were infinitely greater than they appeared, even through the telescope, the spermatozoa – 'bearers of life', as the dictionary proclaimed – turned out to be contemptibly small: something in the region of fifty-five thousandths of a millimetre. As for the outline of the spermatozoon itself, it didn't seem enticing to Jeanne. Consisting, throughout the greater part of its length, of a simple thread, it spent its time chasing about its physiological environment like a tadpole in troubled waters. Upon which subject Jeanne had a dream.

A hole of shifting dimensions, sometimes large, sometimes small, now distant, now close up, and coloured: the upper part green and yellow, the inside black, itself shifting and changing as by the action of a wandering beam of light that revealed, for one brief moment, minuscule, writhing silhouettes – ants, perhaps, but with human arms raised in supplication. Near the top, a row of seated men could be made out more clearly: their legs were dangling above a hole, swinging back and forth. In rhythm with this swinging, a torrent arose: becoming more and more violent, it cascaded down to the bottom, carrying with it dandelions whose entire length Jeanne could see, lacteous roots and all, and tadpoles. The tadpoles came upon her, she could feel their deliquescent consistency upon her skin, she saw their heads from right close up: they were human, the spitting image of the man on the back page of *The Voice of Odessa* illustrating the beneficial effects of 'multispermin'. Jeanne lived her initiation into the facts of life quite intensely.

She didn't like dreams; she never dwelt on them. Always careful to see how the land lay, she would have liked to correct her dreams, to rework them, to act as mistress of her illusions. She was one of those people who calculate their falls.

Nastia would say, 'I'm going to the illusions,' or, 'The illusions were empty this evening.' That's how the cinema was referred to in the language of the day. It was exactly the right word: illusions of a life or illusions of a dream; or, better still, of a dreamt life.

Jeanne became a familiar face at the Odeon Theatre of Illusions at number 28, Cord Street. The woman at the ticket office knew her by her Christian name and would ask after her news. When she went in to take her seat, the pianist would wave her a little hello. He was a very small old gentleman, almost a dwarf, with gold-rimmed spectacles, and was always dressed in a black suit completely shiny with wear, with a celluloid collar upon which he allowed himself a whimsical touch: a very loose knot of orange silk. Jeanne was very taken with this knot: she told him so, and one day she brought him a blue ribbon that she had found amongst Marie-Aynard's things. From then on the knot was orange one day and blue the next.

The old gentleman was called Ivan Semionovitch Filaretov. A former professor at the Odessa Academy of Music, the breeding-ground of the greatest pianists, he followed from afar the career of each of his young colts. He lived in a building near the Opera whose enormous courtyard was divided up into little gardens. He had one to himself, just outside his ground-floor windows. He was very attached to both this garden and his wife; or rather, to the memory of his wife, for she had died young, of tuberculosis. 'A very great pianist,' he used to say. 'An unforgettable touch.' He would also say, 'She was a great friend of mine.' Jeanne liked that.

When, after the Odeon had closed, they strolled along side by side, he scarcely coming up to Jeanne's chest, limping slightly, tired as he was after all the shows he had done, he would still manage to act the part of a perfect gentleman: he would take Jeanne by the elbow, help her to avoid this or that uneven paving-stone, draw her attention to the branches of a plane tree made particularly beautiful by the night, or point out to her a door of intricate cast-iron work. 'So Italian,' he would say, 'just like Florence.'

He often spoke of the cinema, of the films Jeanne had just seen, but above all of what this *art form* was going to become – he never referred to it as anything else. He patiently explained to her how films were made, what the shooting involved and about the work of the actors.

'It must be difficult for the actors,' said Jeanne, 'to be stopped all the time, to advance by fragments, to have to do the same thing all over again.'

'What about when a pianist learns a score? Does playing in fragments prevent one from keeping the entire piece in one's head and trying to find the concordance with the whole? And you as a dancer know all about working on details. You of all people should know how to do it! Doesn't it tempt you?'

'Perhaps,' said Jeanne. 'I could try it. I've got a former teacher who knows lots of people in Petersburg.'

'It's neither in Petersburg nor in Moscow that they're going to make films, but here in Odessa. You know Khanjonkov?'

'I know the name.'

'He's in the process of building studios on the hill at Arkadia: it's not a bad idea at all. There's more sun there, the days are longer. He's bought equipment in America and France, apparently. In a few years from now, Odessa will be the cinematic capital of Russia. There's already a cutting-studio in operation, a few shooting-floors are finished – I think he's even making films there. I recently met some people who work for Khanjonkov, technicians from his film unit, very nice people . . .'

'Here we are at your house, Ivan Semionovitch,' said Jeanne. 'I'll say goodbye.'

'Till tomorrow.'

'I won't be coming tomorrow. This programme's gone on too long. I've seen it enough times. When does it change?'

'Friday.'

'Till Friday, then.'

Ivan Semionovitch watched her go, stumble, lean down without bending at the knee to adjust her shoe, which must have been too big for her, straighten up like a bird about to take wing, and set off at a flowing, rhythmical walk, her arms curving in slightly against her sides.

The next day he awoke early, made himself a cup of coffee, and sat down at the piano. After working for three hours he got up, tidied away his music, and suddenly had an idea. That very day he would go and see Khanjonkov: he would speak to him about Jeanne and ask him to drop by and see her, just like that, as if by chance, one day when she was bound to be at the Odeon. He prepared a great speech, put on the suit he wore for special occasions – shabby, like the rest – perfumed himself with lavender water, knotted on his orange ribbon, and left the house. He went three quarters of the way on a tram packed with swimmers – Odessa's most popular beach was in Arkadia. He had to do the rest on foot, climbing up the hill. His resolve was so firm that he never paused to wonder how Khanjonkov would receive him.

There was a guard standing with a gun at the entrance. A yellow barrier was down, and an open-topped black motor car shone in the sun.

'You an extra?' asked this Cerberus, eyeing Ivan Semionovitch from head to toe.

'Yes,' he hastened to reply.

'They're taking on people in the courtyard there, on the left.'

Some thirty people, young and old, men and women, were standing around in the courtyard, kicking their heels. He picked out a man of about his own age with a goatee beard and spectacles, dressed very correctly in a well-pressed suit and clean shirt, went up to him, and said, 'You wouldn't happen to know where I might find Khanjonkov?'

'Who's he?' said the man.

'The chap in charge. Chap in charge of all this . . .' Ivan Semionovitch indicated with a circular motion of his hand the buildings all around them.

'Is it work you're after?'

'No, no. I've got a proposal to make him.'

'Oh, I see . . .'

'You don't know?'

'Haven't a clue . . .'

The man turned his back on him. Ivan Semionovitch wandered past him, not sure where to go. He crossed the courtyard, went into an empty studio, came out again, and found himself in another courtyard, bigger this time, where a crowd was milling about. He stepped forward to see what was going on. There, in the full sunlight, he saw strange lamps reminiscent of storks, which cast a chill blue light over a set consisting of a bench and a birch-tree made of papier mâché. The birch tree seemed all the more monstrously artificial as right near by, running along the wall of the studio, was a flower-bed of genuine gillyflowers and petunias. In front of the bench stood a man in a frilled shirt and blood-red stock; a woman in a white Empire dress was sitting on the bench itself, a bunch of ox-eye daisies at her side. They were made up as for the stage, in the heavy greasepaint that looks all right under the glare of the floodlights – but not here, in the harsh sunlight made worse by the nightmarish brilliance of the lamps.

'I can't go on,' Ivan Semionovitch heard a voice saying. (It was the actress, speaking to a person some distance away.) 'At least take off that ridiculous cravat . . . I feel so weak, so weak . . . I wish I was dead . . .'

'Now, keep calm, Ninotchka . . . Chin up . . . Just a bit more . . .'

Ivan Semionovitch saw a man standing at the back beside a camera somewhat larger than the ones used by photographers, but covered with the same black cloth. He was dressed in a painter's smock.

'At least the cravat, Ivan Leonardovitch,' pursued the actress, in Shakespearian tones. 'Just the cravat, for mercy's sake. I can't concentrate at all.'

'We're not doing Stanislavsky now, Ninotchka. Imagine the cravat's black. I need it. It'll be black on the film, just the black I'm looking for . . . Now please try a little bit.'

'It's red, red, red.'

The actress was sobbing.

'Five minutes!' called the man in the painter's smock.

The lights were switched off. And now, even with the outrageous make-up that her tears were smudging, she looked young and pretty. The actor in the red stock quit the set and the crowd broke up. Determined to make use of this moment's respite, Ivan Semionovitch planted himself squarely before the man in the painter's smock.

'I'm looking for Khanjonkov,' he said. 'I absolutely must see him.'

As if snapping out of a dream, the other tore his gaze away from the set, looked around to see where the voice breaking in on him might be coming from, lowered his head, and first stared for a little while at the orange knot. His expression softened when he took in the rest of the little man, who was not unknown to him.

'He's in Petersburg,' he said in a soft, rich voice. 'It's not very often that he's down here. Can I be of any help to you?'

'I don't know . . . Maybe . . .'

'Come along with me.'

He took him off to a van. Inside was a chaos of trunks with clothes sticking out of them – boas, crinolines, dinner-jackets, lacy scarves, flowery hats, toppers. Lying on a Persian shawl between two of the trunks was a dog; a very old, philosophical-looking dog, its impassive head resting on its big paws.

The man motioned Ivan Semionovitch to a chair. He himself sat down on a trunk.

'My name is Gauer. Ivan Leonardovitch Gauer. To whom do I owe the pleasure?'

Gauer appeared to be about fifty years of age, with a youthful, smooth complexion which testified to the good health he enjoyed, but with crinkled eyelids, wrinkles at the corners of his eyes, and even more than wrinkles underneath them: real bags. Eyes of light brown. A thick head of hair without a single strand of grey, cropped very short except for the fringe, which covered the greater part of his forehead.

'Filaretov,' said Ivan Semionovitch. 'I'm a pianist. I often accompany films at the Odeon. The cinema in Cord Street – you know the one I mean?'

'An excellent theatre, and your accompaniment is

remarkable, Mr Filaretov. I sometimes go there to see my films again, but it's your playing that really interests me, take my word for it. I close my eyes and amuse myself reinventing my images. You give me a lot of ideas, you know . . .'

'I'm delighted to hear that,' said Ivan Semionovitch. 'The object of my visit is of a completely different nature, and I know that I'm going to seem somewhat importunate.'

'Go ahead,' said Gauer. 'Your word shall be law.'

'It's about a young girl who often comes to the Odeon. She always sits in the second row from the front.'

'Has she bad eyesight?'

'No, no. I think she just prefers sitting quietly on her own.'

'And what of her?'

'She watches the films several times over. I see her laughing, and crying – in really the most wonderful way. It's unusual, don't you think?'

'Most unusual.'

'She's got a walk the likes of which I've never seen. An extraordinary grace. Yesterday evening I was watching her walking along . . .'

'A fine occupation, Mr Filaretov, watching women walk. Sometimes I do it myself. And her face?'

'I'll let that be a surprise.'

'Well, what shall we do? Could you ask her to come here?'

'Goodness, no!'

'You think she'd take fright?'

'I wouldn't exclude the possibility.'

'Are you sure she'd agree to act in films?'

'Why else should I have come?'

'So what do you suggest, then? I'll have to see her. Have to see how she comes across on film, too. It's always different, you know, either better or worse.'

'We change the programme in three days' time, on Friday. She'll come to the Odeon, no doubt about it. If you happened to be there at the same time . . .'

'What time?'
'Nine o'clock, or a bit after.'
'Very well,' said Gauer. 'I'll be there.'

On the Friday afternoon the S.S. *Peter the Great* docked in from Newcastle. Its sizeable crew came ashore and, as the weather was rainy, the low dives of the harbour and its immediate vicinity were soon filled to bursting. Having got plastered to celebrate their return, the sailors – preferably in the company of girls – made their way to the illusions. And on the benches there, fuelling their high spirits with bottles of gin brought back in their pockets from Newcastle, this nautical audience, already very drunk, tried out what they saw on the screen on the girls beside them.

That Friday, *The Haunted Ballroom*, *Scarlet Women* and *Sorrow, Be Still* were showing. The cinema was extremely noisy and full of smoke, and Jeanne, who had not been expecting such a crowd, was on the point of leaving. Ivan Semionovitch saw her in her long canvas raincoat – the same material as is used for sails – wavering at the head of the stairs, wet locks of hair peeping out from underneath the silk kerchief which she wore knotted under her chin. He made a reassuring gesture and pointed out that the two front rows were empty. She stepped forward and took her usual seat in the middle of the second row. Within a short while, what was going on behind her simply didn't exist for Jeanne.

Entirely imperturbable in the riotous atmosphere of the cinema-hall, Ivan Semionovitch was playing the pieces he had selected for the film which was being shown at that point, *Sorrow, Be Still*. It was a passage from Diabelli's Andantino in E flat, intended to convey the inner state of the heroine – a woman by the name of Eva, who, tired of her life as a woman of fashion, escapes from the ball being given by her husband, whom apparently she doesn't love. She is seen walking through a park in an evening gown, trailing her furs behind her; and it was just at the moment that she catches sight of the silhouette of a man at the far end of an avenue that Ivan Semionovitch broke into a different sort of music. It provoked delirium in the house. The rhythm was savage and staccato, and its contrast with the slowness of the scene quite astounding. But this last point passed unnoticed, for no one except Jeanne was watching the screen.

When Gauer entered the house, he couldn't believe his eyes. Beneath the screen – in the central aisle – in every open space between the benches and the walls, sailors were dancing. The ones still in their seats were singing in chorus to the tune played by the pianist the words of a local song then in vogue:

> The night is dark –
> Come with me,
> Maroussia . . .

Not without difficulty, Gauer forged a path through the demented audience, realizing as he went that what Filaretov was performing was nothing other than a popular black tune from New Orleans. He had heard it on his last trip to America, the year before. Where and how, Gauer wondered, could this old strummer from Odessa have heard it? And, above and beyond that, where had he picked up that special way – a way that Gauer had only ever known in blacks – of handling the tempo in new contrapuntal harmonies, in discords? It astonished and amused Gauer – all the more so because *Sorrow, Be Still* was a film of his: he savoured the way Filaretov quite literally exploded the final scene, with which he had taken so much trouble on the day of shooting.

The man at the end of the avenue – tall and handsome in the classic mould, in black tie, his hair blown about by the wind – approached in close-up. Also in close-up appeared his hand and an enormous pistol of the kind used for duelling in the nineteenth century. In the next frame the man was seen from further off, slowly raising the pistol and firing a discharge of smoke. When the smoke cleared, it was the turn of the woman in the furs – who fell to the ground. This image was still accompanied by the same New Orleans music; but under Filaretov's masterly touch, it now took on a different hue. The dry, detached sounds he played produced an effect that was completely chilling. The dancers froze on the spot: the singing stopped. At last Gauer was able to reach the front rows. He caught sight of Jeanne. Only just, in fact, because in the faint glow of the screen he could make out nothing but her small, pointed nose, her white, almost translucent skin, and the slightly childish expression on her face. At that precise moment she was entirely taken up with the trajectory of the fall – falls were her speciality. She was correcting it, mentally tracing another which would have conveyed all the other things she would have liked to be visible – the emotion that could have been there, and wasn't.

A seat creaked. Jeanne saw a man in a light-coloured dust-coat sit down three places away from her. Short-sighted, she said to herself, and went straight back to the fall again.

The sailors went out at the end of *Sorrow, Be Still*. The audience that came in for the next feature was more staid – students, clerks, tradesmen, domestics. The lights were not switched on again between films, and the interval was marked by a general commotion and a musical interlude provided by the indefatigable Ivan Semionovitch Filaretov. Jeanne waited motionless for the start of the next film, *The Haunted Ballroom*. Shortly before the credits – framed in flowery vignettes – appeared on the screen, Jeanne got up to take off her raincoat. Gauer was able to ascertain at close range that the young girl was possessed of no little charm. Yes, he'd try her out, why not – if she really did want to go into this God-awful profession. Gauer did not believe in the importance of actors in the cinema. All right, so they had to be there, with their immense faces; just as long as they didn't take themselves too seriously . . .

All he asked of them was a touch more calmness, a touch more precision, a touch more modesty. After all, they were only models, mannequins endowed with brains. The less the latter functioned when the cameras were turning, the better it was. Unfortunately, this was not the case with the actors he had employed so far, his own wife included. She would concern herself not only with the films in which she was supposed to be appearing, but with all the rest as well: she scrupulously read her way through all the scripts submitted to Gauer, putting notes in the margins. 'Are there laughs here?' she would ask him. 'How many? Yes, let's see precisely how many laughs there are.' Then, she would do her statistics and give her verdict in advance: 'You're barking up the wrong tree, Gauer: this is going to be a crashing bore. How is it that you still haven't grasped the fact that the cinema is something completely different?' She adored scripts with collapsing buildings, storms, conflagrations, erupting volcanoes – catastrophes of all varieties, great and small. 'Your approach is too reminiscent of chamber music, Gauer,' she would exclaim. 'It's intellectual, artistic! That's not what the cinema's about!' Her visit to the studios at Los Angeles had turned her head for good. 'Now, *that's* the scale,' she would say, alluding to her transatlantic experience. 'It moves, it explodes! What nerve! Here in Petersburg we lack daring, we lack sunshine. We adapt all the boring classics – *War and Peace, A Nest of Noblemen!* . . . *Ugh!* And that pathetic salon crowd with their cult of obscurity – all those pOets (she pronounced it pOets, pouring out all her scorn on the O) moping around under leaden skies and turning around in circles with their paltry subjects! . . . And that spitting of blood! All those consumptives getting lost in their own problems! . . . Leave Chekhov to do what Chekhov can do best. In the cinema, rifles hanging on the wall and the hero not being able to make up his mind to take one, all that miserable waiting is *deadly*, my dear Gauer. A film has to hold you right from the start, from the very first moment! And it has to be kept up all the way along! A ceaseless firework display, a festival to end all festivals! Your art should be nothing but that . . .'

'No doubt you're right, Masha,' Gauer would always reply. 'I'll think about it . . .'

Yet he stuck obstinately to his own course, regarding the cinema as first and foremost an art-form which needed no apology. He was just the same as Filaretov on this score. And the pursuit of his art made enormous demands upon him. What he found most vexing was the fact that ever since devoting himself to the directing of films, he had seen less and less of his wife. He had loved her with a love unchanged throughout the twenty years he had known her – a love which was perhaps a little sadder now that he felt its end to be nearer. At a distance, in secret, they were jealous of each other. She was jealous of his work as a director, and of every one of the women he selected for his films. He often changed them, never satisfied with the result, not yet knowing precisely what he should be asking of them. His wife was a greater disappointment to him on the screen than all the rest, being more than the others steeped in the traditions of her famous theatre – she was a member of the Artistic Theatre of Moscow. Gauer found her marvellous in the flesh and bad on film. Despite the populist arguments she mounted for her husband's benefit, Masha had an unbounded admiration for Stanislavsky, following his every advice to the letter, and reading everything that appeared on the theory of the theatre, both in Russia and abroad. And on the stage, employing her highly studied technique, she came across as perfectly natural and true. On film, the effect was crude, false, and out of place.

Gauer loved his wife to distraction – everything about her, right down to her wonderful name, Masha. He loved her superb body, with its full hips and slender waist; he loved her blondness, her dimples, her deep voice, her laughter. He loved her amazing style in clothes – her complicated, rustling dresses, her silks, her stockings, her pins. He loved her very smell, the smell of the Imperial Water that she had sent from Paris by the litre. The only place where he was happy was their house in Pushkino, not far from Moscow. And he became less and less happy, for the days they spent there together could be counted on the fingers of one hand. It was a large, one-storeyed *isba* of rough-hewn wood, in which all the objects they had acquired together were gathered – carpets, chiefly, laid on top of one another to form a mute mosaic of colours, or hung upon the walls. The furniture consisted of two identical glass-fronted mahogany bookcases, with cross-bars of black wood on the doors. The books, of which many were in French, were for the most part extremely old. They would read them together. One of them, which was particularly dear to Masha – she had bought it in Le Havre – bore on its title page a penned inscription which ran TO YOU, MY ETERNAL, INFINITE LOVE, followed by the initials N.C. and the date, October 10th 1760. The paintings in the house were Gauer's choice. There were three of them in total, all portraits. The first showed a woman in a riding habit, extraordinarily alive, a veil half-covering her beautiful face. The second was of an old nobleman in a suit of white satin, an order at his neck, swollen with pride, and exuding an air of profligacy. Above the podium where Masha and Gauer would take their tea there hung the third painting, the only modern one, which was naïve in style. Gauer had bought it at a fair in New Orleans: it was of a young girl holding a red balloon in her hand and wearing a Liberty dress on which every flower was individually picked out.

The Gauer who went to the cinema that evening was a man getting on for fifty, at the height of his maturity now. Born in Prague, the son of a musician from Bohemia, he had spent his youth studying painting. In Petersburg he was considered an absolute master in matters of scene-painting. The Grand Duke Constantine, who had a partiality for Gauer, would have liked to see him at the Bolshoi. But Khanjonkov had got the better of him. Employing Gauer first as a regular scene-painter in his firm, Khanjonkov later paid for him to go on numerous trips to America and France. Gauer embarked on a new course of training in the most reputed studios of the world. He learned to handle the tools of the cinema as skilfully as he had handled a paintbrush. He considered it essential that a director should be proficient enough to intervene in any stage of the making of a film. He learnt about cameras, he learnt about editing. Working for two years at the rate of a film every two months, he had now made twelve. He was inclined to regard these twelve films with a critical eye, seeing them as sketches, as a prelude. People said it was a dazzling prelude. For Gauer himself, these films were of interest only insofar as they gave him the feeling of having with them eliminated everything that should not be done in the cinema. He dreamed of pictures in which people, objects, and space itself would form an inseparable chain, a 'fairy ring', as his friend from Los Angeles used to say, dumb and dead without each other, omnipotent together. He dreamed of a picture that breathes, with an invisible heart that beats, an illusion of life more real than life itself; a picture with sound.

The Haunted Ballroom – in which, we might note in passing, there was precious little of either dancing or ghosts – was nearing its end. When Filaretov had got down from his podium, moving towards Gauer and Jeanne, the two of them – separately, but at one rush – got up and left their seats, each with the intention of greeting him. All three met just below the screen; Filaretov performed the introductions.

He seemed tired, frequently giving a little cough between words. If his bearing was as upright and his gestures as lively as ever, one could tell that it was at the expense of some effort. Gauer himself was all ready to return to his hotel as soon as possible. Throughout *The Haunted Ballroom* an idea had been unfolding in his mind. In the sets that he had just seen, the objects, the furniture, had all been real, they had had as dirty and lived-in a look as one could possibly wish; yet Gauer had been struck by the fact that on the screen they appeared flat, as if they had been badly drawn – just like stage props. They weren't to blame, reflected Gauer. But who, or what, was? One of the shots in the film had made him think of a painting by Rembrandt: the shot showed an old man sitting beside a window. The window had been there on the screen, but it had shed no light; the light-source had been positioned elsewhere, out at the front, just like the footlights in a theatre. In the Rembrandt painting the only light came from the window, and at a stroke everything in the still-dark room came alive: everything was thrown into relief, standing out clearly. Why not, in that case, Gauer wondered, systematically employ a mode of lighting that would issue not just from the side, but from directly behind the objects that one wanted to show up? This would mean that given the set and the positions of the actors, one would each time have to find out the right place for the lights, their right strength, and, above all, work out a way of hiding them – for they were not only expensive, but also extremely cumbersome.

Gauer promised himself that as soon as he got back to his hotel room he would try to work out this technique – concealing the lamps with whatever objects came to hand – so as to light the set of the drawing-room which he was to film the next day, and to see with the aid of candles whether he could put his idea into practice.

Gauer was so preoccupied with the inanimate world that, on finding himself face to face with Jeanne, it took him a moment to recall the actual purpose of his visit to the Odeon. Focusing on her at last, he measured the proportions of her face with a single glance, and pronounced them questionable. He was more tolerant about the eyes: he found the slight circles under them interesting, as also the lips, and the freckles on either side of the nose, which softened a sort of authority in the face. Over and above this, he had the impression, which counted for quite a lot, that Jeanne was easy to get on with. Everything that had happened to date suggested that the cinema had a fatal attraction for hysterical women. The most recent of the series, Ninotchka, was perhaps the worst of all. In the course of his two years' experience, Gauer had developed the habit of carrying, as indispensable tools of his trade, quantities of handkerchiefs, which he would take out of his pocket at crucial moments and sprinkle with drops of valerian. The prophylactic aspect of the same treatment consisted in sending, before each important scene, a basket of flowers or a bottle of French perfume, of which he amassed stocks whenever he was in Paris.

The girl standing before him, enveloped in a heavy overcoat, with her cloud of ash-coloured hair revealing the shawl that had slipped down her neck, with the translucent quality of her skin, and with her air of an amused child, interested in everything around her, her grey eyes wide open, had an obvious charm – all the more so because Filaretov had been quite right in talking of Jeanne's grace, the way she moved, in which Gauer for his part read an unusual familiarity with the properties of space. All this, Gauer had time to reflect, might produce an amplified effect upon the screen, transforming itself into something never yet seen, something fairy-like, perhaps. Instinctively he accepted Jeanne from the moment he set eyes on her; or rather, it wasn't that he accepted her, but that he fell in love with her image, not with Jeanne herself: his heart was captivated like that of an artist painting a canvas who looks at his model and can tell from the start that he is going to make a success of it, without knowing why and without attaching an excessive importance to the model from whom he draws his inspiration.

All these things went through Gauer's mind during the short space of time that the three of them lingered in the deserted hall of the Odeon after the screening of *The Haunted Ballroom*. Without wasting his breath on unnecessary words, he said, 'Mr Filaretov has been kind enough to tell me about you. I make films. I would like – if you've nothing against it – to do a few tests with you. As soon as possible, because I'm just finishing one film and I'll be starting work on another immediately. I think I've got a role for you. An interesting role. When could you come to my studio?'

'Tomorrow,' said Jeanne.

'Tomorrow's Sunday,' said Filaretov.

'Monday, then?' said Gauer.

Jeanne had an unpleasant awakening on the Monday. Still heavy with sleep, she had the feeling that everything had already played itself out – her future truncated, herself without identity, Jeanne without Jeanne, split up, broken into fragmented images that were watching her from every side, as if the walls of her room had suddenly become the distorting mirrors which had remained in her memory ever since the day when, as a little child, she had been taken to a fair by Nastia. She stayed in bed longer than usual, seeking the shelter of the bedclothes and of the silence of her house at Beriozy, regaining little by little her courage and her customary self-confidence. She got up, placed a hand upon the bar which she had not touched since the day of her fall – and a warm, intoxicating feeling gradually spread through her body, liberating it, lifting the heaviness from her. With a light body and a clear head, Jeanne set off for Arkadia. She had a little over three *versts* to cover on foot. It wasn't even a road that she had to walk, but a gravel-strewn path that led through trees which hid the sea from view: the leaves were still wet with the morning dew, and the air was full of bird song.

After walking for an hour and a half, Jeanne arrived at the entrance to the studios. The watchdog with the shotgun who had intercepted Filaretov a week before asked Jeanne a single question, 'For the ball?'

'What ball . . .? No, no – Gauer asked me to come here.'

'Gauer, Gauer,' said the watchdog, not at all pleased with this. 'Always Gauer. Everyone's after him. Get along, then! Wait in the courtyard. It's bound to be for the ball.'

'I tell you it's not for the ball.'

'It'll be for the ball. Move along, now. Don't obstruct the way – there's already enough little chits like yourself making a racket in there!'

The 'little chits' were a bevy of girls around Jeanne's age: they all wore the yoked pinafores and brown dresses of a school uniform. They seemed very excited – shouting, laughing out loud, visibly missing no opportunity for amusement. When Jeanne appeared in the courtyard in her broad-brimmed hat and her dress that was not so much old-fashioned as wholly unconscious of time, they launched into a series of loud-voiced remarks that were anything but flattering. Usually this kind of reaction came as no surprise to her: she had encountered it every time she went into a new class at the Opera and found herself among new people. But today it hurt her. In the past, the initial hostility towards her – springing from the fact that, with her, nothing was the same as with other people – would change quickly enough into tacit affection. Jeanne was a good dancing-partner, and her presence in the room acted as a magnet, polarizing the other dancers, helping them to position themselves better and to perform with more *élan*. Everyone knew that the lessons would be more exciting with Jeanne there. Jeanne never hung about in the changing-rooms of the Opera, and she never walked home with any friend. Her contact with others reduced itself to a minimum. One might have thought her too proud – one might even have thought her a poseur; and this was indeed the opinion of all the girls who didn't know her well. They subsequently discovered that she wasn't like that at all. Jeanne was a Martian, and you don't expect a Martian to go shares in everything on this earth with you.

The Martian was standing in the middle of the cobbled courtyard, which was surrounded on all four sides by walls, near a poplar tree that was growing on its own. She was already getting tired of waiting, not yet knowing that working in films amounts to precisely that – waiting. Gauer had not forgotten Jeanne. He had not been expecting her to arrive so early and then to stand like an idiot amongst the extras in the middle of the courtyard, instead of asking for him.

But Jeanne or no Jeanne, Gauer was completely taken up with his ideas about lighting. Levitsky, the cameraman, viewed his director with the eyes of a governess who has been outstripped by her precocious genius of a child. He had trouble following him, but he followed him nevertheless, putting all his imagination to the task of realizing the boldest flights of fancy of his beloved Gauer, whom he fondly called Vanya. Levitsky was six feet four inches tall. Lean and muscular of build, with an emaciated face and very little hair, he invariably wore a pair of trousers that were completely bagged out at the seat, a sweater of indeterminate dimensions that exuded a problematic odour, high hunting-boots, and the waistcoat of a waiter from the Traktir. At that precise moment he was trailing along behind Gauer with an enormous mercury lamp.

'The good thing about that armchair, Lyova,' Gauer was saying, 'is that it's so big.'

'That much is obvious.'

'If we have Ninotchka standing next to it –'

'It'll be bigger still.'

'We'll have the lamp here. Ninotchka and the armchair together will hide it.'

'You're forgetting that the lamp burns.'

'We'll do very short takes. She can go off and cool down after each take.'

'What if her dress catches fire?'

'One bitch the less,' muttered Gauer.

'What was that?'

'Nothing. What if we had a fan?'

'I haven't got one,' said Levitsky.

'Have one brought here.'

'From Petersburg?'

'Why Petersburg? From the kitchen of my hotel, for instance.'

'You think they've got one?'

'I've seen it.'

Levitsky called an assistant over.

'Micha, go to the Belvedere and ask the manager for the fan they've got in their kitchen. Tell him it's Gauer who wants it. Tell him also that we'll pay a great deal for the hire of it. We need it for a day. Hurry!'

'Vanya,' Levitsky calmly said, once the assistant had gone, 'I'd like to point out that the fan is going to make her dress move.'

'So much the better. We'll put her in something diaphanous and fix up a window behind her, and we'll have it wide open. It'll make a draught . . . When are we shooting?'

'Not before two now,' said Levitsky. 'The time it'll take for the fan to get here and for me to get your window done.'

'Go and get the extras for the ball. They should be here by now. And I'll go and see Ninotchka. It's her last day, thank God. She's bound to be in a foul mood.'

Levitsky had no trouble finding the girls: they could be heard from the other end of the studios. After entrusting them to the care of the dressers, he caught sight of Jeanne, who was standing discreetly beside the poplar tree in the middle of the courtyard.

'You're not with them?'

'No, I'm waiting,' Jeanne replied.

'For what?'

'For Gauer!'

'Are you Jeanne?'

Levitsky took her by the hand and hurried her off to the dressing-room. He talked very fast, rolling his r's as the French do. On the way, he told her a wealth of things about her physique, explained in detail his ideas about make-up, and rounded off the whole with a ceremonious phrase about how it would be both an honour and a delight to him to film such a remarkable, such a magnificent face.

In her dressing-room, Ninotchka was slumped in a rocking-chair with lime compresses on her eyes. A man was curling her hair with a curling-iron; he had the iron heating on a small charcoal stove.

'Who is it?' asked Ninotchka, without removing the compresses.

'It's me – Levitsky. Don't get up. Sit down here,' he said to Jeanne.

'There's someone else with you,' said Ninotchka, sliding the compresses up on to her forehead. 'Who is it?'

'You've got to share your dressing-room with Jeanne today,' said Levitsky. 'There are only two in all, and Igor's in the other one, as you know.'

'And this is the latest find?'

'This is the first,' said Levitsky.

Ninotchka eyed Jeanne from head to toe and replaced her compresses.

'Are you an actress?' she asked, when Levitsky had left the room.

'No,' said Jeanne, sitting down on a stool in front of a three-sided mirror.

'What can you do?'

Jeanne got up and performed a vertiginous *fouetté*, the breeze of which sent Ninotchka's compresses fluttering off her face. She stared wide-eyed at Jeanne going into an arabesque, leg raised to the height of her shoulder.

'Pick up my compresses,' commanded Ninotchka.

Moving with extreme caution, Jeanne picked up the bits of gauze – now covered in sawdust – from the ground, and ceremoniously laid them upon the actress's eyes.

'Are you mad?' exclaimed Ninotchka, tearing off the compresses. 'Can't you see they're dirty? I didn't tell you to do that!'

'Sorry,' said Jeanne. 'My mistake.'

'Call Gauer!' said Ninotchka to her hairdresser. 'And have the dressers come! Then we'll be over and done with it, and I'll leave the place to this . . . Jeanne.'

'That's very kind of you,' said Jeanne.

'Not short of cheek, are you?' observed Ninotchka.

'It runs in the family,' said Jeanne. 'My mother works with Sarah Bernhardt. In the same theatre. They share the leading roles.'

'What are you doing in this hole, then?'

'Odessa, a hole? It's a town with a great future! And these studios are terrific, don't you think? There's Odessa, and then Los Angeles,' continued Jeanne, parroting Filaretov's words. 'Haven't you seen Gauer's film?'

'Which one? He makes so many.'

'*Sorrow, Be Still.*'

'His wife plays the countess in it. What do you think of her?'

'Amazing,' Jeanne was quick to reply. 'She's not very good at falling, but that comes with practice.'

'You've learned to fall?'

'It's all I do.'

Jeanne got up from her stool and executed a masterly fall. She was still stretched out on the ground upon a thick layer of sawdust when Gauer appeared in the doorway.

'That's quite an act,' said Ninotchka. 'Very impressive. I suppose you're planning to build your career around that?'

Jeanne sat up and crossed her legs.

'That amongst other things. I've got a lot of connections. Isaak Storm, for instance. He's an intimate friend of mine.'

'Your lover?' asked Ninotchka.

'More than that.'

'Your fiancé?'

'Lover, fiancé . . .' said Jeanne. 'There are much stronger ties on this earth . . . You see?'

Jeanne took out her revolver. Gauer thought it best to make some show of his existence.

'I'm sorry to interrupt such a fascinating conversation,' he said, taking three steps into the room.

Jeanne got up and resumed her seat on the stool as though nothing had happened.

'Good-morning, Jeanne,' said Gauer.

'Good-morning, Mr Gauer,' said Jeanne, adjusting a fold in her dress.

'Ninotchka, darling,' said Gauer, 'this scene's going to be very different. We're going to have to re-rehearse it. And I must ask you, Jeanne, just to bear with me a bit. Our make-up man will be here in a few moments.'

The make-up artist was a man in his forties, dressed in a white shirt and carrying a doctor's bag. Without saying a word he raised the height of the stool, put up Jeanne's hair in a white cap, examined her face with great care, and finally said, 'It's going to be a very long job.'

He went about his work as if he were painting a water-colour – putting on the make-up, which he thinned with water, in light strokes, spreading it with the aid of a very soft sponge, removing it all with a kind of blotter, and beginning all over again. Whenever he opened his mouth Jeanne caught a whiff of wine mixed with peppermint.

'These paints come from America. Levitsky thought this kind of make-up would suit you best. It makes for a very natural look, you'll see.'

'It pulls at the skin,' said Jeanne.

'I'm sure it does. It contains no oily substances. I'll put a soothing lotion on top to fix it and to prevent it from drying out under the lights. You won't feel anything then. I've tried it out several times on my wife.'

It lasted an eternity. Jeanne got a crick in her neck. And her neck itself had to be made up, and then her hair brushed and curled with a curling-iron. When the treatment was complete, Gauer and Levitsky came into the dressing-room.

'You've done a good job there, Sasha,' said Levitsky. 'I think I'd round off the cheeks a bit. We'll keep that dress.'

'Put a little shawl around her shoulders,' said Gauer. 'Jeanne, I'm inaugurating with you a new system of lighting . . .'

Up to this point, Gauer had spoken as though Jeanne were not there. He looked over her head at his reflection in the mirror.

'. . . and a new actress,' he went on. 'And, if you've nothing against it, I myself shall play the man in this scene. Your partner. Now, you've got three things to do. You're waiting for someone. You mustn't move from where you are. But you can be mechanically arranging the cushion on the armchair positioned next to you, or you can . . . just do nothing. You wait, that's all. Then I come in. You throw your arms around me, wild with joy, and then you suddenly turn away from me, your arms fall to your sides and your face freezes. You weep. We'll have a close-up there.'

'But the tears won't come. I don't know how to cry.'

'We'll give you some droplets for your eyes between takes. That's no problem. Just forget about everything now. Take a rest. We'll have a rehearsal before we do the screen test. The essential thing is for you to be relaxed, very relaxed.'

A week later the developed reels arrived from Petersburg, along with a telegram from Khanjonkov instructing Gauer to take on Jeanne immediately. The screening took place in the Odeon at ten in the evening; it was the day the cinema was closed. Only Gauer, Levitsky and Filaretov were present, not counting the projectionist whom Gauer had had come from America, and who didn't speak a word of Russian. Jeanne's screen test was on the same reel as the final scene of the film, the one in which the star — the armchair — had been so carefully lit. Jeanne appeared after the armchair, without the slightest break or cut. No doubt the armchair helped the impression which Jeanne's face made, so completely one with the light that one could not say where the light wove itself into the face or where the face melted away to become pure light. When the projector had ceased whirring, Filaretov could be heard discreetly blowing his nose. Levitsky made a couple of scarcely audible sounds. Gauer, silent, motionless, was staring at the blank screen.

'This girl,' said Levitsky at last, 'where did you find her?'

'It wasn't me who found her,' said Gauer. 'It was Filaretov.'

'I wasn't aware of that,' said Levitsky, who had turned to face Filaretov. 'I wasn't aware of that at all.'

'Perfection of this degree,' said Levitsky, 'could become . . . well, it could become boring . . . Still, we're not alone in this. If Khanjonkov believes in her too! . . . Shall we have another look at it . . .? Johnny,' he added in English, 'let's have the end of the reel again.'

Sophie Valevsky (triumphant beauty, baroness, coquette) seduces, during the course of a dinner, a young multimillionaire (son of a mine-owner in the Urals). In him she finds the obscure charm of the backwoods, the scent of the steppes, the attraction of a raw and clumsy masculinity. She has a lot of fun with him at the beginning; then she throws him over. In his new townhouse in Moyka Street, the young multimillionaire parades his amorous distress throughout the greater part of the film – until the moment when his eyes, suddenly open to the sufferings of others, light upon the presence of a young girl, the chambermaid. It's Jeanne. He takes solace in her, but at the end of the day marries the baroness. The film ends with a sequence in which Jeanne polishes her master's shoes for the last time, slowly takes off her apron, and, with an unforgettable step, descends the marble staircase at the foot of which her old father, in his porter's livery, is waiting for her with two suitcases.

This cinematic opus would have remained on a level with the average output of the year 1916 had Jeanne not been in it. In the space of the six scenes that she had in the film, she projected a passion so heart-rending that people ferociously believed in it. The whole of Russia wept over the porter's daughter. *Silent Witnesses* became a classic, and Jeanne became Vera Gaiy, 'mysterious and disarming figure of the Russian illusions', as the papers dubbed her. After this film there was a fashion for screen stories in which the star was a coachman, a porter, a cook or a laundress. It was the era of the humble – a great flood of seedy settings, the deprived, the aesthetics of pauperdom. Abroad, Gauer was billed as the master of a specifically Russian language of the cinema. In Petersburg, the serious critics – who had hitherto had eyes for nothing but painting and drama – condescended to talk of Gauer's films in unimaginably high-flown terms.

After *Silent Witnesses*, Jeanne worked with no one but Gauer, refusing the requests of other directors; and this pre-rogative contributed to the legend which grew up around him. As for Jeanne – even when she was on to her sixteenth or seventeenth film, her pseudonym only appeared in small characters on the posters. And her name – Vera Gaiy – had none of the exoticism common to the names of the rising stars of the Russian illusions: in Odessa, for example, there were hundreds of girls called Gaiy. After Jeanne had made so many appearances in darkened cinema-halls, people still failed to recognize her in the street. In her home town she could walk abroad without being accosted, wearing her old dresses – which finally came into fashion – her inevitable broad-brimmed hats, and the shoes that her feet tended to lose.

Her approach to films was the same as her approach to dancing had been not long before – that of a studious worker. The same fatigue was there, and the same self-forgetfulness. On the one hand, there was Jeanne; on the other, the art she practised. The performance of this double act was viewed as a miracle by everyone, herself included. She really was a worker, not knowing, or not wanting to know, just what it was that she brought to films, what kind of actress she was, what kind of face she had, what kind of screen presence she possessed. At no point did either self-regard, or ambition, or capriciousness interfere with her work. One can imagine people asking themselves whether she was really of this world. Indeed, was she? The world went its way. The reporting of the war, ostensibly optimistic, carried with it a foreboding of the disaster to come. The lists of the dead in the newspapers grew longer from day to day. They were printed in heavier, blacker letters than the rest of the page. It was through looking at these lists that Marie-Aynard learned of the death of Serge. She couldn't believe it at first: she read and re-read the name, together with the others, then on its own; she took the paper off to her room and cut out that one line, *Leontiev, Sergey Georgievitch*; then she crumpled up the scrap of paper and threw it in the waste-paper basket. She felt no grief, no bitterness, no regret. Perhaps she felt ashamed – not of this lack of emotion, this emptiness, but of the hopes she had held out of meeting Serge again during those few years that she had gone to Yalta. As a matter of duty, she tried (already in bed and with the light out) to conjure to herself Serge's face, his gestures, the things he used to say, all the debris that she had carted along in her memory over so many years. None of the images which had once been so painfully real came to mind; only that of the line of black letters, which stopped her heart for a second, as though she were bending down and looking into a grave. Doing her hair the next morning, she realized that she had aged, that she didn't want to go to the office, that she didn't want to go to the harbour, that she would have to refuse the invitation to dinner with the French Consul, which was for that evening. She felt quite incapable of examining her conscience, deliciously cold and light, she was the Marie-Aynard of her first years in Petersburg, when she had taken pleasure in trampling the roses of her admirers underfoot. She thought of those roses as she saw Nastia throwing out armfuls of flowers – such as had cluttered up the house ever since Jeanne became Vera Gaiy. Point-blank, without considering for a moment what effect the news would have on Jeanne, in between buttering the two slices of bread that she always prepared for her daughter's breakfast, she announced, 'Your father's dead.'

'Who's dead?'

'Your father.'

'My father?' said Jeanne, without putting down her teacup. 'I've never seen him. He was never there. Whether alive or dead, he was never there. What's his death supposed to change? He's never stopped causing you pain. The only thing that matters to me is that he caused you pain. You've wasted your life on his account.'

'Did I ever say I've wasted my life?'

'No.'

'Who's told you that, then?'

'No one. I just know. You've spent twenty years of your life waiting.'

'I've found happiness through waiting.'

'I don't understand you. I'm sorry, I really don't understand you.'

'Well, that's all to the good. I'm not asking you to be like me. You should be passionate, you should be free, you should indulge your every desire and get exactly what you want, just like that. You should be a bitch –'

'A bitch?' said Jeanne. 'What's that?'

'You have to seduce men. Have them grovel at your feet, make them suffer, get rid of them and move on. Everything suggests that men adore that. There's nothing they love better.'

'Mother, that's just the films people want me to act in. I've just made a mess of one. I'm not cut out for that kind of role, really I'm not. Imagine, a scientist –'

'Yes, yes, you told me about that –' broke in Marie-Aynard. Never had Jeanne known her mother talk so fast, so feverishly. 'You remember that family – I've told you about them – my first family in Paris, where Madame Seyn obtained me a situation as governess? With her son, Yves Seyn?'

'Yes,' said Jeanne: 'with the three little girls, Céline, Cécile and Laure?'

'They must be quite grown up by now. Goodness, yes – Laure must be thirty.'

'What about them?'

'I was in love with Seyn. I fell in love with him immediately, the moment I set eyes on him at the station. He'd come to pick me up.'

'So you were in love with him. What about his feelings?'

'He loved me too. Only I left. What am I saying? I *fled*.'

'Could you have done anything else?'

'I could have taken him.'

'Taken him away from his wife and children? Would you do that today?'

'Without a moment's hesitation. I daren't even tell you what I'd do today. Above all, I wouldn't wait: I wouldn't wait for anybody or anything. You're making a bad start, my little Jeanne. I've been thinking a lot whilst you've been away. Tidying up in the loft, I found your old notebook – you know, your book of the sky.'

'The green one?'

'The green one, with all your calculations and observations. Well, I said to myself: she used to spend her time waiting. One day, Saturn. Another, the aurora borealis. The aurora borealis in Odessa! How you made me laugh!'

'Have you thrown it out?'

'It's there, on the mantelpiece.'

Jeanne flicked through the notebook and re-read three pages.

Odessa, 8 November 1910.

Before three-thirty in the morning of November 1st, the moon, enveloped in cloud, shed only a feeble light. There was a piercing wind, and I was unable to determine its direction, as it was whirling in the trees by which I was surrounded. The Réaumur thermometer showed 3° above zero. I thought I could see scintillations similar to rifle-flashes in the distance. These flashes coming again and again, I commenced my observations at around four o'clock. At that time the sky was covered by billowy white clouds; a few stars shone through here and there, and then disappeared again. The moon was hidden but the brightness of the night made it possible to distinguish objects round about. In the west there was a dark grey cloud lying about 20° above the horizon, perhaps 15° in height and running from SW to NW. For the space of an hour it seemed scarcely to move; then it stretched off towards the north, and, as dawn was breaking, started to come nearer. A number of small, luminous globes descended perpendicularly from the midst of this cloud: they did not flicker, and they left no trail. Their trajectory was short. Sometimes they came one upon another, sometimes at intervals of several minutes. These small spheres were of varying sizes, some of them hardly visible, others larger, and some of them manifestly bigger than even Venus at its rising. They were all pale in colour. I saw them fall from an altitude of 10° to 30° and then suddenly vanish into space. Then, to the north, beyond the cloud, and at a higher altitude, one could see sometimes these little spheres and sometimes what are commonly called shooting stars, leaving a trail in their wake. The latter descended into the west, towards the cloud, at an angle of about 25°. It was the same with the ones that came from the south, also heading towards the cloud, some of them travelling in a zigzag line and others not. Gone six o'clock, there will still some of these spheres and shooting stars, about a hundred of which had appeared during the space of two hours.

In the cloud itself one could from time to time see a sudden glimmer similar to the flash produced when a rocket explodes without a rain of stars. Furthermore, the horizon was in the meanwhile illuminated several times by a flash like that produced on a cloudless night by lightning occurring beyond the line of the horizon, but these flashes were of far less brilliance. Two of these flashes were of greater note, one in the west at around five *o'clock and the other in the north just before six: there was a double flicker which extended for a great distance along the horizon . . .*

'I don't see what there is to laugh at here,' said Jeanne, shutting the notebook. 'It's all the elements of the aurora borealis. I read it later in books . . . It's a pity that I no longer have the time to watch the sky. In my second life I'll be an astronomer. If I have a second life . . .'

'You will have,' said Marie-Aynard. 'You'll have a second life, and a third . . . You're still so young.'

'It's as if you're trying to console me! Do I look as if I need consoling?'

'Far from it,' said Marie-Aynard. 'You're much stronger than me, much freer. You're much more decided. I think I'm going to go.'

'Where to?'

'It doesn't matter. France, perhaps.'

'You're going to leave me?'

'I wouldn't call it leaving . . . There's nothing keeping me here any longer. My Russian period has already dragged itself out too long. It's over twenty years that I've been here . . .'

'What about me?'

'You don't need me any longer. Of the two of us, it's I who am going to miss you most.'

'So you're leaving me?' said Jeanne.

'You're clinging to that word like you cling to your aurora borealis.'

'My aurora borealis was there for all the world to see, but no one was up on the rooftops to watch it. People haven't got time to watch the sky. It's perhaps the greatest luxury . . .'

'People prefer to have children, to kill each other, busy themselves with politics, earn a living.'

'I thought for a moment you were frightened of my aurora borealis.'

'Not the one in the green notebook. The others. I worry

that you're going to spend your life dreaming instead of living
– that you'll go on seeing these auroras everywhere and looking
for them when they're not there.'

'Whether I live my dreams or whatever else I do, I can do it
alongside you, Mother. You've never interfered with anything
I've done. You're the best mother in the world. I just don't
understand you today.'

'I don't understand myself either,' said Marie-Aynard. 'Of
course you're right: one line in a newspaper shouldn't change
anything. And yet I still feel that something has happened to a
part of me, something that leaves me curiously uninterested.
It's not coldness, and it's not emptiness. It's indifference. I'm
getting old, do you realize? One morning you get up, you go
to the window, and you see nothing but windmills turning
round and round.'

Marie-Aynard left during the month following the announce-
ment of Serge's death. Three trunks, packed chiefly with
clothes, was all the luggage she and Nastia took with them. It
was more as if they were going on holiday – the kind of spur-
of-the-moment holiday one takes to clear the cobwebs out of
one's head. At Beriozy and the flat in Richelieu Street everything – the furniture, the linen, the pictures – remained exactly
as it was. When Jeanne went out, a cleaning lady came to do
the house. Grigory, the coachman, came to fetch Jeanne just as
he used to fetch Marie-Aynard. This Grigory was a curious
character. As far back as Jeanne could remember, she had seen
him and his horse on the path leading to Beriozy. Always
silent, always punctual, he was one of the few people actually
allowed into the house. Apart from driving back and forth
between Beriozy and the harbour, he looked after the stoves,
did the gardening , repaired a door that grated on its hinges,
and helped Nastia repaint the house at Easter. The years had
given him wrinkles and grey hair. His horse took longer and
longer to climb back up the hill. In theory, Grigory was

employed by the firm of Liberman & Son, who also owned the horse. Neither Liberman nor his son were any longer of this world. The death duties were still being argued over by distant heirs. The stables and the carriage park ran to seed for want of an owner. Grigory and his horse counted for so little in the balance sheets of the firm that they were just gradually forgotten. The horse slept in the courtyard of the building in which Grigory had lodgings on the ground floor, or rather the basement. In return for the little services which Grigory performed for the man who ran the place, the latter tolerated the animal's presence in the yard. Grigory was a gypsy. A phlegmatic gypsy. The world of clever ruses was quite foreign to him. Heart-breaking torments, the promenading of passions, vicissitudes of all kinds left him cold. He had a roof over his head, enough to feed himself and his wife and daughter; and he had his guitar. He could no longer remember how and when he had come by this guitar. He played it as if it were his whole reason for living, as if he and his guitar had been born together. The only memory he possessed was a memory for music, and he seemed to have no feelings but those which he expressed through this medium. One wondered whether he could actually talk. When singing, he would dispense with words altogether, uttering only vowel-sounds – the gypsy sounds he had heard as a little child.

Some months after the birth of their daughter, his wife found her legs refusing to obey her. The doctors declared the condition incurable. She took to her bed and never got up again. The passage of time scarcely touched her: she didn't age, she just wasted away. She was quite black, practically like an African, with a mouth that kept its youthful rosiness, and large, dark blue eyes that refused to go out. From dawn to dusk she busied her hands finishing off the bridal gowns which the best dressmaker in the quarter entrusted to her. She worked sitting up in bed, just in front of the window. Outside the window, in the courtyard, the horse would be tethered when it wasn't being worked.

After the departure of Marie-Aynard and Nastia, Grigory was all that was left of Jeanne's family, the sole reminder of Beriozy as it had once been. He continued to look after the garden and the stoves, and would drive Jeanne into town or up to the studios in Arkadia. She tried to speak to him, but without success. He would respond with monosyllables and vague stammerings. She knew nothing of him, and she gave up trying to learn anything. His presence was enough for her. It was pleasant to find the house warm and the trees in the garden pruned, and to see his faithful figure waiting with the horse at the end of the drive.

Jeanne was earning very good money at this time; not that the fees she commanded were that much higher than those of the other actors, but she worked so much, spending so many hours in the studio, that it was like – all the obvious differences apart – a worker working more and earning more. She played women, frivolous or serious, from both the working classes and fashionable society; she portrayed abandoned lovers and consumptive prostitutes; she accepted blindly everything that Gauer asked her to do. If one thinks of her days at that period in terms of hills that sometimes lead up and sometimes lead down, then the hours she spent in the studio were all on the downward slope, so relaxed and effortless was her way of working. Ever since Jeanne had been acting in films, Filaretov and his piano had become indispensable to Gauer. Gauer approached film as if it was ballet: he would synchronize the movements of the actors to the rhythm of the tunes Filaretov chose. Every actor knew that when such and such a musical phrase came up, he had a given number of gestures and movements to perform. Unfortunately this was impossible during the shooting itself, because as soon as the camera started turning, the noise it made drowned out the music. One had to rely on the actor's memory and inner sense of rhythm. And Gauer's penchant for long takes made this all the more difficult.

Jeanne brought a certain style to the cinema: an economy of expression, a naturalness, a unique way of moving around the set which owed much to her training as a dancer. There was nothing remote about her beauty on the screen. Supple and pliant, her beauty rested upon the secret charm that is latent in every woman's face, but that only becomes apparent when a look of love discloses it. It wasn't a beloved face but *the face of the beloved*. People saw themselves in Jeanne, and couldn't help identifying with what she did on the screen, with what she was. Jeanne lent masks to the characters she portrayed: her own face remained untouched. She had an endless stock of these masks: it was as if they were a series of layers and sheets that could be removed at will and thrown away. One might ask with what manna from heaven or earth were those masks fed, and from where did her capacity for metamorphosis come?

Her sallies into the world, her life in society, were of the same nature as her work in the cinema. In society she went on appearing in her role as Vera Gaiy. The divide between Jeanne and Vera Gaiy was both so precise and so secret that she hadn't the slightest difficulty in slipping from one to the other whenever she chose.

Her career taking her more and more often to Petersburg and Moscow, it was with a feeling of joy that Jeanne would return to Beriozy, where she would spend a few days completely alone, seeing no one but Grigory the coachman, who received her with his usual mute affection. The effects of the war were not felt in Odessa as they were in the north. It was here, down by the sea, that people came to forget about it all. To forget with the aid of the girls of the port, who exposed their ankles after the latest fashion; with the aid of vodka, the sale of which had been briefly placed under threat by the operations of the Christian Anti-Inebriation League; and with the aid of cocaine, for those of a truly adventurous turn of spirit. It could be purchased either wholesale or retail from

Aunt Agraphya, a seed merchant at Privoz market: in her shop-window, the packets of waxed paper – folded as at the chemist's, and containing a quantity of white powder – would be prominently displayed in the midst of other, similar-looking packets of mignonette and Michaelmas daisy seeds. In the Café Fankoni, which was one of the smartest in town, gentlemen in swallowtails would order, with a pure Petersburg accent, the whisky-and-sodas, the grouse in Madeira, the pineapples and oysters which, war or no war, were still on the menu. There was no lack of English cigarettes, of Havana cigars, of French cognac, or of vodka for the lower classes. The town went on expanding on all fronts. Streets were taken up for new tram-lines to be laid, the Opera was repainted, new 'illusions' opened. The whole of Odessa was present at the opening of a crematorium, the third largest in the world after those in Dresden and London. 'The new age in which we live,' declared the Governor in his speech, 'requires the most modern funerary facilities.'

Gauer left Odessa as winter was coming on. In August he had finished shooting one film, and he was preparing another for the autumn. His rhythm was slowing down perceptibly. Over the winter months he would work on editing the two films in Moscow, where he would be nearer to his wife. Jeanne spent her last day in Odessa, before leaving for Petersburg, playing the part of a nurse. It was the first war film Gauer had made. She was planning to go and see her mother over the winter, at the villa she had rented in Nice. Marie-Aynard was so delighted with the villa that Jeanne had advised her to buy it, and had sent the money straight away. The two films, completed one after the other, had made this possible.

She was intending to spend her last evening with Filaretov. He wasn't expecting her, but that didn't matter. He would be overjoyed to see her: he would prepare for her eggs with fried bread, cooked in butter, and an Italian coffee, which he possessed the secret of making. Perhaps he would play her some

Scriabin. Only perhaps, because he didn't really like playing in the evenings.

His head nodding in time to the rhythm of his efforts, Grigory's horse left the hill behind him and set off down France Boulevard. Here on the flat he perked up. As they were turning into a narrow street littered with fallen leaves that hadn't yet been swept up, Grigory suddenly pulled on the reins and came to a halt. Coming down the street Jeanne saw a young woman of about average height, enveloped in a pelisse of thick grey fur. Her hair, which was black, was put up in a tight bun, and her mouth was bright red.

'Father,' said the woman as she went up to the horse, 'I'm just on my way home.'

'Climb in,' said Grigory.

Giving a slightly embarrassed smile, she sat down next to Jeanne. Jeanne thought her very pretty.

'You must excuse this. It's terribly near, really just round the corner, but I never argue with what my father says. You're Mrs Marie's daughter? After all I've heard about you ... Of course I've seen you in your films.'

The horse set off again.

'I didn't know that Grigory had a daughter. I didn't know he had a family at all. He never speaks to me.'

'Oh, I've given up hoping!'

She leant over towards Jeanne and whispered in her ear, 'He's very good-hearted.'

'Oh, I know! But he's so unfathomable.'

The woman burst out laughing. It obviously didn't take much to make her laugh.

'Can I call you Vera?' she asked.

'No, I'd rather you called me Jeanne.'

'It's the same with me. Everyone calls me Nastia. Nastia this, Nastia that. But my name's actually Dasha. You know the posters? Nastia Polyakova? That's me.'

'And the woman in red?'

'That's me too.'

'Not the slightest similarity,' said Jeanne.

'It's the same with you. We're the two best-known women in Odessa, and we don't know each other. Let's put that to rights straightaway. Can I kiss you?'

Dasha kissed Jeanne on the cheek.

'It's done,' said Jeanne.

'Father,' said Dasha, 'take us home, will you? We're going to celebrate this meeting.' And, turning to Jeanne, she asked, 'You've got a moment, have you?'

'Yes,' said Jeanne, not quite knowing what else to say.

'You'll see that our place is rather poky.'

It seemed anything but poky to Jeanne. The room which Dasha showed her into was more like a cabin in a forest inhabited by some fairy – full of flowers, and wedding dresses, and baskets of lacework, and ribbons of every colour, with clean floor-boards bleached by the sun, a lampshade like a pink cake, and a tiled stove in which birch logs were burning.

'Give me your coat and sit down,' said Dasha, in a tone of command. 'This is my mother.'

The woman who looked like Dasha laid her work aside, smiled at Jeanne without a word, and with a motion of her hand invited Jeanne to sit down on the bed in which she was lying. Jeanne slipped off her shoes, tucked her legs underneath her, and sat down on the corner of the counterpane.

Talking all the while, Dasha picked up the scattered ends of fabric from the floor, smoothed the cloth on the table which was placed alongside the bed, and tidied up the flower arrangements here and there.

'It's only very seldom my father trusts me with the cooking. He does the best marinades in the world. You'll see for yourself in a moment ... But it's with the instrument over there that he performs his real wizardry.'

With excessively careful movements, Dasha removed the cloth that was covering a guitar on a chair at the back of the room, and, without once touching the instrument, put the cloth over the back of the chair.

'Father,' she called to Grigory, 'will you play us something?'

An indistinct syllable was heard from the kitchen.

'He says yes,' interpreted Nastia. 'Father never needs much persuading.'

Grigory pushed open the door of the kitchen, carrying a tray with a decanter of vodka, another decanter of something scarlet, and lots of glass jars with mushrooms, and fish, and little green plums, and olives. Father and daughter sat down opposite Jeanne. Everyone drank a little glass, and then the glasses were refilled. At the third glass, Dasha covered hers with her hand and said, 'Not for me. It takes my voice away, and I've little enough voice as it is.'

'Are you singing this evening?' asked Jeanne.

'Every evening except Monday. But it doesn't start till late. We've got plenty of time.'

Jeanne refused another glass when it came to her turn. 'Not for me either,' she said. 'I can't take it. My head just spins round and round and I've no idea what I'm saying.'

She demonstrated how her head spun. Dasha roared with laughter, Grigory and his wife smiled. Here in this room, Grigory seemed taller and darker and thinner than ever. He didn't say a single word, but his eyes sparkled – the same devilish twinkle that was in his daughter's eyes.

'All right then, Father, your fingers must be warm again now, so . . . We're gypsies, you know' – she was speaking to Jeanne, a note of pride in her voice – 'gypsies from a tribe of musicians with light blue eyes, a very ancient people. No one knows how they came here, or where they came from. They were poorer than the other gypsies, and they had it much harder. Of course I didn't get this from my father. I heard it from my uncle. There are very few of them left today. People often think we're Jews. This uncle of mine had red hair. A

curious race . . . Father, are you going to play something now
. . . ? Go on . . . Jews, I was saying. Yes, and blacks too. We're
supposed to be Jews and blacks at the same time.'

'That's something!' said Jeanne.

'Yes, and it's hard too.'

It was difficult to know when Dasha was joking and when
she was being serious. Grigory wasn't listening to her, seated
now on the chair at the back of the room, the guitar on his lap.

'Ssh!' said Dasha. 'Ssh!'

No one breathed a sound: the silence in the room was
complete, broken only by the crackling of the logs in the
stove.

The opening chords were hesitant, half-opening doors and
shutting them again: other notes crowded along behind them.
There was a rippling – bubbles bursting one by one to leave the
surface calm. Then silence, stillness. The great hand covered the
strings once more, pressing them as though it wished to hurt
them; the head dropped and the face was hidden under the
shock of white hair, the neck looking as though cut in two; and
now the hand, gradually coming back to life, let fall a spot of
light here and there that lit the stars one by one, scarcely
hurrying, fully conscious of the kindness it was performing.
'I've all the time in the world,' said the hand. 'Look how I open
the space, how I liberate the air. Here one can breathe: I've made
a home for you, sweet and mellow, a house of celebration, all
ready for the guests. Come in, come in. Don't push and shove,
there's room for everyone.' And quietly the guests entered as
invited to by the hand, and took their seats in circular rows – the
hand did not like angles – and waited. But the wait seemed too
long, and voices were raised in protest – disobedient voices
which the hand silenced. They started up again, more insistent
this time and more fateful, and yet in their way enticing, just as
certain cliff-faces can be enticing. Now the hand itself lost its
patience. It hurled reproaches. It caressed like a mother. Then it
shook the house and everything fell in a terrible free fall . . .

'Are you frightened?' asked Dasha, whispering because Grigory was still playing.

'What of?' said Jeanne, still lost in her visions.

'I thought maybe . . . It's a tune we play at funerals. And this one now – listen – this is for afterwards.'

'How do you mean, afterwards?' said Jeanne. 'After death?'

'No, not afterwards in that sense. Afterwards for the others, for the living. They go back to the house, and they sing and drink and weep. It's good to weep. We are quick to forget. But you must be the kind of person who never forgets – or am I wrong?'

'I don't know,' said Jeanne. 'I've never had anything to forget. Not as yet, anyway.'

'Every time Father plays something, he plays it differently. You never hear it twice the same. It always amazes me. I'd like to make a song out of this tune. But I can't manage it. Come along with me this evening,' she added without the slightest pause. 'Stay with me this evening. Do come.'

'Where is it you're singing?'

'At the London this evening. I'm not too fond of the place. The theatre's all right, but the audiences are – well . . .'

Dasha made a face.

'You and Isaak will be my audience. I'll try to sing well for you and Isaak. I know that you know him. He's spoken to me of you. If you could hear the way he spoke of you . . . I was actually jealous at first. My being jealous, it's so ridiculous . . .'

Dasha had rattled off these words in one breath. She lowered her head.

'But I'm not any more. Isaak loves me. He says it over and over again, and he shows it. So why should I be jealous? Especially as I see now that he was right to speak of you the way he did. You really are unusual.'

'Jealous . . . Unusual . . .' repeated Jeanne.

'Is it because you're never jealous? Or because you really think you've nothing to forget?'

'I try to hold on to everything that happens to me. I keep hold of it, and I live with it.'

'And your meeting with Isaak?'

'Did he tell it all?'

'I'm sure he didn't. Just the impression you'd made on him. Is it something you don't want to remember?'

'It's something I'm very happy to remember. But to be quite truthful with you, I wish he hadn't told you about it.'

'Are you angry with me?'

'Angry with you?' exclaimed Jeanne. 'I couldn't be angry with you. You're so much like him – it's as if you were his sister. You must suit each other. You're fortunate: he's a good man, Isaak. And he's handsome. I know nothing else about him: it was such a long time ago, before I started in films. But I wish we weren't talking about it. I'm frightened of words. Just like your father . . . Words spoil things. They always miss the point.'

'You close your eyes when you're listening. Do you always do that?' asked Dasha.

Jeanne listened to the music again, and made no reply.

The sound of Grigory's guitar was flowing, soothing, free from care. Jeanne thought of those mornings that herald the fact that nothing has changed, that everything is in its place. The ordinary, the marvellously ordinary. No evil house, no memories, no hint of falls past or to come.

'Are you coming with me, then?' said Dasha, taking hold of Jeanne's hand.

'Coming with you?' said Jeanne. 'Can I go there like this?' She pointed to the dress she was wearing. 'My mother would be furious if she knew I was going out dressed like this – I who never go out anyway!'

'What? You never go out?'

'Well, sometimes.'

'I guess there's a man in your life, though?'

'Scores of them,' said Jeanne. 'Hundreds.'

Dasha cleared the table. Before taking the tray through to the kitchen, she refilled Grigory's glass, then, delving into her bag, produced two reels of white cotton, which she gave to her mother.

'I must be off now, Mother. Is there anything else you need? There's some beef left. You'll have your spectacles tomorrow. Turned out impossible to have them repaired for today. I'll drop by tomorrow morning . . . Thanks, Father.'

On her way to the kitchen, Dasha held out his glass to him. He took a drink and went on playing.

'Is it always like that?' asked Jeanne, when they were in the street.

'There are days when Mother doesn't feel well.'

'Has she been . . . bedridden for long?'

'I've never known her otherwise. The doctors don't know what's wrong with her.'

'And your father . . . ?'

'He must have suffered a great deal, I'm sure, especially when he was young. I often think about it. He's always been very affectionate towards my mother, and then he had me to look after as well – and I was quite a handful. Well, you know what it's like with men . . . Once, purely by coincidence, I saw him walking down the street with a girl on his arm. It was a long time ago now . . . Our paths crossed, and he blushed and looked the other way. He was so embarrassed – just like a little boy. You know, I was ashamed: I was ashamed of embarrassing him by crossing his path like that. And who do you think the girl was?'

'What a question!' said Jeanne. 'How on earth should I know?'

'Well, it's not difficult, really: it was the young woman who lives at your house.'

'Nastia? But she lives with us, she's part of the family.'

'This didn't happen yesterday. The whole thing was over ages ago.'

'Perhaps there was nothing in it.'

'I would find that very hard to believe.'

'And were you hurt?'

'Well, I understand how men work. I always have done. I've always liked men, you know. When I was a girl, I only used to play with the boys: all the gang from the neighbourhood would come round to our place. And I – little chit of a thing that I was – I used to listen to them. They loved pouring out their hearts, even the really tough ones. The tough ones most of all, in fact. Oh, you could hear some amazing things from them!'

'And do you still listen to them?'

'Less and less these days. Things have changed since I've been with Isaak. He takes up too much of my time, what with his business and everything. Sometimes I wonder whether I shouldn't marry him. He'd like me to. He's the marrying kind.'

'What are you both waiting for?'

'Nothing. We're thinking about it . . . I'm more for eternal engagements myself . . . We've got two hours before I go on at the London – would you like to drop in at my place?'

'Your place?'

'My apartment in Pushkin Street. We're almost there already.'

A courtyard, another, yet another, a little garden; and they were at a three-storeyed house fronted with glassed-in balconies. Dasha had three enormous rooms on the second floor. The apartment was full of chandeliers and mirrors; the furnishings were of velvet, the floors inlaid with tiles in different shades of the same colour; there was a smell of candles that had just been snuffed, and a profusion of icons of an unusual, not to say profane, character – suggestive virgins with their breasts exposed. One of them was the spitting image of Dasha.

'That's you!' said Jeanne.

'A sort of portrait.'

'You're beautiful, you know.'

'He didn't like women. You find that sometimes. He really didn't like them. Strange chap . . . He's dead now. I knew him in the Crimea.'

'Do you often come back here on your own?'

'Not very often. Sometimes I do.'

'I wouldn't like that.'

'What wouldn't you like?'

'To come back from work alone and find the house empty.'

'Oh no, it's really nice. I rather like having the house empty. Somewhere to wait in. You need a contrast . . . What do you do when you want to spend the night with a man?'

'Well, that doesn't happen very often.'

'But it happens?'

'Oh . . .' said Jeanne, with an evasive gesture. 'Of course there has to be an emptiness for it not to happen . . . And then another emptiness afterwards . . . But the emptiness, you see, this emptiness' − she pointed to her chest − 'can be there when there's no emptiness all around, and even precisely the reverse . . .'

'Good Lord, you know enough about emptiness, don't you?'

'How very quiet it is here,' said Jeanne. 'So much quieter than Beriozy. At Beriozy you always have the sound of the sea. Here there's nothing at all, not even the sound of the wind and the trees.'

'Well, we're a long way back from the street here, of course. You hear the rain falling, and the birds, but they've all left now. I really like being here though . . . I'm glad you've come. How old are you?'

'Twenty.'

'I'm twenty-two, and I feel I've got about twenty years on top of that.'

'You'll get them back.'

'Get what back?'

'Those years,' said Jeanne, running her hand along a row of books. 'You've got a lot of books here . . .' She took one from the shelf. 'What's this?'

'It's the Bible of our times. An infernal machine for shaking up the world.'

'What, this book?' said Jeanne, waving it around.

'There are two others like that, just as big, and all three are quite unreadable. They're a ticket for Siberia, all the same. I don't mean just that book, but these pamphlets especially. You see the pile down at the bottom there? I call it the "Siberian Collection" – published, I would have you note, at Isaak's expense.'

'And have you read this book?'

'*Das Kapital*?' said Dasha. 'No, of course not. It's impossible to get past the preface, particularly for someone like me. You have to have done all kinds of studies. That book is written for great minds – the idea being that they're going to turn the world upside down, and we've just got to follow them. Isaak says that you have to decode *Das Kapital*, that you have to get to the bottom of it, that it contains the essence of all human thought. Well, how am I to do that? Our orthodox priest was the nearest I ever got to a university. He was a marvellous priest, Father Alexander . . . He taught me to read and write. At the beginning I thought he was trying to save my soul – you know, they all do that. Well, mine was giving cause for concern at the age of fifteen . . . But that wasn't the case, in fact: he loved me for myself, just as I was, with my irredeemable soul and my perforated lungs. And I was so keen! I would run to his lessons, my heart pounding away. We even started learning Greek.'

'And then . . . ?'

'Then he died. At the age of thirty-five. He died of TB . . . For a long time afterwards I didn't want to learn anything, neither Greek nor anything else.'

'And what about your lungs?'

'I got them sorted out – thanks to him again.'

'And your soul?'

'As irredeemable as ever.'

Dasha laughed. It wasn't a laugh. Tears appeared in the corners of her eyes.

'Are you crying?'

'No, no, I'm laughing. I'm just thinking – or rather, I was thinking a moment ago, when we came in – that you might never want to come back here again.'

'And would you like me to come back?'

'Yes, very much,' said Dasha.

'I'll come again,' said Jeanne, replacing *Das Kapital* on the bookshelf.

'If you don't like the pictures, I'll get rid of them.'

'Good Lord, what on earth for? They're very beautiful. I've never seen anything like them.'

'Or the chandeliers, then. They serve no purpose, anyway – I've got electricity throughout.'

'Oh, show me,' said Jeanne. 'We haven't got it at Beriozy.'

Dasha pressed a switch and the whole room was lit up, right into the furthest corners.

'That's terrific!' said Jeanne. 'And you've got it every-where?'

'Even in the dressing-room and the kitchen.'

'What opulence!' said Jeanne. 'You live like a princess . . . My mother has a thing against electricity. We have paraffin at home, and it smells bad. Nastia's just the same: nothing in the world would have persuaded her to have electric lighting. I tell her that the cinema is just electricity and nothing else. She says, 'You're having me on, it's magic . . . She's frightened of trams: she doesn't like the sparks they make overhead. As for me, I love trams . . .'

'It's a pity we never met. We could have had fun. When I think that my father has been going to your place all this time – How long is it now?'

'Oh, a very long time,' said Jeanne, 'as far back as I can think. I can see him with his horse, waiting on the path for my mother . . .'

'It's no longer the same horse. It's the third now.'

'No, it's the second. The first was called Sultan and had absolutely nothing of the Sultan about him . . . Did he never talk to you about us?'

'Oh, he did: he said you were a dancer, and that Nastia —'

'Well, let's not talk about that. It's none of our affair.'

'You have principles?'

'I have an entire civil code.'

'What would you say to a bath? I always take a bath before going off to sing – that's a principle too . . .'

Jeanne followed her out into a little corridor. One of the doors gave on to the bathroom. The floor was of concrete, the bathtub of zinc. There was no mirror, no furniture, no make-up things.

'This is serious,' said Jeanne.

'Isaak calls it my torture chamber. Look out of the window – all those rooftops!'

'The gardens! I never would have thought there were so many gardens in Odessa.'

'Isaak tells me it's the same in Paris. All the house-fronts crammed right up against one another, and, behind the houses, garden upon garden . . . Have you ever been to Paris?'

'No,' said Jeanne, 'not yet. I'll go there one of these days. My mother's lived there. She often tells me about Paris – it's as if I'd been there myself . . . But I think her favourite town is Yalta.'

'What a place!' said Dasha. 'I spent a whole year there – Oh, it was dismal! I shall never, ever go there again!'

'Your lungs?'

Dasha turned on the tap and took off her skirt and bodice. She had on a strapless brassière of cambric with a petticoat to match, very simple in cut, with just a trimming of lace at the hem. With quick and precise movements she undressed, and was soon quite naked. The upper part of her body was frail, but her legs and hips were full.

'What are you waiting for?' said Dasha. 'Hurry up!'

Jeanne slipped off her dress, stepped out of it, and then removed the second dress that went underneath by pulling it off over her head, almost tearing the various layers of thin material.

'You're so beautiful,' observed Dasha, who was already soaping herself in the bath-tub. 'If I were you I'd walk round town stark naked.'

'I think I might wait till summer.'

'What marvellous breasts you have . . . ! And your stomach – what muscles!' Dasha reached out a soap-sudded hand to touch Jeanne's stomach. She ran her hand down it, leant forward and kissed it. 'Come on now,' she said, 'we haven't got long.'

Jeanne got into the bath-tub at the other end from Dasha, sliding her legs in parallel to hers.

'I've got a sister now, you see,' said Dasha. 'I've always dreamt of having one. If I had a real one, she wouldn't be like you . . . It wouldn't be so good . . . But I've chosen you, you're just the sister I need . . . Don't get your hair wet,' she added.

Dasha was the first to get out. She produced a large sheet. They dried themselves with it, each holding on to one end.

'You're not cold, are you?' asked Dasha.

'Not at all.'

Dasha threw the sheet around Jeanne and led her through into the bedroom. Standing completely naked in front of the mirrored door of the wardrobe, she reflected for a moment and said, 'Now, what could you put on? My dresses will all be a bit short on you. It doesn't matter, though, you've got such lovely ankles . . . Try this!'

She took out a tight-fitting dress of white satin, a simple tube with long, close-fitting sleeves.

'There's a fox stole to go with it.'

'What, with the head and tail?' asked Jeanne uneasily.

'Without anything. Here, look.'

Dasha showed her the white fur.

Obediently, Jeanne slipped on the dress over her bare skin, looked at herself in the mirror, and put the stole around her shoulders.

'Fascinating,' said Dasha, in a very serious voice. 'Don't you think?'

'I do.'

'You're going to look unforgettable,' declared Dasha. 'A queen, a real queen of the silver screen.'

'You're a bit of a nanny, all the same,' said Jeanne, sitting down on the bed. 'The great man-eater Nastia Polyakova is nothing but a nanny, just a nurse, and no one in town knows it,' she said, addressing her words to the wardrobe mirror. 'And now for you. I assume you don't actually sing in the nude?'

'Not yet. I'm always afraid of catching cold. With my chest, you know . . .'

She put on a red woollen dress with a very tight waist and knotted a large white shawl embroidered with forget-me-nots around her shoulders.

'Mag–*nificent*!' exclaimed Jeanne emphatically. 'Do you know that?'

'I know that,' said Dasha, in a cold voice. 'You never get anywhere in this profession without all this bit. When you get up on stage, you say to yourself, I'm the most beautiful of all, the most desirable of all, the most this, the most that . . .'

'And does it actually help?'

'It does.'

Dasha put her hand on her hip, threw back her head slightly, and, starting off on a very high note and descending lower and lower down the scale, sang:

'He didn't love me.
Didn't he love me?
No, he didn't love me.'

'Are those clear words yours?' asked Jeanne.

'It's an old ballad.'

'I'd love to listen to your ballads. But I just can't this evening ... I have to leave you. I'll drop you off at the London and go home. I've got to be up at dawn tomorrow. I'm leaving very early.'

'Where for?' asked Dasha, with a changed expression.

'For Petersburg.'

'You're making a film?'

'Yes,' said Jeanne, taking off her dress.

'What are you doing?'

'I'm taking off this dress, as you see.'

'It suited you so well.'

'I'll be back in a month. And as soon as I am, I'll come and have a bath with you and listen to you sing.'

'Isaak will be disappointed. I can already see the surprise on his face ...'

'We'll give him a surprise another day ... Is he as red-headed and handsome as ever?'

'He's more of a red-head than ever: he's got all his hair now. Keep the dress, at least. You might have an occasion to wear it in Petersburg.'

'Thanks, I'll take it. I'll put it on tomorrow. I always go to bed early. I'm in bed by ten, with the feeling of having lived a life, an entire existence. And I wake up the next morning all ready to live another.'

'I always feel I'm singing for the last time. Every time is the last – a whole series of last times ...'

One could see it from afar, right from the top of Nicholas Boulevard, which overhung the sea, running down towards the harbour: the most brightly lit building in Odessa, and the most frequented, too. Everyone who was anyone in the world of finance, everyone who counted for anything in the upper echelons of society, officers of the highest ranks, both Russian and foreign – all came to spend their evenings there. The clientèle was carefully vetted at the entrance by bouncers as discreet as they were awe-inspiring; the cuisine was immensely sophisticated; the orchestra was famous: the whole place functioned as a sort of club. Dinner was served from ten o'clock onwards, and the orchestra took the stage an hour later. People came there to dance.

The main hall of the London Hotel was half the size of the Opera: there were private boxes hung with dark brown velvet, and the tables in the middle of the room itself were spaced an agreeable distance apart from one another. The plates were of English cream-ware, the glasses of Baccarat crystal; the silver-plate was of Warsaw silver; there were arrangements of roses – never anything but white – in all seasons; there was an enormous pastel-coloured carpet on the marble floor. The head chef was French, like the wines.

People started arriving around midnight to see Nastia Polyakova, the heart-throb of the town, step out on stage. The London Hotel was only one of the many places at which she performed. She was paid well at the London, very well indeed – a fact which interested her greatly, for she knew that her career would not be a long one. She was paid for her youth, for her charm, for her novel way of murmuring her songs, for the sudden leaps and plummets of her actually quite weak voice. For the audience, it was like watching an acrobat performing on the high wire. The love that the audience felt for her had something of the thrill, the compassion, and at the same time the sadism that is felt by a circus audience.

From the streets of her adolescence she had kept a hoodlum streak, and from her stay at the sanatorium, a fear – the fear that her illness would come and take hold of her again from one day to the next. She still had delicate lungs, and was all the more desperate to live her days because she still counted each one. She greeted every new morning with astonishment: I'm not coughing, there's colour in my cheeks, and it's not the flush of fever, it's the flush of health, and I've the strength to get up and run about the place. I can cope – what a miracle! At night she would forget this early-morning Dasha: at night she simply lived, without troubling herself with questions. It was only on waking up every morning that she would think in terms of her 'last times'. When she opened the newspaper and found nothing in it about herself, she would be annoyed, sulking all day like a little girl whom someone has omitted to tell how pretty and clever she is. One could print absolutely anything about Nastia Polyakova – the most fantastic lies, the wildest absurdities. It little mattered, as long as she was being talked about. She devoured the reports that turned the spot-light on her conquests, just as she might have read novels: I'm pregnant by the French Consul? A fine idea! The Governor of Kiev is on the point of throwing up his career, his blonde wife, and his darling little angels for a single glance from me! Fat chance! I've never set eyes on the man! But what people wrote about Isaak and her pleased her infinitely less; for it was the truth.

Fortunately, the truth was not a usual speciality of *The Voice of Odessa*, still less of the other papers. As a good citizen, Dasha was not in the least bothered to see her doings reported side by side with other scandalous news items: Snyegureyev, director of the Institute for Deaf-Mutes, systematically deflowered his charges ... There were always scandals. Dasha often drew inspiration for her cabaret from the headlines.

As for Odessa's political commentators, they stuck to the beaten track, never troubling themselves with unnecessary details: everything was the fault of the Jews. They just took care that no real names appeared in their pages: it would have led to unnecessary complications. Abstractions were the order of the day, as was monotony. To alleviate the monotony a little, Dasha had once rewritten a leading article in her own way, setting it to a tango tune and transposing the whole situation two thousand years into the past – she was good on religious history. No one applauded: it had been a mistake to expect the audience to make the imaginative effort required. Since then she had concentrated on more accessible subjects.

'. . . He keeps going on about this scientific certainty. It's the only word he's got at the moment: "scientific, scientific . . ." Yes, it's a scientific certainty that all of this' – Dasha gestured towards the group of ladies and gentlemen in front of the London Hotel, the carriages, a few cars parked at the kerbside, the solicitous porters – 'that all of this will go up in smoke. And before very long, too. Isaak thinks there'll be just one big bang when this war is over.'

'You're talking about a bomb, then?' asked Jeanne.

'Well no, I was speaking figuratively. The Russian Empire is rotten to the core. The whole system's cracking up. No one wants this war . . . Everything's going to change, starting with the distribution of power itself. There'll be no such thing as rich and poor – everyone will be equal.'

'But that would mean a republic, like France –'

'France a republic? With all those people who've got everything, and others who've got nothing at all . . . ? Isaak's friends don't want to see the rich in power, whether they're Royals or Rothschilds – no, they've got no time for these republics. I know what it all boils down to: you've got to do away with private wealth once and for all.'

'Which takes us back to my bomb,' said Jeanne. 'No one's going to part with their wealth without being forced to. And if you do that, if you force them, we'll have a revolution on our hands. Is that what Isaak's working up to?'

'You're obsessed with bombs!' laughed Dasha. 'Isaak, as he says himself, is just a tiny cog in an infinitely bigger machine.

I've seen some of the people Isaak has dealings with. I couldn't believe there were so many of them. Goodness only knows where they all come from – you'd think from another planet. When you think of this Russia of muted voices and shadowy presences, this twilight world of fragile people groping for answers – Well, when you think of Chekhov's Russia . . . But why go as far afield as Chekhov? Just look at you yourself, or Isaak . . . If you could see these heralds of the Apocalypse – their self-assurance, the hardness of their eyes. They don't politely ask Isaak for money: they come straight out with the bills they want paid. Ten thousand roubles for "the people's cause", twenty thousand for the prisoners, five thousand for their comrades abroad. That's what it's like,' sighed Dasha. ' "We need seventy-five 30:30 rifles . . ." I couldn't help asking, "Why not seventy-six?" If you could have seen the look one of those "businessmen" gave me . . .'

'That's a lot of money,' said Jeanne. 'Is Isaak so rich?'

'Well, it comes and goes. He's got a tobacco factory. They make 'Sir' cigarettes – you know the long green packet with the man's head with a moustache and top hat? That's going very well: he's exporting all over the place. He's even got clients in America. And then he's got an import-export agency – all quite legal, and a very good cover for smuggling. But it's the smuggling that really brings the money in. He's not the only one who does it: there's a whole little world involved. And that's where he has to be tough. To make sure that the company performs and that everyone gets their cut, Isaak sometimes has to eliminate the odd person . . . Of course he doesn't do it himself: he's got the boys to take care of that side of things. The *bindujniks*★ are behind him, and he's got a good standing with the sailors. They're all from Moldavanka – it's like one big family. No problems there . . . Smuggling's

★Odessan slang for dockers (author's note).

nothing to worry about: it's as old as Odessa. It's just these characters who have got him involved with the Catalan, the weapons business and the Apocalypse gang who are the trouble. And there I do worry, to tell you the truth; there are times when I fear for Isaak's life. The police don't like it – even here in Odessa, where we've got a kind of republic – not to mention the big men from up north and the spies sent out to track down Isaak's visitors ... Anyway, I try to comfort myself with the idea that they'd need a lot of imagination to get anywhere in Moldavanka ...'

'You exaggerate! The whole business isn't that serious.'

'Oh yes,' said Dasha, 'it's serious.'

· PART THREE ·

Jeanne's new partner, a member of the Artistic Theatre of Moscow (the nursery from which Gauer, his prejudices notwithstanding, often recruited his actors), showed scant sense of decorum when it came to the shooting of love-scenes.

'Do you really have to be quite so precise about where your kisses go?' said Jeanne, during one of the breaks. 'And on top of that, you're suffocating me.'

'Well, it doesn't bother me in the slightest,' interposed Gauer. 'But you mustn't go red like that, Jeanne. These things happen, you know.'

'It's the lights that are making me go red,' said Jeanne, going redder still. 'And I repeat that he's suffocating me.'

Levitsky went up to Jeanne, tidied a lock of hair that was straying from her carefully arranged bun, gave her a kiss, and said, 'Don't worry, my girl, I'll protect your honour! On set, at least,' he added, already back at his lights.

Not to be put off, Jeanne's partner – best known for his interpretations of Hamlet and Prince Mishkin under the direction of Nemirovitch-Dantchenko – invited Jeanne on the spot to accompany him to the Stray Dog that evening.

'It might help clear up things between us. They dance the tango there.'

And, under the gaze of the entire company, he immediately began to teach Jeanne the steps of the fashionable new dance.

'How decadent,' said Jeanne, locked in her partner's embrace. 'Is this going to be the day of my downfall . . .? Why shouldn't I go to the Stray Dog and dance the tango? I've always had a liking for blond men . . . Where is this place?'

'I love your perfume,' said the actor, dancing at arm's length with Jeanne and then suddenly pulling her close. 'Woman, you're more natural than nature herself, and you dance the tango better than the hot-blooded Argentines.'

'Well, it's lovely watching this, darlings,' said Gauer. 'We could make a proper little sequence out of it, but I've still got a load of exteriors to do. Let's get back to the job in hand!'

After ten hours at the studios – ten hours of wearing make-up which she hated, of sweltering, dazzling lights, of the constant din of the camera – all Jeanne's early-morning sparkle was gone. Looking older, her features drawn, she smeared her face with vaseline, washed under the tap of her dressing-room, lay down for a moment to unwind, put on her ordinary dress, and, without saying a word to anyone, left the place.

She walked to the nearest tram stop. It was always the same line she took: the number 9, which ran between the Poutiloff factory and the military hospital. As she walked along, she found herself thinking that her real life was perhaps the one that she lived in front of the camera. Without studio lights, the world around her seemed drab; without make-up, the faces of passers-by looked grey. It took quite some time for her eyes to recover and get used to the badly lit streets. Only then did she begin to make out the outlines of things – faces, houses, trees.

She was particularly fond of this tramline. After the Odessan crowds, she found the people who rode it pleasantly reserved, and she enjoyed rubbing shoulders with them. Sometimes, seeing how pale and slim she was, they would give up their seats for her, taking her no doubt for a nurse from the military hospital, on her way home after a long day's work.

The tram she took that evening was more crowded than usual. It ran along Vassilyevsky Island at a snail's pace, fresh passengers piling in at every stop. Hemmed in on all sides, Jeanne stood on the rear platform holding two copecks in her hand with which to purchase a ticket – an impossible operation, for there was no way she could move. She nevertheless made

the effort, pivoting round on the spot at the risk of losing her
footing, and found herself face to face with a man in a military
cap. She smiled despite herself, so irresistible did his face seem
to her. They remained thus for some two or three minutes,
scrutinizing one another with a closeness that would have been
unthinkable in another place and in different circumstances,
their breath mingling, the warmth of their bodies mingling
too – his through the leather of his jacket and hers through the
wool of her coat. The tram suddenly braked, throwing Jeanne's
head against the man's chest, and he caught hold of her
shoulder as if to protect her – a gesture that was entirely
redundant, for she could neither fall nor injure herself in any
way. When Jeanne lifted her head, her face touched that of the
man so close to her, and this momentary contact produced in
Jeanne such a new, such an acute, sensation that she could have
fainted – in which case the arms around her might really have
taken on a point. But Jeanne's mind was far from thoughts of
cause and effect: it was all she could do to summon the
strength to tear herself away from his face and say, 'This tram
has a mind of its own!'

'A mind of its own,' echoed the man in a voice that was
barely audible, bending down towards Jeanne's ear. 'And you
are an angel. At last I understand: angels don't walk this earth,
they go around in trams.'

'I'm a dog-tired angel,' Jeanne whispered back in his ear.

And as the name of the odour that the man exuded –
chloroform – occurred to her, she added, very quietly, 'You're
a narcotic on legs. One whiff of you would be enough to send
the whole of Petersburg to sleep.'

'I'm sorry,' said the man, giving her a very serious look.

The platform emptied somewhat at the next stop.

'One more stop and we'll have to go our separate ways,'
said Jeanne.

'I know another line where the trams are just as full.'

How amazing this man is, thought Jeanne, her head in a

whirl, how utterly amazing. I must think up something quick, I mustn't let him go, or else – and in a dream, she spontaneously brushed his chin with her burning lips. My God, she thought, I'm going mad, it must be because I'm so tired or something, oh no . . . She freed herself from his arms and said, almost coldly, 'Forgive me.'

His eyes were grey like hers, with bushy black brows and long, curling lashes that were not in the least bit masculine – more like those of a young girl, of a child.

'My name is Alexander Illytch. You'll find life a lot easier if you call me Sasha, or Sayia, but first and foremost if you tell me your name.'

'My name . . . My name . . . I can't remember. I can't remember what I'm doing on this tram, where I'm supposed to be going . . .'

'Try –'

'Jeanne,' said Jeanne.

'Jeanne,' repeated the man. 'There, I've forgotten it too. I can hear other words – basket, wickerwork, jasmine, or something ridiculous and silly like a wickerwork basket with sprays of jasmine.'

'A password for people left behind on the tram? Or perhaps baskets that people have left behind them on the tram, a wickerwork tram . . .'

'I meant the way you smell,' said the man, turning his gaze towards the window – almost with indifference, it seemed to Jeanne.

Empty by now, the tram was going along faster.

'I was getting all ready to court you a moment ago. A long courtship – interminable, to be quite frank.'

'Don't give up the idea, whatever you do,' Jeanne begged. 'I've never been courted by anyone before. I'd like to know what it's like.'

'We've got this evening, and the whole of tomorrow, and then the following morning. On the third day I'm off.'

'Where to?'

'The war.'

'What war?'

'This one.'

He pointed to a soldier who was dragging his way along the pavement on crutches.

'Oh . . . And there's no way you can't go?'

Jeanne and Alexander were standing side by side, their gaze turned towards the window. Night was falling.

'I live right near here. If we get out now, it's just ten minutes on foot.'

Dring-dring! went the tram. There was a squealing of brakes and it came to a standstill. Alexander took Jeanne's hand and pulled her towards the door. They were on the opposite bank of the Neva from the Hermitage, just at the end of the bridge. Alexander let go of Jeanne's hand to take off his cap. For the first time she saw his hair, which was much lighter than his eyebrows and beard. It wasn't really a beard, in fact – just the chin of someone who has forgotten to shave. He ran his fingers over his face and said, 'If I'm to court you, I'll have to shave first. I didn't go home last night.'

'Have you not slept at all?'

'A little.'

He took hold of Jeanne's hand again, sticking it into his pocket as though it were an object, and put his cap in the other pocket. They walked in silence for a hundred yards or so, Jeanne's hand held tightly in his.

'Why do you have to go off to this war?' asked Jeanne. 'Through choice, or through necessity? Or is there some other reason?'

'I'm a surgeon.'

'That must be useful.'

'Simple, too. I deal entirely in concrete solutions. When I'm confronted with a man whose leg has to come off, there's just one thing in my mind: how to get it off. Everything else –

what will become of the man in the end, what he was doing there in the first place, what the whole business is about – you just can't think about these things if you want to do the job properly.'

'And you don't think about them?'

'I do, yes.'

'But you don't want to talk about them, is that it?'

'You could say that.'

They climbed a staircase. At the top was a large double door with a copper plate proclaiming that SENINE K.I., VETERINARY SURGEON lived there.

'Is that your father?' asked Jeanne.

'Yes. He's been at the Front since the war began. He used to have his practice here in the house.'

'What, cats and dogs and things?'

'Horses, mostly.'

'How did they get up the stairs?'

'They didn't,' said Alexander. 'Did you see that outbuilding in the courtyard as we came in? That's the horse clinic.'

'And do you know about treating horses too?'

'I used to help my father now and then,' said Alexander, letting go of Jeanne's hand to open the door. 'They make good patients.'

'And what about your mother?'

'She's on her estate at Pskov. She's never liked Petersburg.'

The walls of the spacious entrance hall were lined with bookcases crammed with books; there were engravings, and all manner of stuffed animals and birds, and antique weapons, and model boats with tatty-looking sails, and a wall map covered with lines drawn in pencil and ink.

Alexander helped Jeanne off with her coat, stretched out his hand towards her neck to take her scarf; she held on to his hand for a moment, and then let go of his hand and the scarf together.

'I don't know whether I've dreamt all this or whether I'm still dreaming,' said Alexander.

The distance between them was as slight as it had been on the tram, and they were talking in a whisper without realizing it.

'And your face is like the face in a dream, flickering and indistinct. I've seen it somewhere before, but I don't know where. What do you do on trams – or can you still not remember?'

'I get about the place.'

'Aren't you ever frightened of being abducted?'

'No. I always carry a revolver. Oh, you mean that you've abducted me? Is that your name for the way you've got me to come here? For me, it's a gift from the gods.'

'Really?'

With the most natural gesture in the world, Jeanne threw her arms around Alexander and laid her head upon his chest. He felt a trifle smothered all the same.

'You must have landed from the moon,' said Alexander into her ear.

'No, from the illusions . . . You're going to give me a child this very night.'

'A what?'

'A child,' repeated Jeanne, looking him straight in the eyes.

'I was always under the impression – entirely outmoded, it would appear – that people got married for that.'

'It's not essential . . . We'll cut a few corners in our – what did you call it? – in our courtship. All those intervening stages that people waste months and years on.'

'And you're going to have no idea where the father of this potential child is – doesn't that bother you?'

'That's why it's so urgent, don't you think?'

'Yes, I do . . . I believe every word you say . . . Can you wait the time it takes me to shave?'

'Of course,' said Jeanne, letting her arms fall.

'Then you can have a look around the place and see if you like it here.'

'I like it here . . . Is that your study across the way there?'

'It's a bit of everything. It's been my bedroom too since I've been on my own.'

'And what's that noise coming from above, those footsteps?'

'That's our upstairs neighbour. He's blind. He hasn't been blind for very long. He's learning to walk again in the darkness: he works really hard at it, and of course he's always sending things crashing. Anything else you'd like to know at this point?'

'No, thanks,' said Jeanne.

'The kitchen's on the right. If you perhaps want to make some tea . . .'

The kitchen had a country air about it. In the middle was a long table with benches running down either side; the wainscotted walls were dark with age and the ceiling black with smoke. There were a few pot-plants that obviously hadn't been watered for a long time, and in one corner an icon depicting a sombre-faced, mistrustful-looking St Nicholas. The enamel sink was piled high with dainty blue-and-gold saucers, and with cups of the same blue, all very badly chipped.

Under St Nicholas's insistent gaze, Jeanne removed the mica top of the little hot-plate, lit the two wicks, replaced the top, filled a saucepan with water and put it on the heat. Then she washed up the contents of the sink and swept the floor. When Alexander came through into the kitchen, Jeanne was drying up the cups. Intent on what she was doing, she didn't hear him coming up behind her; then, sensing his presence, she suddenly turned round, dropping the cup she was holding.

'Leave it,' said Alexander, seeing Jeanne stoop down to pick up the broken pieces. 'I'll sweep it up myself. Honestly – so much fuss over a little cup,' he added, prompted by the tears that were streaming down Jeanne's face. 'And you're bleeding – you've hurt yourself! Let me have a look . . .' He took hold of the finger from which blood was dripping and kissed it. 'It's nothing to worry about,' he said. 'I'll just go and get a spot of iodine.'

'Oh, don't bother,' said Jeanne. She looked at him, her face illuminated with a smile, drying her tears on the back of her hand as children do. 'I don't cry like this every day, believe me.'

'What surprises me a good deal more, actually, is the way you've managed to get that hot-plate going. I fiddle with it for hours without getting the tiniest little flame.'

'It's quite simple,' said Jeanne. 'You have to turn up the wicks, light them, and turn them down again immediately. Shall I show you?'

And with these words, she launched into a performance that was a mixture of dance, mime and conjuring. As she blew on the wicks – of course she had first to put them out – the end of her nose turned black, and her freckles, fading now with the autumn, were peppered with specks of soot.

'And you know about washing-up too?' said Alexander, in the hope of witnessing another demonstration.

'You need water, soap and sand,' said Jeanne, indicating each substance in turn with gestures of her hands.

'Sand?' murmured Alexander dreamily.

'Of course. Haven't you got any? You need it to scrub with.'

'Not stupid,' Alexander said, still hypnotized.

'You're an excellent audience,' said Jeanne, taking the saucepan off the heat.

'Ah, now tea is my forte,' said Alexander. 'May I . . .?'

He took the saucepan from her hands.

'If someone told me you were a conjuror, I wouldn't be the least bit surprised.'

'I'm an actress. I work in the cinema – you know, moving pictures in the dark.'

'Well, not really, but . . . You play parts . . . A child . . . You were saying you wanted to have a –'

'Oh, there was no play-acting there.'

'You do want a child? Really?'

'I want to have a child by you.'

'And it's as clear as that in your head?'

'What, do you think you have children with your head?'

'Yes and no. I have my opinions on the subject. I was going to become a specialist.'

'Is that so?' said Jeanne.

'But I had to break off my studies and come back to Petersburg.'

'Where were you before?'

'I was in Vienna, and then in Hamburg for four years. I'd be there still, but for the war. But don't worry: I'm quite capable of doing a Caesarean.'

'Maybe we could do without that.'

'I'm not so sure at a first glance.'

'Did you put on a clean shirt for me?'

'For you.'

'Really! And you never go to the cinema?'

'I did once or twice when I was in Germany. Not very often, though.'

'Don't you like it?'

'I'll spend the rest of my life at the cinema – word of honour!'

'And you're leaving –'

'I'll be back. Who's going to look after this child?'

'I shall. You're right not to like the cinema.'

'That wasn't what I said.'

'It's a highly imperfect art-form,' said Jeanne. 'Failed novelists write the stories, failed painters direct them, failed dancers act in them, and failures go and see them.'

'Then it must be the most perfect art-form of all!' said Alexander. 'I'm mesmerized by the sight of you washing up a plate – what am I going to do if I see you act?'

'What plate are we talking about?' said Jeanne softly. 'Supposing I lied a little bit when I was washing up, just to keep hold of you . . .?'

'Keep hold of me?' said Alexander. And suddenly, savagely, he grabbed hold of Jeanne as though she were a packet of dried herbs, carried her out of the kitchen, set her down on her feet once more in the entrance-hall and embraced her hard enough to break her bones.

The shooting, a lengthier job than anticipated, wasn't finished until shortly before Christmas. Alexander had left Petrograd at the end of October. Little by little, the life of the capital ground to a halt. The workers laid down their tools on every side. The war seemed to be waiting.

Once Gauer had left for Moscow with the celluloid reels of *The Storks* – his new film, which Khanjonkov was pressing to have edited as quickly as possible – Jeanne moved into the vet's flat, determined not to budge from Petrograd before the arrival of the first hospital train that Alexander was to accompany; it was expected some time at the beginning of January.

The city took on a spectral aspect: from the tops of their boughs right down to ground level, the trees were covered in a permanent hoar-frost, and everything was white and grey except for the apricot or pale green of a house-front here and there. The monotony of perspectives emptied by the great cold was broken solely by the lines of people queuing up outside the bakeries. There was no bread, but the housewives still waited there on the off-chance, wrapped up to the eyes. Jeanne only ventured out on to the streets to go across from her side of the Neva to the Europe Hotel, where she picked up her post. She would cross Hermitage Bridge and then Winter Palace Square, which was swept by gusts of wind as though it were a field somewhere in the middle of the countryside. Quickening her pace, she would push open the revolving door of the Europe and be given a deferential reception by the porters, with whom she was a great success – and it was as if she had suddenly entered another country, another climatic zone. In the coloured light from the stained-glass windows, which intermingled with the light of the electric lamps made of opaque glass and supported by bronze statuettes of Greek youths; beneath the palm trees and green plants which rose all the way to the ceiling; between the camellias flowering pink and white and the miniature fountains on their pedestals of malachite – in this atmosphere of a conservatory, warm and rather humid, one felt sheltered from all disasters, present and to come. Women dressed in silks and furs of black would nonchalantly drift in, whilst gentlemen in evening dress and high-ranking officers chatted casually in groups. Anyone coming in from the street might have thought himself a castaway from the North Pole, miraculously beached upon a warm island in some earthly paradise.

Jeanne's paradise was contained within the little white rectangles of the letters she received from the Front. Without lingering in the lobby of the hotel, she would not walk but actually run back to the other side of the Neva.

Running still, she would rush up the creaking stairs of the vet's house, sit down on the trunk in the entrance hall, underneath the wall maps and patched sails of Alexander's childhood, hurriedly tear open the envelope, and remove the contents. Alexander's rather dry letters contained no professions of love and they ended with an ordinary kiss. With one exception: a New Year's card she had received, with a weird picture of blue fish, and balloons, and the moon, and people like children who didn't seem happy at all. This card ended with the words 'May you always be as much loved as you are today.'

Jeanne had no stamina, no power of endurance. She was a ball of energy, pushing herself to the limit, directing all her forces outwards; and then she would need to withdraw into herself, like a water-lily in a pond that has suddenly been drained. She let the world mark time. Or again, she was like an hour-glass, experiencing an irresistible desire to smash herself to pieces – to scatter the broken fragments, everything she was and was not, and then to put herself back together again in her own time, recuperating inside herself.

She read Alexander's letter:

. . . I'm being helped by two kindly nuns at the moment: the one is called Sister Catherine and the other – I think – Sister Sophie. They're from the Convent of Our Holy Saviour of the Tomb. Have you ever heard of it? It's at Voronej. They're the same size, they wear the same habit, they have the same blue eyes. I can't speak for the rest: I only see them when I'm operating, and they wear masks. The operating theatre is in what used to be the boudoir of the mistress of the house – a woman with an unpronounceable name composed entirely of mushy consonants. The great lime trees that line the drive have just lost their leaves; it's not snowing – not yet, anyway – the fields are black, and on a clear day you can see a chain of mountains further off in the distance. The fighting seems to be at a lull for the moment – we scarcely hear any shooting. The lines are only three versts from here, however. The wounded keep arriving in droves. Those with serious injuries – to the chest, the stomach, the kidneys – we don't even take upstairs: they stay in the hall, laid out on stretchers on the bare floor. I simply haven't the means to operate on them here. I'm constantly sending dispatches to H.Q. As yet I've received no reply. It's so stupid: with an assistant, however poorly qualified, in place of my good sisters, with electric light and one or two more appliances, I could do what was required without exposing them to the dangers of another journey.

All I have in the way of lighting is four paraffin lamps hung from the baldachin above the place where the countess's bed used to be, and where we've now put a long, narrow table which I had brought up from the hall. Sterilizing this table was the most terrible business: all the gilding came off, and the maidservant who had stayed behind in the house, and who keeps a jealous watch over the countess's property, nearly had a heart attack.

When evening comes, I light everything that's lightable in the house, the candles included. The maidservant thinks I'm ruining her mistress, and every evening we have a great scene with her weeping and taking endless drops of valerian. That doesn't stop her being a very good cook, however: the wounded are very fond of her, and she has them eating off the best china in the house — another of her odd whims, for things sometimes get broken, which is the cue for yet another scene.

My nuns are praying: I can hear their thin, penetrating voices coming in unison from the room next door. I sleep in the study — the library of the former masters of the house, who left at the approach of the Front. I think they're in Budapest now. The estate, which is a long way from any town, is at the point where the Austrian, Rumanian and Hungarian borders meet. There are too many things mixed up with one another here. I still haven't fathomed what language the maidservant speaks: it certainly isn't Russian, and if it's German, it's the strangest German I've ever heard. Going through a pile of back numbers of Niva *in the library, I came across a photograph of you: you're barely recognizable under the ghastly white thing you've got on your head, but you're exquisitely beautiful, with the same look you had in the kitchen.*

I'm waiting for an ambulance which is supposed to come and clear the wounded out of the hall here. Despite the enormous doses of morphine I've administered, the place is full of shrieking and groaning and wailing. These men are in a desperate state: I fear they won't manage the journey at all. Ever since last night, one of them has been crying 'Masha' incessantly. His fiancée, most probably — he looks too young to be married.

I must bring this letter to a close. An officer friend of mine is just about to set off for Petersburg on leave, and he wants to take it with him. To get to the point, then: I don't know when or how we're going to be able to see one another again. The train I was counting on — the one taking the wounded from the Front — has already left. There will be others, but I don't know which one I'll be able to take. I'll be staying in Galicia for the time being — and I would like to know that you were in Odessa: we'd be closer to one another, at least on the map, and I would try to find a way of coming to Odessa at the earliest opportunity. Reports I've heard of the troubles in Petersburg also increase my anxiety — why stay there now that your film is finished? I beg you to leave, and I'm even sending you the means to do so, because I've noticed already how stubborn you can be.

Morale is at an incredibly low ebb here: the men can think of nothing but going home. The other day a soldier asked me to amputate his arm. I was driving myself half crazy trying to save it. He said that with one arm less he had a better chance of getting out of the trenches. There are thousands who think the same way.

My friend is waiting – he's already showing signs of impatience. My last piece of news – and the strangest – is this: an odd little character turned up in the countess's house a week ago. At first I thought he must be some relation of pani *Eva's, that quarrelsome woman I've already told you about. He isn't, though. He doesn't belong to anyone. He's just lost. Where, when and how he came to get lost is a complete mystery. We've gathered that his name – which he can pronounce reasonably well – is Igor. As for the language he speaks, it could perhaps be some obscure dialect distantly related to Ukrainian. I think he's just retarded in his development, for he seems to be about five years old. He's quite irresistible, with freckles, a round head and a pointed nose. Very independent and headstrong. Yesterday morning he came into my room to tell me that he likes potatoes: I was happy to understand him for once, but this isn't enough to tell me where he's sprung from. We've asked around in the neighbouring villages. No one has the slightest clue. He came wearing clean clothes, though, which someone had darned. He can't have been wandering about for very long. The whole business is taking up a lot of my time, I can tell you.*

The letter closed with the officer's address. Jeanne went round to see him. He lived on the Moyka embankment, in one of those houses designed for Italy in a hypothetical Ice Age. His name was Innokenti Petrovitch: he walked with a slight limp, wore his army uniform as though it were a velvet frock-coat, and spoke the French of the upper classes and the Russian of the poets. In the figure who presented herself at his door dressed in an old coat and a peasant shawl, he at once recognized Vera Gaiy; and if Jeanne hadn't stopped him in time, if she hadn't, throughout the entire afternoon, brought the conversation back to the things she wanted to hear about, he would have talked and talked about the 'mystic significance' of her screen appearances, of her 'magic', of Gauer's 'message' (he obviously hero-worshipped Gauer), or, worse still, of the hunts in Abyssinia and the archaeological digs in Persia and

Egypt in which he had participated. He did, however, give Jeanne the latest news concerning Alexander and little Igor, who had become the centre of attention at the hospital ever since he turned up there.

According to their most recent questioning, he had got lost in a railway station. He wasn't with his mother at the time, but with an old lady: the word that came from his lips, *baboussia*, could have meant not only his grandmother, but any elderly person, whether a blood-relation or not. They had declined the word 'mummy' through all its forms for him, but it evinced no greater reaction than – to take one example – the word 'chicken'. The drawings he did featured houses several storeys high, and railway trains, but rarely a detail suggestive of the countryside. They had recited the names of towns to him, even of ones as far off as Kiev or Lemberg; they had described the monuments of the towns in the surrounding area: it all meant nothing to him. He was reticent whenever he was questioned: he didn't like being taken elsewhere, even if it was only in words; he was terrified of leaving the house and never strayed beyond the precincts of the park when he was out playing. He slept badly if the main door was not shut and always wanted the light to be left on. The thing he recognized best was a Christmas tree that they had organized for him – juggling the dates – at the end of January. He knew where to look for the presents: underneath the fir-tree, hidden in the cotton wool. He displayed more interest in men that in women, but he accepted the attentions of *pani* Eva quite readily. With the nuns, he was stand-offish. He liked being with an old soldier who was convalescing from an injury, but above all with Alexander, whom he followed about everywhere like a dog. They had the devil's own job, apparently, in forbidding him to enter the surgical wing, the one with the rooms where they put people who had just undergone operations. But he had obtained permission to sleep in Alexander's room simply by marching in there with his pillow and his little coverlet and refusing point-blank to budge from the corner he had found for himself.

Jeanne also learned that, as soon as the new offensive was launched, Alexander would leave to join a flying detachment of the Red Cross, nearer to the headquarters of the Galician Front and five kilometres from Svistelniky Manor – that was the name of the place where he was at present stationed. *Pani* Eva would look after the child until the question of his identity was cleared up.

Innokenti Petrovitch entreated Jeanne to stay for dinner. He introduced her to his mother, a scraggy woman dressed in grey silk and pearls to match. Playing with the diamonds on her fingers, she made reference to the blandness of the veal, the arrogance of the servants and the toughness of the beef – as if the poor quality of the creatures was a direct result of the social upheavals taking place. She pointed out that the pineapples positioned amongst the crystal and the exquisite china in the middle of the table came from Paris, a town where, war or no war, people did not lose their appetite for the good things in life, or the means to procure them, where they knew when to call a halt to change, and how to deal in a reasonable fashion with the catastrophes of which they are indeed fond – 'but good sense triumphs in the end; yes, the French are very sensible when it comes down to it, impetuous as they are by reputation', concluded the lady with the pearls. The main thing Jeanne took in was that her son had been away at the war for three years already, that this was only the second time he had come home on leave, and that this second stint of leave was occasioned by a recent wound. This was anything but encouraging for Jeanne, and she told him so. 'The war's got to end,' replied Innokenti Petrovitch. 'The will to go on fighting just isn't there any longer, nor the means, either. Let's forget about winning: it's not the same thing as admitting defeat now . . .' 'That's a strange prognostic,' said his mother. 'If you start thinking in terms of defeat, you've already begun to lose the battle. That might do for the rank and file. But it's fatal for an officer to talk like that.'

Innokenti Petrovitch offered no reaction to this: he poured out some more wine for Jeanne and his mother, and turned his attention to a large oyster which he pronounced remarkably good. Jeanne judged the moment opportune to give Dasha's ideas an airing. She expounded them in French, embellishing the 'big bang' with a few details of her own invention. 'But you're a dangerous anarchist,' retorted the lady with the pearls, looking at Jeanne with her narrow eyes, which had a definite touch of the Mongol about them. 'Everything you're saying smacks of Marx.' Jeanne noted that Dasha's ideas did not go unregarded in these circles – *even* in these circles. She was pleased for Dasha's sake, and, as for the lady, she thought she was now in a state to hear this final observation: 'Everything that has to do with Marx, madam, is the precise opposite of what the anarchists want. The social laws that he discovered are as absolute as those which govern the' – she pretended to be searching for the right word – 'which govern the stars. Yes, madam, the stars,' she added, with a feigned show of sadness. Hearing this, the lady with the pearls calmed down somewhat, telling herself that this charming artist must be an amateur of astrology who had got one or two things mixed up in her brain.

The disagreement thus smoothed out, Jeanne asked if she could come another time with some parcels: she would like to send something to Alexander and little Igor, she explained.

Buying toys, and sweets, and socks under the falling snow of Petrograd gave a touch of happiness to the last days Jeanne spent in that city, where there was fighting in the streets and the first red flags were flying. She left at the beginning of March.

Jeanne saw her standing on the platform – a slender, motionless figure dressed in black, her face framed by a short grey veil that clung to her forehead and from beneath which a black lock of hair ran down either cheek.

It was half past five: night was just beginning to lift as the fast train from Petrograd gently rolled into the glassed-in cage of Odessa station. Jeanne was at the window, pressing her white-gloved hand against the pane, momentarily confused by the wilderness of empty platforms and the presence of Dasha, standing there all on her own. As the train slowed down, she caught sight of the crowd, held back by a barrier that separated them from the expanse of platforms; a uniformed porter was keeping the iron gateway closed. There was a squealing of brakes; the wheels ground to a halt; the engine stopped puffing – and in a flash, as if they had actually leapt the barrier, the crowd streamed forth, instantly covering every inch of ground around the carriages. Jeanne lost sight of Dasha, then relocated her forging a path for herself through the confusion. Leaving her luggage in the compartment, Jeanne ran down the corridor, jumped out of the train and exclaimed, 'Dashenka, my darling, you're so much thinner! But why all the black?'

'Don't you like it?'

'Oh, I do . . .'

'It's what they're wearing in Paris at the moment.'

'Well, it's not the thing in Petrograd at all. Did you get my letter?'

'Amazing, eh? A republic – and without too many bombs, either . . . Turn round and let me have a look at you . . . Breathtaking! Oh, watch out, here comes our chauffeur-cum-bodyguard,' she added in a lower voice, indicating a man who towered above the entire crowd. Hatchet-faced and inscrutable, he was making his way towards Jeanne's carriage at a dignified pace. 'Which compartment were you in?'

'The second one from the other end.'

The man had come up to them now; and Jeanne recognized him, seeing again the Street of the Assumption and Isaak's barouche that had taken her back home that soft June evening of 1914 – the evening of her fall – and she suddenly felt a blow, as if all the vague, wandering strands of those years had knotted themselves into a heavy ball. She tried to throw it off, tried to free herself of this unaccustomed weight – she who lived from day to day and started with a clean slate every morning – but it was too much for her. Unable to master herself, she said, 'Dashenka, I've come over all strange . . . I don't think I can –'

'What's wrong?' interrupted Dasha. 'Have you got a cold or something . . .? You're just in a bad mood – which doesn't stop you being as bright as a Christmas tree . . . Do you want to go straight to Beriozy? Everything's ready for you there: Father went round yesterday to light the stoves and give the place an airing.'

'Whatever you think's best.'

'Who is he, then?'

'Who do you mean?' asked Jeanne, looking around her.

'The love of your life. Is he an actor?'

'No, he's a surgeon. He's at the Front. His name's Alexander.'

'You stayed on such a ridiculously long time in Petrograd that I of course thought . . . Oh, Jeanne, I've missed you so much!'

'And I you,' said Jeanne, saying nothing more because her gaze had just lighted on Filaretov, who was standing unobtrusively near the station exit, his cap in his hand.

She thought no more about it, remembering now that she had told him too that she would be coming. Filaretov stood watching her, not daring to move, taken aback by the scene that was unfolding before his eyes, by the presence of that Nastia Polyakova, whom he of course knew, having accompanied her on the piano back in her early days. Prudish, concerned about Jeanne's reputation, feeling responsible for her now that her mother was no longer there, he was anything but happy at witnessing these tokens of intimacy between

Nastia and Jeanne. Good God, he thought, this woman wasn't fit company for his little Jeanne, for his pupil, exposed as she was to a world of temptations and danger ... No, no – a gypsy, a prostitute or something very near it, a cabaret singer who led a quite scandalous life – not to mention that lover of hers, Isaak Storm, a thoroughgoing crook, the king of Odessa's criminal underworld ...

'Ivan Semionovitch!' exclaimed Jeanne, throwing herself upon him and kissing him on the forehead. 'I said in my letter that I wasn't sure of the time, that I might come by a later train – and you've got up so early! Good heavens ...'

He blew his nose, as he always did on seeing Jeanne, whether in the flesh or on the screen – Jeanne, his little wonder, the white rose of his heart; Jeanne, the only person since the death of his wife who could give him a reason for living.

'At last you're back in the south. I'm so relieved,' he said.

'Relieved?' laughed Jeanne. 'What at?'

'Just relieved.'

'My dear Ivan Semionovitch, there was no reason for you to worry. And don't try to get rid of me now – don't go trying to pack me off to Nice, as you're always doing in your letters! I will *not* go there! No talk of Nice this year, all right?'

'Gaiy!' Jeanne heard a voice behind her saying. 'It's Vera Gaiy!'

She turned round and saw a young lad who couldn't have been a day over twelve pointing his finger at her. A woman came up and simply planted herself in front of her, and then another.

'Look – it really is Vera Gaiy ...! She's got freckles, see ...? Isn't she beautiful ...? Not if you ask me – she's not the same at all ... But it *is* her! How young she is ... Is that her father standing next to her ...? You know perfectly well she hasn't got a father ... It's the old pianist from the Odeon ...! Ugly sod, isn't he ...? Never seen him on his feet before? He's a dwarf ...'

There was much pushing and shoving, with the whole crowd making loud remarks.

'Let's get out of here quick,' said Jeanne, clinging on to Filaretov's arm.

Dasha led her towards the exit. A motor car was waiting for them just outside the station.

Dasha sat down on one cushion and smoothed out another for Jeanne. Filaretov got in next to the chauffeur – Isaak's old coachman.

'Does being famous annoy you?' asked Dasha.

'Horrible . . . It's like being undressed . . .'

'Well, they're your public: you have to learn to love them. *I* love –' A fit of coughing prevented her from continuing.

The motor car coughed too, shuddered, started growling like an animal and tore away. Dasha went on coughing, her shoulders shaking with the effort: the fit reached a long climax, and then died down. Quickly she tucked away her handkerchief and smiled at Jeanne, who was stunned by both the incident at the station and the sight of Dasha suffering like this.

'Has this been happening a lot?' asked Jeanne, putting her hand on Dasha's knee.

'No, it's just a little attack of asthma, nothing serious . . .'

The mention of the word 'asthma' reassured Jeanne somewhat: she had often heard it at home as a little girl. Marie-Aynard had had asthma, and Jeanne thought of it as a curious ailment, a sort of caprice, something in the nature of a defence against the outside world, a ladies' illness, a whole way of living involving pink bottles of smelling-salts and long eucalyptus cigarettes and impeccably clean lace handkerchiefs; a valid justification for going and spending the autumn in some elegant watering-place. Marie-Aynard's doctor used to say with a smile, 'I'm not an asthma specialist.' And added, 'You don't die of it.'

'Are you singing this evening?' asked Jeanne.

'No, I've taken a month off. Not that it's doing me much good. I just don't know what to do with the time. I sit around reading –'

'Look, I've had an idea: I'll stay here for a week, and then we'll both take the boat to the Côte d'Azur. Can't you just see all the mimosa and orange trees in blossom there? And the climate! If you knew the way my mother went on about the sunshine and the pine forests!' said Jeanne, feigning boundless enthusiasm. 'And I know someone who will find my idea utterly brilliant . . . Ivan Semionovitch!' she added in a louder voice. 'We're going to the Côte d'Azur! We're going to see Marie-Aynard. Do you hear me?'

She had no time to admit to herself that she was lying, that she would never leave this country without Alexander.

'You're dreaming,' said Dasha. 'I can't leave Odessa. I've undertaken engagements in Kiev and Moscow and Sochi . . . Moscow, do you hear? I'm not going to turn down Moscow . . .'

She broke off, glued to her seat, struggling for breath, staring straight ahead of her with huge, empty eyes.

'Have you got a fever?'

Jeanne had taken hold of her hand: it was moist, and very hot.

'That's the only word I hear these days – from Isaak, and now from you,' said Dasha, in a weary, serious tone that was quite new to Jeanne. 'There's nothing wrong with me.' She removed her hand from Jeanne's grip, wedged herself more firmly against the seat, and looked the other way. 'Only yesterday my mother consulted the cards . . . There's nothing wrong with me . . .' Dasha stretched her limbs, and her face softened. 'Spring's on its way – have you seen the chestnut trees?'

In the early morning light they could make out the faint covering of leaves. Spring had begun in October for Jeanne, in the middle of the season of wind, and rain, and dead leaves at the feet of the railings, to the sound of Sunday bells and the footsteps of the blind man on the floor above.

Dasha talked on, and Jeanne registered nothing but the timbre of her voice, which began to grow warmer and more relaxed, recovering its usual confidence and cheerfulness – an accomplishment, a music which, without saying precisely this or that, took hold of the listener completely. Dasha had a beautiful voice, and Jeanne floated away on the sound of it: that fine midday of the spring of her fall, the horses climbing the hill of France Boulevard, this consumptive motor car, this cold early morning, these trees that might be lining an avenue in a cemetery . . . Alexander! she thought. Why wasn't she on her own with Alexander? She was annoyed at Dasha and Filaretov for coming to pick her up; she was annoyed at the car and at the whole world; she was annoyed at herself for having only this one thing – Alexander – that would not, could not change, whereas before meeting him she had managed by herself, always finding her way back to the surface on her own, she who was an expert at falls.

'I'll leave you now,' Jeanne heard Dasha saying. 'I'm going back home to sleep for a bit. Fedor Petrovitch will take you to Beriozy. Ivan Semionovitch, where would you like to be dropped off?'

'Just here, if you wouldn't mind. We're very near to where I live now.'

He kissed Jeanne's hand. A fleeting look of sadness crossed his face. He didn't recognize Jeanne; she seemed so far away. She had always showered him with attentions, asking his advice on things, inviting him along wherever her work took her, making sure that he was well paid and that he felt his presence in the studios absolutely indispensable. Having accompanied films ever since the very start of the illusions, he knew the public better than anyone else, and to the shooting-floor as to the cinema halls he brought not only his cadences and melodies but a completely intuitive understanding of how the public would react – the public that Gauer, lost in his celluloids and his developing-baths as he had once been lost in his colours, tended to forget.

The scene which had just taken place at the station had not – despite the highly unflattering remarks made about him – upset Filaretov in the least. He was an artist, and he knew that the more reactions one got, the better. As a young man he had dreamt of fame, of concert halls held spellbound by the notes planted in the surrounding silence, of all the people come to hear him whom he would hypnotize for the space of two hours with a delicate string of wonders, evoking by a dissonance in F sharp a beloved face seen across a clearing in August, or groping around amongst the flats like a blind man looking for a way out, or reminding them in passing, by means of one or two minor diminished sixths, of the inevitable end, that little corrective to our birth whose tonality is never twice the same . . . Of course it had all come to nothing – well, not really to nothing, for he could see his dreams being realized almost detail for detail in Jeanne. Yet a doubt crept in: he knew that Jeanne's infatuation with the cinema had something of the heliotrope about it: there was really nothing – ambition, desire to be in the limelight, thirst for fame – to make it last, and she was quite capable of abandoning this career as suddenly as she had embarked upon it, and without the slightest regret. There were unfortunately so many different beings contained in this frail person with the freckles. It was quite possible, Filaretov mused, that Jeanne's passion for the cinema had already spent itself. How else could one account for that October day, right in the middle of the shooting of *The Storks*, when she had turned up at the studios like a sleepwalker, rushing off to her dressing-room at every break, utterly indifferent to Levitsky's cables, and not joining in on Gauer's spatial meditations? And why did she always reject offers from other directors – some of whom Filaretov considered to be more talented and interesting than Gauer? Now Gauer had gone off in April on his annual trip to America, a trip that would probably be longer than usual – he thought he needed to improve certain cinematographic techniques! Jeanne would be without work for five or six months, and that was too long in this profession: you could easily be forgotten, elbowed out by one rising star or another . . .

As though sensing Filaretov's sadness, Jeanne emerged from her reverie, gave Filaretov an affectionate kiss, and said that she would come round and see him the next day. Dasha got out her compact, looked at herself in the little mirror, re-powdered her nose, and said, 'I'm not used to getting up so early. How awful I look! There's no one but you can look like this at six in the morning. Don't kiss me – I'm getting out here! Till this evening, then! I'll tell my father to come and pick you up around eight. All right?'

Jeanne made her way through the succession of courtyards and gardens and verandas at a run, impatient to see Dasha again and spend the evening with her. She took the spiral staircase that led up to Dasha's front door in three strides. She had done everything possible to regain her composure – exercised at the bar, taken a walk on the beach, gone up into the loft and examined the telescope which, despite Nastia's efforts, despite the dust-cloth and case, turned out to have been seriously affected by the damp; she had drunk her long fill of the air of the footpaths, and warmed herself up again at the kitchen fire whilst reading Alexander's letters for the hundredth time . . . She was ravenously hungry and had put on the white dress that Dasha had given to her, along with all the accessories – the fox stole, the little necklace of brilliants and gold of which Marie-Aynard possessed the double.

Through the half-open door Jeanne saw Isaak from the side, leaning on the mantelpiece in the flickering light of a multitude of candles – saw his shock of flaming red hair, which had all grown back by now, and the fine line of his nose, and the white shirt casually open at the neck, underneath the black jacket he was wearing. And, as in the past, Jeanne caught a sudden whiff of the theatre, a scent of mandarins with a hint of nutmeg – there were mandarins scattered all over the tablecloth – or was it that the theatre and the smell of mandarin rinds were for some reason associated with one another in Jeanne's mind . . .

Seeing Jeanne appear in the doorway, he didn't move at all, he just turned his head towards her with that smile which she had remembered ever since their first encounter – and that was all, really, just a vacant smile below the line of his sad eyes. And then, before she had even seen him coming, as if the whole thing were a theatrical trick – as if there were just the two of them there, standing beside the out-of-tune piano in the café in the Street of the Assumption – he swept her off her feet and waltzed her madly round and round.

'That's enough of that display,' said Dasha, pulling Jeanne towards her. 'Jeanne belongs to me!'

'It's true,' said Jeanne. 'I belong to a blue-eyed gypsy – *not* to Moldavanka, with its ghastly dens.' No reference to Isaak meant, she added, and freed herself more slowly than she might from his hold; she had felt good in his arms.

The charm of the embrace broken, Isaak went to close the door, then sat down in an armchair near the fire; Dasha went off into the kitchen, returning with a tray of decanters and glasses. There was some hard drinking in Pushkin Street that night.

'How's business?' asked Jeanne.

'Not bad, thanks,' Isaak replied.

'Wars have always been good business,' said Dasha, drinking a long mouthful of champagne. 'But our capitalist here does just as well out of revolutions – it can happen . . .'

Dasha knocked back her glass, poured herself another, and plumped down with it on Isaak's lap, curling up in his arms.

'He's off to Afghanistan tonight,' said Dasha, running a

finger lightly over Isaak's hair. 'I'm staying here to keep a watch over the ideological purity of his enterprises. I'm getting to be a real expert – I need to be, believe me . . . I've got past Chapter Three of *Das Kapital*: I can hold my own against our clients now, they don't intimidate me any longer. I regret to say they're mostly incredibly ignorant – with one or two exceptions, of course. We should have set up a business school a long time ago . . . They're just playing around, they're not serious at all,' Dasha went on, sipping at her second glass. 'They got rid of the bloody Tsar – pathetic, spineless creature that he is – and then, if it really *was* them . . . Well, let's not go into that . . . Having got rid of the Tsar, they didn't even know who to give power to! They gave it to a bunch of inane lawyers! They seem to believe they and everything will be crowned by some great spontaneous mass movement! *The spontaneity of the people, their revolutionary instinct* – those are the phrases they gargle with all the time! As if spontaneity can produce weapons! You can't imagine what they're like, good God! Now they're waiting for Isaak and the Catalan to get them brand new weapons . . . If only I felt they knew how to use them, that one day these weapons would help them achieve something worthwhile, instead of just terrifying poor bloody Nicholas . . .'

'Right, then,' said Isaak. 'We're going to explain Socsec's minimum and maximum programme. Before midnight you'll be fully in the picture, Jeanne.'

'I'm afraid I can't bring any light to bear on what Dasha's talking about,' said Jeanne timidly.

'Light!' said Isaak. 'Oh no, you can't hope for that. You'll be fully in the picture, and as much in the dark as ever . . . There's such a complete fog inside this lovely little head,' he said, kissing Dasha, 'that the Devil himself couldn't find his way there. She spends her time reading, and it's all such a jumble –'

'Egoroff's given me a list! And it's just not true what you're saying, Isaak. Why are you always so discouraging? I'd so like to know where history's leading . . .'

'You think it's leading somewhere?' said Jeanne.

'It's supposed to be,' said Dasha, in a tone of great conviction, 'ever since Marx wrote. You can't live without knowing. You really ought to take an interest in it yourself. What should she begin with, Isaak – any idea? How about *What Is To Be Done??*'

'No, that deals too much with the present day. Engels: *The Role of Work in Transforming the Ape into Man.* The good thing about that book is that it's extremely clearly written.'

Dasha jumped up from Isaak's lap, took a pamphlet from the bookshelf and thrust it under Jeanne's nose.

'Here we are!' she said. 'It's written for children. Will you read it?'

'Of course,' said Jeanne.

'It's obvious,' said Isaak, 'that the business of looking after Jeanne's education falls to me.'

'And that of supplying me with weapons,' said Jeanne, taking her revolver from her bag.

'Was it you who gave her that?' said Dasha. 'I see your dealings went a lot further than I'd imagined.'

'There's nothing to imagine,' said Jeanne. 'The gift of this revolver was the extent of our dealings. I realize now that Isaak's role in History with a capital H is to procure weapons for causes great and small. There are people who distribute sweets, there are people who put on charity balls; Isaak procures weapons. I'd thought myself highly privileged to receive this present, to be quite honest. But I see that I'm just one among many.'

With which words Jeanne picked up the book on transforming the ape and put it and the revolver into her bag.

'I don't like to leave it lying around,' she said.

'You'd make a good activist, Jeanne,' said Isaak. 'That's the quality that's lacking in Dasha.'

'There's no point if you haven't an ideal. I haven't, and I don't think I could summon up Dasha's patience to go looking for one in all these books' – she gestured towards the bookcase – 'but I'll try . . . After all, who knows?'

'I don't have an ideal – ideee–al, as you say . . . It's just that I'm not insensible to the practical aspects of its realization,' said Isaak, going back over to the fireplace.

What a wonderful actor he'd make, Jeanne suddenly thought to herself: he walks like nobody else . . .

'Isaak, do you want to know what I think?' said Dasha.

'Of the March of History? It's all you ever talk about. Going to teach me something new this time, are you?' said Isaak, pushing back with the toe of his highly polished boot a log which was poking out from the hearth.

'It's a dirty business, capitalism, isn't it?' said Dasha.

'Go on . . .'

'He makes the point very strongly . . . I've read the last chapter – you know, the bit on "primitive accumulation". Well, it's all about the origins of capitalism, and it doesn't make pleasant reading, I can tell you. Nothing but blood and violence – theft pure and simple –'

'There must be some good capitalists, though,' observed Jeanne without thinking.

'Well, you've got one in Isaak here,' said Dasha imperturbably. 'And Marx's friend Engels, the author of the book we've just given you – he was rolling in it. Besides, Marx never latches on to individuals – he examines connections, the objective relations between things. It was with Engels that Marx drew up his *Manifesto* for the proletariat – "Workers of the world, unite!" and all that bit. Now, these little paradoxes are what they term *dialectics*. Dialectics explain everything, they sort out every contradiction, they cover up a multitude of sins . . . You must forgive the analogy, Isaak. He can't stand it,' she explained to Jeanne, 'when I take my examples from religion . . . But there are times when it amounts to the same thing. Capitalism is a bit like Original Sin – salvation comes to those who believe. Well, it's obvious, isn't it? Once the capitalists are converted to the proletarian creed, the fact that they're capitalists doesn't matter any longer – they've transcended the limits of their condition, they've redeemed themselves. I'm saying all this for Jeanne's sake –'

'And I'm still waiting,' said Isaak.

'I've lost my thread – where was I?'

'Talking about capitalists redeeming their faults with the proletarian creed,' whispered Jeanne.

'Well, that's just what I wonder – whether it'll really count for anything? When things have gone as far as they can – when the revolution comes . . . Egoroff always stresses the fact that there's a pretty sizeable gap between theory and practice . . . You have one thing in Marx and another in real life – and that's just it . . .'

'I'm still waiting,' said Isaak.

'There'll just be a lot of heads rolling, nothing else . . . Yours could be among them.'

'Why?' said Isaak. 'They need me.'

'As Marx needed Engels,' said Jeanne.

'Excellent! Jeanne's learning fast,' said Isaak, finally making up his mind to snap the log that was poking out from the hearth.

'That's not the point,' said Jeanne, taking a mandarin from the table. 'Everything you say, Dashenka, carries a whiff of prohibitions and guilt. Like the Mass and the Host and Communion – all restrictions. What's the point of following ideas that imprison us further? It's not prisons that we're short of –'

'There's no teaching her! There's absolutely no teaching her!' said Dasha, flinging her head back in the armchair and closing her eyes.

'Let's hope she stays that way,' said Isaak. He took the mandarin from Jeanne's hands, peeled it for her and threw the rind into the fire. 'And as for you, it's time you went to bed. You know what the doctor said – not later than ten o'clock.'

'Oh, these doctors . . . I've had enough of them.' Dasha's voice was suddenly placid, very weary now. 'I hate it when you go away . . .'

'Lie down, and I'll stay beside you as long as you like,' said Jeanne.

'Will you?' said Dasha, opening her eyes.

'I'll try and be back soon,' said Isaak.

He lifted her in his arms and put her down on the couch.

'Yes, come back soon. Please come back soon.'

Dasha was dying: spring had burst into full bloom, it was marvellously warm, and the scent of the blossom on the big wild-cherry tree wafted through the open windows of the room where she lay. Only Filaretov knew how and when the end would come: the same illness from which his wife had died would run its inevitable course in Dasha. The others – Jeanne, Grigory – closed their eyes to the fact, losing themselves in a round of activity: doing the shopping for Dasha's mother, making lace, talking in the courtyard with the doctors, preparing various kinds of drinks, taking turns to sit up at Dasha's bedside at night.

For two days she had been unable to swallow even a spoonful of warm milk or honey; she didn't even have the strength to cough any longer; and when an attack seized her, nothing but a faint wheezing would come from her throat, and a little blood, and some phlegm. She was pale, transparent, her flesh clinging to the bones, and it was only in her cheeks, flushed with blood, that the colour of life remained. When Jeanne sat down on the edge of the bed, Dasha would produce the suggestion of a smile, as if to say that she was sorry for having been in bed so long or to apologize for not drinking this or that potion, knowing that Jeanne had prepared it for her with leaves and roots according to a recipe of Filaretov's. Sometimes she would express a wish to hear her father play, then interrupt him with a gesture that seemed to say, not that one, no, I don't want that one . . . At other times she would decide to get up and try taking a few steps – only to collapse at once, exhausted.

In the Russia that was about to give birth to a revolution, there hovered somewhere above the smoke and straw a presentiment that nothing would ever be the same again. Some – the minority who had a lot to lose – were already leaving the country; others were already shaping the course of History in advance to suit their own ends, or at least trying to do so; and the rest, the great majority, simply waited in hope. In hope of something undefined. In Russia you always wait, you always hope.

In the microcosm of the flat in Pushkin Street, everything revolved around the increasingly crazy movements of the column of mercury in its glass tube, around the number of red corpuscles, which were steadily vanishing. Everything outside could be destroyed, consumed by flames – what did it matter? This little universe rejoiced when Dasha's temperature was a degree lower one evening, or if she could drink a whole glass of hot milk. According to the latest news, Alexander was on a train full of wounded somewhere, bound for Kislovodsk, a watering-place in the Caucasus. Jeanne would have gone off to meet him if Dasha had picked up at all, or if Isaak had been back – but Isaak had been away for a whole month now, and hadn't sent a word.

'Play me that song, Father – the one I used to sing at Fankoni's, remember? How did it go now . . .? Tra-la-lala, Tra-lalalalala . . .

> '*The town's asleep*
> *And dawn is breaking*
> *A fire of hair*
> *A mist of meaning*
> *The wind blows*
> *And this heart is aching*

> *The town's asleep*
> *And you're not here.'*

She murmured rather than sang. 'Pretty feeble lyrics, eh . . .?
But the music was lovely . . . Play it for Jeanne, Father . . .'

'Oh, I like it,' said Jeanne. 'The lyrics are beautiful, too,
with that tune . . .'

'Do you know, I was jealous seeing you and Isaak waltzing
together the other evening – it was such a pretty sight, with
the fire and everything.'

'It wasn't serious at all.'

'I know,' said Dasha, turning her face to the wall. 'Men
don't like invalids and sick-rooms. You see – he hasn't even
written.'

'But you told me yourself that he wouldn't be able to write,
that he'd warned you there wouldn't be any letters, that it
would be unwise –'

'Yes, yes, I know . . . It's true . . . I'm not saying anything
. . . But all the same . . .'

'Dasha, it won't be long now. He'll come back soon . . .'

'Yes, he'll come back . . . Would you read me something?'

'The George Sand there?'

'No, a bit of *Das Kapital.*'

Obediently Jeanne took the tome from the shelf, opened it
at the page marked with a ribbon, and, in a monotonous
voice, resumed the reading:

*'The owners of the forces of production are mortal. In order for them to
play a constant role in the economy, and for money to be continually
transformed into capital, they have to be rendered eternal, "as every living
individual is rendered eternal by the process of procreation". The elements in
the labour force that ill-health or death removes from the labour market have
constantly to be replaced by an at least equal number. The sum of the
resources necessary for the creation of the labour force thus includes the
resources required by their replacements, that is to say, the workers' children,*

in order that this curious breed of dealers may perpetuate itself within the economy.'

'Breed of dealers, you see?' interrupted Dasha. 'That's Isaak: he loves deals and bargains and trafficking and scheming . . . He's a poet of the marketplace: he's not interested in the money, it's the business of dealing that he loves, and everything that goes with it – journeys and ships and foreigners and far-off lands and deserts and horses . . .'

'Isaak is our Christopher Columbus,' said Jeanne, relieved to have stopped reading aloud the string of nonsense that was *Das Kapital* for her.

'Christopher Columbus? Do you think so? How long did he live?'

'He died at fifty-five,' replied Jeanne.

'Fifty-five – what a life . . .! What century are we talking about?'

'Second half of the fifteenth.'

In the middle of a sentence, half-way through a gesture, or even in the silence which absorbed her attention more and more, Dasha would suddenly lapse into a state of absence, as though she were already rehearsing her exit from this world, already sounding out infinity. Jeanne bent down to listen to her difficult breathing, unable to concentrate on the sound because of the creaking of floorboards under Grigory's feet, and a bumble-bee that buzzed around the room for four seconds, and the scent of the lilacs and wild-cherry trees whose mauve-and-white profusion was more exuberant than ever this year. Dasha's last hours were spent in a coma: sleeping peacefully, she scarcely moved, and she breathed her last without the slightest sign of pain: neither Jeanne nor Grigory could tell exactly when it happened.

Dasha's funeral was one of the most lavish entertainments Odessa had ever witnessed: it was in the biggest church, with the most beautiful singing, and the most lyrical sermon imaginable in the circumstances; a sea of people jostled around the coffin until it reached its final resting-place, which was a mountain of flowers, rather than a grave.

Jeanne hadn't set foot in the house at Beriozy for a month, and throughout the entire ceremony her only thought was to get back there as quickly as possible. Right at that moment she would have given anything to have Marie-Aynard with her, to hear her voice, and feel her hands upon her eyes, and cry into her skirts as she had done almost every day as a little girl – for between the two of them there were none of the stupidities that drive people apart, but rather an infinite, mutual gratitude for the life that one gives and that one is given, a fierce and primitive gratitude inscribed in those simple syllables – Mamma – in that magic circle of little tendernesses, traces of which one seeks, right to the end, and without even wanting to, in the face of a spouse, or a sister, or a passer-by, in a whirl of dead leaves, just one of which contains more in the way of hopes and recollections than all the greenery in the world. It wasn't to Alexander that Jeanne's thoughts flew, it wasn't his absence that she mourned in the church where Dasha became a child again upon her final bed; it was her mother, her beautiful foreigner of a mother who had gone off to a country Jeanne did not know. Why didn't she come back, her lovely blonde mother? What letters could Jeanne write, what phrases could she use to explain the feelings that gripped her soul? And how was it that Marie-Aynard could be so unaware of what was happening to her Jeanne? Why were there only those letters – infinitely tender letters, it was true, but still nothing more than ink on perfumed paper, nothing more than words? Jeanne had no faith in words.

On 10 May 1917, Monsieur Yves Seyn, a barrister who had been a widower for twelve years, married Marie-Aynard Forestier at the Town Hall in Neuilly.

It took Jeanne a fortnight to come to herself – if one can come to oneself by cleaning windows and whitewashing walls and tidying cupboards and washing one's hair and swimming in a still very chilly sea and doing suppling exercises at the bar and drinking soup. Filaretov took Jeanne's telescope to have it repaired, and he did his best to change the rusted hinges of the gate at Beriozy. It proved beyond him, however, and they had to wait for Grigory. Grigory himself, after losing Dasha and, a few days later, his wife, had come to resemble his horse: he limped along in just the same manner, his head shaking on his emaciated neck, and he just drank and drank without uttering a syllable. Every two or three days he would turn up at Beriozy with some of Dasha's things in his cart – her chandeliers, her furs, her paintings, her dresses, and his wife's baskets full of unused lace. Moving like an automaton, he would dump the lot in front of Jeanne's house, and Jeanne didn't dare tell him that she was frightened he would just collapse one day, like a sleepwalker. She piled up all these trophies in Nastia's room as obediently as she had read, at Dasha's direction, extracts from *Das Kapital*.

The last object to be brought was the guitar. Seeing it lying on the ground underneath the cascade of clematis, Jeanne picked it up and said, 'Stay, Grigory. Why do you have to keep coming and going like this? You can live with me . . .'

He shook his head, went off again – and returned with his marinading-jars and a few saucepans. For the first time, Jeanne offered a protest. 'Why all the saucepans? We've got lots of the things!'

Grigory, Jeanne and Filaretov dined together that night – by candlelight, with a starched cloth on the table – off a fish that Filaretov had bought at Privoz market. There was no wine; Grigory did without. He wanted to move into the toolshed: no amount of arguing could make him change his mind, and Jeanne was still chary of offending him – all the more so because he remained as stubbornly silent as ever.

Filaretov would have liked to bring his piano and stay there too, but Jeanne didn't ask him. He came to Beriozy whenever there was no evening performance at the Odeon, and sometimes during the day-time too, always arriving with a great load of parcels: there was scarcely any need to go out shopping in that house.

One morning Jeanne received a visit from Marie-Aynard's old friend, the French Consul – a man of about fifty who had occupied his post in Odessa for a very long time, and was now on the point of leaving. With stork-like movements he picked his way among the removal crates and paintings that were cluttering up the floor of the little sitting-room.

'Looks rather like my place,' he said. 'Are you leaving too?'

'On the contrary,' said Jeanne, 'I'm just about to put them on the walls. I'm getting myself settled in here.'

'Well, I have come at the request of your lady mother to try to persuade you to leave. She gave me this mission, which will be my last. I would ask you to listen to me, and I promise to be as brief as possible.'

'Take a seat,' said Jeanne, motioning him towards the wickerwork armchair and sitting down opposite him.

'Do you not read the papers?'

'No, I don't.'

'Fresh strikes have broken out in Petrograd and Moscow. The whole country's in the most unimaginable chaos: the rule of law has broken down completely, and we're dealing with a volcano that could explode from one day to the next. Things here are never going to return to normal, and it's impossible to foresee how they will develop. When the explosion comes – as it will – well, I lack words to describe what it will be like. This country is going to run mad, and there'll be rivers of blood flowing on every side.'

'I must say that I'm aware of all this, without the aid of newspapers,' said Jeanne. 'Although my angle on it is perhaps slightly different,' she added, forcing herself not to smile.

'What is it that's keeping you here? Is it your career? Your friends? You've got no family here, to the best of my knowledge –'

'I do have a family and friends here, and, what's more, I'm simply attached to this land. I was born here, didn't you know? I will not leave this country. Everything that happens to it will happen to me.'

'You – a patriot? Well . . . But you misunderstand me: your mother isn't asking you to leave this country for good. You can come back. When things have calmed down again here, when it's a bit safer again. So please come back to your mother: there's a cabin booked for you on the boat my family are taking. It goes without saying that there's absolutely no trouble with the visas . . .'

'And it was my mother who asked you to come here and say all this?'

'Well, it was partly on my own initiative too,' replied the Consul. 'I saw you at the church the other day. I didn't get the feeling that you were really on your best form. You're still very young, remember: it's not so easy to have to fend for oneself at your age . . .'

'I'm going to give you a letter and a little present for my mother. Would you mind just waiting here a moment?' said Jeanne, leaving the room.

She came back carrying a parcel and Dasha's shawl – the one that was embroidered with forget-me-nots.

'This is my wedding present. I assume you've heard . . .?'

'Yes, I received a wedding-card,' said the Consul. 'I know Monsieur Seyn from a long way back: he's a remarkable man, all heart. He'll be an excellent stepfather to you. Which is just one more reason for you to come to France – but I can see that the case is hopeless . . . Goodbye, then, Jeanne. I wish you well. I hope very much that you'll come to our final reception at the Consulate. It's on the 15th June. I'll have an invitation sent to you.'

'Thanks, I shall,' said Jeanne, shutting the gate behind him.

Jeanne felt suddenly full of energy, perhaps even of joy – the joy of knowing that she was loved, that there were so many people concerned about her welfare. She thought of Marie-Aynard, with her entreaties and her ambassadors with their grey hair and walking-canes . . . It was all that was needed to put her right back on her feet. She had an enormous amount to do. Waiting and making preparations are the most all-consuming activities in this life, and the most enjoyable, too. She hung up Dasha's portraits in the sitting-room – those extraordinarily beautiful portraits done by the painter who didn't like women. She gave all the carpets a good beating and changed the curtains. When everything was spick and span, and the very last floorboard had been scrubbed, Jeanne opened up Marie-Aynard's wardrobe and set about trying on her very old-fashioned dresses: not one of them fitted her, they were all too big, too long, and slightly ridiculous with their profusion of lace and ribbons and pleats. She did however find one: it was of white linen, with a lacy petticoat – a beach dress, really; and, having put it on, Jeanne looked at herself in the mirror, running her hand over her skin. The wind had tanned and toughened it, and her nose was quite red. She decided that she wouldn't take any precautions this summer, she would just let the sun and the sea do what they would – whereas ever since she had been in Gauer's hands she had always had to cover her face and keep it perfectly pale so that the make-up 'rendered' it properly. Jeanne preferred herself like this – and how lucky that Alexander would see her looking this way!

The days passed, and the nights: Jeanne jumped at the slightest sound – a creak of the gate, a footstep on the gravel –; there were plenty of visits and much news, but everything was a disappointment because it wasn't what she was waiting for. Letters came from Gauer in Los Angeles, and one from Isaak, posted in Barcelona: he was staying in Peroutchev's native village and waiting 'for things to blow over', as he put it. That Catalan! thought Jeanne. She was moved by the name of the village itself – Almatret. In the space of those three syllables came and went scarlet sails, and flags, and breakwaters, and shadows, and the friendship of men who didn't exist.

The June of 1917 was a cold month: Jeanne couldn't go bathing, but she went for walks along the seashore to help pass the time. On leaving the house, she would always pin a large note to the gate saying that she was only going off for an hour, and would be back soon. One particular day she forgot the note, only remembering it as she was coming back up from the sea. Suddenly, as if she had gone mad, she started running, tearing the hem of her skirt on the brambles and thistles, getting her legs scratched, not stopping until she was near the house. And her heart gave out on her as it had on the day of her fall, when she saw two figures coming down the top of the hill towards Beriozy – a man and a child.

The
· Barber's ·
Hand

· BERIOZY ·

I

Nine days went by in a whirl of negotiations. Alexander Illytch was looking for an engine to which to hitch up his hospital carriages, stuck in a siding in Odessa. There were no serious cases, it was true – the serious cases had died during the evacuation – but wounded they were, all the same, and in need of attention in some quiet place far away from the tracks, and the wheels, and the clatter.

The orders were for Kislovodsk. An eminently correct document, emanating from on high. From Petrograd. In Odessa the atmosphere was one of evasion, courtesy – all very bourgeois-republican. Oh, these Odessans! Ever since the fall of that poor wretch, Nicholas, it had been: all right, very well, we'll cooperate, why not, but you can't expect the impossible. The captain-surgeon wants his injured moved? Why doesn't he take the boat? A much safer bet, the boat, believe you me! With the railway network in chaos, you won't get there any quicker way. Kislovodsk, of all places . . .

It was hopeless. Here was a captain of what had once been the Imperial Army, all but begging people to remember their duty as Christians. The irony of it! The people who got things done, in Odessa as elsewhere – almost more here than elsewhere – were Jews. A man by the name of Goldman, for instance. He had no civil authority, he had something else. A kind of dodgy independence. Otherwise, he was quite normal.

Alexander Illytch kept a tight hold on this Goldman, who hunted out an engine for him. It dated from the Russo-Turkish war, but at least it moved. A mule of an engine, this one, hooked up already – terribly unfortunate, nothing we can do about it – to ten other coaches carrying hams, sausages, sauce-pans, *Made in Odessa* hashish, Parisian perfumes, Havana cigars: the wealthy were off to the Caucasus, and they were taking their creature comforts with them. An apocalypse? If you insist – but at least let's make it go with a bang! Only the finest perfumes, only the best cigars, and, if we're going to be really decadent about it, let's have it in the foothills of the Caucasus! The air is so pure down there! And the cypresses!

Why was it that whenever Alexander arrived back at Beri-ozy, after one of his visits to Goldman, he found Jeanne washing the child? The little boy couldn't bear water; and there she was putting some on to heat again. She was dandling Igor in a wooden tub. Play with the soap, Igoriok!

'It's bath-time,' Jeanne announced.

What could be more incongruous than bath-time in a country that was in flames? But after the mire of the trenches and the butchery of the Eastern Front, these bath-times consoled Alexander. Let them continue, he thought. Nothing wrong with the jam-making, either. Apricot jam.

'It's the season,' said Jeanne.

Jeanne was making crêpes – using real flour. Alexander understood now why Igoriok had let Jeanne wash his eyes with soap: he adored crêpes with apricot jam. Pink-faced, his hair shining, he was sitting right up at table, gorging himself. Jeanne watched him as he ate, making Alexander jealous. A note like a swallow's kept piping forth from little Igor's lips: 'Ja'. He sang it: 'Ja – Ja – Ja – Ja.' He had eyes and ears for nothing but Jeanne. Alexander was getting used by now to this strange sound, 'Jeanne'. It was such an alien syllable, ending as it did in a mute 'e' – falling away as abruptly as the path which plummeted down from the cliff-top to Beriozy.

Sometimes Alexander would be late getting back. Because of Goldman, of course, who took up so much of his time; but also on account of the wounded in the railway carriages, who had to be kept under constant surveillance: gangrene can set in in no time. Alexander had already performed three operations on a carriage bench.

He would return late after these butchery sessions, bringing with him an odour, his ineluctable odour of chloroform and something else, something stale, blood, perhaps, his pale-complexioned face bristling with more beard and eyebrow than usual. Leaving his cap in the hallway, he tiptoed down the corridor, closing on his way a window here, a window there, and opened the door of the end room, where Jeanne slept.

Jeanne was asleep, which was good: it meant that she felt safe. Alexander looked at the face which had become his life: the features a trifle drawn, the slight shadows under the eyes, the storm of hair, darker than his own, the nose, comically pointed in profile: it was the face of a child. Looking at it, he forgot the stumps and trunks, the caulked veins and torn muscles of all those bodies departing this life. He saw nothing but this room. He didn't go to bed. He had a journey to set out on. If 'journey' was the word for this eternal return to the same harbour, the same bright hearth that was the figure of this woman stretched out on the bed. He didn't dare wake her: he didn't dare touch her. She must be completely exhausted. She had so much to cope with: the child found at the Front, and then Alexander himself, and the war, and the convoy of wounded who needed him. And his own imminent departure.

He would have liked to watch her living, month upon month, hour by individual hour. To watch her bathing Igor-iok, doing the washing, running across the beach towards the sea, swimming. He saw how the child was perking up with Jeanne. The pleasure he took in pronouncing words! Jeanne would say, and Igor repeat: *tomato, orange, foam, star*. Yes: he would have liked the time to watch with his own eyes the way a family can be born of nothing, without the ties of blood.

The journey was looming. He was leaving in two days, thanks to Goldman. He should have spoken to Jeanne, telling her that this separation could not last long, that the war would come to an end, that they were just a single being – Igor, Jeanne and he – and what does distance matter! But a doubt preyed upon him. Not that he was afraid of losing them: he wasn't afraid of anything concerning them – at least, that's what he would have said. But in a patch of shadow in the room, in the staring walls, in the crumpled valleys of pillows and sheets, in the creaking of the front gate which hadn't been shut properly, even in the other-worldly colour of the cliffs, he detected maleficent signs. They tolled a knell.

Jeanne remained calm and cheerful, as if these two days would never come to an end. On both mornings she took Alexander by the hand and led him down the corridor of the sleeping house; and on the threshold she hugged him tight, tight enough to break her own ribs. And then the wave broke and she became herself again, serene to all appearances, scarcely returning the farewell which he waved to her from the top of the cliff – a farewell that was all his own, with the palm of his hand turned in towards his chest and his fingers folding and unfolding, not quickly.

Jeanne had a strict plan which took no account of current developments and was based on what one sometimes believes to be the most indestructible of all things: love. Inspired by this love, she could do nothing but wait for events in Russia to resume a more sensible course. It would not have been good, either for her or for Igoriok – particularly for Igoriok, who had found himself abandoned at the age of five – to give way to panic and do something like leave Beriozy and leap on to a hospital train which was full of nothing but suffering. If she had dared ask Igoriok, and if Igoriok had been able to reply, he would have said that he most certainly preferred their white house with its thick white walls, his bed with its wooden slats, his short-sleeved shirts warm from the ironing, Uncle Grigory with his horse and cart, and even the daily bath with the huge bar of soap which stung. So Jeanne stayed at Beriozy. You can live apart for a long time. You have to trust your memory of arms and lips, your tactile memory, which is the most faithful of all memories. Jeanne had long been full of this memory.

On the eve of his departure, which was a Sunday, Alexander went to visit his wounded, returning in the afternoon. Grigory and Igoriok were at the circus. Jeanne had done Alexander's washing and packed his case. Calm as she was in her daily life, patient as she was, it was more than she could do to look at this suitcase once it was packed. With a mechanical movement of her foot she pushed it under the bed and went to join Alexander, who was in the kitchen, poking the stove. On the table lay the last batch of apricots, washed and pricked with a needle to release the juice: they glowed in the preserving pan, ready to be cooked.

Jeanne, dressed in an old white linen skirt and blouse, carried the pan over to the stove and set it down on the hob with her muscular dancer's arms. Alexander helped her. Jeanne licked her thumbs, which had become steeped in the juice during the operation. Her hair fell down over her eyes, tickling her nose. She blew it away, her thumbs still in her mouth. If only I could see her like this every day, Alexander said to himself, every day of my life! He had known other women, at other times. An endless string of jealousies, separations, reproaches, outrages, regrets. Not now: not with Jeanne. What he felt for Jeanne was more absolute, more serene, with just a hint of incest about it, as if they had been born together. They were like those couples one sees walking along, arm in arm, taking short, well-matched strides, their unmarked faces defying the passage of time under white heads of hair.

Alexander did not have a clear picture of all this. He could only hear the first strains of a muted melody. His train, which was leaving tomorrow, kept him from seeing a number of things. Not six feet away from him Jeanne was licking her fingers as if there had never been a Revolution, or hospital convoys. They drew together, closed their eyes, groped for one another's lips, one another's fingers, tearing off their clothes and throwing them anywhere, in the sink, on the fruit, and they made love in the shared lightning that puts a black nimbus around the sun. Their wildness went on and on, the apricots burned, smoke filled the house, Igor and Gregory would be coming back soon: they ought to get up, make the kitchen look decent, save the fruit, air the place.

II

Alexander left at dawn. 'Don't come with me,' he said to Jeanne, 'it would only make things harder.' Grigory harnessed up the horse and put Alexander's suitcase in the cart. Alexander insisted on climbing the hill on foot so as not to tire the horse, which was getting old. A strange, almost cold wind was blowing. Jeanne stood with her back against the front gate, clutching a shawl to her, the ends of which covered up the child nestled in her arms.

The wind had developed into a storm and rain was falling in sheets when Grigory returned with a letter. 'Take care of yourself and the child. I love you. I'll write to you as soon as I get to Kislovodsk. It'll take around five days, so expect at least as long again before you receive my first letter. Don't worry if it doesn't arrive till later. You know what chaos the post is in. A big hug for you, my little apricot.'

By the evening mail Jeanne received a letter from Gauer in Los Angeles. He was shooting a film: it seemed that people there had taken him up. He was with his Masha, and was in good health. So things were going fine for him, but he was worried about Jeanne. Come over here, he said to her, we can work together. The terms they're offering are out of this world. They're broadminded, these Americans, and they know what they're doing. They're taking events in Russia very well. It's said that President Wilson has offered Kerensky a loan of three hundred and twenty-five million dollars. These democrats must like the idea of a Russia without a Tsar, since they're prepared to part with so many dollars. If Jeanne were to make up her mind to come to the United States, she should go and see a certain David Heller, a businessman from Kentucky: he was in his sixties and extremely well-off, and he ought by now to have arrived at the Consulate, which was just near to the Tauride Palace, accompanied by his black majordomo. He's a friend of mine, said Gauer, he'll do anything for you.

Why do they all keep wanting to drag me away from here? thought Jeanne. First the French Consul, sent along by my mother, and now this one! It's as if the world were falling apart in this town – as if life had come to a total standstill here!

The storm blew stronger and stronger, and it was impossible to put one's nose out of doors. Igoriok, a real little tyrant, wouldn't budge an inch from Jeanne, clinging to her apron, his eyes filling with anguish every time she withdrew from the kitchen to her room.

He had to learn to overcome his fear. He had to be made to feel that every time she left, she would come back again. That she belonged to him. Jeanne had her work cut out. What was all this talk of Los Angeles! If necessary, she would give up acting in films. Having a child on your hands changes your life. And then there was that Protazonov who kept sending telegram upon telegram from the studios in Petrograd: EVERYONE THINKS YOU'RE DEAD, WATCH WHAT YOU'RE DOING, PEOPLE FORGET YOU SO QUICKLY IN THE CINEMA . . .

Let them forget me, thought Jeanne. I'm needed here, what with Igoriok and his fits of panic, and Grigory with his rheumatism, and Sasha with his wounded. Everything will work out: Igoriok will grow up and gain in confidence,

Alexander will come back, I'll buy Grigory a younger horse, even if he wants to keep the other one on ... And then I might perhaps think of working for Protazonov, or even for Gauer in Los Angeles ... We'll see ...

III

Jeanne had no precise visual recollection of the Petrograd tram upon whose crowded platform she had met Alexander ten months previously. She perceived it rather as a kind of never-ending music. To the rhythm of this music, everything took on a meaning for Jeanne – her face, her feet, her stomach, the weather (whatever it was like), the child, the arrangement of the furniture in the house, the soup that she ate with Grigory and Igoriok in the evenings. She no longer washed her hair simply to have it washed; she washed it for Alexander. When she had a new dress made up, that was for Alexander too. Everything was dedicated to Alexander: sleeping, waking, swimming, the games she played with Igoriok. And when she went into town – making a detour via the Alexander Railway Station – she would tear into the Alexander Post Office to pick up her letters.

Those letters arrived by the packet. At the counter of the *poste restante* they had to give her two pigeon-holes: one was not enough to contain the avalanches of envelopes that came for Miss Forestier. The first ones bore the postmarks of all the little towns that ran along the Odessa–Kislovodsk line, like the pebbles of a hop-o'-my-thumb. Then Alexander set off for Petrograd again, via Moscow. Then he returned to Galicia, then went back to Petrograd. The war showed no sign of stopping, people kept being killed and injured: Alexander worked day and night. Jeanne, who had hitherto paid no attention to what was happening at the Front, started reading all the papers that came her way. The war became her war – this bewildering war in which everything was so mixed up: the decrees issued by the new authorities, the speeches of the new leaders, the rows between the political parties, and the military setbacks over which the Odessan press, just like the Petrograd and Moscow newspapers, drew a veil of silence.

In Odessa, the keyword used in connection with all these disasters and mishaps remained the same as ever: the Jews. The fact that prices had increased sevenfold since 1913, that there was indiscipline in the army, that coffee was hard to come by, that mackerel, the Odessans' staple food, was being sold at the price of the carp that the Jews so adored – it was all due to the doings of these traitors. They had sold Our Lord and now they were selling Russia. In Moscow and Petrograd the barometer of public opinion, subtler and less unanimous, pointed also to Germany. Rasputin, Alexandra Feodorovna (the Tsar's wife, and, let it not be forgotten, a German princess), to say nothing of a whole string of generals – all were secretly on the side of the Germans, unbeknown to the Allies and the Tsar. And now the Bolsheviks too, with Lenin at their head. Hadn't he chosen the date of the Galician offensive to stir up the sailors at Kronstadt, the workers at the factory in Poutilov, and the soldiers of the First Machine-Gun Regiment billeted in the buildings of the House of the People? The Galician offensive had ended in defeat. Lenin and his Bolsheviks were organizing the whole chain of germanophiles and spies which led from Rasputin and his Tsarina all the way to the General Staff, the Duma and most of the ministers.

Even if Lenin was not himself a spy, the capital's most respectable newspapers stressed, even if he wasn't in the pay of the Kaiser, hadn't he thrown in his lot with the Germans since his return in April? Hadn't he encouraged Russia to renounce her obligations towards the Allies and negotiate a separate peace? Hadn't he and his party incited the soldiers in the trenches to fraternize with the enemy? He wanted civil war, that was all there was to it! Civil war, to provoke our defeat! These arguments were enough to brand the Bolsheviks as German agents throughout the length and breadth of Russia.

So went the rumour, or rather one of the many rumours that followed one another like waves – overlapping, self-contradictory, inconsistent. The people were being made fools of, still swallowing their disaffection although the *moujiks* were serving as cannon-fodder instead of tilling their fields, although bread was rationed, although nothing had changed since the fall of the Tsar. How the speeches had rung in the early days! Liberty, democracy, everything for the people! And the people just didn't know where to turn: like children let out at play-time, they chased around in all directions, not knowing what to do with this liberty, not knowing whose hand to take, listening now to this person, now to that.

In concrete terms, this chasing around took the form of countless departures, everyone having their own reasons for going. The stations were packed to overflowing and the railway network could no longer cope with the flood of people desperately seeking a centre of gravity. Russia on the eve of her greatest reckoning with fate was like a huge ant-hill that some foot had kicked over. To informed minds, this moment of reckoning seemed inevitable, but they were not able to direct the movements of the ants. Even the colour red was becoming equivocal. In March 1917, Kerensky had put on a red arm-band: a few weeks later, in July, the red of the flags recalled the red of the blood of the workers against whom the troops had charged on the orders of the self-same Kerensky. There would have been even more deaths if a violent downpour had not sent the demonstrators running for the shelter of the courtyards, washing the blood from the tramlines at the same time.

Once more people spread lies about Lenin and his Party. But how long could it go on like this?

IV

The spell of cold, windy weather that had affected the entire area, all the way down to Odessa, came to an end. Fishermen spread out nets to dry on the beach before the houses. They looked pretty against the white of the sand – blue, ochre, moss-green, the colours of the clay in the rocks around Odessa. A smell of burning still wafted in off the sea although the air itself seemed pure, slightly acidic, as in autumn. Then the sun began to blaze and a scorching wind swept the coast. At Constantinople the thermometer registered 55°C. At Odessa it rose to forty-four.

Jeanne would drag little Igoriok off to the beach, encourage him to have a splash, pin a large straw hat on to her head and then set off for a swim in the open sea. Igoriok fretted whenever he lost sight of his 'Ja', jumping around like a wild thing the moment she reappeared. When she came out of the water, he would cling to her legs, kissing her, and they would sing the song they had made up together:

> *Lessenka, lessenka,*
> *Vot kakaïa pessenka*

which meant 'Little staircase, little staircase, And there's a song!' The rhyme, concrete and flashy, sounded entirely avant-garde. The song had come to them as they are descending the interminable Potemkin Steps. They were in fine form that day: five letters from Alexander!

In order not to be without his 'Ja', Igoriok plucked up the courage to jump into the water. He made rapid progress, and was soon doing a competent breast-stroke. So he could follow Jeanne a bit of the way, and when she told him to go back, he made it to the shore on his own. He didn't have so long to wait then, and he felt proud of himself, too. Jeanne gave Igor a great deal of affection, but was careful not to cosset him too much. The future was so uncertain that she tried to teach him to shift for himself, to do up his own shoelaces. She also invented reasons for leaving him with Grigory, or with her friend Filaretov, who of course wanted nothing better. She made him do a lot of walking, put only a light cover on him at night, and took away his pillows. During the daytime he went barefoot. With Jeanne he peeled and chopped the vegetables, with Grigory he groomed the horses – the old one, very stiff about the joints now, and the new one, a real handful, whom they had christened Sultan. Grigory had stopped drinking since the child had been at Beriozy: it happened from one day to the next, as if the sight of this little being had made up for the death of his daughter, Dasha. He no longer feared the fall of night, even his rheumatism improved, and from time to time he would play his guitar.

After the final break, which was called on the spur of the moment, but wrongly, 'the October Fusillades', things started going badly for Russia. In this whole vast land, there was nothing left to feed the people or keep them warm. To crown it all, it started snowing as early as November. That was all right in the north, in Petrograd and Moscow, but here in Odessa the snow seemed a bad omen. It fell and fell upon the black fields, upon the flimsy cobblestones of this almost Italian town. It smothered the acacias and chestnut trees, leaving them idiotically white.

V

Filaretov, who always had his ear to the ground, brought news. He was the only one of the company to keep up his normal social habits. The Odeon cinema, of which he was the pianist, was as busy as ever, if not more so, on account of the bad weather. Foreign films were much in demand at the moment: the Odessans wanted a taste of something new. Jeanne's star was waning, Mary Pickford's rising.

Filaretov suggested a reason for this: Jeanne's last film, *The Woman in Grey*, had not been released in Russia. Gauer had taken the reels off with him to Los Angeles. It was being shown in America – not without success, according to his letters. But in Petrograd they wanted nothing to do with it: it wasn't patriotic. It portrayed the war in a discouraging light. What was worse, it had an unhappy ending, and unhappy endings were not yet the thing. Of all her films from those days – that was the phrase that came to her, 'those days' – Jeanne would have liked to see just that one, *The Woman in Grey*, and no other. Alexander had been there when she was acting in it. Her face in that film was the face Alexander had seen in the tram, falling in love with her on the spot. And in the studios at Petersburg, for the filming itself, she had worn the black kid ankle-boots in which she had kicked her way through the piles of dead leaves near the golden railings of the Summer Garden when she and Alexander went walking there, hand in hand. They would go back to her place, he after his day's work at the hospital, unshaven, with that smell of chloroform about him, she lit up with the idea of having kept some of those dead leaves, some of those treasures, on the soles of her shoes.

One evening – it only happened once – when they had just got back home, she saw him shaving: they were getting ready to go out. They went to a restaurant. And in the restaurant, as she was sitting with her elbow on the table and her hand propping up her cheek, she felt Alexander gently brush her little finger with such tenderness that her head reeled and just floated away, spinning as in a waltz.

What did that waltz have to do with these sudden,

penetrating gusts of dirty snow, with Alexander's journeyings around Russia with his trainloads of wounded, with the sudden fear welling in the eyes of that child – the fear of being left? Or with the latest news? Rumours more than news.

The Voice of Odessa was indulging in its usual hysterics: the Jews were about to seize power in Petrograd. A certain Bronstein, who called himself Trotsky, wanted to buy up the entire Russian army. Kerensky was going to cede his place to him, graciously, as simply as that, 'on a blue-rimmed saucer' – an Odessan expression for the giving of casual presents. And then there were the Soviets: they had set up their headquarters in a convent, the one at Smolny, in a show of defiance against the authorities who had always thought the Tauride Palace the only seat of power.

Filaretov shed a little light on all these goings-on the moment he stepped through the door at Beriozy. The Kerensky government had been overthrown. The new leaders had connections with Jeanne's old friends, Dasha, Isaak Storm, all kinds of strange people – 'Militant socialists', corrected Jeanne, who had lost track of events somewhat, but remembered well what she had learnt from Dasha in Pushkin Street. The allusion to the saucer, Filaretov went on, was justified insofar as the coup had once again been bloodless – just a bit of street-fighting around the Winter Palace, and a few scuffles in the Palace itself – even when the ministers were being arrested. The cannon-shots fired from a ship at anchor in the Neva had been merely symbolic – a martial parody of the bells that rang the moment a new Tsar was crowned. Filaretov stated that the bread ration in the capital had fallen to less than two hundred grams per person, that rents were no longer being paid, and that the promised peace was coming about – that is to say that it had been proclaimed as a fact, never mind the German armies knocking at the gates of Petrograd, or the binding treaties that had been signed with the Allies. As children say, 'I'm not playing with you any more.' The Soviets weren't playing. The question of land had been solved with equal ease: the ownership of land had been abolished without any offer of compensation to the owners.

Filaretov's version was actually much more fantastic than that of *The Voice of Odessa*. And nothing much seemed to have changed in Odessa itself, except that there was panic to be seen on the Stock Exchange, and the Moscow and Petrograd newspapers had stopped arriving. But Jeanne could take money out from the bank every month as usual. And if there were fewer people in the streets, that was partly because of the snow, which showed no sign of letting up, and the icy wind. Old Grigory however betrayed the secret anxiety which had crept over people even in the south of the country: he would go out on his new horse to bring back sacks of flour and potatoes from the surrounding countryside.

VI

With Igoriok at her side, Jeanne kept calling in at the post office. Over the course of several weeks she received only two letters, which arrived by the same mail: they had been forwarded from Petrograd, and were dated the 12th and the 14th of October. Alexander reported simply that he was setting off on his usual trip, first to the Galician Front and from there to the Caucasus.

Deprived of letters, Jeanne could make no connection between Filaretov's news and what was happening to her Alexander. What had become of him? What was going to be his role in this war that had been annulled by a stroke of the pen but which continued for all that, because the troops were still at the Front and no peace had been signed with the Germans?

Jeanne felt overwhelmed by it all. The young lady at the post office told her that the absence of letters was due to the strikes which were breaking out all over Russia. That Jeanne was not the only one in this situation. 'Don't come every day,' she said to her. 'I know myself what it's like to wait . . . I'll let you know as soon as there's a letter for you. How would that be?' Jeanne liked this young woman, who did her work with a big-eyed, freckle-faced baby on her lap.

'Jeanne!'

A man's voice. She turned round. It was Egoroff – the Egoroff who had always been at the flat in Pushkin Street in Dasha's day, the great reader of Marx, and a friend of Isaak's. Jeanne thrilled at the sight of him: this man would explain things to her. He could make everything clear. Even, she remembered, *primitive accumulation, surplus value* . . .

'I called by at your place in Richelieu Street. There were new people living there. They had no idea how I could find you. Isaak –'

He broke off, staring at Igoriok, who was clinging to Jeanne's legs; the child wouldn't take his eyes off him.

'Yours?' he said.

'My son,' replied Jeanne.

'I wasn't aware.'

'You were saying: Isaak . . .'

'Let's get out of here,' said Egoroff. 'Have you got a minute?'

'As many as you'd like . . . Shall we go back to my place at Beriozy? We could have some tea.'

'I haven't got much time,' reflected Egoroff. He looked about him. 'Well, all right then, let's do that. Is it far?'

'We can take my carriage,' said Jeanne, pointing through the window at Grigory and his horse waiting in the street outside.

Once they were settled in the carriage, Jeanne asked, 'Where's Isaak?'

'He'll be back soon. I saw him a fortnight ago, in Constantinople.'

'He's stopped writing to me, you know. I used to get postcards from Barcelona, but I haven't had anything for the past three months.'

'He's not in Barcelona any more. He asked me to come and see you. To give you his news. He had to go to Stockholm. He'll be here any day now, depending on what happens in Petrograd. He's got things to do here.'

'I can imagine,' said Jeanne, who couldn't for the life of her imagine what Isaak had to do in Odessa just now. Even back in Dasha's day she had never been able to grasp quite what it was he did. All right, so there was that front, the import-export business, Turkish tobacco and so forth, and the fact that Isaak seemed to have all the workers of Odessa's docklands at his beck and call, and then his title – his unofficial title – of 'the King of Moldavanka', the thieves' quarter. But why did Egoroff and his 'comrades' take so much money from Isaak's pockets when they made their lightning visits to the flat in Pushkin Street? Where did the money come from? To what extent was Isaak a businessman, and to what extent a revolutionary activist? How great was his involvement in it all? Jeanne could not say. Isaak remained something of a legend – this man who would parade in the company of the local bigwigs (bankers, diplomats, landowners, industrialists and even top police chiefs), but whom one felt to be much more at home amongst the dockers, the *bindujniks*, in the sordid bars around the harbour, or in somewhere as shady as the Café Catalan in the Street of the Assumption in Moldavanka.

An intuitive hunch told Jeanne that anything she might learn from Egoroff would give her a more or less clear idea of what was in store for Alexander. If it really was a question of a Bolshevik coup, of the first stages of a true socialist revolution, then Egoroff would give her proof of the fact, explaining it all clearly – he whom she had more than once heard constructing, with the patience of a village schoolmaster, the set of arguments from which proceeded, smoothly and inevitably, the necessity of such a revolution. Dasha had still been alive at the time, and in her flat in Pushkin Street Jeanne had devoured her library volume by volume – those books any one of which, according to Dasha, was a passport to Siberia.

Jeanne shook with impatience. The mine of information that she was taking home with her in her carriage had to be exploited to the full. She would apply herself to the task.

VII

She applied herself. Egoroff was quite grey: he had obviously eaten nothing, or next to nothing, for weeks. She put out a pâté de fois gras (sent by her mother), a bottle of cognac, likewise from France, a pot of scented tea, and a home-baked loaf – a 'class-enemy' sort of spread. Egoroff spread the fois gras with butter as though it were the last pâté on earth, mixed sugar, cognac and tea in his cup, stuffed himself without saying a word. Sitting opposite him in her black dress, a tightly knotted fichu covering her hair and forehead right down to her eyebrows, Jeanne began to grow impatient. She didn't know Egoroff's Christian names: he had always been known as 'Comrade Egoroff' in the past. She had to put a stop to this feasting, to get through to him, one way or another, in order to begin her inquiries. She was hesitating, racking her brains for an opening, when she heard him say, 'Grain is scarce.'

He said nothing more for a moment, drinking two or three mouthfuls of tea, then launched into an interior monologue in the same cold and neutral tone. Holding her breath, Jeanne looked him straight in the eye as he spoke.

'We can't give the people enough bread. The majority of the peasants aren't going to be with us. We can't give them the machines they need. Fuel for burning, and other things of the utmost necessity, are scarcely to be found.'

His voice was dry, impassive, bitter. This was no longer the Egoroff Jeanne had known. Nothing remained of the impassioned, joyous logic he had once displayed.

'Peace is even more of a problem. The Allies will never accept any peace conference we might suggest. Neither London nor Paris will recognize us. Nor Berlin. And we can't expect any real help from their proletariats. I know, I've just come back from there. I've seen it with my own eyes! We've set out on a course that will lead to total isolation. To civil war. It's inevitable. Isaak told me I could trust you completely. I want you to listen to me carefully. It's very important. Are we alone?'

Egoroff had been speaking fast, in a uniform tone, and the last words, which concerned Jeanne, came entirely without warning. Pulling herself together, she quickly said, 'Yes. Grigory and Igoriok are out in the yard burning leaves.'

'When Isaak and I were in Constantinople, we received messages from Petrograd. We hadn't been expecting any of this to happen, at least not yet. It's rather difficult to explain. I must get back to Petrograd as quickly as possible. You'll see Isaak. He can't afford to show himself in public in Odessa, and he's aware of that. It's up to you to make a move. He'll be at the Café Catalan — do you know it?'

'Yes, very well.'

'He'll have to leave as soon as he arrives. I think the place is already dangerous for him. I have no way of warning him except through you. From tomorrow, you're to go there every day. He should be arriving in the next few days, and then setting off again for Petrograd. You're to say to him, "Parvus and Stockholm are no longer together." Just that. Will you be able to remember it?'

'Parvus and Stockholm are no longer together,' Jeanne repeated in a whisper.

'Signed Egoroff,' he added.

'Signed Egoroff,' repeated Jeanne.

'You're to go there this evening as soon as it's dark. The café's closed. There won't be any lights on. Don't worry about that. Knock on the door. Two long knocks, one short. Twice over. If he's there, he'll open up. Do you have a weapon?'

'I'm sorry?' said Jeanne.

'A revolver.'

'Yes,' said Jeanne, and went to the wardrobe in her bedroom to get the little pistol inlaid with mother-of-pearl that Isaak had given her.

'That's no good,' said Egoroff. 'Take this one.'

Jeanne found herself holding a large Browning, which she placed on her lap. Instinctively she removed her fichu and covered up the thing with it. Egoroff took it back from her.

'It's easy to use,' he said. 'A bit heavy for you – you'll have to hold it in both hands. You hold it like this, and take aim here, both arms fully outstretched. The rest is automatic. Clear?'

Egoroff's voice was becoming more and more mineral. It sounded like an organ of something else, of some other body that didn't belong to him. Despite the tea and cognac, Jeanne felt frozen. Egoroff said to her, 'Take care of yourself, Jeanne. And of that child. After the Catalan, get out of here – both of you!'

VIII

Jeanne followed Egoroff's instructions to the letter. She waited until evening and then, without taking Igoriok (whom she left with Grigory at Beriozy), called in at the post office just before it closed; then, when night had fallen, she went to the Street of the Assumption in Moldavanka and knocked on the door of the Café Catalan, which had a disused look about it.

Igoriok rebelled against Jeanne's repeated absences in the evenings. He wouldn't listen to Grigory, refused to take his bath, wouldn't touch his dinner, and then would go and collect all the pillows in the house, put them in a pile on the floor of the entrance hall, and lie down on them without getting undressed.

On the fifth evening in the Street of the Assumption, the door opened after the prearranged six knocks. At the foot of the stairs stood a suntanned Isaak, wearing a white shirt open at the chest. His huge shock of red hair flamed.

'Jeanne!' he said. 'Jeanne, it's you! My God, with no galoshes! And you're not wrapped up properly! I was just thinking you might perhaps . . . And it's you! Come on upstairs!'

They climbed the stairs, and, as she went, Jeanne suddenly felt she was losing her nerve. That she was losing herself. Something snapped inside her and she was flooded with a sense of abandon. It was like what happens after an over-long swim that has left you exhausted: you're nearly back at the shore at last, just a bit more and you'll be able to touch the bottom, but your strength leaves you. There was no current to help her now, no air for her to breathe – just air, just ordinary air. Everything had been taken from her – her oxygen, her very power of movement. No roof for her, no refuge, no October rain outside the window – that wonderful rain coming from the sky, from the world outside. It was inside Jeanne that it was raining: she was nothing but a colander, dripping wet, full of holes, leaking everywhere. She had no walls around her, no skin to cover her, no protection of any kind. She was open, torn asunder, naked. That was how Jeanne felt as she climbed the staircase. She had no idea why she was there, or that she had something to tell Isaak. And Isaak just talked and talked – words, words, words: Jeanne, her coat, her wet boots, her wet hair, no headscarf – all manner of absurdities. The words didn't really get through to Jeanne, but it didn't matter: they created a presence, an accompaniment, a glow. A marvellous glow which helped light up the stairway a little, bringing back the memory of something that had happened here one day, 'once upon a time' almost, the way stories start . . .

There seemed no end to the steep staircase, narrow and straight: it was so long, so extraordinarily long even for a staircase in Odessa. A ghost staircase, a remembered staircase, recalling prohibitions, and keys, and Bluebeard. It was cold. Isaak however had just that open-necked shirt on, the kind of shirt that men used to wear for duels in a former age when one's enemy was there to be seen, his face exposed. Ah yes, a waltz! She had once had to dance a waltz in this café, a waltz as pretty as a children's counting-rhyme. One-two-three, Bluebeard, white stockings, a waltz, in a café like a boat . . .

Isaak helped her off with her coat – gently, as one does with injured people – and smoothed out her hair by squeezing it with his fingertips to dry it, strand by strand. It was amazing how alone in the world they were at that moment, in this room-cum-ship, this nowhere. Yet they were somewhere, in a house with tables and chairs and a fireplace and a piano; one could live here.

Even if Jeanne was not herself, not at her best, as it was plain to see, Isaak wanted at that moment to know about nothing but the fact of her presence, right there, with her autumn coat and her hair all stuck down and her absent air. She was standing in front of him, within reach of his hand, this being whom for months now he had missed more than anyone else in the world, who at a distance had become his dream, his anchor, his star. For months? For *centuries* he had lived for nothing but this reunion! For eternities Russia had meant nothing to him but Jeanne. The sails of all the ships, the propellers of all the steamers, the boilers of all the railway-engines had taken him nowhere but here, to this meeting. And yet what a mad chance, what a miracle!

Jeanne guessed nothing of the sails and steamers; she was simply there, a stranger to the man's delirious visions, struck by amnesia but nevertheless beginning to realize there was something urgent, something vital that she had to identify amongst the thousand worries which were overwhelming her. She felt a coldness running down her back, cold droplets on her nose. She let herself fall on to the old bench as she would have sat down in the middle of the sea.

'And now you're going to drink, Jeanne,' said Isaak. 'You're going to drink to our health and to my return.'

He spoke these words with great gusto, as though he had taken her in his arms, whilst in fact he had only been filling a thick, short-stemmed glass – a Catalan champagne glass, which gave the impression of holding a great deal whilst really holding very little – with Rancy wine, heavy and red as blood. He looked handsome, tanned not by the sun but by the wind, which gives the deepest tan. His hair flamed like a halo, bristling with chaotic life. His hair, eyes and eyebrows intermingled, like the olive trees at Barcelona that promiscuously intertwine their branches with the architecture of the fountains. That evening he was Christopher Columbus returned from his voyages, still brimming with trees and skies. He might have stayed motionless, doing nothing with the glasses and bottles, saying nothing. It only needed a little patience. Jeanne would have come to him, with a little patience. But his patience was at an end.

It had come to him one day as he was sitting outside a café near the Cathedral in Tarragona, talking with some comrades. He heard himself replying in measured tones to a question concerning a shipment of arms from Belgium to Genoa, and the more he talked, the more he realized that there was nothing to be done: he loved this woman. Odessa was a long way from his thoughts, and everything was going wrong, everything was escaping his control – ideas, and time, and people – there were betrayals on every side, but he clung on to one image: that of a woman who had once, in a café, taken off her shoes and danced for him. The image of this slender, delicate woman, of the way she danced, of the grey horizon of her startled eyes, had taken root in him, and had grown and grown.

No, he had no patience this evening: everything seemed to take too long – the staircase too long to climb, Jeanne's hair too long to dry, her hands too long to warm up, her eyes too long to find their focus. Even before she arrived, the hours had inched by at a snail's pace: the wick wouldn't turn up out of the lamp, there was, as ever, nothing to eat in this dump, the cognac smelt foul, the matches weren't in their proper place, the floor was unswept. And now Jeanne was here and he wanted to light everything he possibly could.

Isaak went back and forth, lighting candles, turning the place upside down. Jeanne, sitting quite helpless on her bench, watched him moving around. She was coming back to earth now, rediscovering him: he had acquired a few lines, just there at the corners of his eyes; one could see them quite clearly in the candlelight when he bent forwards. He must have been through so much. He had lost weight. Hadn't he actually grown taller, in fact? Still in a daze, she started talking to him, telling him about the child and Grigory; on the subject of Alexander, she preserved a silence. And then Dasha's last days, the funeral, the wild-cherry trees; she got lost in details which Isaak couldn't be bothered with, and he interrupted her, saying, 'Here's to our health, Jeanne! And to you! And to the Revolution!'

He put the glass in her hand. Whether it was the word 'revolution' or the few drops of wine that did it, she felt her spirits returning. Her fear suddenly left her. She noticed for the first time that there was a stove in the room. The flames flickered red through the grate. The enormous café, deserted for so long, began to warm up a little. Jeanne's hair, which was starting to dry, became fluffy and hazy and soft. The colour returned to her lips and cheeks. She took another sip of wine. Got up. Took a few steps across the room. Went up to the stove.

'What's Parvus?' she asked.

'Parvus? Why – do you know him?'

'I've a message for you: "Parvus and Stockholm are no longer together. Signed Egoroff."'

'Ah,' said Isaak.

He said nothing for a moment, looking at the window.

'Is Egoroff in Odessa?'

'He's left for Petrograd.'

Isaak got up, went over to the window, and drew the curtains. They were both on their feet now. Isaak was shaken by the news he had just received: the message stated point-blank that something had gone wrong and that he was in danger of his life. He stood there, weighing up the blow. And already his head was telling him how he should at once react. But only his head; for with all the force of his being he was contemplating Jeanne, silhouetted in her black dress against the soft red glow of the stove. Her tiny waist. And, most of all, that storm of hair. In her hair Isaak saw a forest clearing, when the sun comes up shining on the grass, light-ing up the water – drops of dew, revolving round the plants which spring up, happy. This room was derelict, and dusty, and wretched, but with Jeanne in the middle, standing quite straight amidst the reflected light of the candles, it became a temple for Isaak, a temple celebrating life itself. And right at that moment he perhaps loved life even more than he loved Jeanne – Jeanne being the symbol of life, fanning his desire to live, to go on.

'You once told me that I was old, Jeanne. Do you remember? I was thirty-three at the time. I've just turned thirty-seven. Does that still count as old for you?'

'I don't remember,' said Jeanne. 'Everything happens so fast. Time goes by so fast. And such terrible things are going on here. One ought almost to multiply the time by the importance of events, don't you think? . . . What are you going to do, Isaak? I'm frightened.'

'Me too,' said Isaak, in a neutral tone; and Jeanne saw him slowly sit down on the bench and prop up his back against it.

'Isaak, you must go! You can't stay here! Egoroff said the place was no longer safe! He said you should leave immediately! . . . I can't understand why you're just sitting there doing nothing! . . . Do something! At least get out of here!'

Isaak poured himself a glass of wine.

'Don't drink that, Isaak, I beg you! You mustn't! You've got to get out!'

'I don't think so. I've come home at last. Back to my home town. And you're here. And I have nothing in the world but you and this town.'

'Isaak, wake up! You just can't do this! You're not seriously thinking of spending the night on that bench!'

Isaak, usually so capable, so prudent, so clear about everything he did, simply didn't want to move. The words of the message were there, but also, in his consciousness, the certainty that by saving himself he would miss out on something. Or perhaps not even that: it was just that Jeanne's presence swept everything else aside, paralysing him. The survival instinct was no longer at work: he forgot about Egoroff, he forgot about being careful. He experienced a euphoria that he had never known in his life before, he was full of Jeanne and nothing but Jeanne, and he longed for her with a passion that transcended longing.

He said nothing. He sat bolt upright – a flame at the zenith of its combustion, a pure effervescence. The deep red wine before him, he looked at Jeanne, almost with an air of defiance – and it wasn't Jeanne that he was defying. Impatient, distracted, Jeanne felt the anger rising in her. And in that state she was even more beautiful, the flames from the stove and her anger mingling to form a single light in her eyes.

The rest happened very quickly. The candles suddenly flickered, there was a slamming of a door, a clattering on the stairs, and three men dived between Isaak and Jeanne. Before Jeanne could open her mouth, Isaak received a shot in the forehead.

IX

They had all gone by the time Jeanne came to. Stepping over to the marble table, she saw the trickle of red that ran along the arch of the eyebrow, turned a slight corner, and continued down the left cheek. Isaak's head was thrown back, and in his gaze Jeanne caught an expression of happiness unbearable to look at. She didn't close his eyes, didn't put his head on the marble table-top, didn't do any of the things one is supposed to do in such a situation. Without taking her eyes off Isaak – the blood was flowing more thickly now, she saw – she opened her bag, took out the Browning, left the bag on the table and set off down the stairs.

It was very cold outside. Very cold, and very dark. The entrance to the café and the pavement immediately in front of it were in total darkness. Some yards off, on the opposite pavement, three tall black figures could be made out against a lighter-coloured house-front and a bank of snow. Jeanne heard them speaking in low voices. Slowly, silently, she levelled the revolver, holding it as firmly as possible in both hands, and took aim at one of the figures. Someone fell. Despite the shock she experienced in her shoulder, she took immediate aim at a second figure, who was bending down over the first. She brought him down too. The third man came towards her, unable to see her but firing shot after shot in the direction of the café. Wedged in her corner, Jeanne felled him at almost point-blank range.

The Browning fell from her hands; her arm hurt, and her shoulder; she stepped out a little way into the snow and looked at the three bodies in black leather jackets lying curiously flattened in the snow. An image of playing-cards flashed through her mind and she began to run.

She ran as if she had wings. Something icy, half snow and half rain, was falling on her hair. She must have run very fast, for she soon left Moldavanka far behind her. She was coming into the town itself now. She slackened her pace. A woman running through the snow in such temperatures, at two o'clock in the morning, in ordinary ankle-boots and without a coat or hat is not exactly the most normal sight in the world.

The passers-by were becoming more frequent now. She could already see the lights of the London Hotel. One could always get a cab there, day and night. Yes, she could see several parked there. She ducked into a corner to tidy herself up a little, wiped her face on the hem of her petticoat, and then, wanting to give her hair a brush, realized that she didn't have her bag with her. And that she therefore didn't have a single copeck. But she would have to take a carriage: it was a long way to Beriozy.

She gave the cabman the address, climbed in and took her place on the seat buried in an avalanche of old rugs. The carriage set off at a slow pace, and before long Jeanne realized that it was going the wrong way. She called out once, twice. Not the slightest effect. Was the cabman deaf? Or perhaps –? Jeanne experienced a moment of terror. She got up and leant forward. The cabman was dead-drunk. He was asleep, his head nodding on his chest.

With one leap Jeanne was beside him. She took hold of the reins. The cabman offered no resistance, emitting a couple of contented groans and putting his head on Jeanne's shoulder. The horse broke into a trot. It even managed a gallop going down Chestnut Boulevard. Jeanne brought him to a halt at the head of the path that led down to Beriozy. She turned him round in the road and put the reins back into the hands of the cabman, who reeked of all the distilleries in the world. The horse set off again at a walk.

A lamp in an orange shade cast a feeble glow over the entrance hall. His little arms wrapped round a pillow, Igoriok was asleep, making his protest upon the heap of pillows from all around the house. Grigory was sitting on the bench, waiting up for her.

He made no move at the sight of Jeanne. His eyes spoke his anxiety, brimming with unvoiced questions. Collapsing on to the pillows, Jeanne said, 'Grigory, I want you to go to the Street of the Assumption in Moldavanka. To the Café Catalan. This minute. You'll see I've left my coat and bag there. You'll have to move fast.'

Grigory got up without a word. She heard him getting the horse out. Then the sound of hooves on the path. Jeanne ran out.

'Grigory! . . . Try and see who the men are . . . The ones on the ground, in the snow . . . It's important. Leave the horse as far away from the café as you can. Approach the place on foot, slowly, watching all the way. But above all, get back quick!'

X

She went back to the house, bolted the door, checked that all the shutters were securely fastened, put a pan of water on to heat in the kitchen; then, without waiting until it was hot, gave herself a thorough wash-down, rubbing her body with the end of a towel. Then she put on fresh clothes – a white linen petticoat and a lacy bodice – and, picking up the sleeping Igoriok, took him off to bed with her.

Jeanne did not feel tired. Since the moment the leather-jacketed men had burst into the café, she had seen everything as flat, as cut out of cardboard – a fictional world, the world of the studios. All this was happening not to her, not to the real Jeanne, but to her cinematic double, to the actress, Vera Gaiy. She had the feeling – as she always did when filming – that she was awaiting her turn. The lamps were being set up, the lighting and the camera-angles were being tried out, and she was sitting there on the set where in a short time she would be going through the motions of someone who wasn't her. Not her at all. They could just as well make her brandish a Browning which was too big and heavy for her and fell them like trees; and the three men would get up and she would start the scene all over again. And when they were done with the scene they would do a still, right underneath the lamps, of Isaak's face, with the trickle of blood running down his forehead and cheek. And perhaps a close-up of her, with her gaze riveted on him. The whole reel played itself out before Jeanne's eyes whilst she was waiting for Grigory to return.

At last she heard the sound of the horse's hooves. She ran to open the door. It was still pitch black outside, without a single star.

'Are they still there?' she asked, without being able to throw off the feeling of playing the part of someone else.

'Yes.'

Grigory handed Jeanne her coat and headscarf, then went over to the table and put down on it her bag, the Browning, a comb, two more revolvers and a blue-chequered handkerchief, knotted into a bundle with things inside.

'It's time to get out, my girl,' said Grigory. 'They're not going to let you get away with this.'

'No one knows anything, no one saw anything,' said someone speaking through Jeanne's lips. 'There's no danger. They were still there, weren't they? Lying on the ground? And there was nobody in the café? And Isaak –?'

'He's dead.'

'I know.'

'Look, you've got to go . . .'

'No one knows about it. They were all three killed.'

'What about the others? There'll be more and more,' said Grigory, his finger pointing at the little blue-chequered bundle. 'You're leaving at daybreak. If they've killed Storm, they'll track you down. And they won't let you slip through their fingers.'

Still lost in her imaginary cinema, Jeanne wasn't listening to him. She couldn't hear what he was saying. Death, which she had witnessed with her own eyes for the first time, and so intensely, did not seem so dreadful after all, and what Jeanne had managed to do afterwards came as a sort of compensation. In Jeanne's imagination the four dead men were all standing together quite peaceably, calling to one another, flowing into one another. One could say that the dead men simply did not touch Jeanne, at least not yet. She was terrible to behold, sitting as she was on Grigory's still-made bed, all neat and clean in her white summer clothes, her face as fresh as if she had just enjoyed a good night's rest. Buried in his pillows, the child was asleep at her side. Grigory stood motionless, staring at Jeanne as if in terror of her every gesture. He was looking at her as one looks at a mad person.

Like a sleepwalker, Jeanne went over to touch the three revolvers which Grigory had set down together in a heap, as though she wished to assure herself that they were real; then she took the bundle and put it on her lap. Grigory watched her undo the knot in the handkerchief. Inside, there was a tobacco pouch, a pipe, another handkerchief, dirty and crumpled into a ball, a photograph mounted on cardboard, and a small packet

of letters and stamped envelopes, tied up with string. Jeanne
studied the photo for a long time: It showed a man standing
beside a fountain in a cobbled square, with Gothic rooftops in
the background (Germany, could it be? Switzerland? France?
Not Russia, at any rate), dressed in the kind of shirt that is
worn only in Russia – collarless, and with buttons at the side.
He had his arms around the shoulders of a woman who was
laughing out loud: she was pretty and extremely young, much
younger than the man. She was laughing, her head thrown
back, her eyes screwed up, her hair tousled, her teeth all white.
The man was staring at the camera with a serious but happy expression.

Jeanne recognized him: she had seen this man somewhere
before, and that somewhere could only have been Dasha's
house. Yes, that was it. He was one of Isaak's 'clients', as Dasha
used to call them. Not a frequent visitor to Pushkin Street; he
just dropped in every now and then. Jeanne remembered an
evening when the conversation had revolved around a certain
Oulianov – there was always a great deal of talk about this
Oulianov in Pushkin Street. Dasha hadn't been well that
evening: she had a fever and kept coughing: there was a fire
burning in the hearth and everyone was drinking tea and
talking revolution. Jeanne even recalled something Egoroff
had said which had really made her laugh, something on the
subject of Oulianov's prose: he had said that all his writings
should have been entitled 'Brawling: A Philosophical and
Technical Study' or, perhaps, 'The Art of Being Trounced
Politically' – No, that wasn't it, but it was something along
those lines. The man in the photo hadn't liked this and he had
set upon Egoroff, calling him an idealist, a windbag, a re-
visionist, a man of straw, a pacifist, an opportunist – all the
insults that were bandied about at Dasha's place.

Isaak hadn't said much; he had listened to the man, a polite
expression on his face; and Jeanne had had the feeling that it
was really in Isaak that the truth resided, that he was the

essential core of the entire group, that it was he who held all the strings – such was the impression he had made on her. And now neither that impression nor Isaak's death seemed to register with Jeanne. Fleeting images, scraps of memories, flitted through her brain, quite unconnected, stripped of all logic, as she studied the photo and then glanced through the letters she had found in the blue handkerchief. She lost track of time: suddenly a harsh white light was streaming through the shutters, and it was dawn.

It was colder in the room now, and the cold made Jeanne leave off what she was doing. She retied the knot in the big handkerchief, got up – and saw Grigory, who had been standing there all the while. Smothering a yawn, she said, 'I think it's time for bed, don't you . . .? I'm sleepy. You should get some rest too. Igor will be waking up soon. He oughtn't to see us like this.'

'All right, but you're leaving immediately afterwards!'

'Where for?' said Jeanne.

'It doesn't matter where!'

She slept for eighteen hours, fully dressed, with an old fur coat of Marie-Aynard's thrown over her. The moment she awoke, everything which had happened that night at the Café Catalan came back to her, like a nightmare. She sat up. It was over: she was wide awake now and had to forget the nightmare, had to blot it from her memory. Igoriok, amazed at seeing his 'Ja' asleep during the daytime, had been waiting for this moment. He threw himself at her neck, overjoyed to see her up at last. Jeanne hugged his warm, trusting body to her. He slipped into the fur coat. He looked like a bear cub: the fur tickled his nose and he laughed out loud. Jeanne laughed with him.

Grigory was in the kitchen making crêpes: Igoriok watched them being tossed, then wolfed down one after another. Every time she went into the kitchen, Jeanne breathed in the smell of burnt apricots and caramel – a smell which had long since vanished from the place, but which was still there for her, the trace of a sun that had gone. Everything in the kitchen that morning was as it had been in the past: the way the tea tasted and the jam, the feeling of happiness, of the sheer pleasure of being alive, the child's curls, the grey of his eyes – the same grey as Jeanne's – and the calm presence of the old gypsy.

Taking Igor on her lap, she spread the crêpes with jam. She was calm, she was smiling, she was drinking her tea just as usual – and it was this that Grigory found so frightening about her. There was nothing left to him in this world but Jeanne and Igoriok. He was sharp enough to know the extent of the damage which had been done. He was frightened for everyone's sake. He would rather have seen Jeanne weeping and flapping and running off – a Jeanne in a state of panic. Not this Jeanne, playing with the child as though nothing were wrong. She seemed so alone to Grigory, so young and so defenceless. Her mother living far away in France and unable to do anything to help her. No news from Alexander. With this abandoned child and now the deaths at the Café Catalan around her neck. How could she dare stay?

In an attempt to keep his fear in check, Grigory busied himself more than usual – cleaving logs, burning the dead leaves which wouldn't catch light, soaked as they were by the snow, raking the stoves, chopping the wood into smaller pieces. Splitting a large tree-stump, he cut his hand. Jeanne saw him come into the kitchen, holding his injured right hand out in front of him with his left, blood pouring everywhere – not that the injury was all that serious, but he had caught a vein.

Jeanne went white at the sight of the blood. She ran to fetch some tincture of iodine and cotton wool. She stemmed the bleeding. As soon as she had finished dressing the wound, she left Grigory and Igoriok where they were and went off to her room. She was violently sick. The spasms shook her entire body, as though she were trying to retch up her heart, her soul, her very life. She saw blood gushing everywhere, she saw

Isaak's head fall on to his chest, its dead weight making a dull thud. She fainted.

XI

The day was drawing to a close. Sleet was falling, splashing softly at the windowpanes. Jeanne was lying in bed with a hot-water bottle on her chest. She heard the bell being rung at the gate. She didn't open her eyes. Snuggled in the fur coat, she didn't want to know about anything. She was afraid of what she might see.

It was only Filaretov, his little head sticking up out of a beige raincoat, his arms laden with packages containing the chickens, and fish, and butter which by some obscure means he still managed to obtain in a town where rationing had now been introduced. Things were going well for him. Showing a fine contempt for all the social upheavals going on around them, people still kept flocking to the cinema. The Odeon had a full house for every performance.

Filaretov came in. Through the bedroom door he caught sight of Jeanne lying stretched out, her face extremely white; and without a moment's thought, he dumped his provisions and rushed off again.

He returned with a doctor, the one who had treated Jeanne in the past for whooping cough, and measles, and angina, who had listened to her heart that day she fell in the rehearsal room at the Opera, who had become such a trusted figure to Jeanne that the mere sight of him, at a distance, was enough to summon a reinvigorating whiff of the 'King of Denmark's Smelling-Salts' which had had no effect on that occasion. He was as small as Filaretov, and as old, too. His manner was charming, his eyes blending a look of knowing sadness with a marvellously spontaneous smile. And, highly active as he still was, he exuded a sense of assurance, a sense of something permanent, something eternal, like an old piece of family furniture.

To Jeanne, he symbolized everything about her childhood. She pictured him against a background of the low walls and bushes which had seemed so high to her as a child; seeing him, she remembered her mother's lemonade and Nastia's herb teas, with lime- or orange-petals floating on the surface. He was also the doctor who had treated Dasha, and then helped her to die, helping Jeanne watch her die at the same time. Jeanne couldn't imagine the day he would stop taking people's pulses and listening to their hearts, the day he would no longer be able to afford the sick a measure of comfort simply by being there. He was one of those people one hopes will never disappear; and perhaps the real talent of such people, and the sign of their vocation, is their ability to give an impression of immortality, that sense of confidence so necessary to those undergoing a crisis.

The doctor saw at a glance that his patient had nothing physically wrong with her, as they say, but that she was in a profound state of shock. He stayed sitting on the edge of the bed for a long time, held her wrist, examined her tongue and the inside of her eyelids, listened to her chest through a handkerchief; then he went over and whispered something into his old friend Filaretov's ear, and prescribed potassium bromide. After he had gone, Jeanne suddenly felt a lot better. But Filaretov knew otherwise.

Of course he knew nothing of what had really happened to Jeanne – which was fortunate, for if he had known, he would have been the one in urgent need of a doctor, if not a hearse. Filaretov thought Jeanne's illness was all due to Alexander Illytch, and the fact that the man was always away. *He* was the cause of the malady which Filaretov termed, in his old-

fashioned way, chagrined love. More than ever, Filaretov
lamented the absence of a piano at Beriozy. If there had only
been one there, he could have launched straight into Schubert's
Impromptu in C Minor, instead of hopelessly fumbling for
words to take her mind off things; it was a piece she loved, and
she asked him to play it for her every time she called on him.
Indeed, he started his daily practising with it now, out of
affection for Jeanne.

Ever since Alexander's hospital train had passed through
Odessa, Jeanne had stopped coming to see him. She had other
things to worry about, that little boy, for example – as Filaretov
kept reminding himself. But he still went on hoping day after
day that Jeanne would call by. The pianist, the piano and the
Impromptu remained in a state of perpetual readiness, convinced that Jeanne would one day have need of them.

Ivan Semionovitch asked nothing in return for his affection.
Jeanne was there; and that fact alone was enough to fill him
with gratitude. His feelings for his pupil, his 'white flower', as
he called her, were quite unequivocal. He had been the same
way with his wife.

Among all his pupils at the Conservatory, she had seemed to
him to be like a nun: harmony was her church, solfeggio her
faith. Her devotion to music was total; Filaretov had never
known anything like it. Her parents (they were of Greek
origin, and ran a highly reputed grocer's) were anything but
happy about their daughter's dedication to her art. Eligible
young men called at their house in droves; she wasn't interested
in any of them. She wanted to play the piano. Ivan Semionovitch was himself worried about her; for the piano was
not the same thing as life, not life in all its totality. And so,
without actually being in love with her, simply to free her
from her obsession, he had the audaciousness to propose to her
one day when they were at the keyboard. A white wedding,
of course – so as not to over-hasten things and allow her to
concentrate on her music without emotional turmoil.

It took them several winters and several springs to find their way into each other's arms; and then came her sudden death, like a fermata. Over the years, Ivan Semionovitch had come to terms with his grief, but he would still sometimes catch himself living moments with his pupil, as though he were playing a four-handed piece. Living moments with his wife.

Sitting at home late that afternoon, Filaretov had a presentiment that Jeanne's condition had worsened. He went off to fetch the doctor again. The two of them arrived at Beriozy to find that Jeanne was indeed worse. The bromide had had a calming effect upon her, but she was running a high temperature. They changed her sheets, and Filaretov stayed with her to put cold compresses on her forehead.

Jeanne was dozing now. Igoriok had been persuaded to go out for a little walk with Grigory. On the way to Beriozy, the doctor had told Filaretov what little he knew about the child. He had been picked up by a night patrol, somewhere in the Lenberg area. The lieutenant had handed him over to the care of the nuns who did the nursing in Alexander's field-hospital. The nuns tried to locate his family, but without success. It was impossible to keep the child at the hospital: the fighting was too close.

Hearing all this, Filaretov thought to himself that Igoriok would remain Jeanne's child for evermore. But it was a burden for her, all the same. The story also encouraged him to think slightly better of Alexander Illytch. Without ever having met the young surgeon – whom he regarded as responsible for Jeanne's illness – Filaretov was jealous of him, just like a father who is so devoted to his daughter that he thinks there is no man on earth who is worthy of her, no man on earth who won't do her harm.

Filaretov knew nothing of love. What he had known in his musical marriage was something different. He was aware of the fact; and it was perhaps out of a certain sense of resentment that he was always telling himself that people in love merely tear each other apart, look for arguments, bang their heads against a wall, revel in their own misery. He saw love as a terrible sickness which adults cannot but succumb to, just as there is no avoiding childhood illnesses; but love was a much more serious matter, a wicked trick on Nature's part to camouflage with a drama of emotions the revolting animal instinct of reproduction.

And now Jeanne herself had fallen into the trap: according to the doctor, she hadn't received a letter from Alexander Illytch for a month. As far as Filaretov was concerned, this was sufficient explanation for Jeanne's temperature of a hundred and six. Paradoxically, though, Jeanne's fever reassured him. He far preferred the idea of a straightforwardly physical ailment to that of a vague nervous deterioration or a languishing passion.

XII

Grigory and Igor had come back from their walk and were lighting the fire in the kitchen. I ought to be getting back myself, thought Filaretov. So what was stopping him from making a move? Seeing Grigory approach the bedroom door, he realized that he was staying there first and foremost to protect Jeanne. Since midday, Ivan Semionovitch had known that Isaak Storm had just got killed. He didn't want Jeanne to find out too soon. The whole of Odessa was talking about it. The version told by the woman in the box office at the Odeon portrayed Storm's death in a heroic light: he had brought down a good dozen thugs – obviously Bolsheviks sent from Red Petrograd with the aim of seizing power in Odessa – fighting them all off singlehanded before finally succumbing to a bullet right through the heart. Everyone in Moldavanka was in tears over his death: an enormous funeral was being talked about, with Storm apparently to be buried at sea. From this pathos-ridden version, Filaretov gathered two things: that Isaak was indeed dead, and that the news of his death would be yet another shock for Jeanne. It had to be kept from her until she was recovered; Filaretov remembered how shattered Jeanne had been by Dasha's death. As for that brigand Isaak Storm, his whole relationship with Jeanne had been extremely dangerous – what luck that, before getting himself killed, he had been away from Odessa for so long!

Ostensibly accepting everything the woman in the box office told him, Filaretov had managed to piece together a few facts. So Storm had been a Red himself all along! It was as clear as day! He had been a Red, and he had talked like one! Even poor Dasha had been infected by his ideas – and how! She had died with that Bible of theirs, that book on capitalism by Marx. How many times had his blood run cold as he listened to Jeanne reading Dasha passages from it? There was enough gibberish in the thing to bring all the printing presses of the world grinding to a halt. It might be all right as a *philosophy* – but it was utterly, utterly wrong to apply it to real life, to poor, suffering Russia, which was already wretched enough. Yet this was the way things had been going since October. The people didn't want the unfamiliar 'liberty' which was being imposed upon them by force; what they wanted was a father, a strong protector, and as far as Filaretov was concerned, the so-called 'October Fusillades' were nothing but a put-up job aimed at replacing the people's father by a fist of steel, without any velvet glove. The legendary patience and long-suffering of the Russian people were entirely at odds with all the foreign concepts being cried up by a pack of scoundrels. Kerensky's Red ideas, and the equally Red ideas of the Bolsheviks, had fallen on the soil of Russia like snow upon a field of corn in the blade: they were already freezing the earth, which was just the same earth, but they would leave no seeds in it.

Ivan Semionovitch followed these changes, or anyway the language used to talk about them in the papers – in this or that guarded, sheepish report of the kind the editorship of *The Voice of Odessa* were so happy to publish in their 'Open Forum' column, so as 'not to be bypassed by the Great March of History'.

Whilst Filaretov was sitting at Jeanne's bedside quietly fulminating at the newspaper, Grigory was in the kitchen, peeling potatoes and making plans. Jeanne wasn't going to listen to reason once she was well again. There was no means of defending her at Beriozy. Of the three Brownings he had picked up, only one was loaded. He carried it on him day and night. Grigory knew everything there was to know about Odessa. Those men would have their revenge, and Jeanne would be their first victim. The street was deserted, she kept saying, no one saw me! But a street is a street, deserted or not. And the mere chance of a child's getting up in the night to have a pee and catching a glimpse of a woman's skirt through the window would be enough to point all fingers at Jeanne. It was impossible for her to stay there. Why not take the opportunity afforded by her fever, thought Grigory, and move her over to Filaretov's place? Of course! It was the only thing to do . . . Grigory himself would stay behind at Beriozy to guard the house.

He went off to hitch up the horse, then beckoned Filaretov away from the bedside where he had been keeping watch over Jeanne whilst she slept.

'I'll explain everything later . . . Jeanne's life is in danger here . . . I've got the carriage waiting outside. We're taking her over to your place. Igoriok, too.'

'But she's really not at risk now! I have faith in the doctor: it's just a dose of 'flu. And in any case, the hospital's not far, should we have to –'

'That's not the danger I'm talking about! You know that
Isaak Storm was killed last night?'

'Of course. But I fail to see the connection.'

'It's too long to tell you now . . . We're leaving at once.'

'But she's asleep!'

'Precisely! Give me a hand and take this quilt!'

XIII

The train had been standing in the station of a little town for
over four hours. A military patrol – quite who they were was
unclear – clad in uniforms which were neither grey nor beige,
was going through the carriages with a fine-toothed comb,
without saying who or what they were looking for. It was
very cold. The snow was freezing in slabs upon the platforms.
Scraping the frost from the carriage window with her fingernails, Jeanne made out a large sign which read SINELNIKOVO.
She had obtained the seat she was occupying in exchange for a
ring set with diamonds. She was carrying her jewels stitched
inside the lining of her coat. She had also brought with her a
round loaf, some bacon, a little salt, and a jar of sunflower oil,
all wrapped up in half a linen sheet. Enough to keep her going
for a week. But she had been travelling for ten days now; this
was the eighth train she had been on.

She had finally given in to Grigory, who had been begging
her to flee ever since her fever had subsided. It wasn't for her
own safety she had left, but simply because she couldn't wait
any longer: she had to go off in search of Alexander. She had
decided upon Kislovodsk as her first destination. It was the
only thread she had. Of course, Alexander might well no
longer be there. No matter: she was bound to meet people

who had seen him, people who could tell her something of his whereabouts.

The idea of taking Igoriok with her had never entered her head. The railways stations were in utter chaos: people were being trampled to death in the panic. It had been impossible to find milk or vegetables. There was fighting almost throughout the south of Russia. As Grigory stubbornly refused to have Igor with him at Beriozy, convinced that the place could become a hornet's nest, she had left him with Filaretov; at least he wouldn't starve there. She hadn't had the courage to take leave of him as she should. She had slipped off whilst he was asleep, leaving him a letter which Filaretov was to read to him, and a rocking-horse.

Since leaving Odessa, she had covered six hundred kilo-metres in a zig-zag line. She was still very weak from her illness, and very thin. The black overcoat, actually a man's, which served her as a bed when she had to spend the night in a railway station, was dirty and crumpled. On her head, she wore two grey woollen shawls, and on her feet, patched felt boots. Dressed thus, with her bundle on her lap, she looked just like everyone else.

The struggle to find a new train which would take her nearer the Caucasus, to fight her way on board, to forge a path down the packed corridors had taken so much out of her that she was beyond feeling. She was exhausted. It was only when, at the end of her strength, she sank into sleep that she would see Igoriok in a dream, imagining herself cutting his toenails and feeling his little round heels in the palm of her hand; or she would call out to Alexander, whom she saw from behind, standing on the platform of a tram which was disappearing into the open countryside; or again, she would pull at Marie-Aynard's ear-rings, seeing her pretty mother bent over a doll's table buttering bread for breakfast.

The enforced wait dragged on and on. From time to time the sound of gunfire could be heard – quite some way off, it seemed. Two men – obviously drunk, though where they had managed to obtain alcohol was a mystery – were fighting on the platform in front of an utterly unmoved peasant-woman. A young lad of about twelve, dressed in clothes which were too big for him, was selling water from a barrel which he pushed up and down the platform in a wheelbarrow. Jeanne pulled down the window, gave him a handful of roubles, and received a rusty metal can in exchange. The water was very cold and tasted of clay. Jeanne took a drink, then dipped the hem of her petticoat in the water and rubbed her face with it.

XIV

Some hundred yards from the railway station at Sinelnikovo rose a large, ugly edifice of brick: the school. A little white-washed house immediately adjacent to it was the home of the schoolmistress. Her husband had been killed at the Front in 1916. From where she sat, Jeanne could see both the school and the house; and her gaze most probably came to rest on them several times whilst the train was standing in the station.

A month earlier, Alexander had returned to his senses in that little white house. The first thing he remembered was the train, and the snow-covered tracks sullied with lubricating oil and blood. This image fled almost immediately, to be replaced by nothing. He was in total darkness. There was a pain in his head, a searing, shooting pain which rose to unbearable crescendos. He couldn't move a finger. He had no strength, not even the strength to follow the ebb and flow of the pain. Images came back to him: a woman in white running through brambles, a child standing in the embrasure of a door with a pillow in its hand, a pink lung with blue spots on it, a train again, and railway tracks. He lost consciousness.

He woke up again. This time he could feel his body. Not his whole body; just his chest. Something infinitely gentle was stroking his chest, and the sensation was somehow mixed up with the smell of warm bread. The pain in his head was not quite so great now. He realized that he could move a little, because he wanted to touch his head with his hand. He came up against gauze bandages, a great turban of gauze. As his hand fell back, it brushed against another hand, a hand which didn't belong to him. He squeezed it. Fingers were gently massaging his chest and shoulders.

'You've been very lucky,' a voice said.

'Why is it so dark?'

He heard a few footsteps, then the hiss of a match being struck, and the pale oval and black eyes of a woman's face emerged from the darkness.

'Where am I?'

'In the land of the living.'

'What's happened to my head?'

'You're in the land of the living . . . Don't try to talk. Wait a moment: I'll get you something to drink . . .'

His eyes accustomed themselves to the semi-darkness. The faint glow of the candle, positioned on a very low table, allowed him to make out a quilted bedcover and drawn curtains. Was it day or night? Now the woman was giving him tea with milk from a spoon. The tea smacked of mown hay, of stables, and also of the leaves they used to burn at the end of autumn every year on his mother's estate at Pskov. The hot tea made him feel better. He felt completely safe in the hands of this woman, whose whole face radiated tenderness. He had known the same thing, the same permanent freedom from care, in another life. No, not in another life. The smell of leaves, and his mother leaning over his little bed in Pskov . . . He tried to raise his head. He couldn't. Once more the hands were stroking his chest.

'Just lie there. Don't move.'

'What time is it?'

'Very early in the morning.'

'Have I been here long?'

'Three days.'

'What about my train?'

'What train?'

'My convoy of wounded.'

'I found you lying on the railway track. You were unconscious.'

'Wounded in the head?'

'Yes, in the head . . . But you're talking too much. And the children are waiting for me; this is a school here . . . I'll send my Aunt Pacha in to you . . .'

She didn't get up, but went on stroking his neck and chest and shoulders. He could feel her fingers soothing away the pain.

'And has my train gone?'

'I know nothing about your train.'

She got up. He could see her better now. She was not very tall, and was dressed in a black skirt and white blouse, with a white shawl round her shoulders. All he could really see of her face was her very black eyes and her stunningly red lips, obviously made-up. He heard the door close; and was enveloped in a sea of calm.

When he woke up for the third time, she was sitting there at his bedside. He heard her speaking and opened his eyes.

Someone else came up to the bed; a man with a black beard.

'Who are you?' the man asked, in an unpleasant, grating voice.

Alexander closed his eyes and pretended to be asleep.

'I'll have to examine him,' the man with the beard went on.

'No, don't do that, you'll disturb him. You can see he's asleep.'

'He's in a coma.'

'Not any longer.'

'If I'm not to examine him, then why did you send for me, Maria?'

'He's got three holes in the head.'

'Was there a lot of bleeding?'

'Not much.'

'I *must* have a look at him!'

'No, not yet, I beg of you.'

'His pulse is sixty-two – almost normal . . . You say he's a doctor?'

'I saw his papers.'

Lying there with his eyes shut, Alexander wished the man would just shut up and go. He must have gone back to sleep again, for when he looked around the room, Maria was sitting there and the doctor was gone.

'Maria,' he said.

'Yes, Sasha?'

She leant forward to stroke his lips and cheeks with her fingertips. That smell was still there: a smell of bread, and leaves . . . A spasm of pain shot through him and he saw black – then red snow, black railway lines; and then Jeanne, her cloud of hair upon the pillow – Jeanne, whom he mustn't disturb . . .

'Where are we?' he asked.

'Sinelnikovo.'

'Ah, yes . . . I remember . . .'

He was holding her hand, not wanting to let it go.

'You've got a temperature!' she suddenly said. 'It's much higher than yesterday. I'll have to have the doctor come again.'

'Don't go away . . . Stay here . . .'

When he awoke for the fourth time – not the next day, but three days later – it wasn't Maria who was sitting by the bed, but an oldish lady with a pince-nez. She was reading a newspaper.

His head no longer hurt. His fever had gone. In the orange glow of the lamp, he now took in things he had not been able to see before: the pattern of the blue wallpaper, the lace of the curtains, the photographs on the walls, a vase of wilting hydrangeas on a table covered with a Persian shawl, a small white-tiled stove. Yet again, the memory of his mother's house at Pskov, of the peace and security he had only known as a child . . . He tried to get up.

'What are you doing?' exclaimed the lady with the pince-nez. 'After an epidemic like the one we've just had? You must be mad!'

'What epidemic?'

'No one knows. Half the town's down with it, Maria included. You just stay where you are!'

Alexander felt better. He was hungry. He smiled. The smile dropped from his face. Maria? he thought. Where is she? What is this epidemic?

The woman who had been reading the paper went away and came back with a zinc basin, a sponge, a bar of soap and several towels.

'Where's Maria?'

'In the room next door.'

He was lying naked in bed. The lady with the pince-nez went all over his body with the soapy sponge. The feel of the lukewarm water was marvellous: he must have sweated a great deal.

'Is Maria running a temperature?'

'It's coming down now.'

Forgetting to dry him first, she tried to help him on with a striped shirt which was too small for him.

'Is she asleep?'

'Be quiet. You talk too much. I have strict instructions from Maria not to talk to you!'

'Am I supposed to have the plague or something?'

'You're seriously wounded.'

'I'm seriously wounded and seriously famished. I am *dying* of hunger!'

'What impudence!'

With a great display of dignity, she got up and brought him a large bowl of broth on a plate.

'Excellent!' said Alexander when he had finished. 'Is that all I get? I could really manage a potato!'

'Don't go too far!' said the lady, giving Sasha a long look through her pince-nez. 'A potato, these days!'

'What's going on, Aunt Pacha? Is something wrong?'

Maria was standing in the doorway in her nightdress, supporting herself against the frame, her feet bare and her hair unpinned.

'He's demanding potatoes!'

'*A* potato!' said Alexander.

'Go and ask them to cook some for him, Aunt Pacha,' said Maria. She was looking at Alexander with that radiant smile he had seen before.

'Come and sit with me,' said Alexander; and she went over and sat beside him on the bed.

XV

'. . . It's *all* doctors and trains and wounded soldiers, my little one! They need so many of them to keep this bloody war going . . . And then, a train doesn't stay in one place, does it? Well, just take me: I was in Marioupol on Sunday, and I shouldn't be in this place now . . .'

'. . . Tall? Blond? Grey eyes? A captain . . .? What did you say his name was – Alexander Illytch? Yes, I seem to remember him . . . It was on the Galician Front, in a big country house they'd taken over as a hospital . . . There were nuns there and a child that didn't belong to anyone . . . I'd gone there to try and get hold of some antiseptics: they didn't have any left, so the army vet gave me some alcohol instead . . . It was very close to the Front . . . But it's a long time ago now . . . I wonder what's become of him . . .'

'. . . No, I've no idea . . . Means nothing to me . . . Grey eyes? Well, I'm afraid I don't go round looking at the colour of men's eyes . . . *I* was operated on in Petrograd . . . No, it's *your* eyes I seem to remember: I've seen them somewhere before . . . I'm *sure* I've seen you before. On leave somewhere – but where could it have been . . .?

'. . . Oh, but of course! I can see him right now! Terrific man – he saved my arm! He operated on me in a station! I was lying on the ground, on a sheet lent by the mother of the local priest . . . No, it was six months ago . . . Which station? I can't remember . . . I wasn't very with it at the time . . . His train was waiting on the opposite platform . . . The priest's mother told me I had just the same nose as her other son . . . I remember she gave me some grenadine to drink . . .'

I can't take any more of this! thought Jeanne. They're all mad, they think of nothing but themselves . . .! What on earth am I doing here? Igoriok's waiting for me at home . . .

She had been in Kislovodsk for ten days. The beautiful skies, the towering trees, the pure air of the foothills might as well have not existed as far as she was concerned: she took in nothing of them. No one had come forward to help her – although they had all been very kind. At the mere sight of her troubled eyes and her marvellously graceful way of walking, all the doctors and soldiers and officers would bend over backwards for her, trying to give her hope, finding somewhere for her to stay, running to fetch her a bowl of gruel . . . But the more time passed, the more she felt convinced that Alexander was not there, or in any of the towns people had been mentioning to her . . . He was waiting for her at Beriozy, she was sure of it! It became an *idée fixe*, a wild certainty: *Alexander's waiting for me at Beriozy!*

She decided to return home. She had been staying with the director of the local hospital, a cardiac specialist. Wanting to inform him of her decision and thank him for his hospitality, she set off to look for him. Apparently he was to be found in a makeshift operating theatre which had been set up in a corner of the flour mill. She rushed off there. And, as it had become a habit with her now, she started searching for someone to interrogate once more.

The only person not asleep in the place was a very good-looking young man who was sitting on the floor with a coverlet over his knees; Jeanne sensed at once that both his legs were missing.

'Alexander Illytch, Captain Illytch? Oh, he was a marvellous man – not like the rest! If he'd operated on me, I'd have my legs today . . . Are you a relation of his?'

'No,' said Jeanne, filled with a sudden apprehension.

'His wife?'

'No.'

'Why are you looking for him?'

'They asked me in Odessa at the Registrar's Office . . . to make inquiries.'

'I didn't have time to see much. It was in a pretty big station. I can see the name of the place now: Sinelnikovo. I'd just been wounded . . . Through a haze I could hear the medical orderlies calling out, *Alexander Illytch is here, his train has just come in* . . . The moment I saw him, I knew that he'd save me. He had them clear a compartment for me, then laid me out on the seat. He went out on to the platform and started giving orders as he put on his gloves . . . Then six or seven men jumped him – Reds, they were . . . I saw it all through the window . . . I couldn't move. I said to myself, Reds, Greens, what the hell. Captain Illytch'll save my legs . . . He fell on to the track, and they made their getaway – *Miss!* Oh, Miss –!'

He propped himself up on his hands and called out in the

direction of the corridor for a nurse. The only people there were two or three men who had just undergone major surgery and were drugged to insensibility. Unhurriedly, the director walked in.

'Doctor, come quickly!'

'What's wrong?' The director couldn't see Jeanne from where he was standing.

'Quick! On the floor over there! She's fainted . . .'

XVI

A nauseating, sickly smell which Jeanne didn't recognize filled her nostrils as she turned down the path that led to Beriozy. She slowed her walk. The smell was becoming unbearable. She stopped in her tracks. Through the bare branches of the trees she could see that the front gate was standing open. Horrified, she started running: the gate was wedged open by the carcass of Grigory's horse, Sultan.

Her stomach turned and she had to lean against a pillar for support. She took a few deep breaths. Not wanting to pass by so close to the horse, she clambered over the wall some way along from the gate.

A harness, several chairs, and a carriage-wheel were strewn about the yard. The door of the house was ajar. She didn't dare to push it open, or to look in through the windows. She went round the outside of the house.

On the far side of the house, the one which gave on to the sea, Grigory's body was lying half-covered in snow near the edge of the low cliff. She recognized his beige-and-black boots and his big blue ratteen jacket. She was too frightened to go up to him and turn back his head. She sat down in the snow, put her head in her hands and said, *Mother, mother, mother,* knowing no other prayer. A complete numbness seized her. But the word 'mother' gave her a little strength.

Three-quarters of an hour later saw her at Filaretov's house, tugging at the bell-pull in a daze. There was no reply. Puny chickens, the new residents of the courtyard, were pecking at non-existent grains here and there. Standing there with her hair in chaos, her headscarf undone and her coat hanging open, Jeanne started hammering at the door. She was just about to go off and ask at the neighbours' houses when the door opened to reveal the old pianist. He had become shorter than Jeanne herself. At the sight of her, he burst out sobbing and threw his arms around her neck. His hair had turned completely white and his bloodshot eyes were streaming. Before he even opened his mouth, she knew everything. A terrible calm came over her. She pulled away a little, ran her hand through Filaretov's hair, and, taking him by the arm, led him back inside the house.

Settling him on the divan, she went over and sat down on the piano-stool. He was staring straight ahead of him. He seemed to be unaware of everything, even the presence of Jeanne. At last he said, in a childish-sounding voice, 'I'll make you some coffee . . . It's chicory, actually . . .'

He made no move. After a moment, he went on, 'He was carried off very quickly – in the space of a single night. He'd had a terrible temperature that evening. I thought it must be angina. It was diphtheria. He went all red, and then . . .'

His voice trailed off. Jeanne got up, took off her coat, and, folding it carefully, put it on a chair beside the piano; then she retrieved her headscarf from where it had fallen on the floor and folded it too, smoothing out the edges.

'Blue spots.' Filaretov started speaking again. 'He had blue spots all over his face and body . . . He had difficulty breathing . . . Then he began to choke . . . I wrapped him in a shawl of yours, took him in my arms and ran with him . . . This was in the middle of the night. By the time I reached the hospital, the fever had gone. He was quite cold.'

Filaretov was speaking heatedly now, louder and faster than before. He got up and started pacing up and down the room.

'They told me they couldn't treat it. Said that kids always die of it. It was hopeless. There was nothing I could do.'

'I know,' said Jeanne; but Filaretov wasn't listening to her.

'It all happened too quickly, just in one night! The little scamp had been eating icicles! I kept telling him, Jeanne isn't going to like this when she gets home, but it was no use – the second my back was turned, there he was, gobbling the things! And they were everywhere – hanging from all the gutters and downpipes. "I like icicles," he said. "They're ten times better than water." He kept getting up on a box to reach the things. He'd break off the longest ones and suck them like sweets! In the evenings I took him along to the Odeon with me, just to keep him from doing it. I started teaching him the piano. He was amusing, that boy – very gifted, highly intelligent, he chattered away like a magpie! Oh, there were no worries on that score! True, I'd had to take him off to a speech therapist in Moldavanka after you'd left, because he stopped speaking completely. The words these doctors use nowadays! I didn't understand a thing . . . But he likes it at the Odeon. Whenever a film of yours is showing, he recognizes you, and he's so proud! He turns round in his seat and says to everyone in the audience, "That beautiful lady up there's my mother!" Oh, he talks of nothing but you . . . Well, things will get better now that you're here . . . What was I saying . . .? Ah yes, I was going to make some coffee. Do you like chicory?'

He left off his pacing and stood right in front of Jeanne. He looked like a clown. The jacket he wore for special occasions hung right down to his knees, his orange tie was askew, he had one shoe in his hand and the other in his pocket. He was quite emaciated. His bloodshot eyes streamed. He stood there with his mouth open, as though waiting for something.

'Yes,' said Jeanne after a moment. 'I like chicory very much. It smells good and it gives the coffee a good colour. Make me some coffee and we'll talk about – what shall we talk about – about Italy, about Florence!'

'It's cold in Russia and it's night in Italy. People are being slaughtered on all sides. It's the barber's hand at work,' said Filaretov in a clear, impassive voice.

'Don't upset yourself, Ivan Semionovitch,' said Jeanne. She adjusted his tie and kissed him on both cheeks.

'The speech therapist said to me, He needs a quiet life, you must make sure that he gets to bed early. But I've no one to look after him in the evenings! That's why I take him to the Odeon with me. He sees you on the screen and he's happy!' repeated Filaretov.

'He *saw* me, and he *was* happy,' Jeanne said gently. 'Ivan Semionovitch, wake up! Igoriok was here once. He isn't any longer. Do you understand?'

And now it was too much for her. She very nearly shouted, 'He's gone! D'you hear me? They've all gone – Sultan, and Isaak, and Grigory. All of them! And Alexander, too!'

'The barber's hand!' chimed in Filaretov.

'What barber's hand?' said Jeanne, in a more restrained voice now.

'It's everywhere! Look, over there! And there! Everywhere! My poor girl, you don't even see it!'

'I don't see it because it isn't there to see. Now calm down. Sit down. Here, in this armchair. I'll go and make some coffee.'

'It's chicory.'

'All the better . . . I like chicory . . .'

'Chicory, the barber's hand! Everywhere! No coffee, no Igor this evening. The evening you come back. He's a marvellous child. He only has one failing: he eats icicles, and that's dangerous. He has a remarkable ear. He can already differentiate between three octaves of A.'

'There is no barber's hand, Ivan Semionovitch. You must tell me all about it later,' she said, with every ounce of gentleness she could summon.

She kissed him again, took the shoe from his pocket, put it on his foot, and did up the laces.

'You're tired, that's all. I can see you're exhausted. The barber's hand is just a nightmare. You get nightmares when you're all on your own. It's entirely normal. I get them too. But we'll sort things out, we'll put a stop to the nightmare . . . Tell me, Ivan Semionovitch, what have you done with Igoriok's wooden horse?'

'The barber's taken it.'

'Where are Igoriok's clothes?'

'He's taken everything.'

Jeanne reflected that she shouldn't be dressing him, but on the contrary, undressing him – putting him to bed and helping him get to sleep. She knelt down before him to find herself on a direct level with his face and, cupping his head in her hands, said, as gently as she could, 'Ivan Semionovitch . . . My poor thing . . . Listen to me now . . . Igoriok is no longer with us . . . He's dead . . . He died of diphtheria . . . Do you hear me? Can you see me . . .? I wasn't here when Igoriok died . . . I'm Jeanne . . . You recognized me at the front door just a few minutes ago . . . I've just come back to Odessa . . .'

'Jeanne – come back?' stammered Filaretov. 'Jeanne – the letter – Clementi . . .'

'What did you say?' asked Jeanne. 'What letter, Ivan Semionovitch?'

'Clementi . . . Over there!'

He was pointing to the piano. Jeanne got up, and, flicking through the confused heap of musical scores on the piano, found a book of Clementi's sonatas.

'Letter – Clementi . . .' repeated Filaretov.

A letter fell out of the book:

Jeanne, you must leave Russia at once. As soon as you've read this note, go down to the freight office at the harbour. Give the password 'How sweet and fair the roses were' at the gate — it's a line from Turgenev. Ask for Genia Kotlenko. He's expecting you. He'll get you on the first sailing for Constantinople. He has a French passport for you. Don't stay a quarter of an hour longer. Goodbye. Thank you. Good luck to you. Burn this. Egoroff.

She refolded the note and looked at the old pianist. He was sitting bolt upright. She ran a hand over his face. There was no reaction. He had retreated into silence, into total absence. 'If only he'd say something, no matter what!' thought Jeanne. 'Something about the barber or about icicles . . . My God, what can I do for him?'

She began to weep at the sight of his hands, which he was pressing to his knees: they were disproportionately large, with long fingers and prominent, painful-looking veins. She took his hands in hers, bathing them in her tears as she kissed and massaged them. But it was no use. He was quite gone.

· Incarville ·

XVII

The house at Incarville was steadily throwing off its wintry look. The clematis shot up around the gateway in a single night, exploding into sprays of pink and mauve. A bush of some unfathomable species which huddled in the shade near the front door – such a nondescript plant that one was almost moved by pity to pull it up as one went past – suddenly felt the urge to smother its masters in perfume, sending snowy white tufts floating everywhere. One almost had to cover one's nose with a handkerchief in order to approach the entrance.

Jeanne left her bedroom, which looked out over this curious shrub, and went up on to the second floor. A long, straight corridor with doors running down both sides gave this floor the look of a hotel. And the friends of the family, who lived up here, came and went as in a hotel. Monsieur and Madame Seyn had their apartment on the floor below.

Marie-Aynard had been overjoyed to see Jeanne again. The reunion with her daughter, whom she found so greatly changed and yet so much the same – this tall, mysterious offshoot of hers – had brought the forty-eight-year-old Marie-Aynard a sense of well-being such as she had never been able to experience before. Late in life, she had come to know what most people are lucky enough to have at the beginning – a sense of security which comes from being the recipient of affection, the novelty of living with somebody, of being in a married state, the simple pleasure of being able to sleep together when one feels like it, the never-ending joy of being able to reach out one's hand, just like that, and touch the person one loves. Nearing the end of her life, Marie-Aynard began to live for the first time, giving herself up to the experience so completely that she had no fear of how little time was left to her. Time itself had slowed down. Her happiness was constant. It was as if the very seasons had stopped revolving.

This woman who at an early age had gone into self-imposed exile in order to flee one man, who had had to rid herself of another in order to give birth to her child, whose life had been a catalogue of separations, loneliness and waiting – waiting at first with impatience, and then with coldness, and finally without any feeling at all – this woman had found both her first love and her prodigal daughter once more; and it was no less beautiful for being true. To open her eyes at daybreak and see, lying so close to her, the time-worn features of the man she loved, his tangled grey curls, the cross-hatching of lines around the corners of his eyes! Only the failure of a love can change faces. True love always sees the same beloved face.

Yves Seyn would get up first and take his wife breakfast in bed: at the smell of the toast and coffee, she would prop herself up on the pillows. Then he would shave and she would watch him from where she sat on the edge of the bath, smiling. The bathroom might almost have been built so small with them in mind: they were constantly brushing against each other, catching one another by the shoulder or leg, finding in the casual contact a measure of the happiness which had been denied them in the past. This was the engagement they had never had, and it was shot through with nostalgia and gratitude. After those few walks taken together on the beach at Honfleur, they had gone their separate ways. The lives they had lived apart were quite beyond recall. And their awareness of the fact lent an even greater demonstrativeness to their relationship, now that they had the rest of their days to spend together.

And with so much patience in their relationship, so much tenderness, how could she possibly find fault with his wrinkled neck and hollow chest and sagging muscles? For Yves Seyn was not what one would term no longer young, nor even somewhat past his prime: he was almost an old man now. Yet lying there with her eyes closed, she adored the touch of his aged body, filled as it was with a desire to which hers responded. And when she opened her eyes again afterwards and saw her husband stretched out on his back and breathing more calmly, she would almost have to stop herself from laughing at how much good it did the old veteran. Feeling rather as though she were acting in a farce, she would climb out of bed and comb her hair – partly out of mere habit, but more because she wanted to examine her face in the mirror and confirm the fact that she had grown twenty years younger, that her skin was elastic, that there was colour in her cheeks and a sparkle in her eyes. And imaginary spectators, the old sentinels of time, would crowd around her to make their assessment, throwing up their hands in joy at what they saw.

Marie-Aynard let her hair grow, and it was soon almost as long as it had been when, as a governess, she had chased the children in the garden of the *dacha* near St Petersburg, her pigtail bouncing between her shoulder-blades. She only put up her new pigtail when they went out for the evening, or when friends came to the house at Incarville. Making her appearance in the evening with the slender nape of her neck exposed, she made one think of all the freshness of morning. And it was the morning hours which became her best, when she would glide radiantly about in a very pale green dressing-gown of crêpe de Chine – a cross between an ordinary dress and a nightgown, tailored at the waist and with a full, flowing skirt. After Yves Seyn had left for the office – he had a legal practice, with offices in both Paris and Deauville – she would go into the little drawing-room to read on the moss-green sofa. She never took lunch: she wasn't interested in eating without Yves. Nastia, the domestic whom she had brought with her from Russia, had charge of the household: she did all the shopping and planned all the meals, and Marie-Aynard, with no chores to do, spent her time reading.

When Jeanne slipped into the room to give her mother a kiss during her 'study-period', as she called it, she would take the book from Marie-Aynard's hands, read out the new author and title in a clear voice, and then say, 'You'll ruin your eyes.' Or sometimes she would lean over her mother's shoulder and read a passage aloud:

> *'And their children between them like gently ripening seeds. But you, my love, I have no claim on you, and who can say when you will come? Who can know what you're asking of me? You're more of a woman than ever. You whisper in my ear. It's the world you're asking of me!'*

'You do that very well, Jeanne,' said Marie-Aynard. 'You read it quite straight. That's how one should read aloud. It's something actors never manage at all.'

'I didn't understand a word.'

'But you don't have to! It's just there. Like you. It just exists. The meaning here is like life itself. How can anyone understand what you really mean, or me, or life itself?'

'You definitely read too much! You'll ruin your eyes.'

'And you've been swimming again – in this cold! In that freezing water! No one goes swimming in weather like this – you're going to catch pneumonia for me!'

XVIII

Jeanne had indeed been swimming. Every day now she would walk out in the noonday sunshine, cross the forested parkland which surrounded her mother's house and jump into the 'freezing waters of the Ocean', as she called them, laughing. She would just take a quick dip, then dry herself vigorously on a large Turkish towel, quickly put her sweaters back on again and go back up to the house. This sea discipline had become necessary to her, like her daily exercise at the bar or her long walks through the countryside. Ever since arriving at Incarville, Jeanne had steeped herself in forgetfulness – not the forget-fulness which exiles and empties you, and then disappears, but the other kind, the forgetfulness which accumulates like sand, grain upon grain, which prepares you for what is to come, which studies life with you.

Jeanne wasn't somebody to do accounts, too many things had been cut in her life, she had suffered too many losses. She was impulse or nothing at all. (Cut off a person's head, and the heart will still go on beating. Even when laid bare, it will try to beat.) A kind of walking film archive, Jeanne did not let herself go to pieces, she preserved in all their original clarity the images of the pillaged house at Beriozy, of Isaak's head against the wall of the Café Catalan, of Filaretov and his barber, of Grigory's corpse lying near the already putrefying carcass of his horse, of Sasha and his railway tracks. But she breathed no word of this to Marie-Aynard. It was too much. How could she have talked about it? And for what reason? Jeanne knew that her mother's melancholy reveries on the beach at Yalta and the leather-jacketed assassins of Isaak in Odessa belonged to two different worlds. Why should she spoil the tranquillity of her mother's Indian summer? Their positions had become entirely reversed, the daughter drawing a tactful veil of silence over the disasters she had lived through, the mother innocently glorying in her happiness at being loved and cared for at last.

There were times when Jeanne viewed her mother as one does a child: *but of course, whatever you want, just tell me . . .* And she would let Marie-Aynard take her off to one of her dressmakers. Her mind elsewhere, Jeanne would sit cross-legged on a pouf, saying nothing. Marie-Aynard could not fathom why, during one of these fitting-sessions, Jeanne turned round to look every time the dressmaker's son came running into the room, striking at the linen mannequins with his toy sword as he went. Worse than that, Jeanne's face actually clouded over at the sight, she became restive, she wanted to leave the place. Strange, thought Marie-Aynard, she doesn't seem to like children.

The style of the clothes Madam Ramières made – hinting at the contours of the body without following them too closely – suited Jeanne well. Flowing folds subtly suggested the outlines, but one had only a vague impression of the body itself, made hazy by other images of birds or sylphs, evocative of the transience of youth, the transience of all things. Marie-Aynard was proud to see her daughter looking so beautiful in her new jersey clothes: she was well and truly here now, saved from a country going up in flames and decked out in the latest fashion. No more worries needed on her account. Even her colour had improved. She seemed to feel genuinely at home in the house at Incarville, with the trees and the sea. And how could she complain of losing Russia when dancers and painters and musicians were continually turning up at Incarville, making the terraces ring with their melodious Russian syllables?

The big wainscotted room with nothing in it but a Steinway in the centre of the floor was witness to the vertiginous leaps of Slava Mishinsky, a former dancer of the Maryinsky Theatre. The two housemaids – sisters, who came from a nearby village and had never known anything but the typical Norman restraint in matters of dress, even at balls – would stare wide-eyed at the bizarre males who visited the house, with their Herculean muscles and narrow eyes and effeminate voices, their genitals and buttocks all but visible under their minuscule leotards whilst their knees and elbows were wrapped in woollen protectors. Images of pure devilry, they spent their free time jumping high enough to touch the ceiling to the infernal accompaniment of the piano which the sisters had so lovingly polished the day before; and yet, in their quieter moments, these sorcerers possessed a rare gentleness and kindness which the Norman ladies could not but note – particularly Monsieur Slava Mishinsky (whose name the sisters could very nearly pronounce), who was always so friendly and cheerful when he wished them good morning through the open kitchen window, or when, sitting with the others in the drawing-room, he would get up to take the cup of tea they were holding out to him.

They had heard that Monsieur Mishinsky was a celebrity in Paris: people apparently paid a great deal of money to go and see him at the Châtelet. So rich, they said to themselves, and yet so unspoilt! Whenever he let a few more days than usual slip by without coming to Incarville, he would have a black van deliver enormous bouquets of flowers to Madame Seyn's daughter – which struck the two Norman maids as the height of absurdity, for the house itself and the fields all around were already brimming with flowers, actually too many for their taste. Every time they removed the transparent wrapping from yet another bunch of flowers from Mishinsky – carefully interlarded with tissue-paper – they sensed a kind of naivety, perhaps a kind of desperation. Yet their young mistress's spirits visibly rose when these curious migratory dancing birds tumbled out of their open-topped touring-cars to invade the house. As for Monsieur and Madame Seyn, they tended to keep out of the way.

The house in which the two sisters worked was certainly anything but orthodox. Meals were taken at all hours and often in the kitchen. People would arrive without a word of warning and leave in the same fashion, feeling just as free to stay there two months as ten minutes. You might have said the place was like a hotel, only a hotel would never have put up with it all. And then the sisters were in some confusion regarding the exact status of the woman who gave them their orders for the cooking and the housework, the woman whom

Madame called Nastia. Was she a servant? Was she a relation? One thing was quite clear: she was Russian. She couldn't tell a floor-cloth from a towel. Not that there was anything *wrong* with her, oh no – but she definitely didn't act her age, laughing all the time, just as likely to throw curtains as shirts into the washing-copper, putting on light-coloured dresses to wash the tiled floors, flirting with the gardener – *a married man with three children* . . .

The gardener was the most important person in the entire household. In his fifties, with blond hair and piercing blue eyes, he was a real Nordic giant. Monsieur Seyn paid him a handsome salary and he merited every penny of it. Transforming the woods which surrounded the villa into parkland was a complex business, involving all kinds of research into the nature of the soil, the local climate and the various species of trees. He was in the process of creating a large shrubbery, with a host of different varieties. Monsieur Seyn had put him in charge of the house's plumbing system – no small responsibility, for the place was a riot of hot-air stoves and bathrooms and pipes and bizarrely shaped taps, often in the form of animals' heads, which either spouted gallons or else wouldn't produce a single drop.

The gardener's name was Michel, but he was invariably referred to as 'Monsieur Nivois'. During the week he lived in a summerhouse in the further reaches of the park which had originally been conceived as a place for entertaining friends. Every Saturday afternoon he went back to his family in Dieppe. Nastia, who had the whole running of the household, often consulted him. They took lunch together every day in the kitchen, eating off English china and drinking out of Venetian crystalware at the antique table covered with a finely embroidered cloth. The kitchen gave straight out on to the garden. The floor was decorated with pink and black tiles. In front of the windows hung Russian curtains, an heirloom from Nastia's family. The room felt like a veranda. Near to a door which opened on to a little wine-store which was used only for cutting and arranging flowers stood the technological wonder of the house, a 'hermetically sealed refrigerating unit' which kept food cold! The cold was produced by electricity. Monsieur Nivois looked after this temperamental machine.

The rest of the house was in keeping with the kitchen: a blend of the luxurious and the casual, and full of surprises. Period furniture signed by famous cabinet-makers stood side by side with the work of a local carpenter who seemed convinced that every piece of furniture should be a chair, a trunk, a table and if possible a bed, all in one.

Marie-Aynard liked covering the elm parquet of the drawing-room with a mixture of straw mats and tapestries which were actually supposed to go on the walls. The house itself was of recent construction and had been designed by an English architect. There is nothing more depressing than the sight of concrete in the pouring rain, but here, the concrete sang — and all the more because of the clematis which ran along the walls and framed the windows, each of which had its own individual character. There were windows of all shapes and sizes — square, lozenge-shaped, round, oval, Romanesque — some of them done in stained glass and others in a special kind of glass which took on all the colours of the rainbow in the sunlight. Between the flowers and the glass there were a few expanses of bare concrete, almost white in colour, which bore the extremely clear marks of seams or of the grain of the planks which had served for the shuttering. From whatever side one looked at the house, it held surprises. But the best thing about it was its situation. It was on the sea, built on a secluded cliff which ran round three sides of a little beach, like walls. Three high, sheer walls. Between them a large room with a floor of sand, opening on one side to the sea.

XIX

To get to this room, one had to descend a steep, winding path strewn with round pebbles which rolled under one's feet like marbles. Down at the bottom, one was quite cut off from the rest of the world. The sand was brilliant white in the shadow of the cliff walls, speckled with gold on account of its mica content. The sheltered seclusion of the beach made it a natural sanctuary for birds. The sight of Jeanne did not bother them in the slightest: they just went on contemplating in their beady-eyed fashion, or strolling around in pairs.

It was still only April, a weekday, and almost night: there was no risk of meeting anyone down on the beach, so, as the weather was quite mild, Jeanne decided to go for another swim. She set off down the path, whose shade was dotted here and there with white flowers fallen from the trees. At the turning where the path narrowed to become nothing but a little ledge of pebbles, she ran into a man. They stood staring at one another for a moment, then the man backed off and squeezed himself into a hollow in the cliff to let Jeanne pass; and, as she did so, he wished her good evening in an accent which was neither Russian nor French.

The following morning, Jeanne looked in on her mother. For once, Marie-Aynard wasn't reading. She was writing a letter.

'You're looking a bit pale, aren't you, Mother?'

'One of my migraines. And how are you?'

'I didn't sleep well,' said Jeanne, sitting down on the moss-coloured sofa. 'There was someone making a noise up on my floor last night . . . A sort of . . . staccato sound. It would stop for minutes at a time, then start up again quicker than ever.'

'What was it like, this noise?'

'A bit like a machine-gun, but more irregular, and much quieter . . .'

'Perhaps it was coming from the road . . .'
'No, it was in the house. And on my floor.'
'Oh, I know what it was: it was Elliot!'
'I'm sorry?'
'Elliot. He must have been using his typewriter.'
'Typewriter?'
'Jeanne, do you mean to say you've never seen a typewriter? Elliot's a writer. He types everything he writes.'
'Why doesn't he work silently with a pen, like everyone else – like Tolstoy, and Chekhov?'
'Because he's American!'
Jeanne got up, stretched herself thoroughly and gave a deep yawn.
'I'm interrupting you, though, Mother.'
'Jeanne, you know you never interrupt me. The very idea . . .'
Marie-Aynard got up too, gave her daughter a hug and, as she only came up to Jeanne's shoulder, kissed her on the tip of her chin.

XX

Leaving her mother, Jeanne pushed open the door of the kitchen: she wanted to get herself a biscuit. Through the half-open door she saw a man seated in profile against the window. Obviously deep in thought, he was gnawing at an enormous object which he held in both hands and which could only have been a leg of mutton. At least that was the most civilized hypothesis, for his big square jaw and luxuriant mop of black hair made one think of Cro-Magnon Man. Tall, and with a stoop to match, he was dressed in grey velvet trousers and a beige sweater, both of which were too big for him: they swamped him, in fact. Jeanne recognized the man she had met on the path, and, regretting her biscuit, quietly shut the door.

That must be Elliot, thought Jeanne. The Industrial Era at night and the Stone Age at breakfast! They were a strange lot, those Americans ... It was coming up to ten o'clock and Jeanne had to catch the train to Paris, where she gave lessons twice a week at a dancing-school in the Bois de Boulogne. She loved letting time run through her hands in Paris, strolling the boulevards, going to cafés and cinemas. A few days previously she had come across a poster for *The Woman in Grey* outside a cinema in the Rue des Petits-Champs, not far from the Opéra. It was like looking at her own ghost: Jeanne stared back from the poster, clumsily painted, dressed in nurse's uniform and framed by a background of bare trees. She couldn't decide whether to go in or not. It wasn't that she was sad not to be acting – not to have the opportunity to act – any longer. She was done with her career, once and for all. (And had it actually been a career, had it really been her whole existence . . .?) Yet the reels being shown in that cinema were still a concrete reminder of the Jeanne she had once been, back in her Petersburg days. And perhaps it was for that very reason that she wasn't sure whether or not to go in; but her curiosity got the better of her in the end. Jeanne bought a ticket, was shown in by the usherette and sat down in the middle of the almost empty auditorium, her gaze already fixed on the flickering screen.

The woman she saw, dressed in a nurse's pinafore and a cap with a cross on it, was indeed her, chewing her handkerchief as she watched a man walk away down an immensely long corridor; but what Jeanne saw was actually quite different. She was watching another film, one in which Gauer came rushing up to her in that selfsame corridor and told her that it had gone well, that the take was good, and that work was finished for the day. She took off her cap, the big lamps were switched off, and she saw herself in an overcoat, with no make-up on, walking along beside the building of the Poutiloff factory. Then her private film showed her clambering on to a tram – the platform was jam-packed with people, and a man who reeked of chloroform was whispering all kinds of nonsense into her ear: wickerwork, basket, jasmine . . .

In the images that passed before her eyes she saw something else, as do those gifted with second sight, and, like those who possess this gift, she was left exhausted by the experience. When the words THE END appeared, she couldn't have said what the film was all about. Who had left whom? And why? Who was still alive? Who was dead? Everyone in the whole film seemed to be at death's door – women, men, dreams, entire armies. Gauer's film was no doubt an extremely fine piece of work, but how could Jeanne possibly judge that after what she had just gone through in that cinema-hall?

I'll come back and see it again another day, she thought. With Mishinsky. Yes, I'd be interested to hear what he thinks of it. No, I will *not* come back! There's no point seeing it all again. It's all over and I want nothing more to do with it, either with Mishinsky or on my own . . . I won't even tell my mother about it. I won't mention the fact the film is showing in Paris. Let's just hope she doesn't find out about it herself . . .

XXI

Jeanne walked down the avenue. It was still daylight, and the air smelt good – sweetish, with a tang of ozone. Seeing that film has done me no good, she thought to herself. She took a long, deep breath and walked on faster; then, noticing a child perched on the backrest of a bench eating an apple, she suddenly stopped. What had she been thinking of? Of course. She'd left her shoulder-bag on the floor in the cinema, and the tea and biscuits which Marie-Aynard had asked her to buy were in it. The very idea of having to pass the poster once more and go back into the cinema was distasteful to her. She went back all the same. The swing doors of the entrance were standing open, doubtless to air the place. There was no sign of the usherette, all the lights were on, and as she went in a man stood up and held out her shoulder-bag to her – the shoulder-bag she had always had, in which she used to carry her dancing-things when she went off to rehearsals at the Opera in Odessa, and which she later stuffed with all her combs and make-up when setting off for work at the studios of the illusions.

'I believe this is your bag,' he said, in Russian.

His face, underneath a shock of grey curls, was surprisingly young-looking. He was dressed in a work-tunic of the kind Levitsky, Jeanne's favourite cameraman, used to wear to the studios every day, and he had something of Levitsky's old maidish quality too. These tunics, which seemed to belong half to the country and half to the town, had been fashionable in the Russia of the 1910s; one often sees photographs of Tolstoy wearing the same thing.

'Yes, it's mine,' Jeanne replied.

'It's heavy.' He moved towards the exit with Jeanne. 'Have you got far to walk?'

'It depends. I can either walk or take a taxi. I'm going to the Gare Saint-Lazare.'

'That's not far. Let me carry it for you. It's fine weather for walking.'

He spoke a pure, melodious Russian, the Russian of Moscow.

'What did you, ah, think of the film?' asked Jeanne.

He made no reply. Out in the open air he seemed younger than ever underneath his great bush of grey hair. Jeanne felt that his attention was entirely focused on her, although his gaze was directed elsewhere the whole time. His arms were long and the sleeves of his tunic came only half-way down his forearms, giving him a rather clownish look. But the grey of his hair, his long, muscular neck (similar to Mishinsky's when tossing back his head in movements of abandon or joy) and his measured stride, on long legs with big feet, his head held upright, endowed him with an air of distinction, despite his odd clothes.

'Have you been in Paris for long?' asked Jeanne.

'Since the war.'

'The war of '14 or the civil war?'

'I came to Paris just before the outbreak of the war, in the spring of 1914.'

'So all you know of Russia is the good times.'

'If the "good times", as you call them, are a matter of war or peace.'

Jeanne didn't understand quite what he meant by this.

'On account of the war and the Revolution, I've lost a man and a child, and several other people who were very dear to me,' Jeanne heard herself saying, as though she were talking to herself without really knowing why . . . 'It's true I might have lost them without those events – accidents, microbes, assassinations, madness are always there to take their toll.'

'I'm a friend of Gauer's,' he said. 'An old friend. No one here is interested in this film the way we two are. I recognized your bag without even having seen you in the cinema. I said to myself, "That's *her* bag!" There are signs –'

'Watch out!' Jeanne interrupted him, grabbing him by the sleeve. A car was just about to run him down. 'Your days'll be numbered if you go on crossing the road like that! You might be good at spotting signs, but not motor cars . . . I've missed my train,' she went on, looking over the roof of an omnibus at a clock in the Place de l'Opéra. 'And someone was supposed to be picking me up at the other end. I must make a telephone call. Could we go into a café?'

'Not this one. Let's go to that one.' He pointed to the Café de la Paix. 'We could have something to eat there.'

'All right,' said Jeanne, 'it looks nicer.'

She made her telephone call and came back to where he was sitting.

'They say there's another train around half past ten.'

She took off her little hat with its short veil. The man extricated himself from his tunic. Underneath, he had on a vest-like woollen shirt of a mauvish blue. Jeanne saw that his eyes had a touch of mauve in them. He lit a cigarette. His fingernails, unusually delicate for a man's, were rimmed with blue – obviously traces of paint.

'You're a painter,' said Jeanne, closing her eyes, 'and you have a fondness for blue.'

'For grey too,' he said with a laugh. 'The grey of your eyes, the grey of this material . . .' He reached out a finger and touched the end of Jeanne's sleeve whilst running an eye over the menu. 'What'll you have?'

'An omelette.'

'Is that all?'

'And a cup of tea.'

'An omelette and a cup of tea for the lady, please, and a *Bon Soir* for me,' he said to the waiter in French.

'How long have you been speaking French?' asked Jeanne.

'I was brought up by a Breton lady by the name of Mademoiselle Élise. My father spoke French: he used to do a lot of business with France. He was killed in a pogrom.'

'When was that?'

'1902. In Jitomir. Lev Trotsky is my cousin. Ever since that day' – he ran his finger down his nose – 'I've had this head of hair. It looked pretty strange when I was fourteen.'

'It still does,' said Jeanne.

The waiter brought them their drinks.

'Your health!' the man said, proffering Jeanne his glass.

Jeanne took a sip and gave it back to him.

'I never knew my father,' said Jeanne. 'And I can't say that I've ever felt the lack of him. Having a father you love, knowing that he's always there to protect you, and then losing him – 'well, that's a sorrow I've been spared.'

'My name is Samuel. In the film credits your name appears as Vera, but your real name is Jeanne. Gauer's told me a lot about you. About your mother, too. And even about the way you were brought up. But not about your child – did you have it after Gauer left for America . . .?'

'He wasn't my own,' said Jeanne. 'Not that it makes any difference.'

'No, it doesn't make any difference,' echoed Samuel.

'We were very happy together. I never realized at the time quite how much of a support he was to me.'

'You'll have to find another.'

'I don't think it happens quite like that.'

'Waiter, another *Bon Soir* and a bottle of Sancerre, please,' said Samuel.

I don't know about this, thought Jeanne; but there was something about this man which made it impossible to go against him. She picked at her omelette. Samuel downed his second *Bon Soir* and set about emptying the bottle of wine. He drank in a mechanical fashion, without displaying the slightest relish. Jeanne observed no hint of pleasure in anything he did. There was a quality of detachment about the way he held his glass, the way he looked at this or that, even the way he spoke. Not that he seemed weak; it was rather that his engagement with events around him, obvious though it was, was inconsistent. And in this ambiguity Jeanne felt there was a certain grace. She was quite simply at ease in his company.

'I don't like spring,' she said. 'Something about it revolts me. Everything bursting forth . . . One feels one's on an over-lavish stage-set. It always makes me think of larvae, of soft things which haven't come out of their cocoons . . . A friend of mine in Odessa died of T B in the middle of spring one year.

She didn't even have the strength to spit any longer. I was going round spitting at the bushes and the trees! How stupid they looked!'

Samuel twirled the stem of his empty glass.

'It was in the autumn,' he said.

'Sorry?'

'The filming of *The Woman in Grey*: it was in the autumn. It's obvious. The light of autumn is far more interesting. The morning mists, too. Once – not here, a long way away, up on an island in the north – I saw a particular effect of light. It was exactly what I had been looking for. Sometimes, after working for hours and hours, I capture it . . . And I'm deliriously happy . . . The next morning I leap out of bed, and what do you know? The bloody thing's disappeared from the canvas. It's hopeless, absolutely hopeless. Gauer, now: Gauer sometimes manages to catch it . . . Do you remember that scene with the train? You're here' – Samuel stretched out his hands to indicate a carriage-window – 'and the train's here, and it starts pulling out of the station. And what does Gauer do? What do you actually see? Nothing! Not a single soul! Just the light – *my* light! He gets the precise colour of my light, the sod! How does he get the colour to come alive when he has to film everything in black and white? Doing the same thing in paint, I'd have to destroy the colour itself, so that you saw nothing but the light . . .'

'You once loved someone,' said Jeanne.

'Yes.'

'And you're trying to recapture the light of the day you met that person.'

'Nothing to do with it,' said Samuel. 'When I was in love, I didn't even know it. I didn't have my eyes open. And when you do know it's no longer the same. It goes to your head a little, you get on with the business of living, you concentrate on a subject.'

'I told you so,' said Jeanne, 'you were in love once. You're telling me you were. You weren't yet aware of it, but there was a light . . .'

'One ought rather to think of every different kind of light . . . Every light that makes me what I am – all the drawers I've rummaged through, all the doors I've opened, all the heads of hair, the looks, the feet, the dust, the mist, the rays of light . . . Shouldn't one really speak of the lamps of memory?' he said, in a professorial tone, smiling.

'I don't know,' said Jeanne. 'What if we were to stop thinking? As I do most of the time.'

'Oh, that's easy at your age,' said Samuel. 'You're young. Waiter, two hard-boiled eggs and a little bread with just a scraping of butter!'

'What's young? My mother's much younger than me. My skin may be smoother and my features more distinct, but I'm nothing but a box of ashes inside.'

'Your hand, I beg you, box of ashes!'

He bent forward over the hand Jeanne automatically held out to him and ceremoniously kissed it.

'A simple act of homage to the person who produced such a brilliant performance in *The Woman in Grey*. You must come and visit me in my den. I live in Rue de la Glacière. Do you know it?'

'No, I'm afraid I don't know Paris well at all. But I was wanting to ask you to come to Incarville this Sunday. It's Easter.'

'I can't stand services and priests. Do you really believe in that stuff?'

'Yes, I do! As far back as I can remember, Easter has always been a celebration for me. Won't you come?'

'When will you be in Paris again?'

'I'm here every Monday and Thursday. I give dancing-lessons at a place near the Porte Dauphine, in the Bois de Boulogne.'

'Give me the address and I'll come and meet you afterwards.'

'Here you are,' said Jeanne, scribbling the address on the back of an envelope, 'and these are the hours I teach . . . The Avenue du Bois has a huge pavement: we could go for a bit of a walk.'

'We'll try.'

XXII

Marie-Aynard and her husband were coming down the front flight of steps of the house at Incarville, Yves Seyn carrying the travelling-bag which Nastia had packed for them, when the opening bars of a waltz came floating through the open windows of the ground floor drawing-room. It was unmistakably Chopin. They both stopped short and stood quite motionless together on the same step, staring at the trees, whilst the waltz went on playing, a simple story without words, dappled with breezes which stirred the leaves of different memories in the two people who stood there hand in hand, forming a single being.

Five minutes later on that sunny Sunday morning, squeezed up close to Yves in his twenty-five horse-power Peugeot, Marie-Aynard reflected that her life had been nothing but a long process of waiting for moments like this, the impatient waiting of someone who believes that each day will be better than the last, but no, it isn't better, well, let's get through it as quickly as possible, let's get to tomorrow, and so on from day to day, faster and faster – Marie-Aynard glanced at the speedometer: a hundred and ten.

Waiting, yes . . . At the age of eighteen, in the apartment near the Parc Monceau, as on the beach at Honfleur, Marie-Aynard had waited for some word, some sign, from Yves. She had only fled to Russia in order to go on waiting for him, waiting for a letter from Seyn. Later on, she had waited for Jeanne. But little by little as the years went by, she had begun to live each day, each hour, with less impatience, learning to free herself from the compulsion to wait, gradually diminishing it in order to find happiness. The terrible strain she had been under disappeared as she developed a more relaxed notion of time. She was genuinely happy now. Yves – the miracle of finding Yves again after so many years of separation – contributed in great measure to her happiness, but there was more to it than that. Listening to the waltz with Yves, she had suddenly glimpsed the fact that there is a greater equilibrium than one realizes between today and tomorrow, and that one's consciousness, working steadily away in the darkness, makes all manner of preparations which will one day disappear, as the scaffolding of planks and poles disappears from around a white house.

Yves Seyn sat silent at the steering-wheel of the Peugeot, concentrating on the road. Marie-Aynard ran her hand through his hair and let it come to rest on the nape of his neck, feeling as she did so that she was touching a reel of life which had almost entirely unwound itself whilst the waltz was playing and then suddenly wound itself up again as they got into the car. She felt incredibly happy – happy that he was taking her to the house at Honfleur which she had loved for so long, happy that she would be spending the night there with him between the linen sheets which were always slightly damp (those sheets in which she had once spent sleepless nights thinking about him . . .) Today they would be there together: they would collect wood for the fire together, and go for a walk along the beach together, then go out for dinner together at the little restaurant down at the harbour.

'It's good to see Jeanne inviting all these people,' said Seyn.

Marie-Aynard removed her hand from the nape of her husband's neck.

'I'm sorry, what did you say?'

'Jeanne seems to be better.'

'I never knew there was anything wrong with her,' said Marie-Aynard.

'Oh, yes . . . She often looks completely exhausted. You

notice it in her eyes particularly. She's just in a daze. You don't
see these things because she's your daughter, but she's a strange
person, you know. She'll talk, and smile, but she's not really
with us at all. She's living something else, somewhere we can
never follow her. Above and beyond that, she doesn't seem to
be at all interested in men – or in women, for that matter!'

'She's always been like that. But you're wrong. She's not
the introspective kind at all, she's never spoken to me about
her own feelings. She's not a dreamer, either. She often used to
have that absent air, but she was always terribly involved with
things at the same time – first with her dancing, then with the
cinema . . . We'll just have to see what she comes up with
now. I have faith in her.'

'Well, I'm glad to hear that . . . Of course I may be wrong. I
didn't see her growing up . . . I can only see the end result, and
believe me, she's a phenomenon. She's going to be turning a lot
of heads soon.'

'At least she's more sociable than she used to be. All those people
she's invited! She's never forced me to flee my own house before.'

'We're not fleeing,' said Seyn, 'we're chasing something. I
always feel ten years younger the moment I set foot in Honfleur!'

'I just hope this invasion doesn't bother Elliot too much,'
said Marie-Aynard.

'I invited him this morning to come along with us.'

'And what did he say?' asked Marie-Aynard, offering up
silent thanks to Elliot for having left them on their own together.

'He said, "Hordes sometimes inspire me." And anyway,
I've noticed that he works mostly at night.'

XXIII

For the Easter weekend the house at Incarville was full of

people. Helped by Nastia, Jeanne had got everything ready for the arrival of the artists of the Russian Season at the Châtelet. An enormous spread – the work of all present – had been laid out on a table on the lawn, with a host of *kulitches*, and traditional Easter loaves, and pyramid-shaped, pastel-coloured cakes made of cream cheese. Then there was a whole ham, and painted eggs done by a scene-painter from the ballet, arranged in baskets on a nest of wild flowers and grasses, not to mention all the fish – herring, salmon and sturgeon – and the mushroom and cucumber marinades, and of course the inevitable cabbage.

A priest brought in from Paris held a brief service on the terrace which Nastia had decorated with all the icons of the house and the picture-lamps whose tiny flames filled the air with a smell exactly the same as that in Russian Orthodox churches. The priest had been able to make himself available for the occasion for the simple reason that there was nothing to prevent him: he was unemployed, a priest without a parish.

Like an actor who has undergone a lengthy, enforced absence from the stage, Father Cyril put on an inspired performance. Appearing young for his age (he had just turned forty), this emigré from Smolensk made the censer fly and thundered out the Slavonic verses in a deep voice. The improvised choir composed of the invited guests sang the responses – getting a lot of the words wrong, it was true, but demonstrating an admirable musicality and thoroughly enjoying their part. Here in Normandy, they got a little taste of home, and the proceedings were imbued with the homely atmosphere one always finds in Russia on this joyful day of Resurrection, when the Russians open their souls as wide as the windows of a house on a spring-cleaning day.

It was customary on this occasion to lay one's old grudges to rest and to put the ideal of the brotherhood of man more actively into practice. And so these dancers and musicians and painters – creators of the 'miracle' which had impressed the smartest salons of Paris, whose lives were a daily round of backbiting and intrigues without end, and who now found themselves assembled in this mirage of a chapel on the terrace at Incarville – drank deep of the doctrine of the communion of souls and the forgiveness of sins. Quite sincerely and graciously, these delicate flowers of the Russian decadence, dandies and homosexuals, discreet or outrageous, crossed themselves in unison, only occasionally allowing themselves a sideways glance at the artistic poses Father Cyril was striking.

Since the service was being held directly under his bedroom window, Elliot soon found it hard to concentrate. He left his room and went down on to the terrace to have a closer look at what was going on. And there he saw Madame Seyn's daughter, wearing a dress of flowing white lawn, with two white camellias in her carefully arranged bun, singing and crossing herself along with the others. She was standing in the back row, which was less tightly packed than the ones at the front, so Elliot was able to stroll up in an unobtrusive manner and take the empty place next to her. He automatically ran his hands through his hair to give it some semblance of order, for when he was at his desk, not actually typing but groping after an idea, he pulled his hair this way and that. Suddenly he registered the fact that the assembled company was dressed with exquisite refinement, which made him aware of his stained pullover, studded with cigarette-burns, and his cowboy trousers, which had lost almost all of their blue. He had no time, however, to worry himself about the colour of his trousers, for a sudden ripple went through the congregation and, abandoning the passivity of prayer, they started a great round of kissing. The kisses landed full on the mouth, interspersed with sing-song exclamations which Elliot could not understand, but in which the name of Christ clearly dominated: the kissing was both eager and serious.

The first which the dumbfounded Elliot received was from Jeanne: she was standing right beside him and she didn't even have to move in order to kiss him. From close up he saw her grey eyes, in which there was no hint of laughter: the touch of her lips was soft and her smell was reminiscent of the sea. Standing there after she had moved away, he was embraced many more times, principally by men; but his gaze followed her as she made her way through the little crowd. He wanted to see more than her back: he wanted her to turn around so that he could see her face again, not from close up, as a moment ago – one can't see a thing from so close – but from a slight distance; then he lost sight of her completely, because a wall of people came between himself and Jeanne as she walked off, and he received ever more enthusiastic kisses from entire strangers. He heard the words *Khristos Voskress, Khristos Voskress* coming from every quarter; and the sun, which had been behind a bank of cloud until that moment, suddenly came out to shower upon the scene of people embracing, as in a painting by some Italian Primitive, its gracious benediction.

XXIV

Elliot would have stayed on to see how the celebration was going to develop, but it was time for him to leave Incarville if he wanted to be punctual for his rendezvous in Paris, and he did want to be. It was a walk of three kilometres to the station, and he had to shave and change beforehand. Elliot drove a Ford which he had had shipped over from New York, and it was frequently off the road – as was the case today. Going down the Boulevard de Courcelles the previous Wednesday, he had had two punctures within the space of fifteen minutes: one in the front right wheel, the other in the front left. Garages fought shy of repairing his tyres: they weren't the same as the French ones. 'There's no point in fretting,' he had been told at a place in Rue Legendre, where he had rolled up on a scorching wheel-rim. 'You'll just have to be patient.'

Elliot's Ford was a rustic cabin on wheels. Roomy and imposing, with a collapsible roof, it allowed him to do the journey between Paris and Incarville in style, without fatigue or loss of time. The US citizen Elliot Noelting possessed two superb American-built machines: his Smith-Corona and his Ford. Everything else he had came from France. This didn't amount to much: the lady of his dreams and his talent as a writer, which he could only exercise now when he was in Normandy at the Seyns' house.

The lady of his dreams was an actress. A resident member of the Comédie-Française, Madeleine Vallès was touching forty. The public loved her and the press showered her with eulogies. She approached her work with an extreme intelligence and a longing for perfection. Her voice was warm, calm, open; her silences were winning. She moved with great authority. Her body exuded charm at every turn, her gestures were perfectly tailored to the poetry of Racine, and with her sudden outbursts – wild, unexpected, excessive – she could convey the highest pitch of tragedy. She was entrusted with the roles of Phèdre and Roxane, in which she explored – as though rummaging around in the darkness, torch in hand – every nook and cranny of human suffering. Her home life was more prosaic: she lived with a rich, good-natured man, avoiding all scandal.

When Elliot saw Madeleine Vallès for the first time, in the role of Hermione, he was not touched by any special emotion. He was still too new to the French language to be able to perceive the music of Racine or the intricacies of his thought. But as the months went by, he became increasingly haunted by Racine's poetry, and he developed a genuine passion for it – without realizing that his reaction had much to do with the way Madeleine Vallès delivered the lines. He thought it was Racine that he loved, and that Madeleine was just one of his mouthpieces. And when friends asked him what could entice him into the morgue of the Comédie-Française, he would reply, 'I listen to poetry there.'

Elliot took his devotion so far as to rent a box for the year and then to strike up a friendship with the manager of the theatre, whom he had met at the cultural attaché's house in Rue Gabriel – the Comédie-Française was about to set off on a tour of the United States. Amused but at the same time touched by the infatuation of this American writer, who was said to be talented, the manager invited him to come along to watch a few rehearsals. And so it was that the lumbering, ungainly figure of Elliot Noelting became a familiar sight to the actors of the Comédie-Française. Scattering his cigarette ash all over the carpets and seats, lost in the semi-darkness of the auditorium, he spent hours watching shows being got ready for the stage. And it was on seeing her with her hair down and no make-up on, wearing a simple cotton dress or a dressing-gown, that he realized that this particular actress meant more to him than all the others. She aroused a wild, violent desire in him – but, oddly enough, no actual thoughts of seduction. The poetry of Racine was too far removed from everyday life; the boards of the theatre, too. This actress moved in a completely different world from Elliot; and even when he saw her running through a downpour to the taxi-rank in the Place du Palais, he didn't make the obvious connection. She remained, by definition, out of reach, beyond all considerations of lust.

Things might have gone no further had not Madeleine actually been the one to speak to him. It happened one evening in the bar of the Théâtre des Ambassadeurs, where she had been with a friend to see a play by Bernstein. She said hello to Elliot and held out her hand, upon which he planted a clumsy kiss. She introduced him to her friend, said a couple of things more; and it was the same voice, the same gestures, as in *Bajazet*. Elliot's desire rekindled – although he felt a certain hesitation, too. He almost regretted that this had actually happened, or perhaps one should say, that the process had reached its logical conclusion. Stunned, he maintained a semblance of calm, the calm and detachment which women find both enticing and frightening. And he felt that Madeleine's open expression, her smile, her steady gaze were saying to him, Yes, this is how I am – no longer very young. But what does that matter, I can see that you like me . . .

And it was true. That was exactly what they were saying. They spoke on the off-chance, not caring how the words came out. Finding herself face to face with this man outside the Comédie-Française that evening, Madeleine Vallès decided to take the plunge. At first, she had found Elliot's presence at rehearsals irritating. Like all actresses, she suffered from stage-fright, during rehearsals as during performances themselves. But she soon came to realize that this solitary onlooker, sitting there with such concentration, had a calming effect upon her. From a distance, she sensed a warmth and sincerity in his attentiveness. He was like a mirror for her, a yardstick by which to measure her performance, and she came to rely on the support of his silent appreciation. He helped her; and he attracted her, too. She began to think about him, at first unconsciously, then quite deliberately. The moment she stepped out on stage, she would look to see whether he was there. She moved, she walked, she expressed herself entirely for him. And he was too far away from her; she wanted to have him nearer.

Unlike Elliot, she was unable to disguise her confusion during the interval at the Théâtre des Ambassadeurs. She talked in a rush: what she had to say about the first two acts was extremely perspicacious, but it was feverish and intense – as Elliot himself would no doubt have noted, had he not already been hopelessly smitten. He didn't look at her, he didn't listen to what she was saying: he just let things happen. He imbibed her presence, steeping himself in her. Silent as a stone, he was entirely passive and open to her. And she was just as passive, for all her intensity. The preliminaries – highly protracted – had now taken place. They had made no move towards one another, but the play had begun.

The evening wound up in a hideous little restaurant near Les Halles. Everything in the place – the walls, the ceiling, the floor, the tables, the chairs – was painted blood-red. The meat was red and bloody, and so was the wine. Saying that she had an early train to catch to Nantes, Madeleine's friend discreetly slipped away. And it was in this setting, unnervingly reminiscent of a *corrida*, that the liaison between Elliot Noelting and Madeleine Vallès actually began.

XXV

When Elliot took his leave of the huggings and kisses of the Russian Easter so as not to miss the slow train to Paris at Incarville Station, his relationship with Madeleine was already drawing to a painful close. Blessed with a tolerant husband who knew how to turn a blind eye when necessary, she didn't have to go through endless rigmaroles in order to spend what time was left her from the theatre with Elliot. But very soon – the very first time they slept together, in fact – Elliot had found himself wondering whether his Champmeslé was not more thrilling at a distance, in her satins and ruffs, than when lying naked in bed under him or on top of him in the little flat in Rue Git-le-Coeur, which he had more or less abandoned for the Seyns' house. And Madeleine, for her part, did not want displays of potency from Elliot, either. She preferred him sitting in the empty auditorium during rehearsals. Elliot's 'bestialities' – that was how, deep down, she really thought of Elliot's amorous exploits – met with her toleration, but nothing more.

She loved this man: she loved him desperately, as she had loved others before him, because she needed periodically to find someone who could incarnate the faceless, abstract audiences who were her partners every evening of her life. Elliot comforted her, he gratified her more – infinitely more – than any of the others: he was more intelligent, and she was touched by his clumsy good nature, accompanied as it was by a highly complex and subtle sensibility. So touched, indeed, that when in bed with him, not guessing that the whole business left him cold too, she would fake excitement in order to give him pleasure – which only had the effect of confusing him, for he would then see a completely different woman in his mind's eye, the only one whose touch had ever been able to thaw him.

The heavings and gruntings of her lovers were not the only problem Madeleine had. On stage, she was frightened; and off it, she felt ill at ease, all too aware of the approaching day when she would have no place there any longer. She was constantly irritable and peevish – with her impeccable husband, with her relations, with her acquaintances. And with Elliot, too. On her worst days, when she hadn't slept, or – what amounted to the same – when a producer had not paid her enough attention or a critic had had the nerve to go into ecstasies about some actress other than herself – she would treat Elliot to the gloomiest prognoses for the future of their relationship. She deserved nothing. She was ugly, she was old, she hadn't an ounce of talent, she was depressive – she might as well give it all up and die!

These fits of black depression usually occurred when they were in bed together. Elliot would listen impassively, running an index finger over Madeleine's back and shoulders. The sight of her worn, pallid features, and of the panic in her eyes, caused him pain. But not her speeches.

Elliot at his typewriter, Elliot the novelist, was a masterly analyst of the human heart. Indeed, the literary critic of the *Christian Science Monitor* had declared him to be a 'more syncopated Henry James'. But with Madeleine Vallès, as with her predecessors, he was like a little boy. Yes, in order to fall in love with a woman, he had to return to a state of childhood. It would come upon him like the spring or the flu. Pleasure and pain, delivered in equal measure.

XXVI

On the slow train to Paris that Sunday in April, it was mostly pain. Madeleine Vallès had not performed for a fortnight. She had wanted the break herself – but a fortnight away from the stage, with no grandiloquent gestures and heartfelt cries, was bound to produce trouble.

Elliot hadn't even had time to get out his keys before she tore open the door of the flat. She threw herself upon him, smothering him in kisses, and standing there on the stairs in nothing but her nightdress, exclaimed, 'I can't go on! It's *you* I'm married to! I can't live without you! I need the touch of your lips, I need to feel your arms around me, every day!'

'My darling Madeleine, you know perfectly well that I ask nothing better than to live with you,' Elliot said flatly, trying to get her back into the apartment and anticipating yet worse when he saw from her face that she had neither eaten nor slept for several days.

Live with Madeleine? Live together? As he had done once before in his life, with Kate? Oh God, anything but that! He sat Madeleine down on a chair, went back to close the door, pressed his forehead against it, and saw once more the house under the trees by the lakeside in Massachusetts –

'They have factories and stocks and shares, and we have a lake,' said Kate, her head upon Elliot's shoulder. It was a gigantic lake, almost a sea. The birds sang like mad every morning just before daybreak, innumerable performers dominated by a few soloists who came back every year in couples to take up their place, and whose insolent recitals Kate recognized with her eyes closed, long before spotting them on the branch of a beech tree, always the same one, or the corner of a roof: 'That's the blackbird who's got the fat wife with one yellow eye,' she would say, still three quarters asleep, her face buried in the pillow and her legs intertwined with Elliot's –

Don't think about Kate, Elliot told himself, stop now!

He took Madeleine by the arm and led her back into the bed-room.

'But you know perfectly well, Madeleine, that all the ob-stacles are on your side: I'm free and unattached,' he said to her in tones of utter sincerity – somewhat sheepishly, all the same.

Kate gently turned her head upon the pillow, smiled – a farcical smile – and kicked Elliot in the ankles.

'Your career, my career, and Gilles . . .' Madeleine sobbed into Elliot's sweater. 'Gilles could never bear . . . You know there's only one thing he asks of me: to come back every time, to be there . . .'

Creating obstacles and not being able to overcome them, inflicting wounds upon herself and not being able to heal them – that was Madeleine, reflected Elliot as he tenderly stroked her hair; and hadn't he found a certain charm, back in the early days, in her constant pursuit of disaster? Kate used to loathe injuries and everything to do with pain and suffering. What a monument to cruelty she was! How young they had been! And with what terrible simplicity had she achieved her aims!

They had had such an understanding, Kate and he – waking up in one another's arms, walking through the woods together, eating, reading, caressing each other, talking of everything and nothing, swapping glances behind the backs of dinner-party bores, falling asleep lying head to foot or one across the other – such an understanding that Elliot thought he must be dreaming a wild and limitless dream, so wild that he took it almost as a joke when, one morning as they were breakfasting on the veranda, Kate handed him the marmalade and said to the accompaniment of birdsong, 'Suzanna O'Keefe asked me to tell you that the willow needs pruning because if there were a storm, the branches might cut the telephone wires – Blackwell's have telegraphed from Oxford to say that they've found your translation of Dante – they named the price but I used the telegram to wipe the dip-stick when I was checking the oil in the car – I've been in love with another man for the past month – I'm moving out soon – you really ought to put on another shirt to go and see Liebermann – hang on a moment, the tea's gone cold, I'll put some more water on to boil,' – and all this with a straight look and in a measured tone which were all the more abominable for the reason that Kate had not fired off this salvo of multiple-information-in-one with the thought of helping him swallow the pill: Kate didn't even think about the pill, it was just her way.

Struck motionless, Elliot stared at the white line of the lake whilst Kate busied herself with the kettle behind his back. I don't want to know who this character is, he thought, I want to know nothing about the whole business. And he realized that, within the space of ten seconds, Kate had become a stranger to him. A stranger forever. Then he felt himself turning to stone, and the veranda was stone, too. The whole universe was nothing but one big stone. He didn't know how he was going to swallow the stone: it stuck in his throat for months, for years – for the rest of his life.

No, he didn't want to know anything, didn't want to conceive the inconceivable, to search endlessly for ways of explaining this madness. Who? Where? How . . .? As poised as ever, Kate poured out the tea. There's an obstacle? Don't know the meaning of the word, let's just cut this knot, pass me the scissors, will you, look, it's just a tiny operation, you're not a baby, are you? Elliot had nevertheless reacted with a pair of hefty clouts which sent her reeling ˑo the floor.

'Don't worry, my Aricie, I'm here now,' said Elliot. Madel-
cine was weeping more beautifully than ever: he hugged her to
him. 'It's just that you're out of sorts, the weather's very heavy
today. Please don't cry ... There's no need ... There are
people worse off than us — Just think of all those people going
along to the Comédie-Française this afternoon in the hope of
seeing you and coming away disappointed ...' He glanced out
of the corner of his eye at her lips, fearing they might tighten;
but no, he had not gone too far and she calmed down a little.

He had never once seen Kate cry — except, very occasionally,
when making love, and then it was just one or two teardrops
of happiness. They would make love at the drop of a hat. 'It's
marvellous,' Kate used to say to him, 'it's the cure for all ills.
Well, just think, in Ancient Greece the soldiers used to do it
with each other on the battlefield itself whenever one of them
had received a sword-wound in the head. I've read about it in
Thucydides.' If one of them had flu, they would make love. A
sprained ankle, a touch of the sun, an argument, a case of
writer's block, a leak in the boiler and they would make love.
They were happy to be Elliot and Kate, a cosmic unity, a new
astral body. She would spend hours painting unnameable
seascapes in oranges and blues, which she would then wet
under the shower to give them a pastel touch — a Chinese
technique, she would stoutly maintain. She played the piano —
Bach was her favourite composer — and it was torture to listen.
You would have thought she was stomping up and down the
keyboard in hobnailed boots. But Elliot loved these things. He
adored everything about Kate, even the telegram from Blackwell's which had served as a rag to wipe the dip-stick — but
there the ecstasy had stopped: for, a second later, Kate had
hurled the stone.

And from that second on, Elliot had been running away
from Kate. He was still running away from her in France, every
day, from morning till night: he ran away from everything
which even remotely reminded him of her poise, her courage,

her cheerfulness, her full lips, her smooth hands, the lightness of her tread. He couldn't bear the slightest sign of happiness in those around him. He hated intimacy, especially the intimacy of the breakfast table, he hated virtuoso songbirds and dogs that lie at your feet. When he was working in his room at Incarville he would sometimes − really without thinking − draw the curtains as dusk was falling, because the blue of the sky was taking on a touch of orange, or because he had just caught sight of Monsieur and Madame Seyn walking under the trees of the park, arm in arm.

Madeleine, with her Ancient Rome, and her poetry − so un-American, and which she delivered so well − with her tears, and her *Angst*, and her coolness in bed, protected Elliot from the pain of remembering. The existence of her husband Gilles, and her desolate departures in the small hours, the endless complications of a life lived apart, gave Elliot every opportunity to indulge his deep-rooted hatred of what is called 'the couple'. This hatred extended to the books he had written when he was with Kate, and which were his best ones, for they had been a continuation on paper of the absurdities and joys of their life together. Nowadays Elliot saw them as mere trash, mechanical verbiage, the work of a writer who wanted success at any price. Ugh!

A right farce! Whenever Elliot thought back to the day he had been awarded the Pulitzer Prize, and the reception at the Plaza which Kate and he had attended together, that pat little phrase she so often used would come back to him: 'We'll make a right farce of it.' And this is what Kate for her part did, picking up a man during the course of the reception. Elliot had seen nothing, hemmed in as he was by lighting cables and microphones, with idiotic compliments coming from every side and champagne flowing. He couldn't stand the stuff, really, but he drank it on that occasion just to calm his nerves. Through the hideous throng he could only catch glimpses of Kate − her superb bare shoulders, her teeth, her eyes, and the blue rose, wilting and sublime, which she had stuck right on top of her head. On the way back to the country that night, he was surprised that Kate, who was unusually quiet and aloof, didn't notice that he wasn't himself. He was suffering from a migraine and fell asleep at the wheel. They ran into a tree. He wasn't hurt in the slightest. She injured her forehead and broke a knee.

The accident was nothing, she said. Indeed, they were lucky to have come off so lightly. But over the next few weeks at home, Elliot found her too different from her old self. No more water-colours; no more *Well-Tempered Clavier*. She seemed half-dead. He was tempted to wonder whether the doctor hadn't been too hasty about her head X-rays. And after a sleepless night spent trying to devise ways of persuading her to go back into hospital, he found her there in the kitchen, all freshness and cheer, holding the marmalade pot in one hand and a stone in the other.

Kate left. Elliot stopped writing. Somehow, he survived. The spring of 1916 arrived. Elliot enlisted and went to the Front to treat his black despair as others go to a spa to cure their rheumatism. He found the war forlornly tedious, for the madness of the slaughter was nothing compared with the promiscuity, the empty talk, the nights spent lying awake or waiting for the next unforeseeable attack. But he liked France: he liked the villages, the crooked streets, the blue steeples, the irregular walls of the barns and the simplicity of the people. Taking up residence in Paris after the Armistice, he wrote a book in the space of two months in which he killed Kate. He described nothing but the trenches, and the mud, and the cold.

He killed Kate – well, it was easily enough said. Whole areas of his being remained under her sway. She was everywhere. One shameful killing was not enough: she had to be killed every day. Blood . . . Elliot shook himself awake. The periods of life. How long had he been lost in the contemplation of those embarrassing, fascinating bloodstains on the sheets?

Madeleine had calmed down now: she was lying with her eyes open, resting. He had put an end to her tears by taking off her nightdress and caressing her shoulders; and she for once had offered no resistance, almost enjoying the rather less therapeutic embraces which followed. Elliot found something both optimistic and fraternal about the bloodstains, which Madeleine had not yet noticed. It was as if Madeleine were incapable of shedding anyone else's blood, any blood but her own. And it dawned on him, although still only vaguely, that the affection he felt for Madeleine sprang precisely from the fact that she wasn't Kate – because she didn't have the nerve to ditch her husband.

'Where are you going?' asked Madeleine, seeing him put his shirt and pullover back on in a single movement: the incredible agility and speed with which he got dressed never failed to amaze her.

'I'll be back in a moment. I think you ought to have something to eat.'

'But I'm not hungry.'

'You could surely manage a little bit of salad and some compote . . .'

'It's Sunday, everywhere'll be closed . . .'

But Elliot wasn't listening: he was already on his way out. On his return, he found Madeleine fully dressed. She was brushing her hair in the mirror above the mantelpiece. He saw her from behind, with her hair falling about her shoulders: she looked like an adolescent and Elliot thought to himself, not for the first time, that she seemed much smaller at home than on the stage.

'I must be getting back,' she said, turning round to face him.

'And what if you were to stay?'

'What do you mean?'

'Exactly what I said! Only a moment ago you were saying that you wanted to live with me. Well, do it!'

And, hypocrite that he was, he unpacked on to the table

some pike pâté, cucumber salad, chicken *chaud-froid*, lemon tart and a bottle of champagne – all the things which Madeleine loved when, by some miracle, she was hungry, and which he himself loathed.

Oh, it was easy not to go back. It was easy to leave one's husband – to leave the lake, and the beech trees with their blackbirds, and the blue kitchen, and Elliot's strong arms which could hug you hard enough to break your ribs, and his lopsided face, all unshaven and uncombed when he wouldn't drag himself away from his typewriter. It was easy to deprive him of the face he loved, and which was more radiant than ever because it was saying farewell to him. Not the hint of a tremble or a blush. All neat and clean in her light-coloured dress which still smelt fresh from the ironing, quite without malice, quite without regret – at least, not revealing any – Kate simply turned the page. And Elliot, trying to do the right thing, or perhaps in order to foster the illusion that, despite all the bravado, she herself was in need of comforting – Elliot said the most deranged things, things he would never have thought himself capable of saying: *You're right, Kate, one has to have the courage to live one's own life . . . Once you get into habits, they start destroying your soul, and love itself can become a habit . . . You have to be able to break out and go your own way . . . And let's not indulge in scenes, we promised ourselves we wouldn't . . .*

Then he had rushed into the kitchen and poured himself a large glass of water; and, as she was still there when he came back, he called her every name he could think of before jumping into his car and tearing off.

'Elliot, my love, what are you thinking?' – Madeleine's voice came from somewhere miles away – 'You're not here at all . . .'

'Aren't I? I'm sorry . . . Look, there are strawberries, too, the first of the season: would you like some?'

She took hold of both his hands, and looking him straight in the eye, said, 'Elliot, what I was saying a moment ago – I meant it, believe me, you must believe me ... I'd lost my nerve, and then you came along, and I threw myself upon you. I wanted nothing but you – and I was quite serious, as I am now when I say that I love you ... But Elliot, don't hate me for this, don't be angry with me, I beg you – Oh, you'll never be able to understand, I know, but you must try, you must try and help me ... *I can't leave him, I can't not go back ...*'

And Elliot hugged her to him.

XXVII

Once Madeleine had gone, Elliot slowly wandered around the flat, his hands behind his back, looking in a desultory, absent-minded manner for a typing eraser which he seemed to remember having tidied away somewhere. At the foot of the bed he found a tortoise-shell hair slide. He opened the window which gave out over the little courtyard. Then he sat down in front of the dinner which Madeleine had left untouched. She had been right. Elliot had not gone running to the head waiter of the Lapérouse across the road and begged him to make up a hamper because he thought Madeleine should have something to eat, but because he wanted to see her reaction. It had been a test, as the rivals of Frederick Taylor would say. Elliot tried the pike pâté. It was too insipid for his taste. Catching hold of the four corners of the tablecloth, he picked up the meal with one hand and went downstairs to throw it into the dustbin, which had already been put out on the pavement.

He went back upstairs. He sat down in front of the empty table. He wasn't sleepy. He felt perfectly well. Not the slightest twinge of sadness. He was amazed. He tried to tempt himself with images of Kate cycling across the grass by the lakeside; he pictured himself bursting in on her when she was in the bath, with just her head in an incredible rubber cap like a soup tureen emerging from a huge cloud of pink foam. No effect. He was done with Kate. Signs of obsession – none! He felt an enormous emptiness. All he wanted was to get used to it.

It was in this state of numbness that he returned to Incarville. The train was likewise empty. He walked the length of the corridor, looking at the Seine whenever it came near the train, or the ruins up on the heights. The grey blinds of one compartment were down, though not fully, and through the window Elliot could see a fat young woman whose face and clothes and fingernails were stridently coloured: she was in fits of laughter and one of the buttons of her bodice, which was swollen like a balloon, was just about to pop off. She was leaning forward to be nearer the puny little man on the opposite seat: all got up in his Sunday best, his dyed hair carefully pomaded, he was using a silver spoon to eat a cold omelette which must have contained at least a dozen eggs, and which he had on a cardboard plate on his lap. Every couple of mouthfuls, he would feed a piece into the mouth of his companion and they would break out in gales of laughter. There were two bottles of wine propped up on one of the window-seats. They'll soon be wildly at it, thought Elliot, and moved on to another carriage.

Leaving Incarville Station, he set off on foot towards the coast, avoiding the village, whose brown brick buildings he found depressing by night, and taking instead the country road which bypassed it. He could hear the sound of frogs. Suddenly a car's headlamps lit up the road from behind. The car pulled up right beside him: it was the Seyns.

He climbed in the back, secretly annoyed that he would have to find something to say for the next few minutes in order to keep up a semblance of conversation. But the Seyns, who were doubtless on their way back from Honfleur, didn't offer a word, except to wish him good evening in their usual friendly way. He regretted the selfishness of his reaction, settled himself down in the back seat, and then, looking at the dashboard of the Peugeot, said out of the blue, 'Looking at all those square lights, you'd think it was Manhattan.' Feeling, perhaps, the profound sadness of this remark, Marie-Aynard turned round in her seat and gently touched his hand. And Elliot was so struck – despite the darkness – by how terribly ill she looked, that he squeezed her hand in response, far too hard.

Elliot had got on very well with Madame Seyn right from the start. He had been introduced to her by Yves Seyn when they bumped into one another in the Parc Monceau one day. Elliot and she had looked at one another and shaken hands, and a flying football had hit Elliot in the face. They had all burst out laughing and Marie-Aynard had taken a large chequered handkerchief from her bag for him to wipe his face on. He had experienced none of the usual sense of constraint on meeting her: it was as if they had always been good friends. Elliot would often sit in the park with Madame Seyn, discussing books – she was an inveterate reader. They would swap new titles and she would sometimes ask him to bring this or that book back from Paris for her – a Nietzsche that was out of print, or a Chinese Jesuit that simply wasn't to be found. Elliot however knew a bookseller by the name of Bloch in the Rue Saint-Honoré, near the Place Vendôme, who would bring down from the mezzanine to the shop on the ground floor any treasure Elliot asked for: tearing down the spiral staircase, he would bang the books together loudly and exclaim, 'Excellent, young man, excellent! Since when have they learned to read in America?'

A year before Jeanne's arrival, Elliot had spent three whole months at Incarville. The house was still quiet in those days and he had been able to get a lot of good work done. When he felt ready to write another book, he went back there, just as one goes on putting one's money on a winning number. Incarville became essential to him. He felt both protected and ignored in the household, and every day he encountered the evidence of some kindness – a new arrangement of roses on his table, a freshly laundered shirt on his chair, a bottle of bourbon in the drawing-room, and, in the 'refrigerating unit', the remains of a leg of mutton.

Elliot had met Yves Seyn in New York shortly before the war. Seyn had just lost his first wife at the time, and Kate had her leg in plaster. She would lie quite motionless on the couch for hours on end. Elliot was worried: Kate was drawing away from him, silently but at full speed. He didn't want to believe what was happening. He immersed himself in his work, writing night and day. Thinking that Kate ought to have some company, he gave her a dog: it had a soft, red coat and was extremely affectionate. Kate didn't even look at it. The dog, knowing that it was unwanted, went over to Elliot and lay at his feet whilst he was typing. Elliot thought that having friends to stay might help take Kate out of herself. Seyn was one of the people he invited. He spent several days with them, but, having more detachment than Elliot, he very quickly fathomed what was going on: feeling embarrassed by the whole situation, he chose to go off on long walks in the forest, accompanied by the dog, who would bring him back home every evening. Without him, Seyn would never have found his way.

When he was demobbed in November 1918, Elliot called round on Seyn at his flat in Rue de Courcelles. He found him remarried and rejuvenated. His legal practice was already picking up again. Elliot asked him to look after his European copyrights. Seyn had little experience in this field, but he accepted out of friendship. Elliot's books weren't finding takers: Spain was keeping an option on one or two, London and Milan were dragging their heels, and Germany had no paper. In Paris, however, a young editor by the name of Kra bought up his Pulitzer Prize-winning novel and promised to bring out another if the first took off.

Elliot's trust in his lawyer was such that he left his Smith-Corona permanently at Incarville. Elliot's worldly goods consisted of this machine, six pairs of thick woollen socks, which he wore in August as in December (his ankles were sensitive to the cold), a few black jumpers with holes in them, and his eternal cowboy trousers; the only respectable outfit he possessed was a grey herringbone suit he had bought in a shop called Old England to wear when he went to 'listen to poetry' at the Comédie-Française. Elliot also owned a small apartment in New York, on Fourth Street East, which he was loath to give up because his mother had left it to him. It served principally as a free zone for cockroaches and a lumber-room for his friends.

XXVIII

Elliot loved to hear the Peugeot's tyres rolling across the gravel of the drive: the dry, scrunching sound they made always put him in mind of waves running up a beach. Like the Seyns, Elliot had been fondly hoping that the invasion of the house might have subsided somewhat by now. But through the open windows of the library – as the room was called, although it didn't contain a single book, just a piano and some chairs – could be heard laughter, and exclamations, and scraps of Russian ('that Lapland patois', as Elliot called it) and, coming from the piano, some most unusual music. It wasn't the black music with which Elliot was familiar – African music, Chicago-style – although it had something of it, in the rhythm at any rate, and in the violent punchings-out of wild, cleverly constructed chords.

'Is that what they dance to at the Châtelet?' asked Elliot.

'Yes,' Marie-Aynard replied, in tones of resignation, 'but there they have horns and drums and goodness only knows what else.'

Marie-Aynard had insisted on putting Elliot in the most secluded room of the entire house. The outside wall was slightly curved, with a large oval window which pivoted in the middle, through which the view of the surrounding countryside, and people, and even cars and the ultra-modern lawn-mowers Monsieur Nivois used to cut the grass, took on an anachronistic look. The sky was incredibly full of stars that night – very black, and with the brilliantly white stars, which seemed extraordinarily close, leaving trails of gold in their wake. It was far too hot for Normandy, the kind of night one associates with Provence – only the cicadas were missing. The air, full of the scents of plants, was almost palpable. Leaning from the window-sill, Elliot felt far, far away from the interior of the continent, right on its edge, as though he were protected by so much space. He studied the gaps in the foliage and ran his eyes over the great sweep of the carefully tended lawn, which the moon had transformed into a silver tray. The marvellous feeling of emptiness which had come with Madeleine's departure was still with him. He tried to remember a speech he had heard her deliver a few months previously, and which he had proceeded to learn by heart: *De cette nuit, Phénice, as-tu vu la splendeur?* The following rhyme was *grandeur*, he was sure of it, but he couldn't remember the words which would get him to *grandeur*. He wanted to go back and start the speech from the beginning, but suddenly the words just slipped away and all he could hear was Madeleine's voice and the divine music she created out of them. And as when, sailing a small boat not far out from the shore, one hears, wafted on the changing breeze, now the shouts of the children on the beach, now the ringing of a chapel bell coming from somewhere further down the coast, so Elliot let himself be hypnotized by the sublime melody of Madeleine's voice and then suddenly lost it, hearing only a smattering of words – *temps, trembler, Titus* – which, robbed of the music, meant nothing to him.

But it didn't matter: he was just amusing himself, no more, watching in the sky the nape of a woman's neck and her heavy bun trace themselves in filigree upon the round cameo of the moon. He felt fine. He was getting over Kate, the memory of whom no longer caused him pain; he was getting over Madeleine, whose stage voice was all he could hear now, not her sobs or complaints.

There was nothing new in this. Before settling down at his desk, Elliot was in the habit of emptying himself completely: he would put himself into a state of semi-somnolence, like an animal going into hibernation, so as to drift insensibly from the words that made up his life to the life that was in his words. And words became creatures of their own, some huge, some tiny, some happy, some sad, but all entirely real and with their own life to live. Lying patiently in wait, Elliot would then touch upon a real world, whereas during the daytime, moving amongst his fellow-men, he always had the feeling that he was living a lie. Every page he wrote was the result of this nightly wandering and, tucked away inside his real world, he would sometimes catch glimpses of things which had affected him in some way in the borrowed universe of the day. But the things of the day always came at him in complete disorder, fragmented and confused, whereas his living creatures of the night orientated themselves spontaneously around simple axes – birth and death, for instance.

Out of the void swam one entirely clear line: *J'ai cru que votre amour allait finir son cours*, and then isolated words – *erreur, toujours* – lost themselves in the modulations of Madeleine's voice, which Elliot found so transfixing: he forgot where he was, and let himself float away on the sound. Framed by the oval of the window, the perspective of the lawn, with the sharp stars and the silhouette of the trees, became a stage set upon which the actors would appear at any moment. And indeed, at the back of the stage, coming from the side where the greenhouses were, Elliot saw a light blur which moved. It gradually increased in size and then slowly divided into two more slender forms which then drew away from one another – one was Monsieur Nivois, who took the path towards the front gate, and the other was Miss Nastia, who came towards the house. Elliot's gaze followed her for a moment and then, when she was too close and too distinct, he looked across the lawn at a jasmine bush some fifty yards away.

A third light-coloured blur, further to the right, was coming towards the house now, taking a path which would lead straight past the bush. It could only be Yves Seyn's stepdaughter, that Jeanne from Russia, since whose arrival Elliot's Norman retreat had become a kind of dance hall every Sunday. This is all she meant to Elliot: a phenomenon, he thought. Tonight the phenomenon was gliding across the lawn in a white dressing-gown, with a white towel in her hand. Elliot held his breath. Like a hunter. He let her come nearer. Like a hunter. But she suddenly stopped.

From the top of the cliff, Jeanne had seen the phosphorescent glow of the sea and, at the risk of breaking her neck, had gone down for a swim. She was returning slowly, enjoying the feel of the close-cropped grass upon the soles of her feet and mentally preparing her next dancing class, when she suddenly saw the Summer Garden in Petersburg. It was the jasmine that did it. And it drowned everything in its scent – the avenue, the tram, Alexander's eyes, his cap. It was more than she could take. Losing her self-control for the first time since she had left Russia, Jeanne dropped her towel and threw herself on the jasmine bush as one throws oneself upon the neck of someone in whom one has complete trust. She grabbed hold of its branches, burying her face in its mass of blossom, and she started to cry, foolishly.

Had he been his usual defensive self – had this happened during the daytime, that is to say, in the world of men – Elliot

would not have been moved by the spectacle. Cuddling trees?
Why not? There was no knowing what these bizarre Russians
weren't capable of – no need to make a big thing of it! But
standing at the window that night, Elliot's defences were
down: he had already set off into his own world, he was
imagining, he was literally making things out of nothing.
There hadn't been a drop of rain since the morning – so why
were the dressing-gown and the hair which he clasped to him
soaking wet? The dressing-gown was open and underneath
was a naked body with unbelievably long, firm thighs. Her
mouth was moist; he kissed her lips, which had a taste of
flowers both burning and fresh. There radiated an energy such
as he'd never known before, an abandon which at the same
time was a force, that of life itself, and its triumph! Tears
flowed and he drank them, he drank everything, the whole
woman, the jasmine blossom, night . . .

Of course none of this actually happened. Safely hidden
away at his window, Elliot was simply aware of Jeanne's
solitude and the charm of her naked feet. He did not undo her
dressing-gown. But Elliot's creative energy was now unleashed:
he could finally leave the window-sill and start hammering
away at his Smith-Corona. Images and words and, above all, a
certain rhythm, had been liberated: they were free to live and
run and shout, and give rise to a world – not the world of
Incarville and Jeanne in her white dressing-gown, but that of
the Argonne offensive. Elliot was writing another book about
the war: he felt he hadn't said enough in the first. Between a
river and a wood, in a field transformed into a quagmire by
the shelling, two infantrymen, one American, the other
German, keep up a conversation through the night from their
respective trenches. There are stars in the sky and not just the
stars of flares. Elliot could still see, precise in every detail, a
lorry lying there with no wheels, and the broken weathervane
pointing the wrong way on the church spire, and – unbeliev-
able sight – one half of a horse which, flung into the air by an

exploding shell, had lodged itself in the fork of a walnut tree. He could still hear the German phrases which he himself had spoken. And with the tricks the words played on his table in Incarville, as he tried to recreate that night in Argonne, he could not in all honesty have said how much was inspired by what he had been through before the war, with Kate and the birds and the stone, and how much by what had happened since, the whispered exchanges with Madeleine in the semi-darkness of the auditorium whilst rehearsals were in progress, the secret rhythm of the poetry of *Bérénice*, or indeed how much by the image – scarcely one hour old – of Jeanne flinging herself headlong at the jasmine in the middle of the night. Paradoxically, it was the war which shed such a flaring light on the scene in the garden. Thus he wrote – thus one writes, weaving in every direction the unrepeatable threads of the days one has lived through.

XXIX

On the stroke of seven in the morning, Elliot suddenly felt hungry. He went down to the kitchen and set about attacking the contents of the 'refrigerating unit'. He wolfed a herring, pinky-beige and as soft as butter, some pieces of a curious cold chicken dish, very brown and crisp, which had obviously been marinated, as it tasted of mint and plums, and a creamy white pyramid-shaped cake, decorated with little balls of every colour. These Russians may be cracked, he thought to himself, but they certainly know how to cook! And now something to drink . . . There was a crystal carafe covered in condensation with some sort of still drink in it – not entirely colourless, slightly amber, with bits of black leaf floating on the surface. Tea leaves, surmised Elliot: lemonade with tea leaves. After four or five swigs straight from the carafe, his head started reeling. Elliot felt like a fire-eater.

A pleasant, cooling draught came over him and Jeanne entered the kitchen, appearing not to see him; she was wearing a one-piece silk dress which had a mass of tassels at the neck, the waist, the bosom, the knees, the ankles and the hips. It was more like an outfit for a baby. Elliot stared fascinated at Jeanne's oversized swaddling-clothes and noticed the freckles on her forehead and cheeks. Mute and motionless, he stood there with the carafe in his hand, his gaze following Jeanne who, turning her back on him, proceeded to open a cupboard and put a saucepan on to boil.

Elliot had been devouring the leftovers from the Russian Easter with a clear conscience – the conscience of a worker who knows he has done a good job. A nightworker. The sun rises, work is finished, you go home to get some sleep, why not linger a little, not for any particular reason, just for the pleasure of it, just because you feel pleased with yourself . . .

Elliot was no longer a soldier in Argonne. The soldier had fallen into a well. He felt unattached, like a sail which has been loosened and hangs like an old sheet. Was it the effect of that lemonade? He thought so. But, seeing Jeanne, who still had her back to him, warm the teapot and take out a blue tin with the word CHINA on it, it suddenly dawned on him: all that was missing was the marmalade. That old twinge went through him: he was in a kitchen again, at breakfast-time, with a woman. With Kate.

She was lying on a rattan sofa in the kitchen, her plaster cast covered up by a shawl. She had stopped eating rusks; she had stopped eating eggs. She just drank herb teas and lemon juice, and was growing visibly thinner. Drinking his tea, Elliot watched her as she wrote a letter: she was using a breadboard to rest the paper on. Kate had stepped up her correspondence considerably since the accident: she would slip her letters into the envelope and seal it without adding the address. She turned her head away as she licked the envelope and, putting the breadboard down on the floor, closed her eyes. Elliot was beginning to get the feeling that she actually found his presence irritating. In an attempt to drive away this feeling, he went over and sat down at the foot of the sofa. He knew that Kate would have nothing on underneath her dress, as always when she was at home for any length of time: it allowed them to go mad on the spur of the moment. Elliot slipped his hand up her skirt, fondled her knee, went higher, knowing the way by heart: she wasn't naked. She opened her eyes, took hold of his hand and removed it.

Jeanne turned back towards him, carefully holding a steaming cup in each hand. Kate vanished instantly, forgotten. Jeanne set the cups down on the corner of the table. Elliot sat next to her. Jeanne poured some of the scalding tea into her saucer and picked it up with both hands. Elliot was reminded of a cat and also – though why was unclear – of a celebration.

'You do odd things with trees,' he said. 'I've never seen anything like it.'

'It's not me who's responsible for the trees here – Monsieur Nivois does everything.'

'I was referring to the jasmine.'

The colour drained from Jeanne's face and she put down the saucer. Feeling he had gone too far, Elliot hurriedly added, 'Tell me' – his eyes went to the carafe – 'just how strong is that lemonade?'

'About sixty degrees proof,' answered Jeanne. 'I make it myself: it's vodka and lemon juice, with a few tea leaves thrown in. Have you tried it?'

'Just a moment ago.'

'At this hour of the morning? Only the Russians do that! And then only if they've had a few too many the night before. The first thing they do is to knock back a big glass. It works wonders. No good, of course, if you've got the liver, as the French have.'

'Because the Russians don't have the liver?' asked Elliot, tickled by Jeanne's use of the definite article.

'It's something we don't have in Russia,' said Jeanne, calmly.

'And what do Russians have instead?'

'They have the heart.'

'Ah,' said Elliot.

'What about the Americans?' asked Jeanne.

'They have the dollar.'

'Have you?'

'A huge one!' said Elliot, grinning so that his teeth showed. 'As you seem to be a specialist in these matters, could you tell me whether there's an organ of sleep?'

'Well, it's your whole body, isn't it? From your head to your toes – you feel sleepy all over . . .'

'That's right,' said Elliot, rising to his feet. 'I'm wondering whether Russia doesn't act like a sleeping-draught on me.'

'Bravo!' said Jeanne, pouring herself some more tea. 'Now that's what I call knowing how to talk to women! See you very soon!'

Elliot shut the door behind him. 'Good God,' he said to himself, 'what's happening to me . . .?'

XXX

The tea had cooled down a little by now and Jeanne could drink it from the cup. She almost jumped out of her skin on hearing the mewing of a seagull: it was coming from so close that it seemed to be in the kitchen with her. Jeanne didn't like the mewing of gulls: it was too poignant a sound, almost human. She went over and shut the window. She didn't want to stay on her own in the kitchen. It was nothing to do with Elliot; she had already forgotten him. 'I'm not well,' she said to herself – a feeling of helplessness welled in her, and she was on the point of tears – 'I just can't manage on my own this morning. I'll go up and see Mother. No, that's the one thing I mustn't do! What will she and her gentleman think if they see me in this state?'

Marie-Aynard and Yves Seyn, her mother and this elderly man with the big feet and the grey hair one could almost call long, certainly too long for a successful lawyer: Jeanne found them touching. They were strange parents to have: two lovers, two big kids. The lengths Jeanne went to in order not to spoil their happiness! She had said nothing about the pillaging of the house at Beriozy, or the death of Igor, or the disappearance of Alexander. Not a word. She had all the more reason to say nothing about the massacre at the Café Catalan, either – though she scarcely thought about it now, having blotted it from her memory, almost.

When people Marie-Aynard and Jeanne had known back in Russia, and who had now fled to France, told them – either in Paris or at Incarville – about the atrocities committed in the civil war, and the famine, and the gangs of children scouring the countryside in search of a handful of corn, battering dogs and birds to death with sticks, Jeanne would feign astonishment so as to avoid the anxious looks coming from her parents. It didn't cost her much to act the innocent: as far as disasters went, she had had more than her share. What she had to do now was to learn to live again, without being too bowed down by them. And in order to do this, she would distort things in her own mind. It was not a conscious process: she simply played down everything that had happened. Alexander, killed upon the railway tracks by the Reds, or by the Greens, because they had thought he was a White, might just as easily have fallen victim to a German shrapnel shell or a dose of Spanish flu. If the old pianist had to lose consciousness, a cerebral haemorrhage might have been the cause, just as well as 'the barber's hand'.

Trying to dull the pain of the wounds which hadn't healed, Jeanne preferred to think of the Revolution and the civil war as natural disasters, rather like seismographic phenomena, perhaps – bound up with the movements of the heavens and the earth, and not with the class struggle. In her view, no one could be called either innocent or guilty: she had not adopted the ideas which used to be kicked around all night long in that smoke-filled flat in Pushkin Street. But the sparkle, the gaiety, in Isaak's eyes, and then the bullet-hole in his forehead – these things had marked her forever, even if she refused to think about them now.

Less able to forget than she wished, Jeanne was almost daily amazed at the fact that life here – that is to say, elsewhere – went on. That Easter was celebrated. That Paris was raving about her fellow-Russians' ballets. And even that the jasmine was in blossom. Nevertheless, she was a party to all these aberrations, her protest rendered mute by an innate, primitive respect for life itself. She pressed on. She silenced her demons. She didn't like shows of despondency. Yet she felt like crying this morning. Almost eight o'clock, she said to herself: so much the worse, I'll go up anyway – I'd better give Mother a kiss before I catch my train.

XXXI

At the end of the corridor on the first floor, she knocked on the door of the Seyns' apartment.

'Jeanne!' said Yves Seyn. 'What a pleasant surprise! Why don't you come up more often?'

'I was just wanting to say good morning to Mother. I'm off to Paris in a moment.'

'Oh, dear! Your mother's not feeling quite herself this morning and I've got to go to Deauville – I've an urgent brief to deal with.'

'What *are* you talking about, Yves?' came Marie-Aynard's voice from the bedroom. 'Come on in, Jeanne. Don't listen to him.'

Yves Seyn kissed his stepdaughter and picked up a dispatch-case.

'Sit down there,' said Marie-Aynard to Jeanne. 'He's just making a great thing out of nothing. I've got my period, that's all. And at my age it's not quite the same as with you.'

'You had a bad pain the day before yesterday, though . . . Perhaps you really ought to see a doctor.'

'Doctors can't do anything to help! But I'll go along, all the same . . . Yes I promise I shall. And how was your Easter celebration?'

'It went very well. Everyone danced, even Nastia – she looked lovely . . . Mishinsky was at the piano. I thought he seemed happier than he has been recently. He kept talking to me as he was playing – he's going to choreograph a new ballet. It's all over with nymphs and fauns – the dancers will be in tennis gear, on grass, with nothing else, no painted backdrop . . . He showed me an exercise book which was like a musical score: where the notes should go, he puts down symbols to indicate the various gestures and movements . . .'

Jeanne was speaking slowly, not thinking about what she was saying. She looked at her mother. A profound change had come over Marie-Aynard's face. There was a sickness there and not just in the eyes. Something had disappeared from her face, something which one never usually thinks about because it is, if one can use the word, implicit, and which one might call the sum total of all the signs which show that the skin is receiving irrigation. Irrigation by water; irrigation by blood.

By life itself. Stunned, Jeanne realized that her mother's face resembled a parched landscape. It seemed to have been drawn with a hard pencil: there was nothing there but the separate, exaggerated features which, no longer having anything to do with a unanimous life, had taken on another aspect, and had become neutral.

'What day are you going to see the doctor, Mother? I'll come along with you, if you like.'

'Good Lord, this is a conspiracy! . . . All right, so I don't look well. What of it? Neither do you when you've got your period, you don't –'

'Are you in pain anywhere?'

'My insides hurt a little . . . I'm just bleeding a bit more than usual, that's all . . . Tell me about Nastia – who did she dance with?'

'I'll tell you, but now you're going to make me miss my train . . .'

XXXII

Jeanne gave her dancing-classes in a converted joiner's shop, near the flower-garden in the Bois de Boulogne. The glass roof provided the light, and the floor had been relaid. The enormous mirror with its mottled, blackened surface, which covered almost an entire wall, came from the auction of the contents of a large house in the Opéra quarter.

Jeanne's pupils, who were for the most part the children of dancers, and all talented and pleasant to teach, were sent along to her by Mishinsky. Slava took an interest in the way Jeanne prepared her courses: he found a good deal wrong with the manner in which dancing was generally taught. At Incarville,

Jeanne and he would shut themselves up in the library and analyse in detail the exercises at the bar. They couldn't change the movements themselves – the ABC of the art, honed by generation upon generation of dancers – but they tried to find the origins of the movements and then relate them once more to the natural impulses of the body.

At what point does a spontaneous jump become a dance-movement? Where is the invisible divide between the two? Jeanne and Slava set themselves the task of reducing this divide, erasing it in the transition from one type of movement to the other. Jeanne showed how, in the exercise known as *jambe à la barre*, the head would come to rest more naturally upon the outstretched leg if one breathed out at that precise moment, and how simple *pliés* could be performed quite effortlessly, almost *ad infinitum*, if one located and coordinated two centres in one's body – the centre which produced the effort and the centre of one's breathing. All the impression of strain, which counteracted the elegance of the movement, disappeared when *pliés* were performed in this way. The two of them tried to dissect the things which Slava, virtuoso that he was, did without thinking, and to draw their inferences accordingly.

Jeanne talked a great deal when teaching, so as to make sure that everything be properly understood. Each of her explanations was like a story in itself: she took her examples from the movements which are common to all children – skipping, throwing a ball against a wall, swimming, playing with a hoop, or simply rocking a doll in one's arms – and, little by little, these movements became dance. The children enjoyed her lessons. Within a few months, even if the first position was not 'quite there', even if the pelvis was not fully open, they all learned to move in a graceful, balanced way.

'I don't know quite what your Mademoiselle Forestier teaches the children,' one of Mishinsky's partners said to him one evening before the show, 'but she's wrought an extraordinary change in my daughter. You wouldn't recognize Bronia: she's so relaxed and serene! And she's so different at home now – no longer waddling about like a duck with her head between her shoulders. She walks like Karsavina now, and – listen to this, Slava! – she's even giving me lessons . . . It appears I don't get out of bed the right way in the morning!'

'Dancing one's way out of bed,' said Mishinsky, with a smile. 'That sounds like Jeanne!'

It took the mention of Jeanne's name to make Mishinksy smile these days. He had been having trouble with his nerves for some time, and now he suffered from migraine almost every evening as he sat alone in his dressing-room before the show – minutes which had hitherto been the best of his life, marvellous minutes of relaxation. He was never frightened of going out on stage. A sense of calm would come over him as he put on his make-up and gradually slipped his way into the skin of the dancer who was going to go out there and perform miracles.

Little Bronia's mother left the dressing-room. Alone now, Slava Mishinsky started applying white greasepaint to his face with a spatula, putting on layer after layer. Why does he do it? What is he trying to be? What has he got to hide? With his face completely covered, the neuralgic throb in his head subsided somewhat. He broke off for a moment, eyeing himself keenly in the garishly illuminated mirror which had light blue bulbs running round all four sides of the frame. How like his father he was – his father, who had been a circus clown! Hadn't he become, indeed, his own father? He picked up a stick of black greasepaint and extended the line of his narrow eyes, then lifted his already very high-set eyebrows. One should never just slap a greasepaint mask on to one's face: the way to do it was to extend one's features by means of the mask, to become the other person one already is, the person who is already there inside. Don't imitate: remain that other person you are!

Sitting in front of the mirror, Slava felt quite weak. Not relaxed: actually weak. He was bereft of strength, bereft of all energy. No one would have guessed that his silk dressing-gown hid muscles of steel, immensely powerful muscles which were yet so supple and relaxed when he made his superhuman leaps. Slava was waiting for that sense of calm to come over him and for the throbbing in his head to stop completely. The idea that the calm might not come to him today was unthinkable: it always came. Vassily, his valet, came in to say that Monsieur's masseur was waiting. In a state of torpor, growing weaker by the moment, Slava replied, staring at his reflection in the mirror, 'Tell him to get lost. I don't need him any longer.'

He saw that Vassily didn't move; and then the enormous figure of Konyaev appeared in the mirror, with his big gold watch-chain across his stomach.

'Playing the prima donna, are we?' said Konyaev. 'Indulging our oh-so-precious feelings? . . . We're here to work, I tell you – the curtain goes up in fifty minutes.' (He had flipped open his pocket-watch.) 'Now, you just go and have your massage – this instant!'

His words fell on Slava's ears like the cracks of a knout. Slava cringed in expectation of the next one. But it wasn't a blow that came; instead, Konyaev seized a jug and splashed Slava's face with cold water. The black-and-white make-up ran. The whole lot needed taking off with cotton wool and redoing from scratch.

'Don't worry,' said Konyaev, standing behind him and squeezing his neck with both hands. 'You're my God, you're God Himself! You know that, my Slavotchka, my little clown-god . . .'

He stroked the nape of Slava's neck, and his voice took on a confidential tone. 'They'll all be falling at your feet, you wait and see . . . If you knew how many people there were in the auditorium this evening! It's amazing! And what people!'

'This little horse is finished,' said Slava, covering his eyes with his hands. 'He can't take any more . . . He's quaking with fear . . .'

'This little horse is a cretin . . . He's the strongest and most beautiful in the whole wide world! . . . Well, that's enough of that. Silko,' he called out to the masseur, 'get hold of him!'

The masseur grabbed hold of Mishinsky, laid him out on a bench, took off his clothes and set about massaging him. Slava closed his eyes. He was no longer suffering. Thoughts trailed in his empty head like lianas in a forest. He flitted promiscuously from one to another. Spies, the lot of them . . . They're only here to spy on me . . . Eyes everywhere you look . . . They're all against me, they want to destroy me, to rob me . . . To rob me of my God . . . I am God . . . I'm God because I love . . . I am Love . . . They all want something of me and I want nothing. I love . . . They want my death . . . My sister, my life, come over here, near to me . . . Stay with me . . . Put your hands here . . . Oh, they're killing me . . . I'm getting out of here, I'm going home . . . Mother's there, she's waiting for me. Jeanne too . . . He won't stop me seeing her . . . He's evil, but Jeanne's not evil . . . His name is Death . . .

'There we are, sir,' said Silko.

Grigoriev, the stage-manager, stuck his head through the door, 'Twenty minutes, Mishinsky!'

Slava got off the bench, sat down again in front of the mirror and wiped the black smears from his face with cold cream. He redid the white base and dusted it with flour. Not powder: real flour. And then he suddenly reached for the stick of greasepaint and redrew the black lines, as boldly as before, but any old way this time, all askew. He looked at himself in the mirror. He liked the effect. He even allowed himself a smile – but one so discreet that no one else would notice. He didn't recognize himself underneath the layers of make-up which tautened the muscles of his face. He was extremely pleased with himself. Vassily handed him his clown's trousers, chequered blue-and-yellow, his shirt with its zigzag hem, his orange wig and his blue hat with the tassel. Slava put everything on, then sat down again and gave himself a big red mouth, much bigger than his lips, thought for a couple of seconds and then added red marks to his cheeks, like bloody gashes.

The door opened once more behind him.

'Did you call?' It was Vassily's voice.

'No – Yes! Vassya, have a hundred roses sent to Jeanne at Incarville! . . . Thanks.'

The state of grace was coming back to him now: he could feel each separate muscle, one by one – all the way from his hips down through his thighs to the tips of his toes. Aware of his body, he could love it again. He couldn't have said what was going on in his head . . . He fingered the objects in front of him, revelling in their feel, his fingertips tracing the curve of a phial, the corner of a box, testing the elasticity of a waterbubble which had formed on the table-top, the velvetiness of the flour in its wooden bowl. The world of things came back to him. In a moment he would make himself loved.

'Mishinsky, you're on!'

Eyes closed, he made towards the stage. The boards, impregnated with resin, felt springy under his feet. Grigoriev took Mishinsky by the hand and positioned him on a spot marked by a little chalk cross, in between the two actors who were already there – the Dancer and the Arab. The backdrop represented a puppet theatre.

'Slava, what have you done to your face?' whispered the Dancer – Bronia's mother.

'Leave him!' said the Arab. 'He can't hear us now.'

Grigoriev and the stage-hands attached the strings to the ankles and wrists of the three dancers. The orchestra, which had been warming up in the pit, ceased playing their instruments. His eyes closed, Mishinsky crossed himself.

XXXIII

Jeanne found Yves Seyn sitting on the stairs, silently knotting his fingers. He had brought in a doctor from Deauville who was in the process of examining Marie-Aynard. That morning she had tried to move a chest of drawers: it was too near the window, she said, and casting a shadow on the floorboards. Coming up with the breakfast-tray, Nastia had found her on her knees where she had fainted.

'You can come up now,' said the doctor.

Yves and Jeanne went up into the bedroom, their eyes going immediately to Marie-Aynard, lying in bed there quite pale: she smiled at them, made a face behind the doctor's back and rearranged her hair.

'Who usually looks after you?' asked the doctor, using the inside of his sleeve to wipe a mark from his bag.

'No one,' said Marie-Aynard. 'I've never had the need.'

'A fine state of affairs! Well, that's all the more reason to have a few tests done. Four or five days in a clinic – that would be the best way. No need to go to Paris for such a small thing. You could have it done at Deauville, by Dr Dubois.'

'When are we talking about?' asked Yves Seyn.

'Tomorrow morning, if you like. You could take Madame Seyn there on your way to the office.'

'What do you say, Marie?'

'I don't seem to have much choice in the matter,' said Marie-Aynard, with a laugh.

'Oh, but you do have a choice, Madame. You could go to Paris and have it done at Professor Letellier's department. I'll give you an introduction.'

'Which department is this?' asked Yves Seyn.

'Gynaecology.'

'Mother has always liked watering-places. She doesn't like capitals,' said Jeanne.

'What would you choose, if you were me?' asked Marie-Aynard.

'Deauville,' said the doctor. 'The tests are quite straight-forward, and Dubois is very good.'

'Then we'll go to Deauville tomorrow,' said Marie-Aynard.

'If you have any pain this afternoon or tonight, take one or two of these. They're quite harmless, scarcely stronger than aspirin.'

He put a pink cardboard box on the little round table: it looked for all the world like a box of sweets. He was tall, still quite young, and dressed rather as if for a hunt. In place of a tie he wore a silk neckerchief knotted underneath his collar. He had intelligent, hazel-brown eyes and a tanned complexion.

'I'll see you out,' said Jeanne.

As they were going down the stairs, he said, 'This is a very beautiful house. I've never liked modern architecture before.'

'Yes, it is beautiful,' said Jeanne. 'My father-in-law had it built for my mother. By an English architect. He'd seen an enormous place on the Isle of Wight designed by the same man . . .'

And, whilst still speaking, she suddenly spun round on him, blocking his path.

'What's wrong with my mother?' she asked him – not loudly, but with an energy, and a passion in her eyes, which took the doctor aback.

'Oh, I don't think it's anything serious . . . There might be a slight hardening of the cervix . . . But there's no telling at the moment . . .'

Jeanne accompanied him out to his car. It was a De Dion. Her gaze was arrested by the radiator-cap, which was in the shape of a cormorant, its head sunk in its feathers.

Not a case for me! thought the doctor to himself as he drove back to Deauville. The young girl and the old man obviously adore her . . . It's a question of too much love – and there's nothing worse than a situation where love can do nothing . . . I'll send her along to Letellier when the tests have been done.

'He doesn't seem to think it's anything serious,' Jeanne told Yves Seyn, who had been waiting for her outside the door of the kitchen, far from happy. 'I think he knows his job.'

They took dinner in Marie-Aynard's bedroom. Nastia had prepared cold hake, a vinaigrette, and a *compote* of apples, pears and plums – a mixture which did not find favour with Yves Seyn. 'It's the Russian national *compote*,' insisted Nastia. 'Do make a bit of an effort!' Marie drank some cold *bouillon*.

'Slava will be sending me flowers this evening,' said Jeanne. It's the première of *Pierrot*.'

'They're already here,' said Yves Seyn. 'Didn't you see that Nastia had put them in the bath to soak? . . . The première was yesterday evening.'

'Ah,' said Jeanne sadly, noting that, with the worry Marie-Aynard had been causing her, she had been getting her dates muddled for some time.

'I've read the reviews,' said Yves Seyn.

'What are they like?'

'Ecstatic! . . . I'll give you the papers later, I left them in the car.'

'Rather insipid, your dinner, I'm afraid,' Marie-Aynard said to them. 'Why don't we have some champagne?'

'Would you drink some?' asked Yves Seyn in amazement. Marie-Aynard didn't usually like champagne.

'I would with you!'

Jeanne rushed off down to the kitchen and got an ice-bucket, three champagne glasses, a bottle of Clicquot and a tray. In the hallway she ran into Elliot, who had just returned, a cigar in his mouth and an extremely large flat cap on his head. He removed both.

'Having a little party up there?' he asked.

Jeanne shook her head with a kindly smile. Yves Seyn

plumped up the extra pillow which Marie-Aynard now used to prop herself up in bed. Jeanne found her sitting bolt upright in anticipation, and paler than ever. Her eyes no longer seemed to belong to the rest of her face. They were too large and they seemed to be elsewhere, or perhaps lagging behind her other features. Jeanne had seen those eyes once before, in Dasha: she could talk, she could even sing, but her eyes just weren't working. Marie-Aynard raised her champagne glass to her lips.

'I remember one day in Richelieu Street, when you were still just a tiny thing . . . A friend of mine – he was a navy doctor – gave you a few drops of champagne to drink. You went all red and serious, and said, "But Mummy, it tastes of grapes, it's only grapes . . ."'

She lifted her glass so that it was level with her eyes, and slowly recited, '"Only believe in what lies behind the door; I proffer this cup . . ."'

She handed the empty glass back to Seyn.

'And does it go on?' asked Jeanne.

'It always goes on . . . But I can't remember . . . Jeanne, you see that book up there on the top shelf, the one with the pink binding? Do you think you could . . .?'

Jeanne pushed a silk-upholstered armchair against the wall and got up on it.

'Oh, Jeanne, not with your shoes on! . . . Let me have a look, though: are they new? . . . They're pretty . . . When did you buy them?'

'I think it was last week . . . At a place in the Boulevard de la Madeleine . . .'

'You bought them yourself?'

'Yes.'

'Well, that's good! That's the first time you've gone out and bought a pair of shoes on your own . . . It's something you'll have to get used to now . . .'

XXXIV

'I'll have my book finished within the next couple of months,' said Elliot. 'And then I'll have to go to New York.'

Jeanne was kneeling on the floor of the kitchen, pouring milk into a saucer for two motherless hedgehogs which Monsieur Nivois had found in the forest. The words 'go to New York' seemed to register not on her ears, but somewhere between her shoulder-blades.

'Can't you post it?'

'I've got to go there anyway. The contract has to be discussed and I've got to see my lawyer. And there are various things to be sorted out – the lay-out, and the dust-jacket and so on.'

'How long will you be gone?'

'I don't know . . . I've got an apartment over there and I suspect it's falling to bits . . . I might have to undertake some repairs . . .'

Jeanne hated everything to do with departures and absences. She got to her feet. Judging by the way Elliot was attacking the remains of the roast beef and potato salad at this early hour of the morning, he must have worked right through the night.

'I didn't hear your typewriter in the night.'

'I had a hundred pages or so to correct by hand . . . Someone got up in the middle of the night to fasten a shutter that was banging above the garage. I think it was your mother. Is she not sleeping so well?'

'Oh, I don't think so . . . She's steadily improving.'

After the tests conducted by Dr Dubois in Deauville, Marie-Aynard had been taken to Paris to be seen by Professor Letellier. After several days of further tests, she had undergone an operation in yet another clinic. The surgeon told Yves Seyn that he had performed a hysterectomy.

The haemorrhaging ceased. Marie-Aynard had regained her

appetite and a little of her strength. At the beginning of June, Yves Seyn had brought her back to Incarville. She would come down and read in the drawing-room every morning. Leaning on Yves' or Jeanne's arm, she would go out to inspect Monsieur Nivois' plantations: he had plans to grow walnut trees, fig trees, almond trees and even a eucalyptus in the area between the cliffs and the greenhouses. 'We're not in Andalusia,' was Elliot's rather tart remark. 'And we haven't got the Gulf Stream, either,' added Yves Seyn, more gently. 'Just let me get on with it,' replied Monsieur Nivois. 'Back in the days of the English, in the Middle Ages, they planted all kinds of things here!' Towards evening, though, Marie-Aynard would feel tired. She went up to bed early. They all took dinner in her room: Elliot joined them now. He had stopped going to Paris. His meetings with Madeleine, which had become increasingly infrequent, had come to a complete halt for the moment: she was off touring in Rumania and then in Prague.

'What would you say to driving my Ford?' asked Elliot. He had finished the roast beef and was now attacking a Pont-l'Evéque cheese.

'You're asking me?'

'Yes. I'll be leaving it here while I'm away. You can have the use of it. I could try and teach you: there are plenty of quiet roads if you go out a bit into the countryside. Have you ever driven?'

'I've driven horses.'

'Oh, they're much more difficult! When shall we start?'

'I don't know. Yves Seyn is talking of sending Mother and me off to Venice. I really don't know: Mother isn't as well as all that, and Venice doesn't tempt me in the slightest –'

'You're wrong there!' said Elliot. He had never set eyes on Venice, but that didn't stop him from launching into a detailed, enraptured description of the place, culled from a German book which he had just finished reading.

His eyes went to the window as he talked. 'He always seems to be thinking about something other than what he's saying,' mused Jeanne; 'and perhaps that's part of his charm.' She scrutinized him. The only genuine animation she saw was concentrated in his eyes. His body, which seemed to have been hewn with no great care, was simply a dwelling for his eyes, nothing more. It wasn't really a body: it was a shelter, a place of strength and calm. The texture of his skin, the lines upon his face, seemed not to have been made by the passage of time. His body and face suggested a landscape situated in some temperate zone, but his eyes belonged to other zones, or rather, they travelled from one zone to another, eternal migrants. There was an unusual intensity in his gaze, but it lacked all insistence; the intensity was directed inwards, towards some incorporeal inner region which Jeanne perceived that morning as a place which was neither full nor empty, a place of welcome.

'Where do you live in New York?' Jeanne interrupted him.

'Downstairs from a cake factory . . . I can see them up in the sky, moving along on a conveyor belt between two roofs. They make them in white and pink . . .'

XXXV

Jeanne came out from her dancing class, exhausted. The children kissed her goodbye and set off home in pairs, laughing as they went. Across the blind alley stood a tall fellow dressed all in white, like a painter or a mason: it was Samuel.

'I thought to myself that with the summer holidays approaching, I'd probably have less chance of meeting you . . .'

'Oh, but they would have told you the way at Incarville Station!'

'Incarville?'

'Where I live. You've forgotten . . .'

Setting off beneath the chestnut trees of the boulevard which runs alongside the flower-garden, they made their way towards the Porte d'Auteuil. Children with satchels gazed after the horses of a school ride returning from the woods.

'They're speaking Russian,' said Samuel.

'There's a Russian grammar school just over there . . . I'm catching the train back to Incarville – why don't you come with me? The house is empty, or as near as makes no difference. My parents have gone off to Venice. You could swim in the sea.'

'I never swim.'

'Then you don't have to swim. You can brood mysteriously upon the cliff-tops. Your gaze will deign to alight upon something or other before painting it, or even as you're painting . . . You're not going to tell me you spend your whole life locked away in that studio of yours!'

'I'll come along, I promise. But I can't today . . . You wouldn't have time to come back to my place now, would you?'

'Your place? Why not – but I'm all filthy and sweaty from my dancing class . . .'

'There's a shower at my place.'

The driver of the taxi they got into – a middle-aged man with a goatee beard, who threw the car all over the road, remaining in second all the way and braking violently when occasion demanded – had a Russian look about him; but he didn't open his mouth once during the entire journey, contenting himself with giving them severe looks in the rear-view mirror. When, however, they got to Rue de la Glacière, and Samuel made to pay him, he said, 'No, no, there's no charge . . . I used to be a shipbuilder in the Petersburg dockyards. I'd spend hours wandering along the Nevsky, dreaming of meeting Vera Gaiy and being allowed to kiss her hand . . .'

And without another word, he put the car back into gear. Jeanne threw him her grey scarf through the window, 'You'll look good in it! God go with you! . . .'

Samuel had taken hold of Jeanne's hand. 'I haven't been out shopping yet. I'll take you back to my studio, and you can have a shower whilst I'm getting a few things.'

'No, I'll come along with you: I like shopping.'

They staggered back to the studio with their load of salad stuff and cold veal and fruit – dropping half of it, because they had no shopping-bag. Jeanne saw no sign of Samuel's canvases: the curtains were drawn across the great expanse of window. All that could be made out in the darkness were a few wooden boxes on the floor.

Pulling back the hanging a little, Jeanne saw that the recessed window looked out over a dismal concrete courtyard. Plumb in the middle was growing a solitary iris in a stand, a perfectly common iris, mauve with yellow stripes. Jeanne was put in mind of a prisoner, or an invalid – some condemned person, in any case. Not a jot of sunlight penetrated down to the bottom of the courtyard.

'There's courage for you,' said Jeanne.

'I'm sorry?'

'I was looking at that iris in the yard. Why are you laughing?'

'Don't blame me – I can't help it if you make me want to laugh!'

'My mother always tells me I make her want to laugh. I must have missed my vocation. It's all Gauer's fault – I'll write and tell him.'

She spread out on a piece of newspaper some little cucumbers, two tomatoes and a bunch of spring onions.

'This'll make a nice salad,' she said. 'But first, I must have a shower!'

'It's over there. There's nowhere to hang up a towel: I'll hand you one, but take care, I feel like making lo—'

'Well, so do I, so that's quite straightforward!' cut in Jeanne – although the matter was anything but straightforward for her.

Lovemaking had meant nothing to Jeanne ever since she had lost Alexander. But she had not been lying to Samuel. The idea had come to her out of the air, without her feeling anything in particular. What idea? The idea of taking a look at a man again . . . She found Samuel's evident lack of physical desire attractive. She liked his face and his hands, too. He was opening a bottle of white wine. 'Communion wine,' he was careful to explain; 'the cheapest you can get, and really very good. It's made by monks in the Morvan. You're not supposed to be able to obtain it on the open market, but you can see that the dealer has scratched out the label – he's actually only allowed to sell it to the clergy . . .' Jeanne took off her jersey and her woollen skirt, and, with nothing on but her black leotard, went over to the shower.

She washed herself very quickly, with cold water. Samuel handed her not a towel, but a towelling bathrobe which was in a more or less clean state.

'Can I keep it on?' asked Jeanne, sitting down at the table beside Samuel. She peeled and chopped the salad stuff and went over to the sink to give everything a rinse. Samuel downed his communion wine with the same mechanical speed she had noted at the Café de la Paix.

'Do you use oil or cream for the dressing?'

'Both.'

'And lemon?'

'We've got no lemons. Have to use vinegar.'

Without rising from his seat, he reached up, opened the cupboard and got down the bottle.

'Do you live on your own?'

'She lives in London.'

'English?'

'Russian. We were married in Vladimir in 1913. She's a painter too . . . Things are going well for her in London . . . But I can't work with other people under my feet.'

'So work comes first for you?'

'I suppose so,' he replied, with a slightly embarrassed air; and he stroked Jeanne's temple, and neck, and wrist with his fingertips. Then, with what was for once a semblance of energy, he stood up, pressed the light switch and illuminated the studio at last.

Jeanne saw, quite some distance from where she was seated, two paintings; one on an easel and the other propped up against the side of a table. Neither of the canvases offered any clear statement; nothing was directly portrayed in them. They were more like two great expanses of light, one tending towards pink, the other towards blue – but the colour was not important: both diffused the same light. It was a dusty, muted, much-sifted light, a remembered light. And, as if rocking on the gentle waves of this memory, the ghosts of objects would emerge by moments – though what they were was anybody's guess, perhaps a door-handle, or the corner of a half-open drawer, or a saucer . . . But Jeanne would lose sight of them immediately as they were submerged again in the light . . . Jeanne had never before seen paintings possessed of such little external reality. They were there, in the studio; and she could see the table, and the floor, and Samuel, who was standing there with a pensive air, looking at the paintings; and yet the two pictures seemed to be actually inside her, not outside at all. How long did she and Samuel stare at them in transfixed silence? Perhaps as long as an hour.

'It's starting to come,' said Samuel at last. 'But what about the salad?'

He sat down at the table and opened a second bottle. Jeanne turned her back on the paintings. Now that she had seen them, she felt closer to Samuel than before. The idea of making love with him was becoming more of a reality. As a matter of duty, she got dressed again. Then she tossed the salad.

'You remind me of my grandmother,' said Samuel.

'A very old lady?'

'Very old. She had the same hands as you, very small, and she used them in the same way. She would have held that spoon exactly as you're holding it now, with the same concern for the spoon . . . She could touch the very soul of objects. She used to say to me, "Go and rinse out this teapot immediately, otherwise it'll be ill, it can't stand cold tea-leaves . . ." I was always very happy with my grandmother . . .'

'And not since?'

There was a knock at the door. Samuel went to open it.

'Innokenti!' Jeanne heard Samuel exclaim. 'What on earth brings you to this part of the world?'

Jeanne recognized the visitor the moment he appeared: it was Innokenti Petrovitch, a friend of Alexander's. She had been to see him in Petersburg, at his house on the Moyka Embankment, in the February of 1917; he had just come back from the Front, bringing Jeanne a letter from Alexander.

She recognized him, but she found him greatly altered. She remembered him as an elegant, aristocratic officer, a poet who talked about the Middle East and expressed himself in a French which belonged to the eighteenth century. Now he was dressed in mufti and leaning on a walking-stick, speaking Russian and looking old and worn.

'Take a seat, Innokenti,' Samuel was saying. 'For a ghost from the past, this is —'

'We're all ghosts,' Innokenti cut him short. 'Just look at this lady! I'm not dreaming, am I? It *is* you? May I cross myself?'

'But of course!' said Jeanne.

They both crossed themselves and then kissed. Not in the least astonished, Samuel sliced the cold veal, brought another plate and poured the newcomer a glass of wine.

Innokenti stared wide-eyed at the wine, with stupor, almost horror, in his gaze. A heavy silence descended.

'Samuel, old boy,' he murmured at last, 'you wouldn't happen to have anything . . . um . . . anything a little bit stronger, would you?'

'Cognac?'

'Well, if you have it . . .'

Innokenti drank his cognac holding the almost brimful glass in both hands, just as a child would drink a glass of milk. His fingers were chilblained and his lips chapped. His jacket was threadbare at the sleeves. Jeanne had a vision of the dining-room in Moyka Street: the table bedecked with lace and flowers and crystalware, oysters on a bed of ice, golden wine, Innokenti's mother dripping pearls and silk – she could still hear her sounding off against Marx. As if he could guess what was going through her head, Innokenti said, 'My mother died last year. In the famine . . . Do you remember her?'

'I do,' said Jeanne; 'very well indeed.'

'You quite infuriated her with all your talk about the stars and historical necessity . . .'

'I'm sorry.'

'I thought it was a load of nonsense at the time. But you were right. Everything has worked out according to your plans.'

'They weren't my plans,' said Jeanne.

'It's all over with Russia . . .'

Jeanne had been expecting this. How many people had she listened to over the past few months, discoursing about Russia in apocalyptic terms, their pockets stuffed with diamonds? But she felt that something worse was to be expected from this man. He was going to cause her pain. He was doing so already, just with his broken voice and his sore lips.

'Samuel,' he said, 'do you think you could possibly lend me a pullover? I'm cold . . .'

And, as soon as Samuel had left the room: 'Alexander is in Petrograd. He's living with a woman. A schoolmistress. They're not doing too badly. Alexander is entitled to special rations as a surgeon . . .'

Jeanne saw black and felt she was falling.

'Alexander,' she said. 'But – but he's dead . . .'

'He's very much alive, believe me.'

'Sasha . . . But he was killed . . . At Sinelnikovo . . .'

'No, we're speaking of the same man. Alexander Illytch. I saw him at his place a fortnight ago. At her place, rather. His wife is —'

'*I'm* his wife!' screamed Jeanne.

'But — but,' stammered Innokenti . . . 'I didn't know —'

'Imbecile!' exclaimed Jeanne; and, sweeping everything off the table with a single movement, she rushed out of the studio.

XXXVI

July came along, and with it the summer holidays. The dance pupils left. Jeanne didn't set foot outside Incarville. If Monsieur Nivois was to be believed, the summer promised to be hot and too dry, and he was worried about his kingdom, especially the little Japanese trees — they were his latest thing, and he lovingly tended them to the point of no longer going back to his family in Dieppe on Sundays. A fine excuse, said the two Norman sisters, seeing, time and again throughout the day, Nastia and Monsieur Nivois returning from the further reaches of the park, hand in hand. It might do for that Russian, that Tartar — what else could you expect — but Monsieur Nivois was one of them, and a Catholic to boot. And what did that American get up to with Madame Seyn's daughter in the kitchen every morning? Sitting side by side like some elderly couple, she in her négligé, he all unshaven, with his hair not even combed! They didn't dare open the door any longer. What a household it was! Plenty of money, perhaps — but since when did money give people the right to live like heathens? And Madame Seyn, such a respectable lady, was in no position to put a stop to it all: she spent so much of her time in bed now; she was growing weaker again, and when, on rare evenings, she would take a few steps across the lawn, all but carried by her husband, she looked just like a little girl. Such a lovely person, they sighed, and departing this life so early!

Sunday was the sisters' day off. On Monday the house was still reasonably tidy, but every Tuesday, shortly before lunch, the barbarians arrived. And they kept no sort of hours: night and day they swam, and danced, and drank, and sang, endlessly talking – and then their craze for lighting bonfires outside, in this heat!

One Tuesday, as they were plucking ducks beneath the garage porch, they were approached by a man whom they had never set eyes on before. He had obviously got the wrong house, for he was asking after a certain Mademoiselle Forestier. It was the first time they had ever heard the name. At last they grasped that he was referring to Jeanne. Lisette requested the gentleman to wait in the hall, and ventured into the library. Madame Seyn's daughter was dancing an energetic tango with a great brute in tails, bald and with a pince-nez, who struck Lisette as anything but appetizing. Monsieur Mishinsky was at the piano. Mademoiselle Jeanne's cheeks were on fire, there was a haggard look in her eyes, and her dress – an evening dress – kept flying up and revealing her legs. Seeing the maidservant's obvious discomfiture, Mishinsky left off playing.

'There's a gentleman to see you, Mademoiselle.'

'A gentleman to see me! I don't believe it!' – Jeanne hugged Lisette – 'Did you hear that, Slavotchka? I still exist! . . . Show him in, show him in!'

Jeanne had drunk too much champagne that morning. She had been drinking too much for several days now – in the evenings, too, with Yves Seyn. They would sit together at Marie-Aynard's bedside (her doses of morphine were being stepped up all the time), and she would encourage them to

drink a little more than was good for them because it helped
them to talk and to forget about her for a while.

'Samuel!' cried Jeanne, seeing him framed in the doorway
of the library. She was sitting barefoot on the floor. The man
in tails was now at the piano with Slava, improvising a piece
for four hands.

'Sit down,' she said. Samuel did as he was told. They
listened to the music. Samuel began to grow impatient.

'Who are these people?' he whispered in Jeanne's ear.

'The one on the right is Mishinsky and the other, in black, is
the man who wrote the music for *Pierrot*,' said Jeanne, kissing
Samuel on the tip of his nose ... 'You know, you really do
have hands like a gravedigger's!'

'Their fingernails are black, not blue.'

'Ssh! It's beautiful, what they're playing.'

'I'm off!' said Samuel.

He got up and left. Jeanne caught up with him on the grass
outside; she took him by the hand and led him in the direction
of the path which ran down towards the beach.

'You're right,' she said. 'I need the fresh air. I've drunk
about five or six glasses too many ...'

'You'll hurt your feet,' he said, catching her up in his arms.

'Oh, but it's a long way ...'

'You're not heavy.'

'Your hair smells of daisies!'

'Try counting the petals,' said Samuel, clenching his teeth.

Down at the bottom, the sea was grey, becoming whiter near
the line of the horizon. The beach seemed to be floating in a
dense green luminosity. Tipsy as she was, Jeanne saw Samuel's
eyes going to work immediately. He was like a pointer at a dead
set. Quite motionless, an almost sinister look on his face, he
studied the light. Jeanne was no longer there for him; he didn't
see her take off her dress, plunge naked into the water, swim for
a while, return to the beach and run about to dry herself; he was
still there, frozen to the spot, lost in his own mysteries.

'I think I'm thirsty,' he said.

'We haven't got any Communion wine,' said Jeanne, slipping back into her long dress.

He took her up in his arms again. Half-way back along the path, near the clump of wild garlic, he was seized by a fit of giddiness.

'Are you in pain?' asked Jeanne.

'No, no . . . It's the beach . . . It was so beautiful . . .'

She was walking beside him now. In his face she saw the same expression of sorrow she had seen in his studio, when they were looking at his pictures. As they were nearing the house, he said to her, 'I have a letter for you.'

'A letter?' said Jeanne.

They came to a stop on the lawn.

'Innokenti gave it to me . . . He couldn't give it to you himself. You left in such a hurry . . .'

After some searching, he found, in the breast pocket of his shirt, a beige envelope, completely crumpled, and not rectangular in shape: it was a triangle. He held it out for her to look at. She read, in Cyrillic letters: *To Jeanne Forestier*. She knew the writing well enough. Samuel saw a ghastly look come over her: her lips trembled, she burst into tears and, waving the letter away with her hand, she stepped back without taking it.

'Sasha . . .' she said. 'It's from Sasha . . .'

'He loves you, Jeanne . . .'

He folded her in his arms and put her head upon his shoulder. Clinging to him, she sobbed, 'Igoriok loves me, Grigory loves me, Ivan Semionovitch loves me, Sultan loves me – they all love me . . . Why do I have to lose my mother as I lost all the rest?'

Samuel stroked her hair. Jeanne calmed down a little.

'That letter . . .' she said.

'It's here, in my pocket.'

'Sasha . . .'

He held it out to her again; and this time she seized it and screwed it up into a ball.

'It's all dead words . . . I don't want to . . . Samuel, tell me
. . . Tell me what he says . . .'

'Ah . . . Well. That he loves you . . . That he'll always love
you . . . That, finding you gone . . .'

'No,' she said, covering his lips with her finger.

And, averting her gaze, she took hold of his big blue hand,
opened it up, pressed the ball of paper into his palm and closed
his fingers over the top.

'You were thirsty,' she said to him. 'Let's go and ask
Nastia . . .'

XXXVII

What on earth's wrong with her? wondered Elliot. These days
his only encounters with Jeanne were first thing in the morning: the rest of the time, she might as well not have existed.
And they were hardly encounters: she would come into the
kitchen, sit down with a cup of tea, and murmur the odd
word or two, her mind completely elsewhere. Like a ghost
constantly drawn back to the same spot by a process of
tropism. She was losing weight. Was she going to slip through
his fingers and follow her mother? he asked himself. What
troubled him was the way she looked. This was really worry-
ing. He didn't dare discuss the matter with Seyn, because he
had been reduced to helplessness by Marie-Aynard's condition.
All he could do was to stay there, near to his Jeanne, waiting
for some improvement. He scarcely went to Paris any longer,
either to listen to poetry or for any other reason; and if he
occasionally consented to a brief meeting with Madeleine, in a
tea-room somewhere, he would find himself asking whether it
wasn't because he hadn't had the guts to make a complete

break with Kate. No, he concluded, simpleton that I am, I could do it now . . . And in this confessional mood he went on to tell himself that he had his book to finish – only about twenty pages – and that, for achieving this, Incarville remained the island of his dreams.

One evening in early August, Jeanne appeared in the drive. Elliot had just come back from Trouville. She smiled and gave him a kiss. She wanted to learn to drive the Ford. It took only a few lessons before she was handling the car superbly. The business of operating the pedals and the gear stick, and of taking bends, gave her endless pleasure: she would sit there like a child with a new toy, her face flushed with excitement. She started laughing again. Her laughter was too loud for Elliot to believe that she was really happy, but all the same . . . Returning from one of their lessons together, Elliot found a telegram from his friend John Peterson, sent from Dublin: Peterson said he would be passing through Paris soon, and suggested a meeting at the Closerie des Lilas on August 15th.

They had last seen one another in a military hospital in 1918. Elliot had an injured arm, which was nothing at all, but John Peterson was, according to the nurses, a mortuary case. A journalist on *The New York Times*, over six feet tall, with straw-blond hair and a ruddy complexion, he was difficult to ignore; and then he had a talent for getting himself into the most impossible situations in the course of his reporting, trusting always to his lucky star. To get a better view of what was going on, he had the brilliant idea of striding about between the lines with his racing binoculars. He had received a discharge of shrapnel in his chest and his posterior – a posterior of which he was very proud, for it was, despite his size, extremely slim. In no man's land this slimness didn't help him. He had come out alive, as usual. Since then, he had drunk like a fish.

It should be that he was marvellous at holding his liquor, despite the little that was left of his body. On the evening of August 15th, he was on his fourth 'Desert Dream': he went over to the bar to prepare each of his cocktails himself, claiming that the barman didn't have the knack.

Elliot admired John. He was a great journalist: accurate and impartial. And he had a quality which Elliot himself lacked: a presence of mind which allowed him to write things down immediately. Elliot had had proof of his talent when he read, in *The New York Times*, accounts of battles in which he himself had been involved. John was at home in the midst of catastrophe, in living hells, in hopeless situations: he could explain the whole business to you in the space of a hundred lines. He was possessed of very seductive looks, with his soft, black, doglike eyes and his great blond head. Women fell into his arms. He would rock them a little, then set them back on their feet with an encouraging slap on the shoulder. He made no secret of his puerile conviction that he would one day meet 'the woman of his dreams'.

He had met her. Five or six times over. She was never the right one. And it was never reciprocal. Kate had been one of them. He still dreamt of her. He told Elliot this at the Closerie; an hour or so earlier, he had moved on to 'Angel's Kiss', a more deadly mixture. How he had infuriated Elliot, back in the hospital, with his endless paeans of praise to Kate . . .! This evening Elliot was able to listen to them with more tranquillity. But when John, encouraged by such a sympathetic listener, grabbed Elliot by the shoulders to make him understand how Kate had Egyptian ankles, the most perfect in the world, Elliot begged him to change the subject. What was he doing in Paris? He was on his way to Red Russia – Petrograd, Kiev, Moscow, utter chaos. In the cities, the people were starving to death, and the peasants were setting fire to the goddamn countryside! Where else in the world could he go? He downed another 'Angel's Kiss' and was getting angry when he suddenly lapsed into silence, staring in the direction of the door.

A bizarre group of characters were making their entrance. Elliot recognized Mishinsky, white as a sheet, a top hat perched askew on his head and a camellia in his buttonhole. Immediately behind him came Konyaev, his impresario – frilled shirt, gold chains set with precious stones, cigar; a big tall man whose eyebrows were probably dyed. But John Peterson was only looking at the woman who was with them: she was wearing a long grey dress of pleated silk and elegant, flat-heeled golden sandals, and her chestnut hair, caught up in a bun, seemed to form a cloud of mist above the clear, pure lines of her face, with its high cheekbones and troubled eyes. Elliot, who, for the first time since the night with the jasmine, was seeing Jeanne from the outside, as it were, felt his heart miss a beat. As though forewarned, she turned around, spotted him – and her face lit up with such a smile that Elliot thought to himself, 'She must love me a little.'

'You're not going to tell me you know that woman?' whispered John.

'Er . . . Actually, yes . . . She's the daughter of Madame Seyn, the owner of the house at Incarville . . .'

'That house where you work? And what do you do with her?'

'We take morning tea together.'

Breaking away from her friends, Jeanne came towards them.

'That's not a woman, it's a cloud,' said John Peterson, a little foggy himself after all the Angels' Kisses. 'Am I right in thinking that this cloud is coming in our direction? Pinch me, Elliot, tell me I'm not dreaming!'

'Good evening, Jeanne,' said Elliot. 'Allow me to introduce my friend John Peterson. He's off to your country tomorrow.'

'I must thank you,' said Jeanne to Peterson. 'Everyone's fleeing the place: it must feel very much alone. It's good of you to go and see it.'

'John works on *The New York Times*. There's no need to thank him: hells are his speciality. Will you join us for a drink?'

'I'll be back in a moment,' said Jeanne. 'And then you can tell me all about your hells,' she added, to Peterson.

'She's Russian . . .? Sublime!' said John. 'I can see what

you're doing out in the countryside now . . . Of course you're
madly in love with her?'

'I've never asked myself the question.'

More dancers from the Châtelet were arriving in small
groups – the entire fauna of Incarville. The house pianist had
to cede his piano-stool to a strapping fellow with great red
moustaches like Taras Bulba. The lights were switched off.
There was a popping of corks. Gypsy music started playing.
Couples – couples of men, too – got up to dance. Jeanne came
back and sat close to Elliot.

'There's a break in their run tomorrow, so they're letting
their hair down,' she said.

In her dress with its constantly changing colour, reminiscent
of a fan-shaped seashell, she looked like a Florentine. Seeing
her in the midst of all this crowd, Elliot sensed more keenly
than ever what a rare creature she was. She took his champagne
glass from him, just grazing the rim with her lips; and he saw
nothing but those lips, so very pink, and her teeth, like a neat
row of little stars. John was lost for words. But as a good
reporter, he tumbled immediately to what was going on:
Elliot's life was at a turning-point. It's not just her beauty, he
thought to himself, it's worse than that. It's the face of destiny
itself. He got up.

'Excuse me a moment. I'm signing up for duty at the bar. I
think it's now they start serving "Bird of Paradise Fizz".'

Alone at last, thought Elliot. The smoke-filled room was
packed to overflowing. What with the music and the loud
voices, they couldn't even hear what the other was trying to
say. They were wedged close together on the bench. Their
knees touched. Neither of them spoke. They felt good. And
they wanted it to go on: they wanted to be forgotten by John,
forgotten by the whole world. They held hands. The same
blanket of happiness enveloped them both. They were drifting.
They fell asleep together.

'I'm off to bed,' Elliot heard someone saying.

It was John, who could no longer stand up straight.

'I'll come along with you . . .'

'No, it's just the other side of the street! See you tomorrow
. . . Can I give Jeanne a kiss? I don't know whether –'

Before he had got to the end of the sentence, she had flung
herself around his neck.

'The rain'll freshen him up a bit,' said Elliot, as John staggered out through the revolving door . . . 'Shall we go?'

'Yes, let's go!' said Jeanne, wide awake again, smiling like
a child at the prospect of going to a circus . . . 'But –' she
added, 'you weren't perhaps thinking of returning to
Incarville?'

'Yes, I was.'

It was not true. He didn't even know the time. He'd
arranged to meet Madeleine at noon and John at two. He'd
been planning to stay the night in Paris.

The rain had stopped by the time they got to the Pont
d'Asnières. They passed lorries carrying carrots and leeks, and
other white lorries, ice-cooled, carrying sea-food. Butchers'
shops, their metal shutters surmounted by a golden horse's
head, already had their lights on. Jeanne fell asleep, her head
resting on Elliot's shoulder; then she let herself slip right over
on to Elliot. He could no longer change gear. But the road was
empty, so he stayed up in fourth all the way.

By the time they got to Incarville, he had pins and needles
all over. How am I going to wake her? he wondered. But as
they entered the drive of the villa she woke up surprisingly
quickly, and suddenly happy. Whilst Elliot solemnly turned
off the engine, put on the handbrake, switched off the head-
lights, she brushed his temples and ears and chin with her lips,
as though making a methodical study of the man Elliot Noelting. He turned towards her, and looked at her gravely, or
rather, fearfully. It was the look one gives a child who is
showing signs of fever – one's own child, whom one knows so
well, and who is suddenly acting strangely. He might easily

have thrown off all constraint, had Jeanne not suddenly leapt
out of the car and run on to the grass. She stretched her whole
body, lifting her arms high into the air. Her smile reassured
him.

XXXVIII

Elliot stuck his head under the cold tap. He had three hours
before having to go off again. He sat down at his typewriter.
And now the words just came to him, although for the past
few weeks he had had no idea how to write about that
accident involving the two ambulances, which had taken place
in the Forêt de Compiègne – on a road of white sand, under
the pine trees, not far from a village called Saint-Jean-aux-
Bois. He remembered one nurse – a society lady, the sister of a
general, very tall, with a big nose and a monocle and size ten
feet – who had been gathering jonquils as one of the ambulances burned.

He added the little pile of typed pages to a larger pile,
without reading them over. There was no likelihood of meeting Jeanne in the kitchen this morning. But he found Nastia
there, rolling pastry. Waiting for him in the refrigerating unit,
on a plate covered, as usual, with another, was a wing of
chicken and some vegetable salad.

'Was it you who prepared this?' he asked, standing there
and eating with his fingers.

'No, it wasn't me.'

It can only have been Jeanne, he thought. She can't have
gone to bed immediately.

'There isn't any coffee, by any chance, is there?' he asked,
thinking of the journey ahead.

'Oh, but of course!'

Nastia put the coffee-pot on to the hot-plate.

'It's fresh, I've just made it! . . . When are you going to Honfleur?'

'Why on earth should I be going there?' said Elliot, helping himself to coffee without waiting.

'Because Monsieur Seyn asked you to! You know, to see about that roof which was damaged in the storm!'

'Oh, that's right,' said Elliot. 'I'm sorry, I'm just a bit tired. Is Monsieur Seyn up, do you know?'

'He's gone off to Paris in the car.'

'And how's Madame Seyn this morning?'

'She hasn't got out of bed yet. It takes her ages getting off to sleep at night . . . Jeanne's still asleep, too. I get the impression she was out on the spree last night. She's got every reason to do that, hasn't she?'

There was a good deal of provocativeness in Nastia's tone, and no little severity, either.

'Yes,' said Elliot. 'As many sprees as she wants!'

'You're not very fresh yourself this morning.'

'No. I was out on the spree too. Then I came back and did some work.'

'I've put your clean shirts in your room. I turned the collar of one, it was worn.'

'Thanks, yes. I saw. I'll go up and get changed in a moment.'

'I'm told you'll be leaving us soon . . .'

'That's right . . . To arrange about my book . . .'

There was a lengthy silence. Nastia cut up the rolled-out pastry into lozenges.

'Will you be coming back?' she asked, not lifting her eyes from the table.

'Certainly!'

'Soon?'

'As soon as possible . . .'

'You'll be missed!' said Nastia, slamming the door behind her as she left for the garden.

Elliot took a shower and had a shave. He changed his shirt, but kept his cowboy trousers on.

He was due to meet Madeleine at the Régence. She wasn't there. He sat down near the window of the almost empty café. He always enjoyed watching the horses going by, pulling their delivery carts. The sight of a large, very handsome grey, with a swarthy-looking little girl in the saddle and an old man holding the reins, made him think of Joan of Arc – or wasn't it rather that Seyn had told him how Joan of Arc had been wounded here, just thirty yards from where he was sitting now, on the corner of what was now the Avenue de l'Opéra? He felt a hand on his shoulder: it belonged to a white-haired little lady in slippers, who was smiling and holding out a letter to him. The lady was Madeleine's dresser.

Madeleine was at the theatre, suffering as usual. She had back pains. She had a performance this evening and thought it best to rest beforehand. Could he come and meet her at the end of *Bajazet*?

Relieved – in the best of moods – he set off on foot for the Closerie des Lilas, going through the arched passages of the Louvre. In the Cour du Carrousel there were great beds of splendid white tulips. The lawns were fenced off by large interlocking metal hoops. He saw children jumping over them. He tried doing the same and almost twisted his ankle.

John wasn't at the Closerie des Lilas, either. Everyone's standing me up today, thought Elliot. He must be sleeping off his hangover. Elliot ordered a sandwich and a bottle of Bordeaux. The waiter had scarcely gone off with his order when a tall, slim, good-looking man with slightly greying hair, a blond moustache and a very short beard, dressed in a honey-coloured suit, came up and stood in front of Elliot's table.

'Excuse me. My name won't mean anything to you. My wife's name will mean more –'

'Mademoiselle Vallès,' Elliot cut him short, in a neutral tone.

'May I . . .?' He drew back a chair next to Elliot.

'By all means.'

'You know why I'm here?'

'Yes and no.'

'Madeleine's not well at all.'

'Worse than she was a few months ago?'

'She did get a bit better,' said Madeleine's husband very calmly, inclining his head somewhat but still looking Elliot straight in the eye. 'But then she just caved in again . . .'

'And you thought it must have something to do with me?'

'No. But I think you might be able to help now.'

'You really think so?'

'I'm convinced of the fact.'

'Has your wife spoken to you about me?'

'Never. But I found out right from the beginning, through another party . . . You're leaving for New York –'

'You're very well-informed.'

'I don't go out of my way to be . . . Will you be gone a long time?'

'I don't know.'

'Madeleine won't be able to –'

'It's to you Madeleine clings. To you, and to her career. It was impossible with me, she told me right from the start –'

'You don't love her.'

'You've come to me too late in the day to say that,' said Elliot, asking the waiter to bring another glass.

'Not for me, thanks,' said Madeleine's husband. 'I'm playing in a tennis tournament this afternoon. Do you play tennis?'

'I did when I was your age,' said Elliot.

They both laughed, but not more.

'I've read your books.'

'In English? You read me in English?'

'No, I've read them since . . . There are things to be learned there ... About sincerity ... The tone is perhaps a little bragging at times –'

'Bragging!' said Elliot. 'You're the first person who's ever said that to me!'

'Well, maybe it's just the difference in the languages.'

'No,' said Elliot. 'It's perfectly true.'

XXXIX

The weird gang from the Châtelet started drifting away from Incarville. Slava would still turn up from time to time and play a little piano for Marie-Aynard, whom Yves Seyn would carry downstairs for the occasion, wrapped in shawls, and put on a *chaise-longue* in the library. She would always ask for the same Chopin waltz – the one she had heard that Easter morning. To give her mother pleasure, Jeanne had choreographed a dance to the accompaniment of this waltz. She usually danced it alone, although it was actually conceived for two persons; but sometimes, beneath Marie-Aynard's astonished gaze, Mishinsky would get up from the piano and join Jeanne, and they would dance the piece without music. 'They're marvellous,' Marie-Aynard would say to Seyn, in the thin little voice of someone who was dying: 'I can hear the music.' And, lower still, she would add: 'It's so beautiful, I'm ashamed,' and tears of ecstasy would run down her impassive face.

Nastia opened the champagne and everyone sat down on the floor around Marie-Aynard – everyone except Elliot, that is. He remained on his feet, perhaps out of a sense of discretion, leaning up against the piano upon which Slava was playing Debussy. 'This girlish music does me a world of good,' he said. Yves Seyn condescended to smile. Looking at her stepfather,

Jeanne thought to herself that the passage of the years couldn't be so bad, after all, if the end of the road held in store those unruly grey curls and those large nostrils which seemed casually to sniff at every smell on the earth. Jeanne was beginning to feel a filial fondness for the old beanpole.

In fact, though, those evening gatherings were dreadful affairs. There was only one half of Marie-Aynard left on the *chaise-longue*. She weighed four stone. She was becoming quite tiny, constantly receding whilst all the time remaining there, her eyes reflecting the love showered upon her from every side. But on every side the hearts were heavy. Overlong silences kept falling, and no one had either the courage or the insensitivity to break them. Even the damned birds had stopped singing. Many of them, it was true, had already left: one could feel the cold winds of winter coming.

'Jeanne,' said Elliot, at one of their now habitual breakfast-time meetings, 'we ought to go to Honfleur. I think Monsieur Seyn's probably mentioned it to you – the roof, the chimneys, the stoves –'

'Yes, I know.'

'He seems very keen on the idea.'

'Yes, I know.'

'Well, how about going tomorrow?'

'It's entirely up to you.'

And so Jeanne and Elliot's departure for Honfleur – their departure as lovers, need one say? – on the morning of September 14th was decided for purely practical reasons. It was raining heavily when they reached the house. Jeanne was setting foot inside it for the first time in her life. The shutters were closed and the whole place smelt musty. The house had not been aired since Easter.

When Elliot and Jeanne had opened the shutters – not without difficulty, for the hooks and hinges were rusted – and had jammed the front door open with a big log, they saw that they were in an enormous room. It was the kitchen, with three black stoves arrayed in a line along the furthest wall, and an open fireplace in the corner. The wall behind the stove was done in blue tiles, against which the copper utensils, covered in verdigris, stood out clearly. In a stoneware bowl on the big, long table of black oak was a posy of honesty and winter-cherry which had simply been left there, the flowers dried out but still looking like new. The rustic kitchen had a touch of the drawing-room about it: in front of the fireplace, on a thick blue carpet damp as a sponge, loomed a large sofa and two armchairs upholstered in dark leather.

To try to dry the carpet, Elliot had a go at lighting the fire, and Jeanne, one of the Dutch ovens. They used newspapers and twigs for kindling. But everything was damp and the chimney wouldn't draw. The fire only got going when the rain stopped. The sun made an appearance. Branches of hazel rapped against the open windows and the raindrops on their leaves were like diamonds.

After lunching in a hotel near the sea, Jeanne and Elliot went off to see the workmen at the various addresses Seyn had given them. The chimney-sweeps couldn't come till the next day, but they undertook to install in the bedroom a stove which the shivering couple had just chosen – it was like a big, long chest of drawers in cast-iron, with mica windows at the top and a double door below. It produced an infernal heat, they were told, and was of Canadian design, invented by monks in the days of the sailing-ships.

At the close of the afternoon, they made a detour to have a look at the fish market on the quayside, and were fascinated by the bidding of the buyers, whose logic escaped them. The fishing-boats had just come in: the sardines were still jumping, the backs of the mackerel were still pink. They chose for themselves a large silver mullet and some shell-fish. They got back to find the kitchen all warm and full of the smell of burning wood.

Elliot thought that, back in America, he had never seen such an old building. Nevertheless, it made him think of the house by the lakeside – perhaps because of the proportions of the place and the blue tiles. In order to forget this, he went down to the cellar and took out two long, black bottles labelled Saint Julien from the wine-rack. He went back upstairs. Jeanne was cleaning the shell-fish with a scrubbing-brush; she put some water on to boil and added herbs. Elliot prepared the fish for cooking on the open hearth. Then he settled himself down on the sofa in front of the fire, a glass of red wine in his hand.

For the first time ever, he found himself alone with Jeanne in an empty house as night was coming on. He sensed her behind him, rinsing the plates and glasses. He sensed her powerfully. He turned round. She was on her way upstairs. Almost at the top, she stopped, her hand on the banister, and looked at him without smiling; then she disappeared.

Hearing her coming downstairs, he turned round again: her face was hidden by a tottering pile of pillows, sheets, and blankets. He got up to help her, but she said no, thank you, and set the whole lot down on the edge of the hearth, to the left. Then, turning her back on the fire, she sat down on a stool, facing Elliot, her hands buried in the folds of her dress, between her knees.

Then he saw that she had just got changed. She was wearing a dress of pleated leaves of silk. The top layer, which was plain, let the silk underneath shine through, with vague, blended stencil patterns.

'What are you wearing there?' he asked.

'This?' said Jeanne, unfolding a panel of the dress . . . 'Mother and Yves brought it back from Venice for me.'

'I've never seen anything like it.'

'Nor have I . . . You don't think it's a bit too much?'

'Not at all. It's alive . . . Be careful not to get it dirty,' he said – realizing at once, but too late, that this was not a very poetic reaction to such a beautiful dress. He half-threw up an arm defensively, but she understood what he meant, and said quickly, with a frank smile, 'Mother told me exactly the same thing. But it doesn't need much looking after. We've washed it already, with Nastia. It doesn't even need ironing. Shall we eat now?'

Elliot got up, but he didn't go over to the table. He went to Jeanne. She got up from her stool. She was only a fraction shorter than him; their noses were touching.

'I love you, do you know that?'

'Yes, yes,' she said – swiftly, and as though with regret.

She wouldn't quite admit to herself that she was nervous about tonight, that inside her there was a blind terror.

'I loved you,' he said, 'long before I ever saw you. I must have loved you from the cradle –'

'Shut up! That's a horrible thing to say, Elliot. You shouldn't talk like that!' said Jeanne, wincing as though in pain.

She closed her eyes; and, running his fingertips over her eyelids and the tip of her nose, he kissed her on the forehead and mouth. The smell of the sea came back to him – that smell which had been there the first time she had kissed him, without even taking note of him, on Easter Sunday.

'You have dozens of faces,' he said to her. 'They change like clouds drifting across an open sky –'

'And you – you look too much, even when you're not looking at all. If you had windows instead of eyes, I'd put curtains across them!'

'Good idea! I wouldn't be able to see anything. I wouldn't be able to write. I'd become a woodcutter or a shepherd. What a holiday . . .!'

Jeanne was frightened; yet something within her was laughing and crying at the same time. The wine had put colour in their cheeks. They set themselves to the serious business of extracting the shell-fish with pins. Jeanne's face, poised above the pin she was holding, was radiant. But Elliot perceived this glow as though it were not meant for him. They were alone on the earth at that moment, both daunted and inspired; the past had ceased to exist for them; and when Jeanne, getting up from the table, unfolded the sheets and blankets, she wasn't even aware that she was making up their bed. Like an animal, she was making a nest for herself, withdrawing into her shell, trustfully respecting the laws of life.

And everything flowed just as easily that night, and the following morning, and the rest of the day – down by the sea, at the market, and in the house, with the workmen there.

'We need three nights,' said Jeanne, the following evening. 'Everything must happen as in Russian fairy-tales – three times over . . .'

XL

On returning to Incarville, they could scarcely credit the fact that, as far as everyone else was concerned, nothing had changed. For them, everything was different – even the corner of the kitchen table which separated them whilst they drank their morning tea had become impossibly large. Jeanne solved the problem by straightaway deciding to sit on her man's lap. And it was in this position that Lisette discovered them, one morning shortly before Elliot's departure for New York. She was bringing down the breakfast-tray from the Seyns' apartment, and walked in to the kitchen to find Jeanne sitting on Elliot's knees, her head on his shoulder and both arms round his neck – like a tart! With poor Madame Seyn dying upstairs! Lisette all but fainted on the spot.

The end of September was sunnier. Elliot never left Jeanne's side. It was she who had to drive him to Le Havre, where he was to take the liner to America. He gave her a list of all the places at which she could have the Ford seen to if necessary –

the ironmonger's, the electrician's, and so on. And he taught her a little about the mechanics of the car, so that she would know what to do in the event of a breakdown. He also insisted that from henceforth she should never drive without wearing a big wolf-fur which he left behind for her, because the wind came in through the hood of the car.

His final meeting with Madeleine went off less painfully than he had expected. Elliot's departure upset her considerably less than the confession her husband had recently made to her. He had fallen hopelessly in love with one of his young tennis partners and now wanted a divorce. 'Let him play the young man,' said Madeleine, 'but don't let him make a complete fool of himself.' She was rehearsing a play by Marivaux.

In the hurly-burly of the quayside at Le Havre, Jeanne and Elliot stood motionless, holding one another close.

'Now, listen to me,' said Elliot, taking Jeanne's face in his hands. 'If anything should happen to Marie-Aynard, come and join me in America. Take this boat, it's the fastest.'

'What about Yves?' said Jeanne.

'Bring him with you. Promise me, now! ... Say something!'

'There goes the siren,' said Jeanne. 'It's for you!'

He didn't want to let go of her. The quayside was empty before she managed to tear herself free and push him forcibly in the direction of the gangway.

'I'll write, I'll cable!' called Elliot.

'See you in a second,' said Jeanne.

The gangway was raised; the boat cast off, its bows moving rapidly through the water; the tugs approached. Jeanne could no longer make out Elliot amidst the crowd thronging the decks; but he could still see her, in her light-coloured dress and black shawl. She was the only one not to wave.

XLI

During the course of the voyage, Elliot read his novel through once more and made a few final corrections. When the words started swimming before his eyes, he would go out on to the upper deck and lie down in a deckchair in a quiet corner in front of the funnels. A faint smell of burning wafted over him. He would close his eyes and Jeanne would appear, perched on the stool at Honfleur, quite composed, her back to the fire.

The moment he arrived in New York, he threw himself into a frenzied round of seeing people, as though driven by some old habit, or was it perhaps in order to leave more quickly the city, the country he no longer loved. Publishers, agents, journalists, lawyers, photographers ... In Europe he had lost touch with the rhythm of life here. He couldn't keep up with it and he took refuge in his Greenwich Village apartment – if one could call this heap of dust and boxes an apartment.

One panic leading to another, he set to work there, too, getting men in to rid the place of mice and insects, and wash down the tiles and polish the floors. All the trunks belonging to his relations he had removed and taken away to a furniture repository. A vague fear overcame Elliot when the place was finally clean, and he rushed off down Third and Fifth Avenues in search of settees, low tables, house-plants – enough for a park. He also bought a 'refrigerating unit': it was called a Frigidaire here and it was more sophisticated than the one the Seyns possessed.

His publisher was taken aback: Elliot scarcely even wanted to discuss the contract. He seemed on edge. He was wearing a shirt which was far from clean, and he rushed off on the pretext of having to get to the post office before it closed.

Elliot made his way back on foot, stretched out on the bed,

and lay there without moving for a good hour; then he got up, took some ice-cubes from the Frigidaire, and methodically worked his way through half a bottle of bourbon. It allowed him to get his thoughts straight. You get on a boat as fast as you can! You poor bastard. Tomorrow. Carefully he recorked the bottle, then fell asleep.

Next morning, he made a cabin reservation and then asked his neighbour down the landing, an Austrian lady, to water his plants and look after his keys.

Jeanne had replied to his avalanche of letters with just two postcards, laconic in form and noncommittal in tone: she didn't know what to say, she hated writing. But when, on disembarking at Le Havre, he failed to see her on the quayside, or behind the white barriers of the customs-shed, he was nonplussed. All right, so she didn't like writing, but she knew how to drive the Ford! He had sent her a telegram from on board ship. Not coming to meet him – no, that wasn't like her at all.

Whilst waiting for his luggage to come through, he ran off to find out about train times. Yes, he was told, there was a train due to leave any minute – but it was going to Paris. Incarville? No, there was no way he could get there that evening. No, there was no connection at Rouen. Elliot was at the end of his patience. Somebody put a hand on his shoulder: Monsieur Nivois was standing there.

'I've been sent to pick you up,' he said. 'The car's waiting outside.'

'How's Madame Seyn?'

'Bearing up.'

'And Monsieur Seyn?'

'Likewise.'

'And Jeanne . . .?'

'All right . . . She's all right. You'll see for yourself. Would you care to drive?'

Elliot drove Yves Seyn's Peugeot like a maniac. Why hadn't

Jeanne come to meet him? Monsieur Nivois didn't breathe a word. Perhaps he was quite simply frightened at the speed of Elliot's driving.

Coming up the drive – night was falling by now – Elliot was struck by the drabness of the house. The clematis had lost its leaves. None of the windows at the front of the house was lit. And still no sign of Jeanne.

Elliot ran into the kitchen. Nastia was there, preparing a tray. She held out her hand to him.

'Where's Jeanne?' he asked her.

'Ah, Elliot, Elliot! We've been waiting for you. Come on through! . . . Come on into the drawing-room!'

Elliot turned round to see Yves Seyn, or rather, what was left of him: he looked more like a coat-hanger with a jacket thrown over it.

'My dear Elliot! What's wrong with you?' said Seyn, approaching Elliot. 'Are you coming or not?' he almost shouted in his ear.

They went into the drawing-room. Seyn was holding a glass of bourbon all ready. He handed it to Elliot, who knocked it back.

'My friend, there's no need to be worried. Jeanne's had an accident in the Ford. It's all right. She isn't seriously injured . . . Do you hear what I'm saying?'

'Yes,' said Elliot. 'Where is she?'

'In a clinic.'

'Whereabouts?'

'Listen to me now. There's nothing wrong with her . . . It's a miracle she came out alive . . . Marie knows nothing about it. Keeping it from her hasn't been very difficult. She's lost all sense of time. I've told her that Jeanne's away on a little trip –'

'When did this happen?'

'Three days ago.'

'Give me the address. I'll go there now. Can I take the Peugeot?'

'Elliot, there's no point. She's in a state of shock. They've got her under sedation.'

'I want to see Jeanne! Right now! Tell me where she is!'

'All right, go there. But first . . . I'd like to say a word or two –'

'What about?'

'Jeanne.'

'There's no point. I know her!'

'Nobody knows her,' said Yves Seyn. 'Not even her mother . . . After you'd left, we spent a lot of time together. Marie was going from bad to worse and Jeanne helped me to bear up. I tried to help her, too, because you've no idea how much she missed you. We sat up long into the night. Sometimes one comes out with things at night which one could never say during the daytime. Jeanne is an extraordinary person, there's no doubt about that. But I came to realize that something inside her is broken. I was horrified: it seemed almost worse to me at the time than Marie's illness. There are people like that: something inside them is irreparably damaged. They go on like a fully wound-up clock, they act as though nothing were wrong – but something is terribly wrong. They're planning to commit suicide.'

'Jeanne?' said Elliot. 'But that's imposs—'

'The police told me there was no doubt about it. I wouldn't tell anyone except you, but you ought to know.'

'Did she say anything about me?'

'She was in a state of delirium over the last few days. Everything mixed up in her brain. She talked about a person called Sasha, a surgeon . . . And about a child –'

'What child?'

'Some child which had lost its parents and which Jeanne took in . . . Then the name of another man, Isaak, kept coming up: he'd been killed before her very eyes . . . Mishinsky, too – Do you remember him? You've seen him here . . . He had a nervous breakdown. He was taken to hospital and diagnosed as having schizophrenia, according to Jeanne ... He didn't even know who she was ... Sometimes Jeanne would mix up this Sasha with the woman he lives with, but I didn't understand what it was all about; she said an actress at the Comédie-Française had come to see her, but that seems scarcely possible to me –'

'Why didn't you let me know?'

'I was going to, Elliot,' said Yves Seyn. 'It was frightening to be with her. I'm telling you this now, but you can have no idea what it was like – if you'd seen her, if you'd heard the way she was talking: she –'

'And you let her go off in the car?'

'I had to leave the house for an hour, on account of Marie ... The nurse was ill and I had to find someone ... You know what saved Jeanne? That big fur coat you gave her. She tried to drive the car into a tree, but she hadn't noticed a ditch which was full of branches; she swerved, and was thrown out of the car. The grass had just been mown there. The combination of the coat and the grass reduced the impact ... A farmer and his wife found her the following morning ... My God, you're crying Elliot! ... Go ahead, my friend ... I wish I could have done the same ...'

Yves Seyn clumsily caught him by the wrists. They stood there for some while, heads bowed.

'You won't be able to manage if I take the Peugeot, though.'

'I'll find a way. Are you leaving tonight?'

'I'm going this minute.'

'I'll write you a letter which you can show to the houseman. They know me there. They wouldn't let you in on your own.'

'Where is this place?'

'Passy,' said Seyn, already in the act of writing. 'Look, I'm putting it here on the envelope.'

XLII

The night porter, who was half asleep, opened the door. Elliot asked to see the doctor on duty. Shuffling along in his slippers, the night porter led Elliot through a garden to a small outbuilding whose lights were on. The houseman wasn't wearing a white coat. Hirsute, dressed in a crumpled beige suit, and smelling of tobacco, he searched around the floor for his spectacles.

'Mademoiselle Forestier is asleep,' he said, giving a cursory glance at Seyn's letter. 'She's under sedation at the moment.'

'I must see her, whether she's asleep or not,' said Elliot. 'Maître Seyn told me that his letter –'

'Very well,' said the houseman, throwing a dark-coloured cape around his shoulders, 'follow me.'

Jeanne's face lay in shadow. Her eyes were closed and her hair put up in a white night-cap. The room was square. The perfusion tube and its metal stand were lit up by a blue nightlight. Everything was blueish. The doctor went out. Pushing a chair out of the way, Elliot knelt down on the floor, laid his head on the edge of the bed, and listened to Jeanne's breathing. He drifted off to sleep.

He was woken by someone tugging at his hair. Jeanne was sitting up in bed, smiling.

'You couldn't find a slightly more sensible position to sleep in?' she said, in a quite normal voice.

Then she kicked off the blankets, jumped out of bed, stretched to her full height, turned her feet first out, then in, let her head drop, lifted it again, took hold of a foot with her right arm and started lifting it, slowly, slowly, up to the level of her head.

Stupefied, Elliot sat down on the chair.